The Man Who Wanted to Play
Center Field for the New York Yankees

The Man Who
Center Field for the

Atheneum   New York   1983

Wanted to Play New York Yankees

GARY MORGENSTEIN

Library of Congress Cataloging in Publication Data

Morgenstein, Gary.
The man who wanted to play center field for the
New York Yankees.

I. Title.
PS3563.O871498M3   1983   813'.54   82-73020
ISBN 0-689-11358-7

Published simultaneously in Canada by McClelland and Stewart Ltd.
Composed by American–Stratford Graphic Services, Inc.,
Brattleboro, Vermont
Manufactured by Fairfield Graphics, Fairfield, Pennsylvania
First Edition

To Kate

Who was never too weary to help, never too weak to believe, never too selfish to love, all of which made this work a reality

The Man Who Wanted to Play
Center Field for the New York Yankees

Chapter 1

Danny Neuman wasn't certain when he decided to become center fielder for the New York Yankees.

Perhaps it started in third grade. For two months, Danny's full concentration had been focused upon winning the affections of Amy Kessler. She wasn't especially pretty. Her hair was frizzy, her face too freckled, her body too bony—but, like Danny, she wore glasses, giving him hope of a life of shared morning blurriness.

For two months Danny sliced up countless decks of playing cards, leaving the hearts on her ancient wooden desk before school started. After receiving mounds of mutilated Tally-Hos, Amy grew suspicious and inquired aloud where they had come from. Danny hadn't the courage to tell her. His best friend Barry Rhodes spoke up, and he and Amy subsequently went steady. Five years ago Danny'd heard they had been married, then separated, Barry with a drug problem from Nam, Amy with a lesbian affair. Maybe he'd heard wrong. In the third grade they'd only gone steady, Barry depending, through physical coercion, on a supply of cut-up playing cards Danny had had to steal every day after school from the corner candy store on College Avenue. Fortunately, Barry stayed back in the third grade, and Danny went on to the fourth and so his criminal activities ceased. With that came the freedom to dream of playing center field for the Yankees.

But the Mick still played center. Left? Danny knew he could

beat out either Hector Lopez or Johnny Blanchard. All he had to do was remove the hitch in his swing. He practiced on the concrete playgrounds surrounded by steel fences and supervised by deteriorating tenements. He was only nine, he had time. Or so he thought.

His grandfather, however, had other ideas. His grandfather sat at the head of the table on the holidays, drove the newest car in the family and uttered solemn proclamations none dared disobey. And his grandfather wanted *tattelah* to become a doctor. His grandfather told him Meyer Weinstein, head of the painters' union, had clout. He'd get him into NYU Medical School. Danny only knew NY from the Yankees' caps, NYU he didn't know, but his grandfather, and soon his entire family, had decided. He would become a doctor, even if he hated blood and open wounds.

They belittled his thirteen-year-old protests that he wanted to spend his life playing baseball. At his bar mitzvah, everyone referred to him as the doctor. With each pen, with each check, he was the Doctor. Cards were signed, "To the Doctor."

"Doctor, doctor, doctor." When Meyer Weinstein, his breath rancid from herring, had handed him his eleventh pen set, Danny had flinched. How could he be a doctor if herring made him ill? "Don't worry about anything, your grandfather and me got everything taken care of. NYU for sure, don't worry."

Danny didn't worry. Or if he did, he didn't know it was worry. Others had to teach him that. All he cared about was whether Tresh could make the shift to left, whether Maris would ever come close to thirty homers again, much less sixty-one, and when would the Mick retire? Maybe Mantle would stay around long enough to give Danny some pointers about playing Death Valley in Yankee Stadium. How much more was there to worry about?

Try a weak stomach and ineptitude in science, two flaws even Meyer Weinstein and the painters' union couldn't surmount. So much for medicine.

Instead—since nobody from Arizona State and its national championship team saw fit to call Danny, despite a .298 senior year at Springfield Gardens High School—he had to settle for

4

the State University of New York at Stony Brook. There he pursued a degree in political science, concentrated on making the Stony Brook team, roomed with Norman Reiner, boy playwright, and devised means to supplant the usurper Bobby Murcer in center field. There he dreamed, until he met Sarah Golden.

"I can stay forever, can't you?" Sarah Golden had said, tossing back her long, straggly brown hair. Like three-quarters of the girls on the Administration Building floor, demonstrating against Defense Department research on campus, Sarah looked like Carole King. Danny had nodded. "Forever, because doing something like this, this important, can hold one, right? I mean, this is it, saving lives, saving little children from napalm—what else can we do, go to class, get jobs, no, saving children from napalm is what life should be about, right?"

Danny agreed, too ashamed to admit he'd wandered into the demonstration in search of a financial aid officer to choke. After Danny had spent two-thirds of a semester juggling eighteen credits around batting .305 in center field, Stony Brook had written him that he wasn't registered. Once with Sarah, Danny'd forgotten about that. He'd even forgotten about his newest competitor, Rusty Torres. All he wanted to do was sit with Sarah. But of course, Lenny Schnadel, now podiatrist, then procurer of Lebanese red, wandered over and attempted to show up Danny's lack of political knowledge. Though Danny cared little about politics, he'd worked for Charles Goodell and distributed leaflets for McGovern—anything to avoid labeling as a jock. Out of obligation, he hated Nixon, even if he felt sorry for Pat. She did look cold and *goyishe,* and he could never imagine special sauce dripping out of her hamburger roll onto her dress, but still Danny felt sorry for Pat. He never mentioned it, though, because then some would suspect sympathies for Nixon. That was taboo. Next thing, you'd cut your hair.

Which Danny eventually did once he entered law school. Glorious St. John's: Christ on a cross guarding the elevators; professors who made you stand so they had better aim to humiliate you; students who ripped out pages from case books, stole notebooks and kissed ass with professors. Guardians of the Watergate

5

heritage. Danny thought he wanted to be a lawyer until he realized he had to associate with lawyers. So ended that. At least Elliot Maddox tore up his knee, giving Danny's neighborhood softball activities a glint of hope.

The years passed. Danny tried various things, then finally landed a job as a staff writer for a Major National Publication, or at least that was what his mother told her friends without actually naming it. *Auto Service Monthly,* that was its name. Hoses and air filters. What kind of a job was that for a thirty-three-year-old man?

Up in the Bronx, the Yankees surged, ebbed, surged. Danny just ebbed. And then he decided to do something about it.

That's why he was in the singles bar now, having a drink with Norman. He wanted to tell him his decision.

Danny used to go to single bars often, but invariably sat in the corner, spilling Scotch on his pants so he could have an excuse to leave. He wondered why more people didn't spill Scotch on their pants so they could leave. Then everyone could meet on the street corner, compare stains and have something else to talk about besides starting salaries and chic furniture. At least Sarah didn't discuss chic furniture. That's why he'd married her. Or so he thought. Who would know Carole King would metamorphose into Margaret Anderson? That they would live in Flushing, Queens, a place you stopped off on the way to Manhattan? Not yet suburbia, so you couldn't be accused of acquiescing to middle-class values, said his friends the orthodontists and tax lawyers. Not the city, so you didn't have to live with poor people in bad neighborhoods and have your liberal ideology challenged when your lips formed "nigger" or "spic" at the three guys with long knives holding your wallet. Flushing, still a bastion of safety. The front line against *shmutz.*

To Sarah, *shmutz* was as powerful, if not more so, than God. There was *shmutz* on the subway so she took cabs when she had to walk more than three blocks. There was *shmutz* on their rug so they had to buy *shmutz*-free rugs at Bloomingdale's. Instead of God, money decided whether a garment was *shmutz*-free or not. MasterCharge hadn't understood *shmutz* when they'd taken away his card after he'd overrun his limit for the third time in

6

four months. Somehow that had only reinforced Sarah's belief in its omni-importance—an entity so beyond control even Master-Charge couldn't comprehend it.

Faithful, Danny now came to singles bars to watch. Now he was a voyeur. That was what had jolted him into thinking he could supplant Jerry Mumphrey in center. Watching. He watched stewardesses flirt with attorneys. He watched men consume inordinate amounts of booze so they could act sober. He watched people purchase clothes for hundreds of dollars only to replace them the next season. He watched everyone. Sarah with her *shmutz*. Norman with his plays. Mumphrey spearing liners in left center. He watched and kept quiet.

So what did it matter if he was thirty-three and hadn't played baseball in eleven years, though he'd kept active on the neighborhood softball team until quitting three years ago because Sarah wanted weekends to do things? He'd watched, hadn't he? He kept in reasonable shape with an irregular regimen of pushups and situps, enduring Sarah's complaints about his head giving *shmutz* to the floor. He kept his batting stroke sturdy by swinging away at the slow-pitch cage at Adventurer's Inn. His fingers were nimble from typing articles on automatic transmissions. His body was reasonably free of alcohol and dope as he monitored both at the parties where friends who once wore ponytails and hummed Jefferson Airplane discussed life insurance. He wasn't especially neurotic—okay, so that wasn't true. And so he smoked two packs of cigarettes a day and wheezed. Once he quit, the incipient tuberculosis would vanish. He could do it. He could play center field for the Yankees.

"What?" Norman peered suspiciously and ordered another round of drinks, as if alcohol could cure Danny, or at least get them drunk enough so it could be dismissed as empty bar talk. "Why?"

"Because." Danny shrugged. "Because I want to."

"You're thirty-three."

"So? I'm not ready to die. I'm still young."

"Do you still stay up until four in the morning discussing where God came from?"

"No."

7

"Do you ever stay up late?"

"No."

"See?"

"What? Ballplayers go to sleep early."

"You're thirty-three."

"I thought you'd understand."

"And what happens to me when you become a ballplayer? I lose my job, you're the one who covers for me."

Six months ago, Norman had turned up in Danny's office on 56th and Broadway, his latest play venture having gone awry, and with it, Norman. Danny had gotten him a job, but Norman rarely worked at it. He wrote his plays. Yesterday Danny had rewritten Norman's analysis of fuel injection systems. Norman had analogized fuel injection systems with Grecian acceptance of homosexuality. Maybe Norman was right. Maybe Norman would lose his job.

"But what about me?" Danny asked.

"What does Sarah say?"

"Haven't told her yet."

"You're just going to go off to Waterloo and play ball?"

"No, I'm not just. Look, there's an open tryout at the Stadium in five weeks. Anyone can try out, completely open. I'll go. I'll get in shape. I'll do it."

"Uh-huh," Norman said. "Look, did I tell you about this new thing I'm working on? I can feel the second act flowing now, coursing, about to erupt. It's this symbolic thing, see, about South America. The curtain rises on nine frogs in military uniform and they . . ."

On the way home, Danny turned again to his plan, calculating who would be shocked as the E train roared toward Queens. Not his mother, forever mumbling into her oven. His father, the dry-cleaner? Once the conversation passed beyond Martinizing and wire versus wooden hangers, his father fell asleep. Murray, his boss?

"You have no experience in auto parts, right?" Murray had asked him five years ago. Danny had nodded. "But you can write. I see a future with you here. An opportunity to get into

8

auto parts, to dissect them, to write them with a flamboyance that would make Sartre envious." Murray loved existentialism. In one issue he had had Danny write an editorial musing on what Jean-Paul Sartre would've done if he'd developed a car. Danny had written it humorously, speculating that the car would have had no gear except sideways, would require assembly by the owner and have room for only one person. Murray had exploded at Danny's sarcasm, so Danny had rewritten the article, reflecting that Sartremobiles would have no wheels, yet be able to drive across oceans, and wouldn't require gas, for that would imply they had somewhere to go. Murray had nodded proudly and suggested Danny submit the piece to the *New Republic*. That was the issue Danny hadn't brought home.

No, Murray wouldn't understand. Who else? Certainly not his grandfather, who'd passed away muttering that if his grandson had been a doctor, he wouldn't now be receiving intravenous feedings from strangers. His older brother, Nathan the Rabbi, currently preparing to re-enact Moses' march across the Sinai for the *New York Times Magazine*? Who would care? Everyone would care, except five youths sauntering into his car. No, they would care, too, Danny thought, watching them grab a fat lady's purse. If he were in Waterloo, who else would they rob?

"You're going to do what?" Sarah didn't drop his electric toothbrush into his iced tea. In fact, she attempted no violent acts. Worse, she sat on their unpaid-for *shmutz*-free couch and laughed, for ten minutes.

"Yeah, so, why not?" Danny got defensive. He rarely got defensive, for he rarely had anything he cared enough to get defensive about. How could he get defensive about grammar in a shock-absorbers article or whether the lawn should be watered first in the front or the back?

"Why?" Sarah chuckled.

"Because, I don't know, something I want to do."

"It's ridiculous. You're thirty-three, what are you going to do, make the Yankees at thirty-three?" She still hadn't stopped laughing. Danny grew angry. Maybe that's when he first detected wrinkles about her eyes, the stretch marks on her bare

9

upper arms, the way her lower lip sagged to permit the convulsive chuckles to explode out of her fleshy throat. "What, do you think you'll become a millionaire, like Dave Winfield, is that why you're doing this?"

Because I didn't have the courage to tell Amy Kessler who sent her the cut-up playing cards, or the stomach to utilize my MD bar-mitzvah pens, or the character to see law school through, or the determination to finish any of the three novels I've started. He didn't say that.

"No, because I don't know, I don't. I just decided to do it."

Sarah offered no rebuttals attesting to his previous impulsive actions. Any prior impetuousness had long since been buried. Until today.

"Then why? Christ, Danny, you want to make a fool of yourself to satisfy some childish whim? Is that it?"

What childhood, he wondered. Just yesterday he was watching old men play for the Yankees. Today they were lean youngsters. Whose childhood was she talking about?

"I'm getting into shape and going to the open tryout at the Stadium. Anyone can try out, anyone. I'm going to exercise and maybe get back on the softball team and I'm going to do it, okay, that's it, the end of it. I'm going to do it."

"Uh-huh." Sarah grinned. Just like Norman. "What kind of salad dressing do you want?"

Chapter 2

Then again, maybe it wasn't such a good idea. Danny pressed down the snooze alarm for the fourth time and scowled at the clock. Five-forty. What the hell am I doing up at five-forty?

He'd always hated the mornings, associating them with Death. He'd come to this because, as a child, his evenings were often interrupted by the vaporizer designed to alleviate his chronic croup, a condition his mother blamed herself for.

"It's the germs, I protect him, I try and protect him from the germs, what can I do?"

When one goes to sleep coughing and wakes up shrouded in steam with parents whispering incantations of puzzled guilt, it seems like morning, even if it is only eleven at night. This is especially true when a tall, cherubic man in top hat and tails is standing by the bed, peering at you through the steam and poking your chest with cold instruments: the Angel of Death, otherwise known as Dr. Schultz, an old-fashioned GP who had actually left a wedding to rush over and frighten an eight-year-old. So when you have the croup at eleven at night, which you think is morning, and can't see through the steam and wonder if it's coming from your body and you're in Heaven, like on Tom and Jerry cartoons, you tend to associate everything connected with the experience to Death.

Like this morning, sitting on the edge of the bed, wondering if he were doing the right thing.

Sarah shifted, no longer felt his body, and so swerved per-

11

fectly counterclockwise, like the minute hand of a clock, to inhabit both sides of the bed. She groaned and Danny watched her. She used to groan a lot, back when they'd first started dating and first married. She'd groan and he'd groan and the coffee would boil over but it didn't matter. One on top of the other. Sex. Early in the morning, late in the morning, before dinner and after dinner. Sex. No more. Now she just adjusted like Big Ben and groaned to herself.

Who are you thinking of, Sarah? Danny wanted to stroke her hair, but knew that bothered her. She hated to be awakened in the middle of her sleep. Who? A movie star, maybe? Not me, that's for sure. Who then? He wanted to shake her for the answer, as if it would explain why he no longer knew why he loved her. Not that he didn't love her—just that he didn't know why. It escaped him, this love, actually nagged him, gnawed him, the girl suddenly gone, replaced by a slightly overweight woman who loved him for his side of the bed.

He rose, debated whether he should actually play the *Rocky* theme, then realized it was too ridiculous. If I can't do it without Rocky, I shouldn't do it. Danny tugged on heavy white socks. Children's socks, Sarah called them, but he'd worn them when he was young, along with the white bucks and shorts and shirts his mother threatened he'd better not get dirty. So, of course, he would get them dirty, diving headfirst into bases, scraping his knee along the concrete playground. Once he'd torn up his knee. He'd hobbled back, holding his knee together until he'd reached his mother's mah-jongg game, then spread his hands to allow the blood to hit the sidewalk. He'd spent forty minutes in Lebanon Hospital getting sewed up while his mother had lain in the emergency room for two hours, fainting. He and his father had visited her that night. He remembered the doctors sewing up his fat legs where the Mallomars had gone after digestion and hearing his mother wail that her son would be an amputee. He'd come out of it even more determined to hurl headfirst and incur danger. They called him Screwball Neuman back then. He'd ram into fences and chase fly balls through traffic. He didn't do that anymore. He couldn't remember when he'd stopped. Just had. Even when he'd played ball in high school and college, he hadn't dived quite as much as he'd once done. And he couldn't remember why. Maybe he'd stopped caring.

But he wouldn't stop wearing his white juvenile socks. Sometimes he wore them to work, sometimes to a party. He knew that infuriated Sarah, his wearing of the white. He didn't do it to infuriate her. He didn't want to infuriate her anymore. Maybe that's why he didn't know why he loved her anymore. They never fought, ever. Even last night when she'd ruined an album of his.

He'd put on Jimi Hendrix, the *Are You Experienced* album. He hadn't listened to it, nor had any desire to listen to it, for years, but he'd put it on anyway. Sarah had come out of the kitchen, speckles of raw chopped meat affixed to her blouse, and calmly run the needle over the record. She'd displayed neither anger nor irritation nor even glee—nothing. Emptiness. He thought he could see fear, but that was only his paranoia and he was paranoid enough, something she never stopped telling him.

"I'm telling you, I think that's a whole CIA operation up there." Danny had said the day they'd moved in, pointing skyward and pausing before a carefully wrapped box of dishes.

"You've lived in this apartment thirty-seven minutes," she'd said, always precise—eventually he expected her to add seconds, then beep on the hour and half hour—"and already you're suspecting people. They seem nice."

"See, listen, hear that?" They'd heard rolling sounds and maniacal laughter. "What do you think that is?"

"They seem nice."

He had to admit Sarah had been right, though they'd switched positions and he'd taken a liking to their upstairs neighbors, whereas Sarah now couldn't abide them. They didn't seem bad, just a little strange, but she called them names and said they should be locked up. He would've defended them, but that would've caused an argument and they never argued. So he just shrugged, listened to the constant rolling upstairs, and her complaints, and kept still.

Maybe they weren't normal enough for Sarah. She adored sanity. Everything in its place. Sanity. Security. Clothes neatly folded, bills paid timely. He'd never cared much about such things but found, as marriage proceeded, that it was better to accede to such orderliness. After a while he lost all his bad habits, except the white socks. That seemed to please her, as if she were Professor Henry Higgins reforming him. If only he could remember why he refused to give up his white socks. He knew why, but it made no sense. If he could give up everything else, why not his white socks? Perhaps for the same reason he finally decided to put on *Rocky* at 5:55 A.M., flinging Big Ben off the bed.

"What the hell are you doing?"

DUM*DUM*DUM*DUM*DAH*DAH*DAH*DA*DAH*DUM.

"Exercising." Danny did jumping jacks.

"Danny"—Sarah seized the alarm—"it's fucking six o'clock in the morning."

"I gotta wake up."

"Can't you do it quietly?"

"Why? You don't have to go to work today."

Sarah had been a buyer for Bloomingdale's, then left when they'd gotten married. She'd thought he should take care of her, that she shouldn't have to work. He hadn't protested, though it became embarrassing when he had to bring oranges to work for lunch. He let her have her way. But not this morning.

"I'm going running," he insisted.

"Then go." Sarah burrowed under the blankets.

GONNA FLY NOW . . .

"In a second."

"Will you just turn that damn stupid music off?"

"The answer my friend, is blowing, in, the wind, the answer is blowing in, the wind." Danny remembered how Sarah had sat cross-legged, strumming the guitar, surrounded by doped-and-boozed faces. Danny had been neither, but he, too, had listened intently, had watched as Sarah's shining face had grinned and she'd sipped from Boone's Farm Apple Wine, bowing. She had a great voice. She could've sung professionally. Danny didn't like to think it was his fault she hadn't, because she'd had to work to support him a year and a summer-school session in law school, only to have him purposefully flunk out. Sarah never mentioned it, but he knew that if she hadn't had to work, maybe she

14

could've done it. Then again, maybe not. Maybe it wasn't in her. Maybe that's why she hated music so damn much. Maybe, maybe, maybe. Danny turned off *Rocky,* panting.

"Thank you," she said coldly from beneath the pillows.

"You're welcome."

Danny started for the door, realized he didn't have his sneakers on, then struggled to lace them while standing up before stumbling back out.

"When will you be home?"

"Depends how long I can make it."

"Five minutes?"

He would've sworn she sneered.

"Maybe ten with a respirator," he snapped, jogging through the living room and out the door. He stopped once he saw the roller skates lying at the foot of the steps. After three years in the lower half of the two-story home in Flushing, he knew to look down lest he fly off on one of his upstairs neighbors' roller skates.

How far will I run? Danny did jumping jacks on the lawn. Three miles, four, five? How long should I run? Should've kept one of those books, no, that would defeat the purpose.

How to Break the Four-Minute Mile; Running for Fun; Lungs Are a Man's Best Friend; Legs, Legs, Everywhere Legs; I Run and I'm Seventy, Why Not You? Danny had examined the books in the store near his office.

"May I help you?" a slender man vacillating between asexuality and effeminism had stood by, coughing slightly.

"Oh, yeah, just looking." Danny had squinted at the titles.

"Are you a runner?" A glance at Danny's lower torso. How could he see my fleshy calves? Danny had wondered, inching away. The clerk had followed.

"Are you?"

"What?"

"A jogger?"

"No."

"Then why are you looking here?"

"Just curious."

"We do have books for beginners."

"I don't want any books."

15

"You'll run without proper exercise or regimen?"

"Maybe."

"So you *are* a jogger."

"I'm a browser, okay?"

"We don't encourage browsing."

"Then how do I know what to buy?"

"If you tell me what you want, perhaps I can help you."

So Danny had bought three books: *First You Wheeze, Then You Soar, A Layman's Guide to Ghetto Jogging* and *Nutrition, Your Body or Your Life*. Then, he'd thrown them away, disgusted he'd even bought them. Sarah would be proud of the way he'd tossed them into the garbage.

"You can't just throw them away." Danny had stood behind her in the tiny kitchen of the rented Catskills bungalow they'd taken for two weeks several summers ago.

"I can't get the filth out of this pitcher." Sarah had peered into the beige container, making a horrified face at the cruddy iced-tea odor.

"It doesn't belong to us."

"So?"

"You just can't throw it away."

"I should just leave this crud here, in the cupboard until next summer, and have some poor innocent person pour iced tea or something into this pitcher, then die because you wouldn't let me throw it away?"

As always, Danny had relented, fearful of some felonious warrant issued for his arrest for the purposeful poisoning of an elderly couple from Bensonhurst who had died while drinking from a cruddy pitcher.

He looked over at the Long Island Expressway. Even at this hour it sagged with traffic, disgusted motorists honking irritation at some unknown enemy which forced them to approach the Midtown Tunnel at six miles per hour. Danny glanced away, sucked in his breath and started humming *Rocky* as he felt the twinge in his back. Don't need my back, just my legs. He massaged them, felt their flabbiness and stopped, looking around. No one watched him. No one was up yet.

Danny bolted down the hill, pumping his legs, his arms rotating wildly, his eyes closing in agony, his chest heaving with pain,

16

sweat dripping down his cheeks and his hunger for a cigarette intensifying as he neared the bottom of the hill.

Go for it, go for it, ball's in right center, go for it, stretch the mother, stretch it out, he fumbled the ball, go for three, go for three, cap's comin' off, go for it, do it, do it . . .

"Just starting?" A lean, gray-haired man with perfectly muscled legs ran up alongside Danny as he weaved around the corner and down a side street. Danny glared at him.

"Yup," he replied, not out of curtness but because he couldn't manage anything else.

"Your attire is wrong."

"Yup?" Danny tried to swallow, then tried to speed up but couldn't move ahead of the man wearing monogrammed jogging shorts, monogrammed shirt, jogging shoes and a smug grin.

"You can't run in sneakers."

"Yup?"

"You need running shoes." The man raised his leg to show Danny. The moment to accelerate. Go for three, go for three, Danny thought as the man hopped on one leg, keeping pace. "That is, if you are sincere."

"Yup?"

Danny felt another man flank him. Good, I'm about to be mugged by joggers. Actually, through the sweat dripping into his eyes, he could see an almost exact replica of the other man jogging alongside.

"Hiya, Sam."

"John, how are you?"

"Did you discuss those tax options with Harry?"

"No, we're having lunch today."

He could barely breathe and they were discussing this morning's *Wall Street Journal* over his head. Okay, shortstop fumbles the ball, gotta chance for a round-tripper, you can do it.

"Who's this?" John asked.

"A fellow jogger. What do you think of his attire?"

"Not good."

"I think he should get supportive shoes."

Danny whirled around a corner and they easily maintained the pace.

"Is he just starting out?"

17

"Yup?" Danny responded, his lungs filing emigration papers.

"Do you think we should be running with him?" John asked. "Doesn't look good, running with someone not properly dressed."

"Oh, give him a chance, he's just a kid."

Danny grinned.

"Perhaps you would like to attend a meeting of the Flushing Roadrunners Club?" Sam handed him a card. Danny couldn't lift his hand because he couldn't feel his hands or his throat, and besides the second baseman had retrieved the ball and was about to fire it home.

"Yup?" Danny allowed them to shove the card in his front pocket.

"Of course, if you are merely working on short-term distance, um, how far did you say you were working for?"

The plate loomed ahead.

"Inside-the-park-homer."

"What?"

"Want, to, run, an, inside, the, park, home, run."

"Why?"

"Yup?" Danny hoped that would placate them. It didn't. They ran just ahead of him, almost blocking his path.

"How long is that?"

"Three, hundred, and, sixty, feet."

"You are running a mere three hundred and sixty feet?"

"Seven, hundred, and, twenty, case I get up, twice."

They laughed and shook their heads.

"Race you along the service road?" Sam asked. John nodded, and Sam slapped him on the back, nearly knocking him over. "See you, son."

"Yup?"

Danny stopped a block from home. He'd run in a circle. Figures. Run, inna, circle. Base, paths, a, circle. Want, a, cigarette. Gave, it, up. Want, to, die. Too, early, to, die. Danny sagged against a light pole and consulted the clock in Nimsons' Hardware Store. Six-thirty. He'd run an eighth of a mile. He couldn't go home yet. Sarah would know he'd only run an eighth of a mile. Not that she cared. But this she would care about. Maybe she would ignore him. He couldn't go home yet. What was open besides massage parlors? Danny tried to stand up straight, buckled and decided to sit on the curb.

He saw several cigarette butts. Filthy city. He reached for a butt. Smell it, it'll make you sick, then you'll realize why you quit. He picked up the butt, sniffed. It smelled good. Too good, nope, gotta quit, how the hell you ever gonna get in shape if you don't quit?

So I can't go home yet. Danny managed to stand up, though hunched. Why should I be afraid? I have nothing to be ashamed of. I ran for a while, long enough, that's all. Danny started home, stopped, sat back down on the curb. Maybe I can kill a little time. Make it look as if I really did run far. He stared across the street at Moscowitz's Bagel and Bialy House, got up and went over.

"A bagel is God's sacred food." Moscowitz, whose first name Danny didn't know, held out a sesame bagel. Steam hissed out of one of the ovens and Danny flinched. He wouldn't allow himself to associate bagels with Death. "It is bittersweet, no? A salt bagel, to me, a salt bagel embodies what God meant, what he said to Moses."

"Moses didn't have bagels, Moscowitz."

"So, that was his fault? Those lousy Egyptians." Moscowitz spat into his knee-high *"feh"* container. Every time something displeased Moscowitz, he spit into his *"feh"* container, as if his spit could somehow punish three thousand years of injustice.

"Two garlic," Danny asked, figuring he'd make a peace offering to Sarah.

"Garlic?" Moscowitz shook his head. "You want to smell like garlic when I offer God's fruit, a salt bagel, speckled with God's freckles, the hand of God on this food and you want garlic?"

"My wife likes garlic. Me, I don't care."

"What is she, Italian?"

"No, Jewish."

"A Jewish girl who likes garlic instead of salt bagels?"

"Moscowitz, what can I tell you, this is what I'm supposed to buy, you want to get me in trouble because of a biblical interpretation?"

"Ah, you hen-pecked, afraid to stand up for your religious principles?"

"Moscowitz, I could eat a plain bagel, an onion bagel, a bialy, this isn't a question of principles but where I sleep tonight, okay?"

"An atheist, huh?"

"What?"

"You would spit"—he spat—"on God like this?"

He bought two salt bagels. Then he contemplated smuggling them into the house, realized Sarah knew every crevice, and threw them away. But he wasn't afraid of her. Her habits of throwing things away had just rubbed off on him. When she threw things away, it was out of determination. He, out of fear. Maybe it wasn't fear but apathy. She considered more things important than he did. Almost everything was important to her, almost nothing to him. Apathy, not fear. He wasn't afraid. If he was so afraid, why did he wake her at six in the morning to go running? Not afraid, Danny crossed the street, glanced back at the house, and loitered for about fifteen minutes in front of the delicatessen, the pizza place and the dry-cleaners. Steam obscured the window of the dry-cleaners. Maybe he associated steam with Death and his father. But how could he think evil of his father? His father was a sweet, decent, kind man who pressed all day and watched television all night. Freudian? Oedipal? What was the term? Why hadn't he ever gone to psych class to learn if steam and Dr. Schultz and Death and his father and Moscowitz's ovens were interrelated? Maybe he'd have learned why he was afraid. Apathetic, Neuman berated himself, buying a pack of cigarettes. Apathetic, apathetic. You love your father, Neuman.

"A game of catch, Dad?" Danny would adjust his NY cap, slap his glove and block the doorway. His father would smile at him. His father always smiled, except when Gorgeous George was getting beaten up on TV and Dennis James was simulating broken bones by cracking nuts. His father wouldn't believe wrestling was fake, even later, after Danny had taken a job at the leading wrestling magazine and would explain how he made up all the stories.

"You think Bruno Sammartino isn't a nice man?"

"I don't know about Bruno Sammartino, Dad. All I know is I make up all the stories, everything, quotes, everything."

"Ah, and you think if these people weren't really that way, they would let you make this up?"

So his father would turn off wrestling and prepare to go back to the store and Danny would stand in his way, slapping his glove and wondering if Whitey Ford would pitch until he was fifty.

"I have to work, Daniel." Always Daniel. Sometimes *shmendrick*, always Daniel. To his mother, Danny. To his older brother, the Little Shit. "I have an entire wedding party to press."

Press, steam, press, steam. Maybe that's why his father never got the croup.

"After work?"

"There's a steel-cage match on tonight."

"Before dinner?"

"You want to make us sweaty for your mother's meatloaf?"

"No."

"Tomorrow, Daniel."

Tomorrow never came. They never played catch. Maybe because his mother didn't want the future surgeon's hands ruined by a blazing fastball. Maybe because his grandfather owned part of the dry-cleaning store and blackmailed his father. Maybe, maybe, maybe.

Danny paused on the lawn. He wasn't sweating. How could he go into the house an hour later and not be sweating? He turned on the hose and drenched himself, then sniffled. Good, pneumonia. Danny continued soaking himself, then paused to look up at the maniacal sounds and the laughter. Their upstairs neighbors.

The tall, muscular one with bony cheecks and bony knees screeched down the steps on skates, clad in a Lone Ranger outfit. The short chunky one with mushy cheeks that must've been pinched a thousand times followed, clad in an Indian outfit. The tall one stopped, the chunky one stopped, grinned at Danny, who grinned back, and started circling him on the lawn.

21

"Hi, cutie." The Lone Ranger kissed his forehead.

"Hi, lover." Tonto kissed his chin.

"Hi, guys, where you going?"

"Out to play." The Lone Ranger giggled as they held hands and spun around and around. "Sadie thought we should get an early start."

Sadie laughed and did a little dance on the concrete walk. Sadie, otherwise known as Frederick Arnold Simpson, once owned an S&M shop on Christopher Street called Aunt Sadie's. Whips, chains and belts. Sometimes a twofer deal. According to Pistol, a nickname whose origins Danny feared inquiring into, the shop was taken over by the Mafia in a relentless sweep of the Village S&M stores. Sadie went out of business. Actually, he was paid off. Now neither one worked, ever. All they did was roller-skate and screech out of their apartment in different outfits. Danny wondered why he liked them. Maybe because Sarah hated them. Maybe he had his own reasons. He liked to think the latter.

"What are you doing, cutie?" Sadie asked.

"Running."

"How wonderful. You should try skating," Pistol pealed.

"No, I'm not . . ." Should he tell them? "I'm getting in shape. I want to become the Yankees' center fielder."

"Wonderful." Sadie nearly leaped off his skates. "Really and truly?"

"Really and truly."

"When?"

"Soon, I'm, I'm going for a tryout in five weeks."

"Well, the best of luck, honey." Sadie pumped his hand, first removing his glove. Then he glanced past Danny toward the street. "Look, kimosabe, a great green bus." Sadie peered into the distance as they held hands.

"Come, Tonto, catch bus." And off they skated. Danny watched them. They liked it. They really did. Great, I have one thing in life that I ever wanted to do, and the only ones who validate its meaning are two insane homosexuals on skates.

Danny fluffed up his curly brown hair as he entered the kitchen. Sarah looked at him.

"You're drenched."

"Jogging's hard work."

"You were running all this time?" Disbelief and irritation. Why? he wondered, removing ingredients from the cupboard.

"Well, yeah." Danny shrugged. "Ran a long time."

"Did you pass the deli? We need cream cheese."

"I ran a mile."

"You didn't get the cream cheese?"

"Two miles." Danny held up three fingers.

"Milk?"

"What, I ran three miles, what milk?"

"I told you we needed milk."

Sarah left him notes. Every Monday, his checklist of things to do. A copy taped on the bedroom, bathroom and kitchen doors. Sarah insisted she felt less like a housewife if she didn't have to do all the errands. So they became his errands.

PICK UP CLEANING (1). She always put the numbers last. Maybe to be different? GET YOUR HAIR CUT (2). BUY CREAM CHEESE (3).

"Why couldn't you buy cream cheese?"

"That's your job."

"Why is it my job?"

Sarah actually flinched. How dare he criticize their system? He'd never refused to buy cream cheese in all their years of marriage. Because, she said, about to launch into some well-constructed rationale why his duties included buying Philadelphia Brand Cream Cheese. He listened, dully, stupidly, staring at her while she spoke. Nothing infuriated Sarah like him not listening to her. She finished and returned to her bagel. So they'd had bagels after all. He watched her carefully spread the last of the cream cheese on the bagel, ensuring each and every spread was even so one side was covered in a light, methodical *shmeer*. She always did this, everything methodical, cautious, even as she used a different knife for the butter and started to layer the other half of the bagel. Then she would drop both halves on top of each other, examine it, smell it and make sure it lay just right before biting. Danny pressed down the blender and she nearly fell out of her chair.

"What are you doing now?" Sarah held the butter knife.

23

"Mixing a health thing."

"Couldn't you wait?"

"For what?"

"Until I finished my breakfast."

"Can't we do both at once? I mean, why not?" Danny turned the blender off, though his finger stayed on the button.

"And what are you doing with that . . . mess?" She gestured with the knife.

"Making breakfast, healthy things, I don't know, lots of healthy things."

"You're going to drink that with coffee?"

"I gave up coffee."

"What?" Her knife edged outward. "Why?"

"Too much caffeine, not good for me."

"Since when?"

"Since I decided to get back into shape."

"And you're really not going to drink coffee with me any-more, is that it, no more coffee?" Sarah scowled, her pretty, lumpy features hardening in a rage he couldn't understand.

"No, I . . ." He hit the blender, she purpled and he turned it off. "I quit."

She shook her head and returned to the bagel, her movements no longer quite so methodical. He whirred the blender and poured his concoction of carrot-zucchini-carob-dill-three kinds of vitamins-and-sugar into a glass, then drank it as he watched her. Sarah shook her head and chomped on the bagel.

"What's wrong?" Danny sipped.

"Don't forget Nadine's party tonight." She lit a cigarette.

"Yeah, tonight?"

"We're going," she said flatly.

"Okay." He didn't want an argument. "So what's wrong?"

"You smell like garden hose," she said over her shoulder. "We're expected at eight."

"I can't stay up too late."

"Now what?" She whirled. Danny put down his drink, took a cigarette and slipped it into the side of his mouth, not bothering to light it.

"I need my sleep."

24

"For what? Tomorrow's Saturday." She held out a lit match and he innocently blew it out. Sarah sighed in disgust and leaned back.

"I have to run."

"And we have to lose our friends because of . . ." Sarah ditched her cigarette, lit another and stared at the *Times*. "Eight o'clock," she said softly.

"I'll be there." He put out the unlit cigarette. "Do we go in separate buses?"

"If you want."

"Is that what you want?"

"No."

"Then?"

"What."

"Then what's wrong?"

"Eight o'clock. We can dress casually."

Chapter 3

Danny bounded up the subway steps and onto Lexington, then down a block to 50th, clutching his jogging shoes in a white plastic garbage bag. Already the line at the bus stop was swollen, but Danny didn't care about the line. He did care about being conspicuous, so he moved to the end and fingered a token while slipping out of his shoes and into his sneakers. Danny looked down 50th. The bus was two blocks away. Danny twisted from side to side, loosening up. He stretched to the left, then to the right as the bus paused at a light, a block away. Now he lifted his arms over his head and rotated them, attracting a few curious glances, no more. He'd have to wear antlers to get any real attention at a Manhattan bus stop during rush hour. Now the light changed color and the bus sputtered forward. Danny backed away, waiting until the passengers climbed aboard, giving the bus all the chance it needed. Waiting for the door to close. Waiting for the cars and taxis to pass so the bus could pull out. Poor bus, Danny thought, crouching. I'm gonna whip your butt, little bus. He tensed as the 50th Street crosstown bus eased into traffic.

And we're off, Danny thought, racing ahead of the bus. A foot between them. Two feet. Five feet. The bus hit a clear patch and roared ahead of him again, but Danny stayed with it. Go for it, go for it, he panted. Despite the agonizing chest pains, despite his blurring vision, despite the throbbing legs bruised from smashing around pedestrians, Danny caught up and passed the bus again midway between Fifth and Sixth. He never stopped, joyfully kicking up his heels until he hit Broadway, where he suddenly tottered on the sidewalk and staggered to a newsstand, hoping people would interpret his wheezing as a need for this morning's *Times*, and not a stroke.

Ten minutes later, still puffing but exhilarated, he reached his office building.

"What floor?" Jeremiah the elevator operator drawled. Danny had worked there five years and every day it was the same.

"Thirty-six," Danny said, smiling both out of his accomplishment and the fact he could again breathe without seeing his ancestral village in Galicia. Danny glanced around at the other passengers, none of whom knew what he'd just done. Should he tell them? Nah. He turned his happiness upon Jeremiah's short, black frame drooping unwanted age. "Great day, huh, Jeremiah?"

"What about it?"

"Terrific day. As Ernie Banks used to say, great day to play two."

"Two what?"

"Games. Baseball games."

"Who the hell would wanna do that?"

By Mother's Day of every season, Jeremiah took to wearing an Atlanta Braves cap in honor of his favorite team. Mother's Day had passed a week ago and all Jeremiah wore were the remnants of his hair.

"Thought you were a baseball fan?"

"Was. No more."

"How come?"

"Bunch of babies, don't hustle, bunch of millionaire babies."

"Hey, not everyone."

"All of 'em."

"Some of 'em hustle."

"None of 'em."

"Lotta guys put out."

"None of 'em."

"Well, some do."

"Who?"

"Lots."

"Like?"

"I . . ." His stomach departed on the twenty-eighth floor. "Lots."

"Name one."

Me, Danny thought. Look at it, not even in the union yet and I'm defending the faith. Christ. Danny shook his head, not wanting to bother arguing the point.

"Good morning, Mr. Neuman," his young secretary smiled.

"Danny, please. Good morning, Lisa."

"You have some calls, Mr. Neuman."

Lisa never called him Danny because she said such informality unnerved her, which was much the same reasoning she used for why typing his stories without errors or writing his letters or mailing his correspondence or even relaying accurate phone messages unnerved her. Murray said he liked the way Danny answered his own phones, that it showed the personal touch. But Danny never complained. Why should he get her in trouble? Where else could she find a job that paid nearly three hundred a week and not have to do anything else except make him coffee?

"Coffee?" Lisa held out a plastic cup containing a tea-y solution.

"Quit." Danny sniffed, angering his headache. He fumbled in his pocket and lit a cigarette. Tomorrow I'll quit, just have to work into it.

"Why'd you quit?"

"Because"—he leaned over her desk—"I'm getting in shape. Listen, don't spread it around"—he saw her fingers inch toward the phone, ready to spread it around—"but I'm getting in shape, gonna be a baseball player."

Lisa giggled.

"What's so funny?"

"You'd look silly doing jeans commercials."

"I'm not doing jeans commercials."

"They all do."

"I, I don't want to do jeans commercials. I want to play baseball."

28

"Maybe you'd look good in tight jeans."

Danny flushed and started into his office, grabbing the coffee and ingesting half the cup in one fetid swallow as Norman came up from behind, followed him into the office and sat in Danny's chair. Danny turned, saw Norman and spilled coffee on the floor.

"You wanna kill me?" Danny snapped, brushing coffee off his pants.

"You hungover, too?"

"I didn't drink yesterday, you drank."

"Right, right, listen." Norman locked the door and returned to the desk. Danny glanced over "Wheel Alignments: Fact or Fiction," sighed and pushed the half-finished story away. "Hey, you want to get away early today, Friday, maybe take in a movie?"

"No, have to work out after work, have to talk to Murray about that."

"What work out?"

"You know, work out." Danny mimed lifting weights, touching toes and pushups. Panting, he said, "Ran this morning, too."

"You ran?"

"Yeah."

"What for?"

"To get in shape."

"For what?"

"I told you yesterday. I'm going for that tryout at the Stadium." Danny stared at an enlarged photo of a fuel pump. Beneath, the caption: YOUR ENGINE'S DEATH MAY START HERE.

"I thought you were just drunk."

"You were drunk."

"One of us were drunk." Norman giggled. "You're not serious?'"

"Why not?"

Norman rolled his eyes.

"So you're running?" He smirked.

"Yeah, yeah, I'm running."

"At your age, right?" Norman picked his fingernails. "You want a heart attack? You get a heart attack, what happens to me?"

"Oh, that's nice, always worrying about yourself, thanks. Ever stop to think of me, huh?"

"I am thinking of you. You get a heart attack, you're dead. I just lose my job. Which is worse?"

Danny wasn't sure. Yes he was. Positive.

"Norman, maybe you don't take this seriously, but I do."

"Danny, Danny, I know you from way back when. We lived together, so what's this silliness? Come on, you're thirty-three, stop this. It was fine in college and everything, but don't get carried away."

"What are you doing?" Young Norman Reiner inched back on his bed as Danny poured Franco-American spaghetti into a pot.

"Eating."

"That?"

"All I can afford."

"You'll die without nutrition."

Danny shrugged and poured in a can of tuna fish, Bumble Bee, naturally, and stirred the concoction.

"You're gonna eat that?" Norman cringed.

"Yeah, it's good, wanna taste?" Danny held out the fork. An hour later Norman spoke to the housing office about moving out. No vacancies, so he was stuck with a man whose dietary habits consisted of canned spaghetti and tuna fish, coffee, cigarettes and beer.

"Will you talk to Murray for me?" Norman finished cleaning his right pinky fingernail. "I think he's pissed at me about that story I wrote."

"Which story?"

"The one on steel-belted radials."

"Jeez, Norman, I warned you not to have each of the tires as separate characters."

"I thought it would be cute, with dialogue and everything."

"It's not cute. Look, I, I can't keep rewriting all your stuff."

"Oh, you have time to run like a lunatic around Queens, but you don't have time to help me out, right, that it? Which is more important, huh, which is?"

Danny sighed and relented.

"By the way"—Norman started on his left thumb—"Murray wants to see you."

30

"About what?" Danny constructed a baseball diamond on his blotter, decided to wait until Norman left before pulling his baseball glove out of the briefcase.

"Your fuel injection story."

"*Your* fuel injection story."

"My name's not on it."

"Norman, you're a prince, you know?"

"I would've handed it in the way it was."

"Yeah, you would've been fired and the Gay Liberation Front would've been in here picketing." Danny sighed. "Okay, okay, is he in already?"

Murray Camus, formerly known as Murray Edelbaum, grunted as the door opened, then grinned broadly as Danny entered. Murray viewed Danny as a son and insisted he call him Dad. Some people even said they looked alike, though Danny couldn't see the resemblance. Maybe the hair. Danny's was beginning to recede. Murray had a long pointed nose, fleshy body. Danny's body wasn't fleshy—okay, a little flabby. He could take care of that.

"Hi, Dad."

"Son, son, sit, sit," Murray urged, though Danny had already sat.

Years ago, Murray had been a newspaper reporter, having worked at a string of papers until the local bars and managing editors' patience had snapped and he'd been forced to move on. Finally he'd landed a position at the Associated Press in Cincinnati. He'd been covering the bus drivers' strike in Dayton, filed his story and was returning home, when his car broke down in Lebanon, Ohio. Eleven-thirty at night, no gas stations open, no one on the road, no liquor stores to deliver, his AAA card no longer in his wallet. As legend had it, Murray had decided to fix the car himself. He started examining the car piece by piece, until he descended into something of a religious experience. As Murray told it, he understood that car was like man. Some nasty ones said that Murray was tanked on Anti-Freeze Summer Coolant. Even Murray wouldn't drink that straight. Anyway, come six in the morning, the entire engine lay in pieces by the roadside. The state police found Murray fondling his battery cables, mumbling.

"Okay, mister, what's the problem?"

"It's a small intestine, you know?" Murray had looked at the two patrolmen. "A small intestine. So lovely." He'd gestured about the pieces of the Chevy engine. "Like a human body, frail, so lovely, you must treat it well."

After making bail, Murray had quit his AP position and decided to open *Auto Service Monthly*, the very least he could do as a paean to this thing of beauty.

"So son, how are you?"

"Fine, Dad, yourself?"

"Wonderful. And Sarah?"

"Fine."

"The kids?"

"Don't have any."

"Why?"

"Just don't, Dad."

"Ah, someday, you'll understand children." Murray fingered a scale model of a V-6 engine. "So, what's new?"

"Norman said you wanted to see me."

"Who?"

"Norman, Norman Reiner, my associate editor?"

"Oh, him." Murray's face twisted in disgust. "No, whatever, it wasn't important."

Danny started to stand, then fell back down.

"Listen, Dad, uh . . ."

"What, son, what's on your mind?"

"I was wondering, uh, if I took a shorter lunch break, well, if I could try and get out of work half an hour earlier?"

Murray considered this request for three minutes, opening the tiny doors of a miniature Monte Carlo and squinting to watch the miniature passengers.

"And do you think that's so wise?"

"What, well, you know, usually by the end of the day, my work's completed and . . ."

"I miss my Janet."

"Who?"

"Your mother, the one you never met."

"Oh, right, Mom."

"And you want to ruin the same thing, the same way?"

"I, I just want to get out a little earlier."

"So what's her name?"

"Who?"

"Your mistress."

"I don't have a mistress."

"Son, son, you can tell me."

"What, I, I have to get out a little early. I'll make it up, even bring work home to stay ahead. I'm always ahead."

"Go to a professional for your urges."

"I don't want a hooker."

"You want a number?" Murray studied him. "I just don't want to see you destroy your marriage on some little girl who'll take you to the cliffs and drop you over the edge. I hurt your mother, Danny."

"I know."

"Don't you do it. A hooker's the same thing, almost."

"Okay."

"Feel better?"

"No."

Time to get serious, Danny thought, making his way up Fifth while trying not to run outside the base line and into the path of the downtown bus. Or time to remember what it's like to get serious.

"Are you putting all your effort into this swing, Neuman?" Springfield Gardens High School coach Spud Bateman glared at him.

"Yes sir."

"Are you giving it your all?"

"Yes sir."

"Then go up and hit a home run."

Danny had struck out. But at least he had been serious about it. Not until he'd gotten to college did he become less serious. Not even less serious, just more confused. Grades, classes, friends, women, career, acne, beer, baseball. Everything pulled and bewildered him. He couldn't get into the jock towel-slapping-beer-guzzling-God-am-I-horny atmosphere. Besides, varsity baseball at Stony Brook wasn't exactly Arizona State caliber.

33

HASIDIM, HASIDIM, HASIDIM, the Stony Brook crowd chanted whenever they played Yeshiva. No one took it seriously. To be a real jock without living in the real jock world left you with one other choice.

"Just one toke, I'm mellow."

"Me too."

"Maybe another."

"Who has the Oreos?"

Six people sharing a bong, lolling eyes and listening to mellow music. Guzzle beer or mellow out until dead. He belonged to neither that world nor the world of the studious, so he stayed within a small circle of those who didn't belong, either. He started giving up what he wanted because he was afraid: afraid of being different, afraid of just enjoying himself. Baseball and making the Yankees suddenly terrified him. How could he honestly believe he could make the Yankees coming out of Stony Brook. So what was he doing playing baseball? And why was he smoking dope? Either you participated in all the rituals they demanded of you, or you didn't. Either you knew how to keep the pipe lit or you were mocked in a room full of stoned people intensifying your paranoia. Either you talked dirty to girls and fucked the jock-sniffers or you were weird. Just because you simply wanted to hit the ball.

"And then what happens?" Sarah had asked as they watched the 1973 World Series.

"On the fourth ball you go to first."

"Why four?"

"Because."

"Because why?"

Lovely, inquisitive Sarah, always asking questions. If he couldn't provide a suitable answer, then it couldn't be worthwhile. Merely telling her it was the rules wasn't enough. So Danny had sought to involve her in baseball through more spiritual realms.

"It's the tranquility, don't you see? The utter timelessness, the link with the past, the small human drama on every pitch. One man against one man, it's so simple, yet so complex."

That had held her for a while, especially since they were dating and she had wanted to understand what was so important to him that he could sit hunched over a radio or memorize *The Sporting News*. Then Sarah had discovered feminism and realized there were no female starting pitchers. Or even utility infielders.

"It's demeaning, those batgirls."

"Why? They have boy batboys."

"Batgirls, serving men. Where are the female managers or players? Ech, it's a disgusting male province, disgusting."

So the woman he loved thought his love was disgusting, and you couldn't see the signals from the third-base coach through the clouds of Acapulco Gold from the stands, and who could get excited about beating Yeshiva when their players couldn't dive headfirst because they'd risk losing their cap and yarmulke and so offend two thousand years of Talmudic law? At least if he'd had reinforcement from someone, but there hadn't been any, only pressure. Except for Joe. His best friend. A man who had vacillated between thinking himself Mr. Spock and Jesus Christ. His inseparable companion, whether playing football at three in the morning, or sharing chicken salad heros, or smoking an ounce of dope, or playing chess completed wrecked out of their minds.

He remembered the time he'd been stoned to the edge of comatose with Joe, when Salmon Face Levine had come in. He'd been amused by them, often studying them like zoo animals. Salmon Face had watched for a few minutes, or hours, both Danny and Joe ignoring him. Then he'd giggled and turned the album from 33 to 78, waiting for their response. Obviously he'd thought speeding up the music would flip them out or enhance their head or some such nonsensical term. He hadn't understood that they didn't need anything extra. Then again, no one seemed to understand. That much Danny could already see, whether it was in some dormitory room or in his own office. Or house.

Danny stepped inside Herman's Sporting Goods store, and immediately decided he hated everyone in there. Over there, the one with muscles grafted onto muscles in a T-shirt. The tennis player swinging an imaginary racket and not even breaking for lunch. The gymnast with broad shoulders and muscular legs doing handstands in a three-piece suit. Even the bowlers had better physiques than Danny. He hated them because he could tell they viewed him with contempt, so much so, in fact, that no one even looked at him. Not even worthy of a look of contempt—well, I'm not in that bad a shape, Danny thought, picturing himself as he had stood before the mirror that morning.

"I don't know what you're talking about." Sarah had watched him suck in his stomach. "You're in good shape."

"Then what's this?" Danny had seized the sides of his waist. "Huh, what's this?"

"The aging process."

"Hah, aging process, does Jack LaLanne have these?"

"He's older than you."

"Exactly."

"And he's been at it longer than you."

"Right, right, so I'll start and catch up."

"Why, Danny? Don't worry about your body so much. There are more important things."

Her more important things, he thought, smiling at a weight lifter, then paling as the Schwarzenegger clone winked and rubbed his tongue across his lips. Good, that's what I need, to get raped in Herman's. Danny waved his arms, warming up for what, he didn't know. His shoulders were still fairly broad, if stooped; his arms still somewhat lithe, even if the triceps didn't shoot back in the opposite direction from the biceps, which didn't shoot out, either. Right now, he could pass for a golfer. Maybe. Actually his expression was too pasty for a golfer. Maybe a ballplayer. A ballplayer who didn't play in the sun. Oakland? Minneapolis? New York? Exactly. Paste, the tan of pollution. Get serious.

"Nice machine." Danny patted the seat of an exercise bicycle, talking to a reedy man with veins bespeckling his pointed nose. "How much?"

"Depends." The man eyed Danny.

"On what?"

"You know, this is top-of-the-line merchandise. Best on the market. Has the lowest ratio of heart attacks per user in the country. Only three heart attacks per eight hundred users. We're damn proud of that mark."

"Well." Danny rubbed the seat, then withdrew his hand before the man's jealous glare. "I'd like to buy it."

36

"Not so fast." The man circled Danny, inspecting him. "How old are you?"

"Thirty . . . twenty-nine."

"Uh-huh? Exercise much?"

"Run, swim, tennis, golf, karate, water-ski, hang-glide and polo on weekends. Hey, you take a check, cash or what?"

"All right, okay." The man held up his hands. "I just wanna make sure you won't screw up the statistics, that's all."

Just to prove he wouldn't screw up the statistics, Danny purchased a hundred pounds of weights. Just to tone his muscles. He would've added a heavy bag, but wasn't so sure he wouldn't screw up the man's statistics.

At home, Sarah watched him assemble the machine in the basement. "Danny, I don't want to be late."

"We won't be."

"When will you get ready?"

"Soon."

"How soon?"

"Soon, soon. I want to try this out."

"Now?" Sarah lit a cigarette.

"Yeah, so, why not?"

"You want to go sweaty?"

"I'll take a shower."

"And we'll be late."

"If we're five minutes late?"

"I hate to be late."

"I'm just trying it out."

"American Express bill came in the mail today." Sarah examined a price tag. Danny glanced back, then climbed on the bike. "They said our account was delinquent for the third month in a row."

"Yeah, we'll pay it."

"And Bloomingdale's came in." Sarah laid the cigarette pack on the box.

"Okay, fine." Danny revolved his legs, feeling pain, enjoying it.

"Saks, too." She offered him a cigarette. Danny allowed her to slip it into his mouth.

"All in one day?"

"Also Macy's."

"Isn't there some kind of law against them sending out bills on the same day? Emotional harassment?"

"Well, you would know about the law, wouldn't you?"

Danny stared at a two-foot mound of law books.

"I just can't take it anymore."

"You're just tired." Sarah rubbed his neck.

"It won't work."

"Just rest."

"It won't, I can't, it's not, it's not—shit, I don't want it."

"You sure?"

"I gave it a shot."'

"I know."

"And then they'll talk."

"Who?"

"Everyone, saying I couldn't make it."

"Fuck 'em."

"Everyone?"

"Fuck 'em all, do what you want. Don't be miserable for them."

Danny groaned as the bicycle dial slowed. Sarah started up the steps.

"Please be ready by seven-thirty."

"Make it, seven-forty, five. Norman's coming." Danny wheezed.

After Danny had rewritten Norman's story he'd let it slip that they were going to a party that night. Norman had asked to come. Begged, in fact.

"Why? He wasn't invited."

"He knows them."

"He wasn't invited."

"What is it, a wedding, with meals paid for? He went to school with them, too."

Sarah had hated Norman ever since he'd moved in with them following his eviction two winters ago. He'd lasted two days on the couch, and would've stayed another few but Danny hadn't wanted to join him.

"They're not his friends."

38

"Not mine, either."

Maybe they were. No, they weren't. They were the remnants of the hall that had ostracized him and only found him legitimate once he'd been married. He'd become saner for them since his marriage. Actually they were Sarah's friends, and she legitimized him. He had a ring on his finger, so he couldn't be expected to smoke up all their dope, or start a match fight in a living room, or any of the extreme measures he'd once undertaken to resolve his confusions. Like sliding headfirst. Danny had few friends. There was Norman, and sometimes he didn't even know what category Norman fit into, which relieved Danny because at least there was one category he didn't categorize. And Joe. Joe, who now lived in Alabama and had attended grad school in philosophy; Joe, his best friend in the whole world, with whom he wondered how much he had in common anymore. All they had was their love and the memories, since they had no present to build upon the memories. Joe, who wrote him of fishing and hunting . . .

"Put it back," Danny had screamed at Joe, as a helpless fish dangled from the fishing pole. Joe and his wife had taken him to a farm during Danny's visit to Alabama. The last time Danny would be allowed to go anywhere alone. "Look at it, you're killing that fish. Isn't it bad enough to eat them, do you have to kill them?"

Joe had stared at the fish, an amalgam of reflection and guilt sweeping his long, angular face and those clear blue eyes forever darting near madness or utter calm, or both. He had inspected the fish for several seconds before he'd plucked the convulsive frame off the hook and flipped it back into the lake. Joe had looked at him with that distant knowledge, that one look which had always connected them, always would, no matter where they went. It had both knifed and relaxed Danny, and he'd grinned.

"Indeed." Joe had smiled faintly.

"Indeed." Danny had grinned . . .

"And please don't tell anyone tonight about this." Sarah poked her head back down.

"What?" Danny leaned against the machine.

"This, this nonsense."

"Why, you embarrassed by me?"

"This isn't you. This I'm embarrassed by, not you."

"Same thing now, Sarah."

"I'm asking you not to embarrass me."

"And I'm asking you to understand." Danny gestured around the musty basement. "Okay, just understand."

"Will you do this for me?"

"What makes you think I'll say anything?"

"Because I know you, I know how you tell things."

"What, I've told no one."

"You tell everyone. You told your secretary, she mentioned it to me when I called today about the cream cheese. If you told her, you'll tell our friends."

Bitch. Traitor. Monday morning she learns to type.

"Why would I tell them, they're not my friends."

"They're our friends."

"The hell, they're your friends."

"Don't turn on your friends, Danny."

"I'm not turning on anyone, damnit. I ask for some lousy understanding from my wife and I get this shit—be silent, like I'm some goddamn retard or something."

"Don't embarrass me in front of our friends. They've been very good to us. Will you promise?"

"Yeah, yeah."

"Swear."

"The hell, isn't my word good anymore?"

Sarah turned and walked up the steps.

40

Chapter 4

What do insomniacs do when they stay up through the night and don't smoke? Danny wondered, sucking on a cigarette in the dark living room. Watch TV? Eat? Danny was hungry. He'd cut down on his caloric intake. Hadda get in shape. Hadn't even smoked during the entire party, neither pot nor Marlboro though he'd wished desperately for a cigarette. He'd chewed gum the whole night. But he hadn't made a similar effort to conceal his unwillingness to get stoned.

"What do you mean, you don't want any?" Tall Jeffrey, formerly known as Eb, had accosted him with the burning tip of a joint. Tall Jeffrey who, upon moving into the hall his freshman year, had insisted on being called Eb, a strange enough nickname for a tall Jew from Forest Hills. They had all been from Forest Hills, originally, hence the name, the Forest Hills Gang. Except Danny. But then he had never been part of the Forest Hills Gang. Eb had held this nickname until the night he'd ingested a small amount of LSD and watched himself scurry up and down the side of his guitar for several decades. After that Eb, now known as Jeffrey—even if everyone still called him Eb, except Danny, to whom Eb/Jeffrey was eternally grateful—had taken to walking through the woods surrounding Stony Brook, chanting yoga and dispensing eloquent soliloquies upon the flowers. Now he worked in the management end of Wendy's. Danny had rather liked him when he'd wandered through woods speaking to flowers instead of discoursing upon hamburger buns.

He didn't like him this way. He didn't like any of them. Fuck their rituals. I'll do what I want.

"Uh, you know, just my lungs."

Everyone had stared at him. So he wanted to stand among them straight? To observe them? To watch for little eccentricities that could be used against them later? Jeffrey's wife had whispered to Sarah, who'd made no comment except to suck extra hard on another joint. Yellow paper, expertly rolled. Some things they didn't forget, even if they couldn't remember why they smoked in the first place.

"Why not?" Jeffrey had insisted.

Go for it, Danny had thought. Say it, fuck them, who needs them, why can't I just do what I want? Maybe someone would understand. Maybe they would be pleased he'd agitated the evening beyond discussions of IRA accounts. Maybe someone would even empathize with him. Maybe, maybe, maybe. He'd shrugged and heard a voice from the exiled corner—Norman, who for the past fifty minutes had just sat in the corner, ignored by everyone except Danny.

"He wants to be a Yankee," Norman had said. He'd meant no malice. At least Danny wanted to think he'd meant no malice. He'd just wanted to be accepted, and so selected the side of greater numbers. Them. "He's going for a tryout at Yankee Stadium, can you believe that?"

Norman had snickered. Unlike the others, Norman hadn't meant to snicker, just that he'd been nervous at this sudden attention and quickly realized what he'd done, so he'd buried his head. Not for long, though. Several had approached his exiled corner and probed him for information. Sarah, flushed, had wandered near the dip, at once vigorously shoving sour cream and cream cheese on a chip into her mouth and glowering at Danny. She'd mimed toking. Danny had shaken his head. Again she'd mimed. Again he'd shaken his head. She'd nearly bitten off her lower lip and whirled toward the wall. Several wives, sympathetic since their husbands weren't going to be Yankees, had whispered at Sarah. Danny had seen a handkerchief applied to Sarah's eyes, her mascara running.

Jeez, what did I do so wrong?

Soon they'd surrounded him. Who would be his agent? Would hitting in front of Winfield help or hurt? Center field? Well, Mumphrey's still young. Ahem. Maybe if you had a drink you'd feel better. When do you become a free agent?

Afterward Sarah had coldly asked Norman if he'd mind not walking with them toward the subway. Norman had nodded guiltily and mumbled an apology to Danny, who'd clasped him on the back. God love Norman, sometimes, shit. Danny had been irritated, but not at Norman. Not even at those smirking assholes. Not at Sarah, though she had asked him where he was sleeping that night. No, Danny had been incensed with himself. He should've said it. He should've been the one.

Danny rose and went down to the basement. He consulted the blackboard littered with chalked exercises, grunted and leaped onto the bicycle.

Whir, whir, whir, Sarah heard through the floor. I don't believe it, she thought. Three in the morning and he's exercising.

It wasn't that Sarah was so embarrassed by him. Just that she thought Danny could do more. She had always believed in him—at least until she saw the pattern of his half-finished life, starting and stopping. She thought he could do better in life. Even when he dropped/flunked out of law school, Sarah thought he'd go on to something, become a something. Then he'd started writing for those idiotic wrestling magazines and going to work in sneakers and jeans. And never completing any of the novels he'd started. Maybe it was more than whether he'd ever become anything. Maybe it was because Sarah was counting on him to become something so she could become something. Which she hadn't. She'd planned on teaching after college, then realized a lifetime of rubbing running noses appalled her, and so sought a business career. Initially she had found success and fulfillment, then grown bored with deciding fabrics and fashions. Too material-oriented. But she'd wanted material goods. Then again, she hadn't. So she'd stopped looking for work. Danny became her vocation. Make Danny something.

He'd been a disappointment. How to tell him he'd been a disappointment, that she feared he'd never amount to anything, and then she would never amount to anything either? Okay, she could go back to work, but that terrified her. What would she do? There wasn't anything she wanted to do. Nothing interested her. Only Danny, and he seemed determined to spend the rest of his life at that silly car magazine. Now this. No children, a rented home in quasisuburbia, bills up their behinds. And this. It was so typical of him that he would get excited about something as ludicrous as this, only to vent all his energies and their money, and then finally give it up. Give up what? He really thought he would make it. Deep down, really believed he would make the Yankees. Then what would become of her? Stupid, Sarah berated herself, listening to the weights being lifted and dropped. He won't make it, so you'll have to scoop up the pieces again, and they're your pieces as well. With each creeping collapse of his ego your own ego falls apart. For what? Why was he doing this? And why wasn't she doing something? She had. She'd tried to guide him, encourage him. Obviously she'd failed. He'd failed, she'd failed. Failures together. Now she could see how their marriage was disintegrating as well. Danny the child. Refusing to grow up. Refusing to accept responsibility. But what about me? Did I ever pursue anything? At least I took responsibility for marriage, for fiscal soundness. At least I've tried. He never had, never. Now this, this ultimate in irresponsibility, he goes and tries to get in shape so he can embarrass himself. And me. No, not embarrass me. He wouldn't understand he really wasn't embarrassing me. Disappointing me. I look around that party and see those people and I think of us and Danny waking up to run and what do we have? We have nothing. And whose fault? His fault for failing, mine for allowing his failure to be mine as well? Whose fault is it, anyway? I love you, Danny Neuman, she thought, hearing a loud groan. Probably dropped a weight on his foot. Should go and help him. Why, so he can continue? So for the next four and a half weeks I have to live with this nonsense? And he refused to involve me. He wouldn't listen to my comments, my opinions. Perhaps because they're not important to him. Perhaps because I'm not important to him. Chasing a stupid little ball. This is to be our life, watching him chase a stupid little ball and come home from that silly tryout all dejected and then what? Christ, Danny, then what?

44

So far not good, Danny thought, sitting in his office. He had smoked through half a pack of cigarettes inside of half an hour. Of course, he had only smoked a few puffs before ditching them, which, he told himself, couldn't be too harmful. The wretched pain in his chest had to be from the bench press falling there, not from emphysema. Actually it wasn't the chest pain which bothered him but the pile of cigarette butts on top of his desk. Not even the pile of cigarette butts but what they represented. Failure.

How many tobacco leaves died for your sins, Neuman? he asked the butts toppling atop each other. How many? You shouldn't be on my desk but on the floor, where you belong. He sighed, which produced pain, which produced irritation, which compelled him to try and stand, only to collapse back onto his desk chair because the ankle weights he wore everywhere except into the shower generally kept him affixed to one spot. They were supposed to make his legs stronger, but after five days he felt he belonged on a telethon rather than a baseball diamond. He fiddled with his pencil, flipped a butt in the air and swung the pencil. He missed. He flipped another butt in the air, swung the pencil and missed. Again. Again he missed. Shit. Should have live pitching, Danny grumbled. What's the use of fungos? Timing, Neuman, timing. Like your subway escapades.

On the way to work that morning, Danny, fortified by his conquests over the crosstown bus, had decided to see how long he would wait before dashing into the crowded subway car. Just as the doors had started closing, Danny had leaped in, which hadn't been easy with the ankle weights. Successful the first time, Danny had decided to repeat the process. At each stop on the E train, Danny had gotten out, hovered at the edge of the crowds swarming into the cars, then dashed back in. Unfortunately he had been nearly mutilated at Willetts Point when a fat woman, whose entire life was apparently devoted to the care and eating of hero sandwiches, had moved ahead of him, leaving Danny in the closing doors. He'd screamed and twitched until several people had come to his aid. He hadn't tried it again, resolving to wait to practice riding the subways until they were less crowded. Good, so my timing will be down and I'll get mugged, he thought, disconsolate as yet another butt tumbled to the desk.

Fuck.

At least his waistline was receding, undoubtedly due more to Sarah's unwillingness to speak to him and his inability to digest food across the table from a sphinx. Five days of running with no progress. Five days of lifting weights, and all that seemed to do was eviscerate his ability to open a jar of ketchup. Five days of wearing ankle weights, and his gait resembled not Bruce Jenner but Walter Brennan.

I am doing something wrong, Danny thought, his hands swollen from swinging a bat. He pecked at the intercom.

"Lisa, come in here, please."

Lisa straddled the chair and stared.

"Uh, could you take some dictation?"

"I don't know dictation, you know I don't know dictation, Mister—"

"Danny."

"Neuman." She started crying. "I don't know dictation, when you hired me you didn't ask if I knew dictation, please, I don't know dictation."

"Okay, okay, fine, then, uh"—Danny could barely move his fingers—"but I have to get some stories out."

"I'm sorry."

"Okay, listen, it's okay, Lisa, really. Just that my hands are real sore and, you know—"

"You want to fire me."

"No."

"Yes, you do."

"Lisa, no, really." He smiled. "Maybe you can get me some coffee?"

She brightened and returned with a cup of tea-y coffee. Danny sipped it. First of the day. First. No more with Sarah. He was supposed to have quit yet still drank coffee. Except with her. Jeez.

Danny knew he should've called Murray's office before popping in, but whenever he called, Murray's secretary was away

46

from her desk, leading Danny to wonder what the secretaries at *Auto Service Monthly* did for a living. He knew what Murray did, which is why he never popped in, lest he interrupt the editor in a running dialogue with a new water pump. But this was important.

"Son, sit, sit." Murray had been communing with a radiator hose. "You know, they don't make hoses like these anymore."

"Not since *West Side Story.*" Danny hid his swollen hands in his lap.

"Eh?" Murray didn't like it when anyone insulted auto parts. He wasn't certain whether Danny had been insulting auto parts, but he frowned just in case. "So, son, what can I do for you?"

"Well, Dad, I was wondering, you know, maybe if—uh, well, I'm a little short and I could use a loan because, you know, I need to buy this machine."

"A machine?" Murray glared at Danny's swollen hands, forcing him to slide them into his pockets. "Whatever happened to normal sex?"

Danny chuckled faintly. "No, not that kind of machine. You use a bat, you know, to practice baseball."

"Baseball? What's this about baseball?"

"I'm a baseball player."

"Since when? You never told me."

"Since always."

"I don't understand . . ."

"Dad, I'm going out for the Yankees, okay, and I, I need some equipment to get in shape, to practice up."

"You're going out for the Yankees and you never discussed this with me, your father? You're leaving me, without discussing this?"

"No." Jeez, I hadn't even thought of that. Good, terrific, Neuman, consider all the angles. You can't work long-distance from the minors. "No, just, you know, really, I can't go into it all, but . . ."

"I gave you your start, Danny."

He had. Once Danny had worked for Zebnal Publications, the leader in professional wrestling magazines. Danny'd found that job after departing law school.

"Headline time." The editor-in-chief would call them around once a week. The editor had come to the magazine from a job announcing sales at Gimbels. The managing editor/photographer, from a feeble act entertaining liver-spotted audiences in the Catskills. The copy editor from the obituary page of the *Staten Island Gazette*. And Danny. Every week they would receive a packet of photos from stringer photographers around the country, sometimes Japan and Puerto Rico. They'd study the photos, decide which wrestlers were hot and would sell magazines, which ones the promoters were pushing as gate attractions, and fabricate a headline and angle. One angle. Animal hate. Animal hate carried Danny through three years of concocting stories. "The Secret Agony of . . ." "Why Andre the Giant Will Never . . ." "Fury in Florida: The Savagery of . . ." They'd concoct angles and Danny would make up the stories, make up incidents, make up quotes. Write stories about a wrestler's nightmare which he would never tell anyone yet miraculously Danny knew. Or describe someone alone in the dressing room, refusing to admit the press. Then how did Danny get in? Three-page stories, short fiction. The only profession where he could call someone the lowest, meanest, nastiest, stinkiest SOB that ever lived, and have some overweight, geriatric man with a forehead scarred from cutting himself with razor blades to evoke blood call and thank him.

But that wasn't the only reason Danny had enjoyed working there. The atmosphere. They had been his friends. They could write and slave all morning until their publisher left, then devote the rest of the afternoon to playing whiffle ball or poker or Strat-O-Matic baseball. It hadn't mattered because he could go in his college outfit of sneakers, T-shirt and jeans. That's what had incensed Sarah, that her husband went to work dressed like a junior in college. After a year, she had begun pressuring him to quit.

"You're better than this." Sarah had ignored the magazines he'd brought home. "Better. Wasting your talents on garbage like this."

"*Time* hasn't called yet, have they?"

"Have you tried?"

"I tried them all, remember? This is the best I could do."

"Try again."

"Maybe I like it."

"You told me there was no creative satisfaction."

"Maybe for now, maybe it's good for me."

"What are you waiting for, huh? You have to start a career now, build the foundation now. Where could you possible go after writing this garbage?"

Murray blinked tears now.

"I took you under my wing and this is how you repay me."

"Dad, listen, I, I'm not leaving."

"Are you going to try and succeed?"

"Succeed." God, how strange that sounded.

"And should you make it, then what? You play for them. Can you still come to this office and play for the Yankees?"

"No."

"So you would go behind my back and leave me in the lurch, after all I've done for you, walk out with a day's notice?"

"Give two weeks," Danny said hoarsely.

"This you do to your father."

Jeez, you're not my father, Danny thought.

"Dad . . ."

"It's Murray. You're no son to me. You'll just up and walk out after all I've done for you. God, I'm glad your mother isn't around to hear this. Hah, I bet you're malicious enough to call her in Fresno and tell her."

"I don't have her number."

"And I do? She walked out on me like you just did. After everything, it comes to this."

"Listen, maybe . . ." No, damnit, don't say it, don't back down, for once in your fucking life don't go the other way. Stay, stand, damnit, you can do it. "It's something I have to do."

"Then I must think of myself. I have to cover my bases." Murray paused. "Danny."

"What does that mean?" Danny trembled. "Are you . . .?"

"Yes."

"How can you . . ."

"And how can you?" Murray zoomed a miniature Cadillac across the desk. "I have a business to think of."

"When?" Danny closed his eyes.

"This week."

"Tomorrow's Friday."

"Then it's tomorrow."

Danny emptied his desk into a carton. Television always showed people requiring cartons to clean out their drawers. Danny could've used a manila envelope. At least he had more than when he had finally quit the wrestling magazines. There, all he'd taken were some paper clips and an autographed picture of Bruno Sammartino.

"Well, so now what?" Norman stared.

"I don't know."

"You're about to get me fired. Happy?"

"Shit, I won't get you fired, you'll probably be promoted."

"Don't want it."

"Norman, this has nothing to do with you."

"You covered for me, Danny. You saved my life, now you're responsible for it."

Good, terrific, Norman quoting Chinese proverbs because I rewrote his fuel injection story.

"Norman, you're crazy, really. Murray'll move you right in here. You have the most experience."

"Can't."

"Why not?"

"Just can't."

"Norman, listen, I'm sorry, really. I never meant to get fired, believe me. You think you got problems, what about me? Sarah'll have my balls."

"Don't tell her."

"Oh, good, how am I supposed to not tell her? Just go out every morning and when she wants to pay the deli for the twelve packs of cream cheese, then what?"

"I'll help you if you help me."

"Norman, what can I tell you?" Danny started to steal the stapler, slid it back into the drawer.

50

"When you get your next job, take me with you."

"Won't be a next job." Shit, damn, this is it, all the bridges up in smoke over my butt. "Why get another job when I'll be playing for the Yankees in four weeks?"

"You're insane. I thought you just did this to get out of here, really."

"Shows what you know."

"Danny, you can't do it."

"Don't tell me what I can do, okay? Just don't. I'm sick of, all my life, people telling me what I can't do. Christ, Norman, get off my case, okay?"

He did get off his case. And out of his life. Norman didn't attend the impromptu farewell party the office organized Friday afternoon, everyone grouped around, giving him presents. Murray sent down a poem about fatherhood.

> What is a father, if he isn't
> A father to his son?

Danny ripped up the poem, but kept the check for the next four weeks' pay. Helps to have a wealthy ex-father. Lisa gave him one of those one-cup Melitta coffeepots. Someone else gave him a silver cigarette holder. He was compelled to try both. Jeez.

So he spent the next couple of days standing in the backyard, flipping the ball up in the air, catching it, mumbling a play-by-play of his flipping the ball in the air and catching it. There was no one there. He'd told Sarah. He couldn't lie, not merely because it was ludicrous to lie about this. They didn't believe in lying. At least not about small things, like spending a dollar over their allowances or not mailing a letter or getting fired. Big things, like how they felt, those stayed submerged. Somehow they both believed the small lies wouldn't grow into big lies. Maybe the reason they were so compulsive about confessing small lies was their respective guilt about not confessing big lies. Maybe, maybe, maybe.

Her reaction had puzzled him. She hadn't thrown anything or threatened divorce. He might not have cared about either one.

Yes, he would've. He didn't want to lose her. She didn't want to lose him. Yet she had simply looked at him in abject disappointment, held her head in her hands the way his grandmother did when he refused to get his hair cut, and left the room. Nothing more. Except that she turned around and said dully, "You go to your parents' house alone Sunday."

Sarah got along better with his parents than he did. They liked her better. She and his mother linked neurotic arms in sisterhood. His father appreciated her sarcastic sense of humor. His older brother, the *nachis*, liked Sarah because she was Jewish and her spreading thighs would admit her into any Hadassah meeting. They liked her better than him and she didn't want to go with him? So they wouldn't go, he said.

"Go on, hurt them, that's what you want, hurt your parents. Look how much they love you and now you turn against everyone. Right, Danny, go on, you don't care who you hurt anymore, just go on and hurt them."

That's how he had come to stand in his backyard in Queens, New York, a place you stopped along the way to Manhattan, flipping the ball up in the air, catching it, flipping it higher and intensifying the difficulty until he finally missed one and, satisfied and dejected, squatted on the ground.

"You squat sooooo nice." Danny heard the high-pitched voice and looked toward the kitchen window, hoping it was Sarah. Their curtains were drawn, their lights out. Where was she? Danny sighed and examined his ancient Ralph Terry model glove he'd had since he was eleven.

"Hunch over, we love it."

He really knew where the voices originated but didn't want to admit it. Slowly he turned his head up and saw a Bea Arthur look-alike standing in the bedroom window. Their house was laid out the opposite of his.

"At least we don't have to hear their noises at night," Sarah had once said, though neither had ever heard noises like the ones she meant, only skates rolling above their heads.

"Hi," Danny said weakly.

"Whatcha doin'?" Bea alias Pistol grinned.

"Playin'."

"Havin' fun?" Sadie appeared at the window, long black shoulder-length curls draped to his bare shoulders.

"No."

"Wanna come up?" Pistol smiled seductively.

"Come up?" Shit, why not?

Danny knocked hesitantly. He could've sworn that his downstairs door had opened as he ascended the steps. But he knew it wasn't so. Or wished it were. In either case, Danny stood at the forbidden dark brown door. He knocked twice.

"Well, hello, look who's at our door and without any magazine subscriptions." Pistol, in a beige, sleek evening gown, and skates, waved a beige gloved arm and ushered him in. Danny hesitated. "Do come in, we don't bite."

Danny peered past Pistol into the living room. Living room? Two chairs shaped like a head with the seats a protruding lower lip. One had a tongue jutting out, the other didn't. Nearly enveloping the walls were movie posters. *Gone With the Wind. Casablanca. Bonnie and Clyde. The Blob. Abbott and Costello Meet the Wolfman.* A chandelier swayed from the ceiling, two black gloves affixed to its bottom.

"That's when we play Robin Hood." Pistol skated around on the hard wooden floors. "I play Robin, Sadie plays Maid Marian. Or sometimes he plays the Sheriff of Nottingham and I play Little John."

"I never play Robin Hood," muttered Sadie.

"You're not tall enough."

"I can wear heels."

Danny looked at Sadie's heels locked into the skates.

"Like them?" He picked up a skate.

"I don't know."

"You look in shock, sweetie," Sadie said over his shoulder as he skated into the kitchen, clinked glasses and skated back around the other side, lowering a pitcher of fruity liquid onto the glass-and-chrome coffee table.

Danny had yet to move from the doorway.

"Are you afraid?" Sadie asked.

"No." Danny trembled. "I . . ."

"I what?" Pistol grinned.

"Never been in here before."

"And why do you think that is?" Pistol rolled to the chair with the tongue, sat down, giggling, and crossed his skated legs in a yoga position.

"I don't know."

"Then why are you here now?" Sadie poured drinks.

Danny shrugged and shifted his weight from foot to foot. Sadie and Pistol exchanged grins.

"We don't bite, you know," said Pistol. "We are harmless. We won't attack you. We don't even attack each other."

"You don't?" Danny inched forward, angry that he suddenly felt less threatened.

"No, no." Pistol adjusted his hair. "Too time-consuming. Too much energy involved. Too many fights arise. I want it, he doesn't. He wants it, I'm not in the mood. If you ever calculated all the times both people were in the mood and subtracted them from all the times they weren't, well, you'd have a very high plus figure."

"Two hundred and eighty-three last fiscal year." chuckled Sadie.

Danny relaxed and searched for a chair. Pistol leaped off the seat, raced into the bedroom and returned pushing an ottoman the shape of a Snickers bar. Danny plopped down.

"I, I just thought . . ."

"What?" Sadie grinned.

"You know." Danny smiled.

"Good."

"It is?"

"We don't care."

"You don't, do you?"

"Uh-uh."

"So then, okay."

"Okay what?"

"I don't know."

Christ, I'm thirsty. Danny thought. He stared at the pitcher, hesitating. Sadie caught his glance and handed him his glass. Danny sipped it and they laughed.

* * *

"Where were you?" Sarah asked an hour later.

"Uh, I dunno, just talking, that's all."

Sarah twisted her face in disgust.

"You have lipstick on your cheek." She glanced upward.

Danny grinned, even as she stormed away and slammed the bedroom door.

Chapter 5

For five days after he lost his job, Danny exercised by himself. Swinging a bat until his hands puffed. Flipping the ball in the air, announcing his stumbles, announcing the deep drive to left, announcing how Neuman races to the warning track, announcing how the wind seems to be taking the ball and, holy cow, if only Neuman hadn't gotten dirt in his eye he would've made the catch, but that rookie showed a lotta moxie taking the ball directly on top of his head. Running toward a goal of one mile only to barely make a quarter and, in fact, spending more time nibbling Moscowitz's bagels. Lifting weights whose weight magically increased on every set. Riding his bicycle until he realized he was going nowhere, and didn't know why, didn't know where the resolve had suddenly gone or why it was so damn hard to get back into shape.

He did know he was terrified by what he was doing. That's why he ran so early in the morning, so he wouldn't see the commuters pouring toward the subway stations and be reminded he no longer had a job. That's why he still went to bed at the same hour, why he still brought his clothes in for cleaning, why he went and purchased a week's supply of tokens, because the abnormality of his dream was too much for him to deal with.

And then they'd come to him and asked if they could help. And he'd accepted. Why? He didn't know. Yes, he did. Out of fear, loneliness and desperation, because he knew he'd gone too far to give it up now. Sadism, too, though, was a definite possibility.

* * *

"Take your clothes off." Pistol handed Danny a hanger.

"Why, uh, why do I have to do that?"

Sadie and Pistol rolled their eyes.

"Are you afraid?" Pistol, arms folded across his turquoise dress, asked Danny, who lowered his eyes, nodded and pouted. "Of us?" Danny nodded. "That we'll do something to you if you take off your clothes?" Danny nodded. "Well, don't be." Pistol chuckled.

"You don't have to be insulting." Danny's head bobbed up.

"We're trying to help you."

"Can't I maintain my dignity while you're helping me?"

"Do you want to do this or not?" Pistol snapped. "We can be doing other things, sweetie. We don't have to waste our time on you."

"Okay, okay, just, can I at least undress somewhere else, is that okay?"

Danny took off his clothes in their bedroom. He did it by rote because he was afraid to open his eyes in their bedroom, afraid of what he would see and half-expecting them to come charging in at any moment.

"Pretty bad." Pistol studied him from the front.

"Lats aren't good." Sadie jotted down notes.

"Delts could be better." Pistol inspected.

"Tris are almost nonexistent."

"Stomach could use some tightening." Pistol shook his head. Danny glanced down to look at his stomach, which he knew couldn't be that bad. Okay, maybe it was. But not that bad.

"Jump." Sadie poked him in the back. Danny trembled. "I said jump."

"Why?" Danny touched his stomach, and Pistol slapped away his hand. "I mean, according to you guys, I'd probably have a stroke if I exerted myself."

"A stroke'll be the least of your problems, honey." Pistol grinned and Danny didn't like the grin. He didn't like standing in his underwear while two guys in dresses skated around sniffing disdain at the remnants of his physique. Nor did he like the idea of jumping, because he knew he couldn't jump very high.

"Is that how you jump for a fly ball about to take off?" Pistol feigned nausea, then sighed. "We'll start with your legs first. Now bend over, grasp the edge of the counter and press your face a few inches over the counter." Danny wasn't too hot about bending over. They noticed that.

"He has homophobia, as well." Sadie giggled.

"We'll cure that," Pistol snapped, shoving Danny's face down so his rear jutted out.

Had to happen eventually, Danny resigned himself, knowing the underwear would slide off and . . .

"Ow, hey," Danny screamed as Pistol sat on the small of his back, facing away from Danny. "What are you doing?

"Raise me up." Pistol grabbed onto Danny's waist. "Push up your legs, this'll strengthen the back of your legs."

"I can't." Danny wheezed, trying to lift up his feet with Pistol's sudden weight. "I can't."

"Come on, come on, honey, do it."

Danny pushed up. One. Two. Three times before he slumped against the counter, heaving.

"Not bad." Pistol bounced off, spinning gracefully on a skate. "We'll do three sets of these, as many as you can do."

Ow.

Next came running. At nine in the morning?

"You're supposed to run early, my—my bagels haven't digested yet," Danny protested as they skated him outside. People with jobs congested the streets. Danny tried to think of an excuse. He knew they wouldn't go for his wanting to watch a *Beverly Hillbillies* rerun.

"You run how much?" Sadie skated circles around Danny.

"Oh, you know, few miles." he shrugged, self-conscious over the bemused looks people gave him since two transvestites were circling him in skates. He blushed.

"He runs quarter of a mile, tops," Pistol said, clutching Danny's elbow. Sadie did the same and they skated him toward a steep hill. A very steep hill, perhaps even a mountain, perhaps rivaling Mount Everest.

"I can't run uphill." Danny smiled at a couple of people he recognized.

"A minor slope," Pistol said, smiling as he removed a small black box and dangled it at his side. "You can do it."

58

"I can't." Danny stopped, irritated at them, more irritated at himself because they'd caught his blushes and saw his sheepish looks at people staring at them, knew they knew why he was ashamed. But they didn't say anything, maybe because they understood what smirks were all about. Maybe they remembered how it was for them, and had a way to deal with all this, the guilt, the shame, the bewilderment.

Danny suddenly felt a bit more secure, though still embarrassed and afraid.

"Don't worry about them," Pistol said. "I'll bet few of them could even run a quarter of a mile."

Danny smiled gratefully, his smile twisting into puzzlement as he heard a scratching noise and felt them skate him to the top of the hill.

"What's that noise?" Danny asked. They grinned, their wigs blowing in the wind as they accelerated, Danny unaware he was nearing the top of the mountain. "I hear music."

"You're the baddest," Sadie whispered.

"The meanest," whispered Pistol.

"None one's badder," Sadie shouted.

"You're the champeeeeen of the world," Pistol laughed.

"Hit it, baby," Sadie shouted.

And from that black box which had slept inside of Pistol's dress Danny heard the music. *Rocky.* Heard the inspiration and saw their wide, elfin grins and felt himself peel over the top of the ridge, his arms windmilling at his sides, the wind smashing into his face and the sound of their skates racing side by side.

GONNA FLY NOW.

Danny ran, unable to conceal his deep crimson colors at the people laughing at him, the people who saw a thirty-three-year-old in cutoffs running like a madman down Queens streets, flanked by two men who must also be madmen. He pushed aside the paranoia and concentrated on not getting hit by a sanitation truck. They wouldn't let that happen to him.

ROCKY HIGH NOW.

They cut across a red light. Danny had slowed down but they grabbed his elbows and lurched him forward. He distantly heard cars honking and people swearing, but they kept abreast, skating furiously and whispering encouragement over the din of *Rocky* and the sound of his heart hammering inside his head, until finally they pulled up, a block from Moscowitz's.

"Ha, ha, ow, ow, ha." Danny slumped onto the sidewalk. "How far, was that?"

"Half a mile."

"I ran, half, a mile?"

They smiled.

"Do I get a chance to rest?" Danny wanted a cigarette, remembered he'd quit, remembered he'd smoked three in a row in the shower, remembered he wasn't supposed to remember such violations.

"For a few minutes." Pistol said as Sadie skated back to the house for some mysterious equipment. Probably a whip and a chain.

"How do you feel?" Pistol clamped a gloved hand on Danny's shoulder.

"My body hurts," Danny panted.

"Good."

"I knew I could count on your sympathies."

"Sweetie, you don't know what pain is like until you're run in full pads and equipment through spring drills in ninety-degree weather."

Danny turned slowly.

"You played football?" He asked Pistol's body, for the first time aware of the muscular physique, the massive forearms, albeit unshaven, stuffed into white gloves, then back up at Pistol's bony face. They didn't go together, Danny realized.

"Of course." Pistol said it casually, though it was forced, pulled by an abrupt pain which violated his pretty-handsome face. "Quarterback. Made All-State my junior year." Pistol's struggle to speak continued and Danny feared encouraging it, feared allowing his astonishment to show lest he insult him. Yet he knew he had to let it show, that it would be dishonest otherwise and he couldn't be dishonest with people who cared enough to bring a taped version of *Rocky* along on a run. "All-State. Yes." Pistol stood.

"But . . ." Danny gestured at the neatly tailored dress. "I mean, your—you know."

60

"I know." Pistol smiled without humor. "So did they, after my junior year. Funny thing, I never made the team my senior year." His gaze seared Danny. "All-State. You've never been All-State, have you, no." Danny cringed without knowing why. "I played baseball, too. Hit .380 one year. Darndest thing, they didn't seem to have room for me either after that. No one did."

Danny didn't get a chance to ask how it had happened. Not that he would've. That would've violated some rules he barely understood, the rules of the club into which he had found himself initiated—an organization he wasn't so certain he wanted to join. He waited silently for Sadie to return.

"Now what's all this?" he asked a few minutes later as they slipped shoulder pads and knee pads on him in the playground, and shoved a glove on either hand. Joe Pepitone model on the left, Bobby Richardson on the right. Jeez, where did they ever find these? Danny examined the glove, then looked up to see Pistol backtracking with a bat and softball, while Sadie approached with a helmet.

"Football doesn't start for a few months, you know," Danny said.

"This is for your timing," Pistol sighed.

"My timing? All this . . ." Danny's voice was muffled by the helmet Sadie plopped onto his head. "Mmmmmhhh."

"Are you ready?" Pistol flipped the ball in the air.

"I can't breathe," Danny screamed.

"Yes you can. Sadie dear, you put a nose protector on him."

"I can't breathe." Danny jumped up and down, flailing his arms.

"Sorry, darling." Sadie unclipped the guard and Danny gasped.

"Wait, wait." He held out Richardson. "Just a sec, what, what are we doing?"

"I will hit the ball to you. You will try to catch it. You probably won't, which is why we gave you a helmet and pads."

"That's encouraging. Uh, don't you think maybe you should back up a little, you're kinda . . ."

Thwap. A softball the size of an ICBM shot near his shoulder. Danny flung up his glove and missed the ball, but his shoulder caught it. Despite the pads there was pain. Tremendous pain. He was now an amputee, a cripple determined to make the Yankees. Shades of Pete Gray, but not for long, because Pistol rifled one at his left and Danny flung up his glove and again allowed his arm to take the blow. Now he was a paraplegic. They're going for quadraplegic. Danny backed up against the wire fence, feeling the familiar metallic iciness of the playground fence, the kind he used to crash into all the time. That fortified him a little, though not enough to refrain from begging for mercy at one point, nor enough to enable him to make one catch.

More timing and reflex exercises. They draped a carpet of pebbles in front of him at the park so Pistol's grounders would hit the pebbles, simulating the dreadful conditions of a minor-league field. Danny didn't do too well in those either.

"Can I have my helmet back?" Danny asked Pistol, who grinned malevolence and whacked a ball down, finding a pebble, or maybe two or three—Danny couldn't count because they sprayed his knees. He groped for a pebble instead of a ball, and found the ball had dashed about eight inches to his glove side. Better catch the pebbles. Maybe if he caught enough pebbles they would let him be.

"You know, the fields really aren't that bad, this is the Yankees organization and . . ."

Thwat, another sizzling grounder found a pebble, then his thigh. Danny fell to one knee, determined not to rub, doubly determined not to rub because Sadie bounced up and down and shouted, "Error—Neuman—error—Neuman," and Pistol laughed.

"You bastards," he screamed.

Pistol chuckled and lashed another grounder which, naturally, found a pile of boulders which ricocheted into Danny's groin. At least this time he moved in the direction of the ball, even if he was a few seconds late, or maybe hours.

"You're moving right," Pistol shouted.

Which was, frankly, more than he was able to do later that night, or for the next several nights. A full day of running. Calf exercises. Flailing at grounders, few of which he caught. Search-

62

ing for fly balls in the dusk because minor leagues have poor lighting, they said, to which Danny countered that the massive skull fractures he would incur from balls landing on his head would prevent him from ever finding out firsthand, to which they replied, no pain, no gain, to which Danny gave them the finger. Swinging at Pistol's fastball and Danny wondering why he wasn't in the Hall of Fame. Missing Pistol's fastball, convincing Danny it would be a while before he was in the Hall of Fame. Playing catch. Playing tag-up from third, each time Danny thrown out at home on Pistol's Yaz-like pegs. Running, situps, pushups, throwing, fielding, hitting, running throwing hitting catching pushups situps.

Danny had two death wishes. One concerned suicide, one the hatchet murder of two encrazed transvestites.

But he didn't dare complain. Not that he wanted to complain. That was a lie. He did want to moan and groan, even though the pain and frustration satiated him in a perverse way. But who would he moan and groan to? The *boychiks?* Hardly. Their idea of sympathy consisted of not beating him when he fell down. Sarah? Hardly Sarah. He would've spoken to Sarah if she'd ever spoken to him. But she didn't, or only to tell him there was a note on the refrigerator outlining his errands—chores which he did, primarily out of guilt. Of course, if he'd dared ask why he had to do all the errands when he barely had time for epsom salts, Sarah would've told him she was too busy looking for a job. If she spoke to him, that is. And if she did speak to him, he would've asked why she never went out to interviews, how the ubiquitous classified section of the *Times,* blue-circled pages scattered everywhere, never once led to a job. Or an interview. Again, he dared not ask why and she never told him, feeling it sufficient that she returned half an hour after leaving the house, every day. Either the subway never came or the bus never came or she forgot her purse or the want ads or Manhattan was closed today. That much she told him, flashing defiance, a look he hadn't seen for so long. And then she would shut up, and he would shut up, and the silence would continue.

After nearly a week on the set of *Gays and Dolls,* Danny, however painfully, felt some progress was being made. Just a little. His breaths weren't quite so short. His fumbling flailing at balls not quite so feeble, his stomach not quite so flabby.

Okay, not enough to be placed on the All-Star ballot. But still, something.

Chapter 6

"New game, new game." Sadie bounded up and down. Danny noticed they had selected a Saturday afternoon when they knew the streets would be especially crowded to subject him to another exercise. He still hadn't gotten over his embarrassment, but it didn't bother him as much. He knew the others were not only laughing at him, but at Pistol and Sadie. Somehow that diluted it. Not completely, however.

"Rundown play." Pistol announced in that firm, commanding voice. "Jackie Robinson, all that, Danny sweetie."

He'd been looking down at the ground. Probably more people'll be watching me than watched Robinson in Ebbetts Field.

"Yeah, I'm here."

"Good, darling, we'd hate to lose you now, what with all the fun just beginning."

Great, terrific, Danny thought, watching Sadie go behind him with a glove, Pistol in front, amused shoppers on their way to Alexander's brushing past.

"You just gonna chase me?" Danny asked Pistol, who nodded.

"Back and forth, back and forth, until you can stay in it as long as possible."

"Well, that's all fine, you know, but—" Danny gestured at Pistol's skates. "Not really fair, uh, you guys got skates on."

"You want a pair?"

"No, but I think it would be fair if you took them off."

"Too bad," Pistol sang and charged at him. Danny stumbled back and fell.

"Yer outta dere," Sadie screamed from behind as Pistol applied the tag.

"Not so difficult, is it, sweetie?" Pistol helped Danny up.

"I'd have more warning in a game."

"Aw, poor baby." Pistol kissed his forehead. "Give up?"

"Fuck off." Danny wiped off his pants and waited. Pistol charged and Danny retreated sideways, keeping his eye on Kate Hepburn—Pistol's guise for this day—and waiting for the throw over his head to Sadie, whom Danny could feel behind him. Pistol faked and Danny paused, grinning. Pistol moved forward again. Pistol faked, which Danny didn't know was a fake so he ran forward, slamming into Pistol and knocking them both to the ground.

"Yer out." Sadie hooked his thumb up as Danny panted atop Pistol. "But you guys shouldn't do that in public."

Both Danny and Pistol laughed.

"Aside from your sexual overtures," Pistol began and Danny gave him the finger, "you should try watching our eyes. I don't think the catcher would enjoy your grinding atop him as much as I did."

"Hah, hah, very funny."

"Not at all." Pistol grinned and retreated. Danny tensed. "Now," Pistol called out. "Our eyes, or anyone's eyes, should widen when they're about to throw. So watch for that."

Danny did. He believed Pistol. He kept believing Pistol as he was chased toward Sadie, kept believing Pistol as Pistol's eyes widened, which convinced Danny he was about to toss the ball to Sadie, so Danny again ran toward Pistol, who never threw the ball.

"Yer out, hah-hah-hah-hah," Sadie chanted as Danny reddened.

"You told me to watch your eyes, your eyes widened when you were about to throw, jeez, you told me that."

"So I fibbed." Pistol shrugged. "First lesson. Never believe anything a man with mascara says to you in a rundown play."

So Danny didn't watch for eyes. He didn't watch for anything. He tried to go on instinct, which didn't work, because he spent an hour being tagged out several thousand times, trying to elude them, never managing to elude them for too long.

66

Though he tried. Certainly not the way he tried to elude others. Danny needed approval from someone. He knew he had their approval, knew that was the most important thing, yet he was obsessed with finding someone he'd known before all this had happened who would say it was okay. But he couldn't. He dialed the office and heard Lisa announce it belonged to Norman. He dialed Murray and hung up after the first ring. He even called Norman at home, receiving his answering machine.

"This is Norman Reiner. I'm currently in a meeting with Michael Bennett at the moment, but if you leave your name and message, I'll . . ."

You're full of shit, Norman, Danny wanted to leave, but said nothing. They were all full of shit. That didn't make his isolation any easier, however, nor did it diminish his mental doubts that something was very wrong with a man who wanted to be a Yankee and whose instructors were two transvestites.

On the other hand, he *knew* there was nothing wrong with what he was doing. Not a damn thing. Maybe he was fooling himself, but if so, was it any less a delusion than anybody else's? That's why he ignored Sarah leaving the Brillo outside the shower when his ankle weights bled off black dye because he'd forgotten to take them off and forgotten about the added weight, and nothing would rob him of that tiny victory. That's why he berated himself at his self-conscious blushes whenever people pointed a finger at them and laughed. And that's why he refused to question his sanity, even if the whole world did.

Like his parents.

He had delayed going to his parents' for as long as possible. He knew it wasn't out of fear for the inevitable confrontation, or shame for what he was doing. Instead, Danny wanted to avoid hurting anyone. He knew nothing would dissuade him now and knew people who loved him would get hurt.

"Wonderful, wonderful, you'll get fresh air," his mother said. "Clean air is healthy."

Danny glanced at Sarah to see her reaction. There was none. Both understood his mother. Danny could lop off both hands and announce he was going to play the fiddle at the Grand Old Opry and his mother would approve. Superficially. Deep down, she would prepare the Kaddish, and that mourning would no doubt be communicated to his father when his mother would stare tearfully at *yahrzeit* candles in Waldbaum's, which would in turn be reconveyed to Danny.

"Do you think you should play touch football in new jeans, Daniel? Nu, Daniel, I don't think we should upset your mother like that."

Always his father using "we," as if to assuage the guilt when Danny came home late for dinner. Somehow by using that pronoun his father believed responsibility would be shared, the sin lessened. The only thing they'd ever really shared.

But Sarah said nothing, just ate. She knew his mother, probably better than Danny. For some reason, Sarah appreciated his mother's eccentricities, like her stocking up on so much food his parents' basement resembled a Waldbaum's warehouse. Who would ever need fifteen large jars of Hellmann's mayonnaise or a dozen packages of Ronzoni spaghetti? You never know who'll show up, his mother always replied. Danny was convinced that if Hitler arrived at his parents' house, his mother would fling bagels down the Fuehrer's throat before accepting relocation to a concentration camp. Always be prepared, his mother believed. Somehow Sarah accepted his mother's weirdness while she wouldn't accept Danny's.

"You can get hurt, Danny," his mother said.

"I won't get hurt."

"You'll tear up your knee again." His thin mother who cooked, never ate, lit another cigarette, chain-smoking. As Sarah did. As Danny wouldn't, though he'd snuck smokes in the bathroom, not out of guilt, but because every time he entered the room where Sarah was chain-smoking, Danny suffered coughing convulsions and had to leave. Or maybe he had to leave because she was there.

Danny made his preparations for leaving the table by shoveling a handful of rugelah into his mouth, which would both eviscerate his mother's insistence he eat for all of Jerusalem and justify his eventual declaration of the need for a walk.

"My knee's fine. They took the stitches out almost twenty-five years ago, remember?" Danny mumbled.

"Drugs, I hear athletes use drugs, drink. Nathan, isn't that so?" His mother turned to his brother the rabbi, calmly dissecting a mandel of all its nuts. Danny couldn't get away with that, but Nathan could. Danny wondered if he could get away with stuffing Nathan's nostrils with mandel bread.

"Good evening, everyone, this is Marv Albert. On top of the news tonight, phenom Danny Neuman was given his unconditional release by the New York Yankees following his arrest for the alleged mandel-manslaughter slaying of his older brother . . ."

"You mustn't drink, Danny," Nathan said. Danny popped the sesame seeds from a bagel. "Our people aren't alcoholics, Danny." And then his brother the rabbi recited statistics about the low incidence of alcoholism among American Jewry. His brother the Reform rabbi, who believed in the sort of assimilation which would result in all American Jews wearing yarmulkes and looking like the Cleaver family. Danny felt if you were going to do something, do it all the way. Grow *pais. Daven.* Don't be a Methodist with a knish. How long had it been since he'd felt that way? It felt good. Then if it felt so good, why did he want to kill his brother?

"And also, I wanted to ask you a question about my article." Nathan folded his hands and stared at Danny, who felt about seven, as he always did around his bother. He dropped the half-shredded bagel onto the plate.

"Yeah, sure, need help?"

"Actually, I was wondering if you could suggest a writer to help me polish up the piece once I've done all the legwork, someone experienced I could trust."

"What am I, Captain Hook?" Danny began to scrape onions off the rye. "I'm a writer." He held up his hands and saw they were fisted with sesame seeds and onions.

"Well, Danny, you're leaving us."

"If you would stay, the two of you could write together, be a famous brother writing team." His mother was at the oven, searching for a grease spot.

"Not exactly, mother," said Nathan. "After all, my name would have to be the only one on the piece. But anyway, you're leaving so . . ."

"And if I stayed would you share the by-line?" Danny snapped.

"Danny, I am the authority. I'm the one trekking across the Sinai to . . ."

"Maybe you and Danny could trek together," his mother said into the oven. "Danny, you know how you love figs and dates."

"Well, that's specious, Mother. After all, Danny has another career now." Nathan smiled. Through his rage, Danny wasn't sure if he had reached for the cream cheese knife while Nathan was talking, or when he started smiling/smirking. It really didn't matter, all that mattered was stabbing Nathan in the heart and watching the blood pour over the cream cheese and scallions. Danny really would've done it, he believed, if his father hadn't tugged the knife, ever so gently, out of his fist.

"Daniel." His father hadn't, up to that point, said a word. Now he prevented a murder. Danny glared around the table, shoved away and bolted out the door.

"What, what? I hear a door, is someone here, do I have enough bagels?" his mother shouted into her oven.

"It's Danny." His father stared at the still trembling front door.

"Touchy, isn't he?" Nathan shrugged and made an egg salad on onion roll.

"I don't know." Sarah sighed, really not knowing. "Mom, can I help you?"

Danny panted inside the garage. Panted and stared around, stared in bewildered rage until he sighted the opened cartons of old magazines. Old *Sporting News.* 1965. Jimmy Hall, Bob Allison, Tony Oliva, Earl Battey. Harmon Killebrew. The Minnesota Twins. 1966. Jim Palmer and the Robinson boys, Frank and Brooks, of the Baltimore Orioles. 1967. A rookie named Seaver. 1968. The new-look speedy Yankees.

Danny relaxed as he walked absently toward the rear of the garage, tripping over a childhood of useless junk his parents had seen fit to save, until he could reach, and slide out, the bat. His Lee Maye bat. A pretty fair hitting outfielder for the Milwaukee Braves. An official Lee Maye bat. Danny started running his hands up and down the fat part, then over the handle, taped because it had cracked and that's how his aunt, his mother's sister, whom everyone in the family except Nathan despised, had gotten it for him at Shea one night.

70

He swung the bat, gently, trying to remember how long it had been since he'd swung this very bat, when he felt his father nearby. Danny swung again for effect, to set up a protective screen.

"So, Daniel, what's new?" His father looked everywhere but at Danny, now assuming a stance, measuring his swings.

"Nothing much, Dad." Danny swung easily, knowing he didn't have to set up a protective screen with his father, for all the wrong reasons.

"So much junk in here," his father said, still scrutinizing the cartons.

"Yeah, well." Danny looked around. "I have to clean this place out for you one of these days."

"What, no, no, you have no room in your house. Leave them, I don't mind."

"Dad, you can't even fit your car in here."

"My car, that abortion, it needs a house? I'm hoping it'll run away some day."

They both chuckled. Danny looked at his father, who looked off in a corner.

"You lost weight, Daniel." His father still stared into the corner.

"Nah. Yeah?" Danny instantly thought of Sadie and Pistol and wondered what would happen if he ever brought them home for dinner. Home. It was home and he hadn't thought in terms of this house as home for—well, just hadn't. But standing here swinging his old bat, surrounded by his magazines, fulfilled by the same hate he'd always had for his brother, Danny felt at home. He swung again. Double down the right-field line.

"Those pants are a little baggy, Daniel. Maybe my tailor should take them in."

"Nah, I'll throw 'em away." Can't wait, Danny thought, crouching. Look for the curve on three-and-one.

"You'd waste good pants like those?"

"Yeah, they never, you know, look the same when they're taken in."

"My tailor will make them look like they just came off the rack. Give them to me." He stepped toward Danny.

"Dad, come on, you don't have to."

"Come, come, give them to me." His father started reaching for Danny's pants.

"Dad." Danny laughed uncertainly. "I can't go home in my underwear."

"I'll find you something to wear, I'll have them done right away." His father seized Danny's belt loops.

"No, please." Danny backed away, knowing the real reason he was backing away had nothing to do with his father trying to undress him in this musty garage. Then Danny stopped, because he didn't want his father to know why.

"Security, Daniel." His father blurted out. "You just don't throw away pants, money, you know. Security, Daniel."

To his father, security was everything. His father also had the advantage of omnipresent spaghetti and grass stains and funerals and weddings.

"Has nothing to do with that, Dad."

"Security." His father awkwardly patted Danny's arm. "You throw away security?"

"Dad, I have to do this."

And then Danny realized this was the first real talk they'd ever had. His father twisted his fingers in an uneasy ball and Danny squirmed. The first real talk they'd ever had except when Danny was late for meatloaf.

"You don't make it easy for us, Daniel."

The Emancipation. "We" transformed into "us." He was no longer on Danny's side. He'd given Danny his freedom. A child with freedom, as if that would scare him back into normalcy.

"Dad, wasn't there ever anything you wanted to do?"

"Lots."

"So?"

"I didn't."

"Why not?"

"Wasn't done. I had responsibilities."

"But don't you miss that, don't you regret, ever?" Danny squeezed his father's hand, who responded, then tried to withdraw. Danny wouldn't let him.

"I wanted to be a CPA," his father said softly, avoiding Danny's eyes.

"So?"

72

"So, I married your mother. Your brother, bless him, was born. I didn't have time to go back to school."

"But don't you wish you did?"

"No."

"I don't believe you." Danny squeezed. "I don't believe you don't regret that, that you don't wish you could just go back to that point and start again."

"No."

"Yes you do, Dad, you do. You do understand me, please, tell me you understand that what I'm doing is the same as what you wanted to do but never could."

"I love dry-cleaning."

"You don't."

"I love your mother, our house, you children. I have no regrets."

"Dad, please tell me you wished you were a CPA."

"I love to press, to steam."

"Dad, don't lie to me, please. This—please don't lie to me."

"I love to put the plastic on the clothes."

"Damnit, don't you wish you were the firm that counted the Academy Awards balloting, that it was your name on TV?"

"No." His father closed his eyes.

"Don't you wish you went to work in a nice place, came home not covered with other people's filth on your own clothes, your hair, but were doing what you wanted?"

"No."

"Don't you ever wish you did what you wanted, had the guts to do what you wanted? Please, be honest with me."

"Security, Daniel." His father kept his eyes shut.

"Fuck security," Danny screamed.

"Don't ruin your life like this," his father screamed back.

"I don't want to regret what I wanted to do and have to lie to *my* son, don't you see? I don't want to have to lie to my son."

Eyes now open, but unseeing, his father left the garage. Danny picked up the bat and swung some more before carefully sliding it back into its niche.

It would be a while before they spoke again, but at least that talk would be different. Danny didn't know that. Not right now, anyway.

Chapter 7

It had to be a conspiracy: a vast conspiracy intertwining the public school system, Virginia tobacco growers, Heinz ketchup, the New York City bureaucracy, gypsy cabs and private businesses.

How was it that Danny no longer had to wrestle a 44-ounce bottle of Heinz ketchup to the ground? How was it that streets which once slithered beneath his feet as he tried to elude Pistol and Sadie in a mock rundown now gave him traction? Sand, of course, they'd sanded down the streets, on orders. The same orders which flowed into public schools, instructing teachers to instruct pupils to allow the slightly (slightly?) out-of-shape neurotic thirty-three-year old, often accompanied by two men in dresses, to hit two- and three-sewer shots in neighborhood stickball games. The same orders which compelled the genteel folk at Philip Morris, Inc., to prepare special packages of Marlboros which no longer produced addictive joy but instead hacking and coughing. The same orders which the city and private businesses received to overload their employees with work so they wouldn't have time to pause and laugh at Danny. The same orders which told cabbies to slow down so Danny could run and keep pace with them.

Yes, yes, everyone was in on it, and who had told them to make it seem that Danny Neuman was actually getting in shape?

Bette Davis and Joan Crawford, that's who.

Bette Davis winding up and firing a fast ball which was not quite as fast as it should've been, enabling Danny to pull the ball, where Joan Crawford mysteriously lagged behind so the ball seemed to travel further than it actually did. Bette Davis unleashing a peg from left to home which wasn't quite as ferocious as it once was, allowing Danny to slide under the tag. Bette Davis, who didn't fungo those fly balls quite as twisting as she/he/it once did, allowing Danny to get a better jump and move to the spot and catch the ball.

Yeah, the gals arranged the whole bit. Called Phil Morris and Mr. Mayor and all of them, and then covered their bases by never once letting on that Danny was making progress.

And if they had, would Danny have accepted it? No, Mister Mental Health would not have accepted it because he wasn't quite up to accepting the implications of it all. He couldn't and wouldn't—which is why, a week before the tryout, they sat him down.

"Yeah, well." Danny sipped his marguerita as Pistol and Sadie sat across from him on the couch. "Week to go, huh?" He grinned crookedly and sipped again.

They said nothing, just stared at him, discomforting Danny way too much, so he poured his glass full and gulped some more.

"How am I doing?" Danny asked.

"How do you think you're doing?" Pistol asked.

"I dunno, you're the specialists."

"Think so?" Pistol glanced down at Sadie, who shrugged and slid away to allow Pistol to stand, skate into the kitchen and return with some cheese and crackers.

"Don't you? I mean, maybe not, the tryout's only a week away, I don't know that I'm ready." They said nothing. "Uh, am I ready?"

"Do you think you're ready?" Pistol whispered.

"Are you going to keep repeating my questions or what?"

"Until you ask the real question."

"Which is?"

"No help from us."

"Well, great, I don't know what I'm supposed to know or ask or anything."

"Tell him," Sadie whispered, nudging Pistol, who bounded up.

"No, he has to feel it, has to deal with it. Or else he'll never make it." Pistol snapped, harsh, brittle, with the same expression he had when demanding Danny do a particular exercise, an expression which always puzzled and frightened Danny. Like now.

"Uh, it's okay." Danny held up his hands. "We'll talk about—"

"No, we won't change the subject, honey, no." Pistol trembled and resisted Sadie's tender tugs. He just stood there, balancing himself on one skate before he sagged back onto the couch. Pistol leaned forward, jabbing a polished finger at Danny, and hissed, "You're scared, aren't you, sweetie?"

"Well, no, I'm not scared . . . uh . . . yeah, okay, I'm scared."

That seemed to satisfy Pistol, for he leaned back, only to jerk forward again.

"What are you scared of?" Pistol shoved aside the platter of crackers. "Come on, darling, tell me, what?"

Danny looked down.

"I dunno."

"Come on, come on, tell us. We already know, we just want to hear it from you."

"Peter . . ." Sadie said his real name and Pistol stiffened, started to sag back into the lining of the couch only to spasm forward again.

"Of what, that you're not good enough, is that what you're frightened of?" Danny nodded. "Of failure, is that it?" Again Danny nodded. "Well, you are good enough. For what you want to do."

"Thanks," Danny snapped. "I appreciate that, I really do. God knows I'd never heard you say a damn nice thing before, huh?"

"And what good would it have done?"

"I don't know, okay? I, I just would've liked some encouragement on occasion, all right? Something, a kind word or . . ."

"Kind words, Danny. Is that what you want? How about Laguna High's chances of repeating as conference champions rest on Peter Foley? The All-Conference quarterback must at least duplicate last year's fifteen touchdown passes and deliver the same sort of leadership if the Lions are to repeat. Kind words, Danny? How about the Lions' lineup depends on left fielder

76

Peter Foley and his torrid bat. If the team is to go anywhere this year, it'll have to be Foley who brings them there. Those the kind words you want, Danny?"

Danny shivered, stole a look at Sadie, whose head was lowered, his hands clenched tight.

"What else, Danny? You want clips, I'll give you clips. You can borrow mine, anytime you want. How about sideline chatter, you want some of that? You want me to bring in a coach to slap your butt for you? You want that coach to speak to one of your teachers to fix a grade for you? You want a hot girl to grab your cock in the back seat, huh, those kind of kind words?

"Or do you want the truth, Danny? Because all the clips and kind words mean shit, understand, sweetie? They have as much relevance as your announcing yourself on the field, all your holy cows. Because you're never good enough for *them*, Danny. And because you're never good enough for them, you're never good enough for yourself.

"So what the hell is good enough? Good enough means not accepting what they say. It means accepting your own idea of failure and success, if you have the guts, which I never did.

"You know what I did instead, Danny? This is a good one. I decided to come out. Yeah. Right after my junior year, in the most spectacular way I could think of. I wore a dress to the junior awards banquet. Wigs, makeup, everything. They laughed themselves silly—good old Peter, what a joker—until they realized I was serious and then suddenly it wasn't so funny anymore. Suddenly I had a hard enough time not getting kicked out of school, let alone playing on any teams.

"And you want to know why I did it? I told myself it was because I couldn't live a lie, that if people couldn't accept me for what I really was, then I didn't give a fuck about them—and that was all bullshit. I did it because I couldn't stand being Superjock anymore and having to perform game after game to *their* expectations. And so instead of rejecting them, I arranged it so they would reject me. Neat, huh? Except that I never did find out what I could do.

"And I didn't want that to happen to you, understand, sweetie? I saw you running around out there, stumbling and dropping the ball, and I knew you were setting yourself up for the same kind of rejection. Do you know what I'm saying, darling? You were already preparing the excuses you'd use for the rest of your life, making sure you weren't good enough for yourself *or* them. So I decided to lend a hand." He paused, then looked down, smiling crookedly. "More bullshit. It wasn't just for you, Danny, it was for me too. I wanted to see if I could remember what it felt like to care about this nonsense, to see if what I was, was what I really wanted to be." He looked up again. "That's why I never showed you any kindness, Danny. For your sake and mine. I jumped on my own case and pushed myself with every exercise you did."

"And?" It was Sadie who asked, not Danny. Sadie who looked at Pistol with an expression of love, and apprehension.

"It was a good speech," Pistol said sadly, leaning back against the couch, arm around Sadie's shoulders.

"That it?" Danny hunched forward. "Nothing else, a good speech and that's all?"

"Yes." Pistol stared at him. "Yes, nothing else. Though you won't believe it, you're ready. Whether you make the Yankees or not, you're *good enough.*"

"And you?"

"I've already gotten in shape to make the Yankees, Danny." Pistol adjusted an earring. "There's no difference."

He had delayed going down to Adventurer's Inn until the last possible moment. The batting cages. He knew Pistol's fastball was nearly the equal of any machine, but there they had people. Lots of people, and all watching him. He was afraid, too, because of the finality of it. Even though the calendar said the tryout was only a few days away, Danny knew it wasn't the calendar he was swinging against, but his mind.

Sadie and Pistol wore shoulder-length black curly wigs and ice-cream vendor uniforms as they trailed Danny near the entrances to the batting cages in Adventurer's Inn.

"This one." Danny stopped, handed them a five and waited for the twenty quarters from their silver change machines.

"Uh-uh." Pistol shook his head, pointing to the sign. SLOW-PITCH. Inside, youngsters lunged at 55-mile-per-hour pitches.

"What, that's good. Come on, guys, that's fast."

"Listen, Neuman, we haven't given up daytime television to have you punk out on us at this point."

Shit, damn.

Danny wandered down, aware of some snickering, though only dimly. He stopped in front of the MEDIUM cage, but not for long since two pairs of manicured hands nudged him all the way to the end. The last cage. A vacant cage. With good reason. SUPER-FAST.

"So?" Sadie spread his hands.

"Yeah, so." Danny stared at the cage.

"Are you going to ask the Oakland pitchers not to throw hard when you come up?"

"No."

"Then?"

"What, then what?" Danny never took his eyes off the cage until he heard someone snicker. "Fuck." Danny grabbed the quarters and stormed in. The machine enlivened to the feel of three quarters and fired a pitch past his awkward lunge. Danny stepped away and they made faces, so he stepped back in and again missed. They applauded.

"What are you applauding for?" He held his bat, leaning away, glaring at them.

"Because you need it."

Danny rolled his eyes, clenching the bat and watching another pitch whistle past. He didn't swing. Go on, Neuman, all this and you're afraid, afraid of a stupid little machine, a silly little machine programmed by some idiot who never faced live pitching, huh, what are you afraid of?

And then he heard the voice.

"Danny Neuman, an exciting youngster with a world of speed," shouted Sadie. People drifted over and Danny crimsoned. Another pitch went by. Pistol held the microphone, though Danny wasn't certain if it were a banana or not. Both squatted, Yankee caps upon wigs. "Neuman tore up the minors on his way to the big club, batting .458 and slugging sixteen homers in just fifteen games, and Steinbrenner believes that Neuman will fill the hole in center for a long, long time to come."

Danny gulped and saw more people, some snickering, many bewildered, line up behind the broadcasting duo. Another ball whizzed past as he focused on Sadie and Pistol.

"Scooter, what do you think of this Neuman kid?"

"Holy cow, the guy's another DiMaggio," Pistol screamed. Now the entire complex spilled back behind the two transvestites in ice-cream vendor suits miming a play-by-play account of a thirty-three-year-old too frightened to swing.

"It's a great day for a game, Danny Neuman still looking over those pitches, waiting for his pitch."

Danny grinned, swallowed, and set up. And hit it.

"It's a long drive, deep left . . ."

And hit again.

"Down the line, extra bases . . ."

"Holy Cow, another . . ."

"Three-base hit for . . ."

And the applause. And shouts.

Danny swung and swung and swung until his hands swelled and his quarters ran out. After an hour he stepped out and nearly eighty people applauded.

"And we have with us the star of today's game, Danny Neuman." Pistol shoved the microphone under his mouth. It was a banana. "Danny, how's it feel, tell us what it feels like?"

Danny blinked, uncertain of tears or sweat.

"Go on," Sadie encouraged him. "Don't be shy, tell us your feelings."

Danny looked over the microphone at the two lunatics, grinning and loving him. He gulped and kissed them flush on the lips. The crowd erupted in approval.

On the day before the tryout, Danny discovered a package on the bed. With a note. "From Sarah." Nothing spectacular, nothing romantic, just a note. "For Danny." And the package. He opened it, unaware she was watching from the bedroom doorway. A new uniform, from head to toe. New York Yankees, official, complete with cap and warmup jacket, even a glove.

"Like it?" she asked softly. "You can wear it to the Stadium, all summer long."

"Thank you." Danny trembled and didn't look up.

"Try it on." Sarah stood next to him. He laid the cap back in the box and covered the package. Sarah tensed. "Don't you like it?"

"Great, wished I'd had one a long time ago."

"So?"

"Nothing. Can't wear it."

"Why not? Don't you want to look the part?"

Danny turned, expecting a smirk, instead finding somberness and hurt.

"No."

"No? I thought that was the whole point of . . ."

"Not the point, don't you see? Wearing a uniform like that defeats the point. I, I want to wear my jeans, my sneakers, a T-shirt."

"Like you were ten?"

"Yes, right, exactly."

"A little boy."

"Yeah, a little boy, that's the whole damn point, that I used to be able to crawl onto the field and go out in a pair of sneakers and . . ."

"You can't go back."

"Why not?"

"You can't—I, I won't let you."

"Oh, oh, you won't?"

"No."

"Why?"

"Because I can't go with you."

Suddenly she seemed old. Old and scared.

"You can . . ." Danny reached for her hand, but Sarah jumped back, eyes widening.

"No, no, I don't want to go forward, either," she said, "but that's all I know. You want to go back, and I don't want to."

"For a while, a second."

"Not even for a second, Danny. You step back there, into your childhood, your little childhood which you never lived except in your head, and you can't come back here so easily."

"I can always . . ."

"No, as what? A failed boy? A foolish middle-aged man? How? You can't live out your dreams anymore, Danny. Don't you see?" Sarah tugged her short brown hair. "That's why I'm not going to be a folksinger anymore, why I cut my hair, because I don't want to be reminded of that. But I can push that aside. You, you watch the television, you keep your dreams and they infuriate you because you never tried to live them."

"Neither did you. You were a helluva guitarist, good voice, you could've done something with it."

"No, I knew I couldn't. I knew it was a dream. But you don't. And you're going to go out there tomorrow and they'll squash your dream and you'll have nothing, because if you had anything really important, you wouldn't be doing this in the first place. And then you'll be coming back to me, to this, and it'll always be second choice." Sarah backed through the doorway and spun away.

"Hey." Danny chased Sarah, grabbing her arm near the bathroom. "Won't you at least come, huh, at least see me? Maybe I'll surprise you, maybe I'll make it, damnit, huh?"

Sarah caressed his arm, smiled shakily, and walked away.

Chapter 8

God, I'm gonna die. Danny lay perfectly still. He hadn't fallen asleep last night. Or if he had—around four, the last time he'd squinted at the clock—it didn't feel as if he'd fallen asleep. He felt drugged and terrified, unable or unwilling to move his legs.

"Danny, get out of bed, time for school."

"Oh, Ma, I feel sick."

"Sick? Again? Always on a Monday, wait, I'll get the thermometer."

This time he couldn't feign illness. He had to get out of bed because it was seven in the morning and he had to get out of bed. Sarah rustled next to him, then bolted up. She looked from the clock to Danny, her stare lingering. He returned it, then she slid out of bed. Danny watched her pad across the carpet and out the door.

Can't get a note from my wife, have to do it, have to get outta bed. He heard Sarah bustle around in the kitchen, heard the cupboard open, close, jars bang against the counter.

Please God don't let there be a fight, don't let her use the hair dryer or fight with me or anything that'll ruin my nerves worse than they already are.

He heard a whirring and covered his face with the pillow, praying the noise away. It didn't work. Forsake me, Lord, thanks. Danny shoved the pillow onto his face, still heard the high-pitched whirring, then it stopped. Thank you, God, sorry. Danny made no effort to remove the pillow from his face or even move a finger. Through his mute terror he heard Sarah pad back toward him.

"Hey." She jabbed him in the shoulder.

"Huh?" His voice was muffled beneath the pillow.

"Danny." It was soft, almost gentle. His hands gripped the edges of the pillow, but didn't pull it off. She did. "Here." Sarah handed him a juice glass.

"What's this?" Danny stared past the filled glass at Sarah, something resembling a tender smile on her face.

"Your health thing."

"You made it?"

"Yeah."

Danny took the glass, propped up in bed and watched Sarah stand uncomfortably by the side.

"So?" Danny whispered.

"Yeah." She looked down. "So, uh, I have to take a shower, uh, you want to take a shower first?"

"I dunno, took one at two, uh, you can."

"Yeah?"

"Yeah, sure." Danny looked into the glass. "Thanks."

"Okay."

Sarah stayed in the shower for nearly half an hour. He waited until she was in the bedroom dressing before he soaked himself for twenty minutes. When he stumbled out, she was sitting in the living room, smoking. He wanted to say good-bye, realized she already had, and maybe even wished him luck in the silent, awkward process.

Danny staggered out the door, resisting the urge to lie down and vomit. He pulled open the front door. Bright, sunny, warm. He closed it and looked up the steps. He forced himself up, then sagged against their door.

SOMETHING TO CHEW ON. The note dangled above a package of Dentyne Sugarless gum. Danny pocketed the pack, listened at the door and heard nothing. They hadn't offered to accompany him because they understood, and he didn't want anyone coming with him, just because. But that was yesterday. Today he wanted someone, needed someone. He paused at the front door, glancing back at his apartment. He wanted to go back in and take her with him, but didn't. He had to do this alone, even if he was petrified, on the verge of repetitive regurgitation and knew he hadn't a sliver of color in his face. Maybe green, that's all.

He let two trains pass. They weren't filled enough and he didn't feel safe, he told himself. Then a third came and was too crowded. So that one passed. By the fifth one he realized how stupid he was and leaped into the car, edging his way to a far corner, away from everyone else. Then he inched back to the center of the car, in case someone wanted to stop him. No one did. Not the fat black woman clutching two small children nor the comatose drunk nor the well-dressed man talking to the window. No one wanted to stop him because no one cared. Except him, and it was too much for him. Even squeezing his glove didn't help because nothing could shove away his weak fear. Nothing. If he thought about the tryout he got sicker, and if he thought about anything else, he chuckled insanely, realized he was chuckling insanely and stopped, which allowed thoughts of the tryout to come back in.

The train stopped at the Stadium. He rose, then stopped. Maybe it was silly, maybe I should go home and buy a baseball board game and get a job at *Knitting Digest* or something like that. Danny jumped past the closing doors and stood on the platform overlooking the Stadium. He felt nauseous again. Good, afraid of heights. He hurried down the steps, landing at the bottom, and sighted the long line of hopefuls. All clutching gloves and bats and numbers, winding around the far side of the Stadium.

Jeez. Danny shrank, retreating. No, no, forward, your feet go forward, shmuck, he muttered until he found the place to register and found the end of the line.

Danny had to wait an hour. One torturous hour of deciding against this and deciding for that, of staring at the kids who had to be in better shape than he, of wondering how many people would laugh and how he didn't care and how he did and wouldn't it be nice to be still asleep.

Then he entered Yankee Stadium, already having filled out the brief questionnaire, whose clause at the bottom exculpating the Yankees from any legal responsibility for any damages incurred during the tryout did little to calm Danny down.

Home plate. Danny stood behind home plate and stared

dimly, the grass curling about his sneakers, the dirt fondling his feet. It smelled as he'd always hoped it would. As it had to smell. Fresh-cut grass and smooth infield seduced by a soft breeze. The sort of breeze which wriggles the flag and dries out only part of the perspiration on the forehead. He heard the shouts, no longer from his competitors but from umpires signaling Maris out at second and Richardson safe at home. A booming, imperious voice exploded out of a microphone, no longer instructing but sounding a bit like Phil Rizzuto.

"Uh, yes, sir, that's what his card says, thirty-three." Yankee PR Director Paul Peterson spoke into the walkie-talkie connecting his presence on the field with the presence of the Boss in his box overlooking the stadium. "I've double-checked sir, seems to be his real age," Peterson continued, watching Danny approach home.

Someone told Danny he had eight swings. He didn't hear. He didn't hear because the outfield walls were stripped of their sacrilegious blue, the heretical modern scoreboard gone, the monuments again visible as idols of the outfield. Beyond, the Bronx Courthouse stood as it always had, the subway rattled past as it always had.

Feels the same. Danny squeezed the bat. Thought it would slip out of my hands, but the sweat's gone. Maybe I don't notice it. Maybe I just thought I'd notice it. Maybe I'm too close to death to notice it. Danny started to knock the dirt out of his sneakers, stopped, then stared at the mound through the protective screen at the batting practice pitcher until both the screen and pitcher were gone, only Sam McDowell towering, glaring back. Now he knocked the dirt out of his sneakers, glancing down for the signal from the third-base coach. Frank Crosetti gave it to him, not from the grave where Crosetti was but from the third-base box at Yankee Stadium. Christ, Danny didn't know if he was breathing, was positive he wasn't when Ellie Howard came to life in the first-base box and clapped his hands for encouragement.

Danny nodded, dug in, examining the defensive alignment. The infield played him deep, the outfield deep and shaded to left. Somehow the nervous jabbering of the infielders steadied his trembling. Somehow the muttering of the ghostly catcher and the distant breaths of the umpire and the deafening shrieks of the crowd failed to unnerve him. Or penetrate. Suddenly the sounds all meshed, became one, became as natural as his slight crouch and his concentrating squint.

Danny was guessing fastball. He guessed right. McDowell fired a rising fastball which Danny stepped into and met dead on, sending the ball up the left-center field alley. It rolled and rolled, touching the monuments, even if they were safe beyond the outfield walls.

"Well, uh," Peterson kept his eyes on Danny, knowing the Boss's binoculars could just as easily swivel from the figure at home to his own figure near the Yankee dugout. "Our reports say he's just average and . . . yes, sir. I know you know average when you see it."

Danny slashed a curve ball, this one from Camilio Pascual, down the left-field line.

"Our people don't look at him as a major league prospect. Excuse me? Yes, I know they told you to make that deal with Kansas City, too, and that didn't work out, but—" Peterson shut up, bracing himself for yet another of the Boss's brainstorms.

Danny cracked a Mudcat Grant pitch off the end of his bat into right field.

"Yes, he is a local boy. Grew up in the Bronx, yes." Peterson's brain was starting to click now. Actually, this idea wasn't so bad. "Yeah, I think I see what you mean—local guy dreams of making the Yankees, finally gets an opportunity to prove himself, and we give him the chance, right? And he's thirty-three years old, so he's an inspiration to armchair jocks everywhere, right? Yeah, we oughta get some great press out of this—it'd take some heat off that Kansas City thing and—what? Oh yes, sir, of course, and it'd be a terrific humanitarian gesture. Who else but you would have the compassion to give him this chance?" God, give me a break, thought Peterson.

On his last cut, Danny slammed a Jim Lonborg pitch into left center. Single, maybe a double, if Yaz doesn't field it.

"Where would we send him? I don't know, I'd have to talk to the farm people. Where? Greensboro? Yes, I think there's a slot open there, I guess he could fill it—no, I wasn't guessing, sir, of course he could fill it. Should be perfect ... His name again? Wait a minute, it's right here ...

"Neuman, Danny Neuman."

Chapter 9

"Hey mister, wait up, hey, mister."

Danny paused until the tiny kid of eleven with the autograph pad and Hornets T-shirt caught up. Ahead lay the players' entrance to Hornets Stadium, behind the rented car that had overheated three times, twice in Maryland. Danny laid down his valise.

"Hey, gimme your autograph."

"You sure?" Danny took the pen.

"Hey yeah, I collect 'em all, every one of you guys, yeah, just sign it there, hey thanks." The kid stared at the name. Danny's smile faded as the youngster shook his head, glanced at his roster, back at the pad and then ripped the page out and flung it aside.

"I'm a ballplayer," Danny said weakly as the kid stormed toward another gate. Ten hours of torturous driving only to be insulted by some yokel in Greensboro. Great, terrific. Danny stifled a yawn and started back toward the players' entrance, clenching his valise . . .

"You serious?" Danny had looked at the Farm Director, then up at the pictures of Them. Joe, Babe. Lou. Mickey. Whitey. Then back at Him, smiling and shoving a contract across the desk in the executive offices of the New York Yankees.

"We want you to be part of the Yankees organization." The Farm Director smiled. "Read the contract, try and return it by tomorrow. We'd like to get you on your way to Greensboro as soon as possible."

Can't really lose on this one, he thought, looking on and studying the pale, trembling lump in the seat. Gotta give the Boss
credit, signing him's good PR, makes the Boss look human. If
that's possible. Greensboro'll be happy we're sending someone
down instead of always recalling people. If he falls apart, no one
can blame us, because we gave him a chance. If by some miracle
he does well, we look humanitarian, and maybe the Boss can
find some future use for him. Either way, it's worth the lousy few
bucks. Not that I think he'll amount to more than a little favor-
able press for a couple of days. Poor dope can hardly sit up
straight in the chair.

"I'll sign now." Neuman. *N, e, u,* Danny tried to remember.

"Read it first, please. Have an attorney go over it with you, if
you like. But we do want you to read it first."

Read? He could barely read the Yellow Pages to find an agent,
then realized he wouldn't be able to afford an agent. On what
they would pay him, he could barely afford the subway ride
back. But who cared about money? He would be getting six hundred dollars a month. Ten dollars a day meal money. He could
live in regal splendor on that. He'd done it before when there
was no point to it, starved in school and starved looking for a job
and starved because they had too many bills. Now he had a reason to starve. Greensboro. Greensboro, his Paris. Greensboro, a
magical sound. If it was so magical, why was he so terrified? . . .

"Neuman, Danny Neuman," he told the guard at Hornets
Stadium.

"Ain't onna list." The guard stared suspiciously.

"Could you look at the list?"

"Been doin' this for thirty years. I seen all you people come
and go. I know you ain't onna list."

"I'm sure I'm on the list."

"I knew Peanuts Bombo, Herbie the Popcorn Man, Cool Brew
Barbara. I knew 'em all."

"Barbara? You had a female ballplayer?"

"Worked the concessions here. I knew 'em all. I don't know
you."

Danny laughed limply.

"No, I'm a ballplayer."

And the guard laughed . . .

"So, you'll send me your uniforms, I'll dry-clean them," his father had said.

"Dad, look, I appreciate that, really, but, but I can't ship my uniform up North every time I slide into third, you know?"

"You always liked the way I dry-cleaned your clothes." His father's voice was barely audible on the phone.

"And I still . . ."

"Danny, this is Nathan."

Danny could hear crying in the background.

"You living there now, Nate?"

"Danny, someone has to look after them. They're pretty upset."

"I see, okay, and that's my fault, right?"

"No one blames you, Danny."

"Jeez, Nate, I'm not doing anything so wrong."

"No one says you are."

"Then why won't Daddy discuss more than Martinizing with me, and Mommy only whether I want rugelah or mandel sent, why?"

"They must deal with this tragedy their way, as you must your way. I am only here to help."

Right, yeah, good ol' Nathan, help your little brother. Like always, right?

He remembered what a pal Nathan had been after Danny had finally broken up with Laurie. Laurie, his *shiksa* girl friend of his sophomore year whom he loved and whom his parents wouldn't let into the house. Then again, Laurie's parents didn't like him either. An Italian Catholic. A Jew. "You can't blame them for not wanting her in the house, Danny. You're young, you'll get over her," Nathan had said.

"I love her, is that so terrible? Nate, please. So she's not Jewish, okay, but I love her. Talk to them, ease things up with them."

"I'm sorry, Danny, but I agree with them. You'll get over her."

Let's bow our heads in prayer, right, Nate? You put on the tallis and I come home with scraped elbows. You get A's and I get hit in the mouth with a fly ball. You marry a bitch whose heart belongs in Tiffany's and I love a nice girl cursed with a her-

91

itage not from the shtetls but from Sicily, so I'm the outcast. Yeah, right, Nathan, square everything.

"I wanted to get on the line, both to wish you God's luck"— Nathan paused now—"and to give you a number of a *shul* in Greensboro."

"There's a *shul* there?"

"There are *shuls* everywhere. We have no geographic boundaries when it comes to serving God."

"But in North Carolina? Persia, Babylon, even Staten Island, but North Carolina?"

"I want you to speak to my colleague, Rabbi Jacob Gottlieb, a fine and brilliant man. I've already told him you're com—"

"Why'd you do that? What do you think, I've got time to attend Friday night services?"

"You never have, Danny."

"You never asked."

"Because you never showed an inclination."

"Maybe there's a reason."

"Will you call him so you can be among your own kind?"

My own kind, Danny thought.

"We don't want to lose you, Danny."

"I'm not converting."

"He'll help you, if you have problems, it's someone to speak to."

What about my own brother? Shouldn't I be able to tell him my fears? Or my mother? Or my father? Or my wife?

He had wanted to tell someone of his terrified delirium, but there'd been no one to confide in. There'd been no point calling the office so Lisa could put him on hold. He'd been terrified— cold, naked fear. If he'd shown the fear they would have used it against him to urge him to reconsider. If he'd acted flippant they'd have bombarded him. No one knew what to do with him. When he'd been dreaming, he was just a painful amusement. But now . . . now he was serious. Actually serious. He had a contract, a place to go, a locker waiting and a bat and a glove. If he could ever get past the guard . . .

"Okay." The guard put down the phone. "You're on the other list."

"Which list?"

"Players list . . ."

Pistol had worn a chiffon evening gown, Sadie a tux. A farewell party. They were the only ones who showed. Maybe because they hadn't invited anyone else. Pistol said he'd asked Sarah, but she'd walked right past him.

"I'm sorry, I apologize for her, really . . ." Danny fumbled.

"You don't control her," Pistol said.

"Still . . ." Danny had stared into his drink. At first he thought it was simply that he had no one to tell of his fears, but he realized that was bullshit because he could tell Sadie and Pistol. He simply didn't want to admit how terrified he was, for somehow that would reinforce the terror. If he was mute, it would go away.

"Bet you hit .400." Sadie grinned.

"Yeah, yeah." Danny rolled his eyes.

"You will."

"Okay."

"You have to have confidence. What happened to that confidence of yours?"

"Dunno, I'm—I think—you know, this is it."

"Exactly."

"Yeah, but, I mean, this is *it*. I'm going down there, I'm . . ."

Say it. "Maybe they just signed me as a gimmick, you know?"

"Everyone's a gimmick," Sadie said.

"Not what I wanted to hear."

"Whatever you do, you're a gimmick. At a job, you're used, you're a gimmick. In a relationship, you're used. People don't bother with you, as much as they love you, unless they think they can get something out of you—love, support, companionship, whatever. What's the difference?"

He knew he could play. But what if he couldn't?

"What's this?" Danny fingered the little black box with the yellow ribbon.

"Open it." Pistol grinned.

"You know"—Danny fumbled with the wrapping—"you didn't . . ."

"Have to do it and why did we spend the money. Just open it."

Inside rested a gold chain with a gold baseball cap. "NY" was etched on the cap. They were the only ones who'd given him anything . . .

"Why are you taking all three pairs of jeans?" Sarah stared at his valise the next morning.

"I need 'em." Danny squished clothes into the corners.

"All of them?"

"Well, yeah, Sarah, I can't live in one pair, you know?"

"Danny, for a while you can. I'll wash them." Sarah grabbed the jeans, he grabbed them back and rolled the faded dungarees into a ball.

"Honey, please, I'll wash them down there."

"You don't know how to wash."

"I do too." Danny didn't, but wasn't about to compound doubts with detergent questions.

"Danny, you've never done a wash."

Danny shook his head and zipped the valise.

"Should I cancel the *Times?*"

"No, why?"

"I don't read it."

"You read more than me. I just read the sports pages."

"So I'll save them for you."

"Sarah, they'll collect *shmutz.*" Danny grinned and Sarah blinked back tears.

"I'll dust," she whispered.

"You want a big pile of *shmutz?*"

"What, a couple of weeks' worth?"

"Honey, season doesn't end for a couple of months, nearly into September."

"Three, maybe four weeks."

"Sarah." He wanted to touch her, didn't. "You can still come down and live with me. We'll get a furnished apartment."

"Like a Howard Johnson's motel room?"

"They must have some nice places. I'll call the Rabbi, he'll find us something."

"For two weeks?"

Danny pulled the valise off the bed and dropped it on the floor.

"Don't you think I can do it?" He stared at her. Sarah closed her eyes, though her face stayed eye-level with his.

94

"Yes." she whispered. "I'll save the sports pages for you, uh, Sports Monday, okay?"

Sarah watched him leave. She wanted to kiss him, to hug him, to caress and squeeze him so his shoulders would break and he wouldn't go and leave her. Alone. His going merely supported her feeling she'd lost him forever. Somehow she'd hoped that once this was out of his system, he'd come back, settle down. That hadn't happened. He was really going to play baseball in the minors, to eat cheap food and ride on buses and do God knows what with God knows who. And leave her all alone. She hated her selfishness. Sarah wanted him to succeed, but didn't want him to succeed at something like this. So how much could she want him to succeed, and how much could she love him if she felt this way? And did she love him, or just need him?

And what was she going to do? She couldn't live on what he would be making. She'd have to get a job, eat alone, be responsible for changing the toilet paper. Stupid things. They had never talked anyway. But at least Danny had been there if she had something to say. Now she had no one. She could commiserate with friends but talking about it would only enhance the depression. She could call his parents but they would only cry. So who? And could she go to parties with friends when everyone would be paired up? It had been so long since she'd not been paired up. Long time. Years. In a body and mind she no longer had. She'd be embarrassed. Maybe they'd try to fix her up with someone. She couldn't kiss anyone else. Bad enough she fantasized about it, but she could never kiss anyone else. And what would Danny say if he came back after striking out three million times in a row, only to find another man in his bed?

So she'd wait. For what? She had to eat. Sarah burst into tears thinking about making a smaller pot of coffee.

Danny had looked so afraid when he'd left. She wanted to tell him not to be afraid. But she couldn't be brave anymore. She couldn't force it. She'd forced too much for too long. Maybe they were just going through a crisis in their marriage. Maybe she had to wait until he passed through his crisis before they could get together again. But he would be down there, all alone, meeting people and doing things without her. How could she listen to him talk about things and people she hadn't seen or met? That's why they had always done things coupled. That's why she always went to his office parties, so she could know whom he was working with. And do what, approve? She had never approved and she didn't approve now, but it was so damn important to him and every time she acted casual he was hurt that much more. And the one time she asked if he was at all afraid, he exploded and said there was nothing to be afraid of. So she left him alone, unable to share in it.

Really, what could she do? Make like June Allyson and wave good-bye at an airport or a train or bus station or a toll booth? What could she do except wait and make smaller pots of coffee and avoid his side of the bed.

Chapter 10

Not exactly Yankee Stadium. No pictures of the Babe and Joe D. and Lou and the Scooter and the Mick and Reggie and Rapid Ron along the freshly painted walls. Not even freshly painted walls. Not even walls, but cardboard separating offices.

Danny squished along the tiled floor, paused, then hurried past the signs. Not Old-Timers Day but Cow-Milking Day. Not Helmet Day but Banjo-Picking Day. And pictures of former great Hornets of the past. Actually one former great Hornet of the Past: Dummy Dudley.

Dummy Dudley swinging a bat. Dummy Dudley racing for a line drive. Dummy Dudley posing with Miss Tobacco Chaw 1956. Dummy Dudley, with a distended stomach like the Babe's and thick legs like Thurman Munson's, sipping from a can of Dummy Beer. Dummy Dudley crashing into a wall. Dummy Dudley's funeral—from the beer or the crash or what? Who the hell was Dummy Dudley? Danny pushed open the door marked EXECUTIVE OFFICES—GREENSBORO HORNETS. ALL WELCOME.

"Hi." Danny laid his valise up against his shaking leg. "I'm Danny Neuman."

The secretary was gracious enough to swallow her bubble gum bubble, pause at the ancient manual typewriter and slip her glasses upon her long nose.

"So?"

Danny cleared his throat.

"I'm here to see Mr. Antonheimer." Danny smiled weakly. "I'm reporting. I'm uh, the new player."

She just stared and smiled.

"Miss?" he whispered.

"Mrs. Dudley."

Oh-oh, his widow?

"Mrs. Dudley, I just signed with the Yankees organization and I'm, uh, reporting, uh . . ."

"Newberg?"

"Neuman."

"Neuman, Tony?"

"Danny. Danny Neuman."

Mrs. Dudley shrugged and stood. She also had a stomach like Babe Ruth's and legs like Thurman Munson's except she chewed gum, not tobacco. She disappeared into the inner office, which must've provoked the loud shouting, a scream and a piece of furniture overturning. Danny looked at the inner door. Could probably go through a wall and hit the car in five minutes and be back on the interstate in just over an—

"He'll see you now." Mrs. Dudley adjusted her beehive hairdo, blew a bubble and resumed assault on the typewriter.

Danny heard clacking as he opened the door, then mumbling as he closed it. Jefferson Antonheimer stood polishing a moosehead jutting out from the far wall. On both sides of the moosehead were bookcases. One filled bookcase stood three feet high and held only one title: *A Call to Ball,* Author, Jefferson Antonheimer. The big, broad-shouldered man with billowy red hair who mumbled to the moosehead had spent his entire life trying to get a big-league franchise. At first he'd attempted it with money, but he wasn't wealthy enough nor did he have wealthy friends eager for tax shelters. Then Antonheimer had tried to lure big-league teams into Greensboro.

Antonheimer knew the only way he'd attract a franchise was by demonstrating a broad enough appeal in Greensboro. Hence the promotions. Hence the team newsletter, *Hornets Life.* Hence the Christmas cards to the Commissioner of Baseball, George Steinbrenner and the owners of every other major-league team. And every January, when he'd receive a card back, Antonheimer chortled and pointed to the progress he'd made. That had been going on for nearly thirty years.

"Why are you still up?" Antonheimer said, polishing the

moosehead. Danny wasn't certain whom he was talking to, so just touched his valise for comfort. "Well?"

Danny looked around the office. More pictures of Dummy Dudley and several other Hornets players of the past, an autographed picture of President Eisenhower and another of Captain Kangaroo and Mr. Green Jeans at home plate.

"Sir?"

"Sit, sit." Antonheimer patted the moosehead and turned to Danny. "So, you're Neuman, huh?" Antonheimer slid into his desk chair. Danny took the opposite chair, dragging his valise over by his shaking feet. "Your stuff?" Antonheimer pointed.

"Yes, sir, I, I haven't found a place yet."

"You have a place here."

"Here?"

"Right here, a new home."

"I was thinking of a furnished room, sir, I don't know . . ." Danny glanced at a picture of Reggie Jackson to the right of the moosehead. How was it Jackson was older than him, yet looked younger?

"We want all our boys to think of Hornets Stadium as home. Your home. Everywhere else you live is away from home. Every time you go out those gates, you're on a road trip, understand?"

"Yes?"

"Good." Antonheimer flipped through several folders, discarding them on the floor until he stopped, flipped one open, grunted and grinned. "Have a good report on you, Neuman."

"Thank you, I, well, I thought I did well at, the tryout, uh, and all, my hitting . . ."

"Says here you're bright, intelligent, articulate. Wonderful, God only knows we can use those attributes."

"Thank you. I, I do have a good arm."

"What?"

"Arm. Good arm." Danny shook his right arm.

"Oh yeah, well, that's not my concern. That's Jones's problem, what he does with you on the field. I never meddle, never once have I told a manager who to play or where to play someone or who to bench. Fact is, well, I don't want to dump too much on you too soon. You're terrified, aren't you?"

"Yes." Danny felt relieved to say it.

"Well, don't be." Antonheimer slammed his thick hand against the desk, knocking over an ashtray and jiggling the moosehead. He jumped up. "I don't want fear from my boys because then I don't get action, understand, action?" Antonheimer stormed at Danny, bashed his hand against Danny's chest, bounded to the door and wrenched it open. Danny heard footsteps, Mrs. Dudley yell, Antonheimer scream, then silence as the owner returned to his seat. Danny had kept his eyes on the moosehead all this time.

"Action, do you understand?" Antonheimer glared.

"Well, I, I do bunt well, get a good jump off first, don't know that I'm another Maury Wills or . . . ."

"Action, action." Again Antonheimer leaped up, again punched Danny in the chest, bounded through the doorway, exchanged screams with Mrs. Dudley and returned to his desk, heaving and lighting a cigarette. He offered one to Danny, who refused out of fear he would drop it on his lap. "Now do you understand?"

Danny didn't, but couldn't withstand another blow to his body.

"Yes sir, I do."

"Then explain it."

"Explain?"

"Explain what I mean, I hate parrots, can't abide them. Do you see a staff here?" Antonheimer gestured. "I do all the promoting, write the newsletter, hire and fire, make the deals, everything, hate yes-men, okay?"

"Yes, sir."

"Don't yes me."

Danny smiled and nodded.

"So? What do I mean?"

Danny had hoped the five-second interval would've erased Antonheimer's memory.

"Action, uh, well, excitement, right?" Antonheimer nodded. "Uh, more excitement, action, uh, lots of excitement, lots of action."

"Good, good." Antonheimer beamed. "We'll be able to use you. By the way, you married?"

Shit, he wants to fix me up with Mrs. Dudley.

"Yes."

"Good, fine, like to see married ballplayers, keeps them on their toes, gives them someone to answer to, don't always . . ." Antonheimer's eyes moistened. "Much as you do for people, sometimes, they just"—he swiveled toward the moosehead— "you know. So go on, report to the clubhouse, they'll take care of you, see you sometime, I'll be in touch."

So he wasn't exactly George Steinbrenner. Or maybe he was. He'd heard strange things about Steinbrenner. But at least he'd gotten out of the office alive and was now winding his way beneath the stadium toward the clubhouse. Danny paused, staring at the bare concrete corridors. Okay, so the Yankee Stadium tunnel was nicer that day of the tryout. Only a little. No corridors look so nice. Save money for clubhouse and treating players well and giving them an extra bat. Danny slowed. Now don't be too cocky. Walk naturally. Casual, no, don't slouch, casually, I said don't slouch, now you're too stiff, you're not with the Seventh Army. Just walk naturally, casually, not arrogantly, not a superstar, be yourself, right, now move the left foot, then the right, then the left, got the hang of it, Neuman? You forgot how to walk and you're supposed to play center field? Danny stopped at the edge of the clubhouse. Now don't get your hopes up too high, only the minors, probably doesn't even have carpeting.

It barely had floors. Scratched wooden floors, a wooden piece of table from Robert E. Lee's army which stood gnawed and burned in the center of the clubhouse. Naked piping ran along the walls, spying upon tiny, cramped lockers suitable for a junior high school team. Empty paraplegic stools stood before the narrow lockers crammed with clothes, after-shave lotions and magazines. Ahead were the showers and toilets. Only one ballplayer was there, thin, lean frame bent into his locker so that his black hair fell over an attractive face absorbed in a book. He didn't notice Danny, nor did a wrinkled man near eighty whittling at Robert E. Lee's table.

Danny coughed loudly, still uncertain whether he should cough to attract attention or stand there and wait. The player's head bobbed up, held in curiosity as Danny grinned limply, then fell back into his book, though it was obvious he was no longer concentrating. As for the old man, his whistling preoccupation indicated he was far from finished.

"Excuse me." Slivers of wood flew onto the floor. "Sir?" More slivers and a song. "Excuse me, uh, I'm Danny Neuman, I'm the new player?" The old man was whistling "There Is Nothin' Like a Dame." "I, uh, excuse me?" Danny bent.

The old man looked up, stared straight through Danny and jerked his head down the far end of the clubhouse.

"Last one." He resumed his whittling and Danny shuffled toward his locker. He passed the player, now staring up into his own locker, and paused at a tiny cubicle. He knew it was his locker because it read: NEWMAN. 34. So much for spelling, he thought, just standing there and staring.

The player, four cubicles away, rose, coughed and Danny turned.

"Pete Kelly." He extended his hand. Danny reached over, neither really moving toward the other.

"Hey, hi." Danny smiled. "Danny Neuman."

"New guy, right?" Kelly smiled shyly.

"Yeah, fresh off the boat."

"Excuse me?"

"Never . . ." Danny wanted to stare into his locker. His locker. His space for his uniform and his glove and his bat and his jock strap. His locker.

"You're the guy from New York, huh?" Kelly now sat on an adjacent stool, the legs shaking.

"Oh, yeah." Danny started to touch his uniform, stopped, embarrassed.

"Go on." Kelly smiled. "Your first time, huh?"

"How'd you know?"

Kelly shrugged. "Can tell. 'Member my, remember my first time, uh."—Kelly squirmed and Danny didn't know why. "The feelings of, uh, the first time, shit." Kelly reddened, shook his head. "Not the way I meant to put it."

"Put it fine."

"No." Kelly shook his head. "Been said better."

"I guess." Danny didn't exactly know what they were talking about. "Uh, what do you play?"

"Center." Kelly looked down. "What do you do in the off-season?"

"Never had an off-season."

"Before this, then."

"Writer, sort of."

"Really?"

"Yeah." Danny sat on the stool and Kelly rose, again reddening. "What about you?"

"Nothing much." Kelly fumbled in his locker, seemingly hiding whatever he was reading. He grabbed his glove and started out to the field. "See ya out there, Danny." He stopped. "Hey, uh . . ." He stared at Danny, shrugged in inner decision, bounded away.

Slowly, Danny put on his uniform, piece by loving piece. He never thought it could feel so good to itch, to mess up his hair as he pulled on his undershirt, to button buttons or zip a fly or buckle a belt or lace a pair of shoes. Not until he shook himself awake did he realize the uniform was about three sizes too big.

"Uh, excuse me." Danny waved his arms within his cotton tent. Sam, the clubhouse man for twenty years, glared up. "Do you have anything a little smaller?"

"No."

"Oh." Danny sighed, scooped up his glove and bat, stopped near Pete's locker and saw some philosophy books. Spinoza. Nietzsche. Kant. He squinted into an adjoining locker and saw *Playboy*, shook his head and started off toward the runway, toward the sounds.

"What's them?" Sam blocked his path.

Danny followed the stare and they both looked at his feet.

"Shoes?"

"Them socks."

"Right, my socks."

"Ain't regulation."

"Oh, listen, uh, these are my lucky socks . . ."

"Ya wanna go through them doors, ya take off them socks. I don't bust my butt dressin' you punks to have ya screw up the uniform."

Christ, just what I needed, not to be able to wear my socks, terrific. Danny undid his shoes, slipped on the regulation Hornets socks, tied the shoes, ignoring the fact that relacing them was not quite as magical as the first time.

Danny saw a lump asleep on the bench. Since he was twice the age of the other uniforms, Danny assumed, correctly, that the lump was the manager. Danny didn't know that Horace Harding Jones was preparing for the game. Sleeping on the bench was one of the many personality traits Jones had adopted from his hero, Casey Stengel. Of course, when Stengel fell asleep managing the Mets, he was pushing seventy, whereas Jones had just turned forty-five. Which meant, according to Jones's thinking, by the time he reached seventy he would've perfected falling asleep and other Stengel tricks.

Like platooning. Jones took platooning to another dimension, often yanking a righty batter and pinch-hitting with a lefty against the opponent's lefty pitcher, simply because the other team had a righty warming up in the bullpen and Jones wanted to get in the first shot. So it was against the percentages. Jones believed there was another baseball philosophy beyond percentages, even if he had observed it from last place during his nine-year managerial career.

Or double-talk. Jones had perfected double-talk while managing winter ball in the Dominican Republic. During a playoff game, gunfire and artillery shells started landing beyond the left-field wall. Calmly, Jones continued managing up to the point when the revolutionaries entered the dugout and announced they were claiming the bat rack and the water cooler in the name of the people. In broken English and Spanish interspersed with pig Latin, Jones convinced them to await nationalization until the game was over. Proud of himself, even if his team had lost and he never saw his shortstop again, Jones embarked on a career of double-talk, believing if he could stave off revolutionaries, he could climb to the majors.

Finishing last didn't bother him. He knew he would be vindicated, often pointing to Stengel's early failures with the Boston Braves before triumphing with the Yankees for twelve years. Jones didn't even mind his players laughing at him. He just wished they would only laugh and not stick lit Winstons between his fingers when he dozed during the game.

"Uh." Danny hesitated. Jones snored, a cigarette burning down between his fingers. Just like Casey. Danny wasn't sure if a fire would start, but certainly wasn't going to be a hero during batting practice. He'd wait until the game. "Sir?" Jones snored. "Uh." Danny coughed. "Mr. Jones?" Danny touched Jones's shoulder and the manager bolted up.

"All right, run and bunt, let's get something going, last of the fifth, need . . ." Jones looked at Danny. "You're not him, are you?"

"Who?"

"Does it matter?" Jones peered. "What does matter is hitting the ball, right?" Danny nodded. "If you don't hit the ball then the other team has nothing to do and it's a pretty boring game if they sit out there all day long. You think you can draw flies to something like that?"

"No sir."

"Well then, I've talked long enough. It's your turn. Who are you?"

"Danny Neuman?"

"Aren't you sure? You need confidence, son, confidence. You can run around the outfield all day long but if you don't make a catch you'll never know if you can do it and if you don't know if you can do it then you'll stop running and what happens when the ball is hit because the other fella decided to hit it and then you're there standing still and we're down a couple runs, think that makes my job easier?"

Danny thought he'd like to go home.

"I don't think so."

"Aren't you sure?"

"Yes I am."

"Well good then, so already I've built up your confidence, that's my job, I have a whole team to slap butts and slap heads and sometimes the good ones need a kick in the rear but the others don't and you gotta figure out who needs what or else the water coolers get smashed and then I'm not watching the game and we're down a run and maybe we shoulda sacrificed." Jones squinted. "So, who are you, our new batting-practice pitcher?"

Danny sighed.

"No, sir. I'm a ballplayer. Danny Neuman." He touched his uniform and immediately started scratching. "I, I was just signed."

"You, huh, you're the one, well, I've heard a lotta 'bout you. Now, I try and know all my players, you have to know what makes them tick. I've heard of you, I'll figure you out later. Until then, what do you do?"

"Play the outfield."

"Outfield, outfield. You know, I used to play the outfield. Back in, well, maybe it was ought-six-four or ought-six-five, one of them years, and I think I can show you a thing or two."

"I'd like that."

"Why?"

"I don't know."

"Thought we took care of that confidence, huh, do I have to ream your rump a little, that it, you one of them fellas I always gotta stay on top of, huh?"

"No, sir, I just, uh, would like to play ball."

"So would I, what do you think you're here for?"

"I—"

"That's good then, you have no confidence in yourself and you're doubting me, you think it was my fault our starting pitchers can't finish a game just because they get tired and so I have to go out there and I don't enjoy that much either and then both of us get booed, do you?"

Danny shrugged.

"So what do you play?"

"Center."

"I gotta center fielder." Jones jerked his blistered hand toward the field in the direction of Pete Kelly, easing under a fly ball out in deep left-center field. "He's my center fielder." Danny wouldn't look out there.

"Well, that's my best position."

"And when you've got confidence in me, you'll see I can make these decisions."

"Uh well, just that, sir, I have experience playing center and all."

"Good, you're getting back that confidence of yours. Fine

106

then, show me what you can do so I don't have to yell at you and I can save my strength for hollerin' at the umps who, as you know, don't like it but you have to yell at them every once and a while or else they give you the wrong calls like back in ought-six-nine when this blind bum signaled out and then changed his . . ."

Danny sucked in his stomach and looked onto the field.

"One-two, one-two, get down, get down, one-two, one-two, get down, get down."

"Who's the best?"

"Stony Brook."

"Who's the best?"

"Stony Brook."

Danny hung back, inconspicuous beyond the stands, just watching. He hadn't wanted to tell the coach he was coming because then he might've had to speak. And what could he tell them? All he could do was stare at the suddenly youthful kids in his uniform on his field. He didn't want to saunter over and be the Graduate to them. He'd seen that already with Kent Popowski, star pitcher when Danny had been a freshman. Popowski had signed with the Phillies organization and lasted one year before being cut. Yet Popowski had claimed the manager had it in for him, that he was merely working at his uncle's ski lodge to get in shape for another tryout with another organization. No one had believed him. But they'd allowed him his lie. Danny hadn't even a lie. So he hung back, watched and walked away, listening to the kids in his uniform on his field.

Jeez, they're all so lean. Danny stepped onto the field at Hornets Stadium. And young. Lean and young and I'm flabby and old. Flabby-and-old, meet lean-and-young.

"Hi." Danny stood near a gaunt Latin sitting cross-legged near the first base line, pounding his glove.

"Oh, sorry, sir." The kid bolted up and danced around first, missing a throw from the diminutive shortstop who now moved to third. Minutes ago he'd been playing second.

"Sir?" Danny laughed, waving his glove. "No, please, not sir. I'm Danny Neuman, how you doin'?"

"Sorry, coach, still working on this position, name's Heddy

Arturo, just shifted me into first, still learning." A throw bounded in the dirt and Arturo swiveled his face away from the ball, his bony face twisting in fear.

"Coach?" Danny sucked in his stomach a bit more, adjusting his cap. "I'm not a coach."

Arturo stared, heard another throw whizzing toward him and flung up his glove to protect his face, though the ball sailed eight inches off to the side.

"Really, look." Danny spun around to show his uniform. NEW-MAN. 34. He'd find a U somewhere. "I'm a player really. Just wanted to introduce myself, that's all."

"Hey you, git on out there, shag some flies." No one looked around except Danny. Arturo took the chance to gesture once more at Pee Wee Schaefer, the diminutive shortstop, to throw the ball waist-high.

"Me?" Danny poked himself in the chest, smiling at Jones.

"No, not you." Jones shook his head, pointing beyond him. Danny clutched his bat for comfort, trying to keep his eyes on the front of their uniforms so he wouldn't see their faces. Or sloping shoulders. Or lithe legs. Or pimples or faint whiskers. He kept looking at their uniforms to convince himself that his massive uniform was the same as theirs. Though it wasn't. He wanted to dash onto the field, but didn't. Fear. Not fear. He just didn't know if his cap were slanted just so, or if he could keep holding in his stomach and run at the same time. So he stood there, holding the bat, the glove, touching the beak of his cap and staring at the uniforms until he finally squinted around. He saw the cluster of uniforms flipping a ball in a circle behind the batting cage as a tall blond with acned forehead whistled "Sweet Georgia Brown." He saw the sprints along the warning tracks and the jockeying for twisting flies and savage liners. He saw the uniforms, still only the uniforms, and knew he could do it. If he could keep his stomach tucked in. Danny raced onto the field.

Okay concentrate, just concentrate. Danny hunched over in left. He was alone. The others were grouped together in left center. He could've moved toward them and introduced himself but he didn't want to be "Coach." So he stayed where he was. They could've come over to him, he thought. But they didn't. Better

108

this way, show them I can do it. Better show yourself you can do it, too.

"Who's that?" B.K. Evans yawned, holding the fungo bat near the batting cage.

"New guy," a player replied.

"Ain't that the old guy we heard about?" Again B.K. yawned. With his incessant yawning and casual stroll, he appeared nonchalant, almost lackadaisical. That way, when he slammed a shot into the stands or dived for a line drive, his actions seemed that much more palpable.

"Think so."

"Shit, this team's in worst shape than we thought."

A whistling liner sailed into left center. Danny didn't move, instead watched it soar past him and heard a thud as it disappeared into a glove. He tensed. Another liner rampaged toward the alley. Far away. Not so far if he thought he could get a good jump, but if he'd run for it he might've bumped into someone, and he still didn't know the signals.

"This is run." The Little League coach rubbed his chest. "This is bunt." He touched his cap. "This is swing." He touched his nose. "This is take." He touched his lip. Danny could never remember the signals. He never tried to remember them. Back then, he was forgiven because he was the star.

A lazy fly, not too high, moved toward him. Okay, be ready, get a bead on it, don't stagger. He staggered. Both hands up, be casual. He almost vomited. Just reach up and ... the ball popped off the tip of his glove. He gulped, picked it up and fired a savage throw back to the infield which had to roll to make the pitcher's mound. He heard laughter and knew it was for him.

Too lazy, wind got it, Danny thought, cursing his blush. Wind takes it and how can I make the catch? If they gave me a harder shot I'd make it, hey, how come they don't hit it as hard to me?

Danny clenched the bat. He would've used some pine tar to help his grip but one of the other players, Kelly it was, had it, and Danny didn't want to bother him. Besides, Kelly avoided him out in the field. Danny didn't know why. Kelly would nod, Danny would smile and Kelly would redden. Danny hadn't the faintest idea why, but he wasn't about to risk humiliation by going over to Kelly, standing with some of the other players, and asking for the pine tar when he had no right to ask for it.

The batting-practice pitcher was Reggie Leach. The blond kid who whistled "Sweet Georgia Brown." Danny didn't know if he always whistled, though he thought he heard Leach humming from behind the screen. Danny also heard the players muttering that Leach was throwing his knuckler again in batting practice. Danny was terrified to hit a knuckler. He wasn't sure he could hit a change-up, much less a knuckler. He also didn't know Leach would be cut that night. In two days Leach would be back in Athens, Georgia, asking the same people who had cheated for him when he was a high school star for a job. At least he could lie.

The pitch came slow. A super-dooper slow pitch. So slow it could've changed its mind and returned to Leach. Danny swung and grazed it with the tip of his bat, dribbling a ball down the first-base line. Several players shouted encouragement.

"Way to take a cut . . . good swing, good leverage . . . getting your hips into it," several shouted as he grazed two more, missed another, then blooped a foul into the stands.

"Thank you." A fan waved his souvenir at Danny.

Blushing, Danny stepped back away from the plate.

"Hey, throw it a little harder."

Leach couldn't throw much harder. That's why he'd developed a knuckler after throwing out his arm at nineteen. That's why he'd be back in Athens, Georgia, in two days.

Again the pitch came in, a bit faster, though still slow. Danny missed, now annoyed. Again he heard laughter from the stands. Shit, I don't even get boos, just laughter. Bet they're just making it easy for me because they don't think I can do it, don't think I can hit. Pistol had a better fastball. So did the machine at Adventurer's Inn. I can hit it, okay, have it your way. I'll cream your change-ups, your junk pitches, see how you feel.

Danny stepped forward and delivered a level swing, the fat part of the bat cracking flush on the ball. It felt good to get all the bat on the ball. He smiled, expecting to see the ball slash past Leach and past Pee Wee and over the fence. It did none of these. He hit it with all his strength and it dropped lazily just beyond third base.

"That was good," yelled Evans. "Got into it now, pretty good."

Danny blushed, stepped back, laid the bat down, started for his glove, realized that was silly, too, and just retreated a few feet away, alone, to watch the children play baseball.

Chapter 11

"Well, you wanna come down with us, uh, to this place, have a few drinks, not a bad place, probably not what you're used to. I usually don't go much, try not to drink much but, sometimes I need it, so . . ." Kelly studied him.

"Uh, well, I should shower, you know?" Danny was still in uniform while the rest of the team had already dressed. He was embarrassed to strip in front of them. His blowsy uniform could conceal just so much.

"Shower?" Pete smiled politely.

After three games, Danny still had no reason to shower. He hadn't done anything more strenuous than sit on the bench. For several minutes, he'd debated where to sit on the bench. He thought it'd be nice to sit in the middle, then realized he didn't know everyone's names and so couldn't shout encouragement. He didn't want to scream, "Do it, number eleven," when everyone else was screaming, "Go, Willie." That's why he had sat at the far end, waiting for everyone else to scream before he screamed, for everyone else to clap so he could clap. He never even considered he'd get into a game. Jones ignored him. At first, Danny hoped it was because Jones couldn't remember who he was.

"I'll work you in, we're inna pennant race"—they were sixteen games out of first—"gotta lot to think about, think about too much and then we've blown a five-run lead and I'll miss somethin' else and then we'll never catch up."

Danny hadn't asked to play, had simply slid his bat back into the rack. He wouldn't dare ask about any particular spot for his bat, just as he wouldn't dare sit among the players.

So how can I prove myself if I don't play, and why should they let me play if I can't field in practice? And how can I get any better if they don't give me any difficult chances, but then why should they if I muff the easy ones? Danny slowly undid a button, tossing furtive glances around the clubhouse. At least the players were nice, if condescending. He could tell they were condescending. They were too nice. If he were any good they wouldn't try and help him so much because he would be competition for them.

"Should use a lighter bat," B.K. had said. "Less strain on your arms. You can borrow this one." He brandished an ancient, skinny bat first used when he was a senior in high school. "Anytime, just ask if you want it."

Fat chance he'd ever get to use it.

"My spare glove's broken in real fine," Pee Wee had said, patting a battered mitt. "Think I got rid of all the errors in it."

I'll put 'em back in for you, Danny thought, incredibly depressed, nearly shoving his entire body into the tiny cubicle as he undressed and dressed. Already depressed. In fact, depressed beyond depression and he'd only sat on the bench for three games. He hadn't any failure to point to because he feared he wouldn't get the chance to fail. So he was depressed. Depressed and scared. That's why he went down with them to Dogner's Grill.

"Let's get some pitchers here, hey, Danny, you wanna play guzzle?" Pee Wee neatly arranged each of the three ashtrays around the table so he could flick his ashes into any of them. Danny shrugged, smiled, looked around at Pete, leaning back in his chair and nodding distantly; Heddy, blackish eyes flashing suspiciously around the bar; B.K., holding a yawn; Pee Wee, nervously adjusting the ashtrays just so.

"Guzzle?" Danny had to shout above the music he no longer recognized.

"Yeah, guzzle, fill up a cup." Pee Wee took his empty cup, fingered it, laid it back down and swiped Heddy's cup. Heddy

113

glared into the table, fiddling with the tips of his long fingers and shaking his head, pausing only to shoot up his eyes toward the entrance, then lower them again.

"Man, you get reamed doin' that." B.K. grinned as Danny held the full cup near his chest.

"Yeah?" Danny grinned.

"Shit, speakin' of that, you guys catch Leach's smoke?" Pee Wee smiled.

"Fastball?" Danny asked. They looked at him in wonderment.

"No," Pete said softly.

"Smoke, pot." Pee Wee sucked at his fingertips, then wiped them off on the table. " 'Bout all the smoke Reggie's got left."

"Look at them," Norman said. They sat in the James College Pub. Once their home. They'd lived a flight up from the basement bar and some nights didn't even have to put on shoes to go down. Sometimes when they did wear shoes, then came up without them.

"Unbelievable." Danny stared at the people. Unfamiliar people. Strange faces. No longer friendly faces willing to share a beer or buy them a drink or sit with them. Even the interior had been painted. Spruced up. Gone was the dingy cellar brown, replaced by a bright yellow already peeling.

"If only these people knew it was Thursday night and what that once meant," Norman said. The pub was half empty.

"Let's go."

"No, come on."

"Norm, I dunno, it's depressing me."

"Maybe someone'll come in."

"Who, no one comes here anymore."

"You never know, maybe someone had the same idea we did."

"Wasn't a formal reunion, Norman. Didn't mail out invitations, we just drove out, that's it. Let's go."

"Let's hit on some chicks."

"I see some nice ones." Pee Wee waved at several girls by the bar.

"Guys are with 'em," Heddy mumbled, jerking his head toward a few cowboys staring at the same girls.

Danny followed their stares. The girls were eighteen, nineteen. Thin straight hair. Even, smooth faces.

"We used to go here." Norman had corralled two bored girls and lured them to the table.

"Yeah?" said the one with wavy black hair.

"Oh yeah, went here, lot different back then."

"How long?" asked the plump one with layered auburn hair as she took one of Danny's cigarettes. Danny smiled, feeling guilt because he was recently married. She shrugged back, disappointing him because he at least wanted her to respond, so he could respond, so he could have that sense of satisfaction even if he wouldn't, under any circumstances, do anything. Even in college, they had called him Father Neuman.

"Four years ago, right, four it was?" Norman had asked him. Danny nodded, even though it was five. "Place has changed, used to be real lively on Thursday nights, wouldn't believe the crowds, people dancing and screaming, drunk and luded out and stoned."

"Still is." The girl with the wavy hair poured herself a beer.

". . . Eva and Linda and Norma and Patty and Chris." They said their names and sat down. Danny got Norma. Or was it Chris? He wasn't sure, even less certain what to say to them. Chris/Norma had bony shoulders and a thin slender nose and dirty blond hair parted in the middle, falling down over firm breasts.

"Don't you think?" Chris/Norma asked.

"Huh?"

"Don't you think this is a nice place, huh? Great crowd, huh?"

"Oh yeah, terrific, yeah."

"I stopped coming here for a while, I used to come here a lot with my boyfriend, old boyfriend," she emphasized. "He had a great car, five-speed Camaro, shit, it could go, we'd just race up and down the strip, over on Evans—you know where that is?— bunch of people would race up and down on weekends until the cops would . . ."

"The Furnace." Norman grinned and jerked his thumb at Danny, who was mutely inspecting the foam on his warm beer. "Also a drinker. Doesn't look like it now, but he can drink with anyone. Banzai, buddy." Danny hesitated. Norman bulged his eyes and Danny complied, gulping down the cup. The girls smiled in awed respect. "This guy could smoke anyone under the *table, we'd be through an ounce of dope in a night, just me and him. One time we had a contest between the halls. Of course, I was the champion roller, still am."*

"I'm terrible," said the plump one.

"Yeah, I can't roll, either," her friend agreed.

"Well"—Norman tapped his jacket pocket—"I've got some stuff, real great stuff, if you're interested."

Danny shook his head.

"One time this guy had a Trans-Am, shit, what an animal, you know what I mean?" Chris/Norma asked. "Great power. Hey, you ever drive a Trans-Am?"

"I have trouble with Fords."

"Hah, I like you, you know, you're kinda cute, you know?"

"Norman." Danny leaned over, hissing at his friend's ear. The two girls had wandered over toward the cigarette machine, then back to the pinball machine, debating whether to accept Norman's offer. Neither the girls nor the two machines had been in the Pub five years ago. Or was it four? Or ten? "I don't want to."

"Why not, come on, relax. Listen, I won't tell Sarah."

"It doesn't matter, I don't want to do it. I, I feel ridiculous, okay? Just ridiculous. Christ, they could be my sisters."

"What, you're Methuselah? So, they're twenty or so, we're only twenty-six, come on."

"Norman, I don't want to go, to, to some room. The smell, okay?"

"What smell?"

"The smell, always the same smell in girls' rooms here, makes me sick."

"Drink up, you won't feel so sick."

"Usually the stuff in bars is watered down, they don't say that, you know what I mean?" Chris/Norma sipped Danny's beer as he tried to figure out what all the empty cups were doing in front of him. "But I had a boyfriend here once, almost got married, what a creep, thought I was pregnant, you know what I mean? Hey, you don't mind my telling you this, do you?" Danny shook his head, caught Pete smiling at him, saw Pee Wee arranging matchsticks in an ashtray while Heddy whispered hotly at his girl, uncertain whether to respond or leave as her friend was led onto the dance floor by B.K. "Anyway, he was a bar-

116

tender, at this place, and he told me the owner never let them water down the beer, or the drinks. When you order a drink, you get a real drink, not too much ice, hey, can I have a bourbon?"

It did smell the same. Danny never knew why all the girls' dorm rooms smelled the same. He couldn't figure it out when he was a junior and he surely couldn't figure it out when he was an old man following two giggling girls down a hallway he'd tramped down too many times to forget. Or remember. They fumbled with their keys. On both sides music blared. On his left, rock. On his right, folk. Stereophonic memories way too loud, making him ill. Very ill.

"What?" Norman whispered.

"Bathroom," Danny mumbled.

"Okay." Norman hesitated. "Just hurry back, hey, you're not too fucked up, are you?"

"I'll show you." Pete half-rose as Danny wavered slightly.

"I can find it."

"Sure?" Pete searched him. "Kinda tricky back there."

"No, I can do it, yeah, I'm okay. Just a little dizzy, I think."

"If you need help, just holler." Only Pete watched Danny stumble through the crowd. Kelly turned his head, smiling gently to himself, then turning back to the table.

Girls' bathroom, Danny thought. He still thought in terms of girls' and boys' bathrooms. Sarah had slowly obliterated the distinction. At least their bedroom didn't smell like the dorm, a smell making him progressively sicker as he wheeled away from the bathroom entrance and stumbled down the staircase and into the fall night.

"Wrong one." Danny heard someone say something. He paused at the door. LADIES. No I can't go in there, why not, does it smell? "I don't mind, but some people might think you were strange."

"I am?" Danny said to the door, hoping the sign wasn't talking to him.

"I don't think so, hey." A hand turned him around, gently, firmly, forcing Danny to stare into a wide, pretty, freckled face, layered red hair swooping across a grin, a pair of bright green eyes twinkling, large breasts jiggling beneath a conservatively styled sweater as she stood before him. "Need help, little boy?"

117

"When we get the money, that's all, okay, when we can afford it." Sarah seized her breasts and squeezed them in front of the mirror.

"I like them."

"Danny, they're sagging," Sarah said sadly, one hand reaching up to touch the facial wrinkles she insisted were there and he couldn't see.

"I like 'em." Danny grinned, moving toward her.

"I don't want pity." Sarah shrank away.

"What pity? I like your tits. Always have liked your tits."

"You liked them better when they were firm, admit it, when they were firm. They're not firm anymore. Just promise me when we have the money someday I can get them firmed up, okay?"

Danny nodded, flushing as the woman's smile widened.

"I have this thing about public bathrooms." He shook his head. "I don't . . ."

"What?"

"Never mind."

"You get embarrassed?"

"Yeah."

"Do you have much of a choice?"

"No." He laughed, sliding onto the bar stool next to her. "Guess I can wait till it clears out."

"In this place?" She threw her head back and laughed, a deep, booming, utterly joyful laugh. "You'll have to wait till they close."

"You know this place, huh? I mean, you come here often, jeez, did I say that?"

"Yeah." Her eyes twinkled.

"Wasn't a line, I mean, I, I'm not trying to pick you up."

"Not here to be picked up."

"Then why are you here, I mean, no, you can be here, I mean . . ."

"Sporting of you." She smiled, her fingers shaking slightly as she lifted a glass, perhaps some kind of brandy, to her full lips, sipped, never once taking her eyes off him. "I come here because I know the owner, he's an old friend of mine. I feel safe here, I nurse one drink, I talk to friends, I listen to music, I go home." She studied him. "Usually alone."

118

"What's safe about this place?" Danny searched the cowboy hats and alien expressions and bombastic music and billows of tobacco smoke.

"Maybe not to you. To me, it's safe, secure. Aren't many places you can go where you feel secure. Here, I'm secure. If I went into a strange bar I'd get lines. I don't want lines. I want to sit and talk. That's all. Strange to you, right?"

Danny sighed heavily.

"I don't know. I used to have a safe place, where I'd go, where everyone knew me. No more."

"Where'd it go?"

"Got invaded by the present." Danny paused. "Can I buy you a drink?"

"No, I'll get you one."

"I can buy you one."

"Why?"

"I . . ." Danny shrugged. "I dunno."

She laughed, ordered him a beer, herself some ice water and they stared for a few seconds. They exchanged names. Hers was Colleen O'Toole. He learned she worked in a battered-wives clinic, had two children, one, a son, an artist in Portland, the other, a daughter, a mongoloid, who was in a state institution.

"I couldn't take care of her, when I put her there." Colleen's eyes softened. "Now I could. Too late for that. Taking her out would be my way of assuaging my guilt. She deserves better than my guilt."

"Love?"

"Too tangled up with my guilt. So, I visit her, every Sunday."

"Isn't that guilt?"

"Yes, but at least when I visit her, I can fool myself about my love, on the trip up, on the way back. To have her constantly would be guilt. So I compensate, okay? The love I feel for her and can't give her I try and give out to others."

"In a bar?"

"Is a bar any different than a street, a supermarket, a party?" She shook her head, a veil returning to her eyes, bringing back a twinkle. "Doesn't matter, long as you give, right? It's what others put on the giving that changes it. If I give someone directions, I'm a good neighbor. If I counsel a battered wife, I'm a sensitive sister. If I talk to you, it's either because you think I'm trying to pick you up, or because I feel sorry for you because you're afraid of public bathrooms."

Danny winced, suddenly remembering, and she laughed loudly, her laughter warming him, reassuring him.

"I'm having fun," Danny said softly, stiffening lest she think it was a prelude to something.

"Why shouldn't you be?"

"Because I'm married. Did I tell you that?"

"Three times." She grinned. "Would you feel better if you called your wife and told her you were having fun talking to a perfect stranger who happened to be a woman?"

"Probably." Danny grinned. He sensed someone near, saw it was Pete, neither smiling nor frowning, simply watching. "Hey, Pete, uh, this is Colleen O'Toole."

"Hi, Pete." She shook his hand and he tensed. "Sit down."

"Uh, no, it's okay, really." Pete bent over to whisper into Danny's ear. Colleen leaned back, bemused. "Guys are goin' now, and, uh, want us to wait for you, or what?"

Flustered, Danny looked between Pete and Colleen. He saw her smiling, studying Pete, and saw Pete, frowning, reddening, perhaps with jealousy.

"If you need a ride, Danny, I'll drop you off. I was thinking of some coffee. Like to join us, Pete? Talk for a while?"

"Uh no, okay, no." Pete stared at Danny. "I'll leave the door open, okay?"

"You can go, Danny," Colleen said softly.

"Yeah? No, I . . ."

"I won't rape your friend, Pete. Promise."

Pete blushed.

"And you can stay, come back to my place for coffee, talk for a while. Open invitation, you can bring your friends if you like." Colleen gestured to the players swaying several feet away, watching.

"No." Pete backed away. "It's okay." He turned to Danny. "I'll leave it open for you."

"Coffee sound good?" Colleen asked after a few minutes. "Can go to a place near here, back to my apartment." Danny flinched. "Perfectly safe and you can still call your wife. Collect, please."

Colleen could've worn her apartment, it was so much her. Intelligible art prints on the wall, beaten, comfortable-looking furniture. Clean, neat. Throw pillows scattered and lots of books and an old-fashioned hi-fi with records piled onto an adjoining table. She took care of her records, they didn't take care of her.

Colleen pushed open a door and Danny held his breath.

"Think you've waited long enough," Colleen gestured into the bathroom. Danny smiled limply. She announced she'd put up the coffee. He closed the door, locked it, listening for a second at the sounds of water running, sniffing at the tidy bathroom. Then he unzipped his fly, careful to pull up the seat and aim straight.

He didn't need to call Sarah. He'd already talked to her that morning. "You have a lotta mail here," Sarah had mumbled.

"Yeah, anything good?" Danny had gripped the edge of the pay phone.

"I don't know, I haven't opened it."

"Why not, go on."

"No, I'll wait for you."

"Sarah, what if there's something important? Maybe I won something from *Reader's Digest.*"

He heard her flipping through the mail.

"No, nothing from *Reader's Digest.* Macy's."

"Just pay them the minimum, I'll send you a check soon."

"Okay."

"You okay?"

"Yeah, great. Find a place?"

"Staying with some of the other players."

"Please call your parents and give them your new address."

"Yeah, okay, you got a pen?"

"You call them."

"I want to give it to you."

"I'll get it next time we talk."

"Can give it to you now."

"I'll wait."

"Sarah, you mad at me?"

"No."

"Just don't be mad at me, okay? Please, I mean, I'd rather you hate me than be mad at me."

"It's not you I'm mad at, Danny."

"Then who? My parents, they say . . ."

"Call me Sunday night, okay?" her voice had wavered, then the phone had clicked dead . . .

"I was careful." Danny plopped onto the couch, muffling a yawn as she handed him a cup of coffee.

"What are sponges for?" Colleen eased into an opposing chair, crossing her legs. She stared at him, forcing down his face. "If you're nervous you can go."

"No, I, I don't want to go."

"Good." She stood and walked over to the hi-fi. "Like jazz?"

"Love it." Danny yawned. As he laid his head back on the couch, he vaguely heard Charlie Parker, heard her ease back into the chair, heard her sip. He shoved his head back up.

"Relax," Colleen said gently.

"I'll fall asleep."

"Then fall asleep."

"No." He shook his head as "April in Paris" oozed through his abruptly exhausted body. "Just rest my eyes, you know?"

"I know."

Colleen watched him slowly slouch in the couch until his head lolled sideways and his breathing eased. She liked watching men sleep, telling herself they were most vulnerable then. She knew that was part lie, concocted because she could barely penetrate the conscious defenses, and so needed to see what they looked like when they weren't trying to impress her. She was never impressed by the totality of a man, only bits and pieces. But as she watched Danny's chest rise and fall, she wished to wake him. She wanted to stay up all night, talking to this cute kid who was about twelve years her junior. She didn't want him to sleep because he was vulnerable awake. But Colleen wouldn't disturb him. She sat there for an hour, listening to Charlie Parker and Danny Neuman speak to her, until, around three, she draped a blanket over Danny, quieted Charlie, and disappeared into her bedroom.

Chapter 12

"I think, you know, the truth?" Danny whispered into the phone a week later, forcing away both the blaring music from upstairs and his accelerating guilt. "The truth is that, you know, things uh, I haven't played much . . . fact, not once at all, been here all this time and haven't played and I don't think I'm any good and . . . well, you know . . . maybe, maybe this, uh, wasn't such a good idea. I mean, you know, I dunno . . ."

"Do you want to come home?" Sarah closed her eyes.

"If I come home, I'm a failure."

"You're not the failure."

"Yeah, I am, I mean, I haven't done anything I said I'd do, or wanted to do. I'll look stupid, I'll be an asshole, okay?"

"At least you tried."

"Yeah, well, so?"

"More than most people do."

"Okay then, so I tried. So, what do you think, huh?"

"At least you tried." Sarah twisted the phone cord.

"And failed."

"Better than someone who never tries."

"Yeah, yeah, so—what do you think, huh?"

"I'd like you to keep trying." Sarah's voice trembled.

"You would?"

"Yes."

"Don't you want me back?"

"Keep trying. Please." Sarah dropped the sweaty phone back into the receiver.

Nothing would've pleased Sarah more than Danny coming home, nothing—until she realized she simply didn't want him back. Not yet. At first she thought it was just because she didn't want to scoop up the pieces. She wasn't surprised he was so miserable. It was ridiculous to begin with. Or maybe it wasn't. At least he was trying. Something.

His absence forced her to try and figure things out. Like her life. Not that she'd been so successful, but his leaving forced her into things.

Initially she'd just stayed inside, constantly. She had the supermarket deliver her food. She dashed out to retrieve the paper and dashed back in, lest someone see her. She stopped using makeup because there was no reason to use makeup if she never went out and if Danny wasn't around to see her. Which is why, she had told herself, she stopped answering the phone. She was out of practice talking. That's what she told herself.

"Ma, I don't know, didn't you talk to him?" Sarah had finally answered the phone once she'd found herself screaming encouragement to contestants on *Bowling for Dollars*.

"Yes, so, he sounds happy. Is he happy?"

"I guess so." Sarah lit a cigarette. She was up to two and a half packs a day. Neither the fetid smoke nor the chest pains bothered her, only the fear of running out of matches.

"He told me he hit home runs, he did well, so, isn't it time he came back?"

"I don't know, Ma, what can I tell you? This is his decision."

"What, it affects us all. You, look at you, all alone."

"I'll live."

"Don't you miss him?"

"Of course I do."

"Then tell him that, lie, tell him your life is a shambles, get him back home."

"I can't do that, Ma. I can't tell him what to do. Who the hell am I to tell him what do do?"

"You're his wife. He's making a fool of himself, talk sense to him."

"He wouldn't listen. He has to come back on his own."

"If you talk sense . . ."

"Ma, I can't order him, he'll hate me."

"So, for a while."

"Forever. I can't."

She told herself she couldn't stay inside indefinitely. That's why she started answering the phone. That's why she accepted an invitation to one of her friends' parties. Just this once, she told herself. She would put on makeup. Then she decided against it. Then she applied makeup, terrified what she'd look like to them without it. Even more terrified what she'd look like to herself.

"So what do you hear from Slugger?" Jeffrey had smirked.

"Doing fine." Sarah looked away.

"Tearing up the league?" Someone else asked.

"I, I think he's doing well."

"I look at *The Sporting News* every so often and I haven't seen his name in the Class A roundups." Salmon Face smirked.

"I, he's doing well, just starting."

"I'd think some old guy coming down there, who was hitting well, they'd mention him."

"Maybe they're behind in those roundups. He just got there, okay, give him a . . . just got there."

Sharon took her aside. Sharon was Jeffrey's wife. Sharon was also Sarah's friend. Until that night.

"Jeffrey and I decided, we talked, we can lend you some money until Danny gets his head on straight," Sharon whispered, though everyone watched. Obviously everyone knew what she was whispering. Communal charity. Sarah blushed and shook her head.

"No, thank you, I'm doing okay."

"He can't be making much down there."

"It's okay, I'm getting by."

"I know it probably isn't much of a drop in salary from what he must've been making at that magazine." Sarah reddened, started to respond, didn't know what she could say and so just let her head drop. "But let us help you until he comes back."

If she let them or anyone else help her, then she'd be acknowledging Danny was crazy. And was he really? She'd thought he was, but maybe not.

And anyway, it really wasn't Danny anymore. It was her. No

one ever assumed, for the briefest of moments, that she could survive alone. No one. Not even herself. Even when she mustered the strength to shop in the supermarket, or stroll along the stores, never once going in, whoever she'd meet always asked about Danny. And when they asked about her, it was how she was doing without Danny. No one understood the courage it took for her to go outside, alone. Nor did anyone understand that when she quickly changed the subject from Danny to something else, it was out of her shame, not his.

And maybe that's why she didn't want him to come home, just yet. Even if he were a failure, which, in everyone else's terminology, he might be, she was more of a failure. At least he was trying something. More than she had done. More than sitting home and cleaning and watching television and deceiving herself that there really wasn't some kind of job she could do. Simply, she didn't want them asking about Danny. She wanted them asking about her, about her life, on her own, about something she had done, or was trying to do, or was contemplating. Something more than putting on the silly makeup and wandering down the canned foods aisle as if that were some act of rare courage. For it wasn't. Perhaps progress, but only to her. Not to anyone else. And not even to her.

Sarah wouldn't accept she was that much of a loser. Maybe she was, but she wasn't entirely certain. If Danny came home, he'd be depressed, despondent, whatever, but at least he'd have some stories to tell her. What would she tell him? How she'd changed the toilet paper? How Waldbaum's had a different delivery boy? How she'd witnessed a traffic accident? What would she tell him that wasn't a lie? Exactly. To make her life worthwhile, if only to herself, she'd have to lie.

And maybe she was tired of lying.

Chapter 13

Guilt. All Danny felt was guilt. Guilt for drawing a salary for doing nothing and guilt for bothering a coach to hit a ball to him and guilt for leaving Sarah and guilt for cheating on his wife, if what he was doing amounted to cheating on his wife.

"Talking, I like to talk, uh, at college they called me Motor Mouth, among other things, and I just enjoy talking." Danny squirmed on the couch. She still sat directly across from him, still studied him with warm amusement, still laughed loudly at his jokes and, sometimes, just at him.

"What about listening?"

"Oh shit, I don't do that?"

"You do that fine."

"No, not enough."

"I just think you've been running off for the past hour because you're still nervous."

"About you?"

"I don't know. Are you?"

"Yeah, well, I feel guilty."

"Why, because of Sarah?"

"Yeah, no, I don't know, I, I've always been faithful."

"And you still are." Colleen smiled, shoving across a plate of cookies. "We haven't slept together." Her eyes twinkled and her mouth pulled apart in sly humor. "Yet."

Yet. Danny blanched. That's all he'd thought about in the last week and a half since they'd met, and started spending every night in her apartment sipping wine and eating cheese and nibbling cookies and listening to jazz, and feeling guilt, and wondering when, and dreading yet.

"Uh yeah, I uh, meant to ask you about that."

"What?" Colleen grinned.

"Uh, you know, about sleeping together." Danny's voice dropped.

"Are you making a pass?"

"No, no, sure, no."

Colleen grinned and even Danny smiled.

"Would you know how?"

"Well, yeah, of course." He chuckled at his foolish machismo. "No, see, if I make a pass at you I'm cheating on my wife. And if I make that pass you'll think that's all I want. But maybe you're the sort of person, I think you are, who doesn't like passes and wants to make them yourself, but then maybe you don't want to seem too aggressive, so you won't and we'll both sit here wondering."

"My God, Danny, it isn't that complex. Wouldn't it make it easier if it just happened naturally? If it happens."

"Will it?"

"I don't know. Do you want to?"

"What?"

"Danny."

"Yeah."

"So do I."

"Good." He twisted his fingers, caught her grinning at him and grinned back. "So, uh, now what?"

"Now what, what? We don't have to. I'm attracted to a lot of men I don't sleep with. Maybe we shouldn't sleep together. Maybe it would be all wrong, so we should just keep talking. I don't sit here undressing you with my eyes. I just like being here. But if it happens, it happens. I just wonder if you can do it without feeling guilty, then I'll know you feel guilty and I'll . . ." She threw her head back and roared. "My God, Danny, I'm sounding like you."

He did just relax with her. Spoke to her as a friend. They didn't need to go anywhere or do anything. They could just sit

128

and talk. About his life. About her life. And all the while, she watched him. Initially that had discomforted him, because he didn't know what she was watching, exactly, except that whenever he gestured crazily or rambled on for ten minutes without a comma, her smile would widen and her eyes would twinkle and she'd just shake her head. He could be himself with her. He didn't have to worry about years of pent-up resentments triggered by a casual comment. He could say whatever popped into his mind and not worry. At first he'd thought it was because he didn't care that much. Then he realized it was because he cared a lot. And so, as she shook her head, he tried to follow the direction of that mass of red hair, wondering where it was all leading.

At least in the clubhouse, he'd managed to make progress. He still cultivated a forest of splinters, still accepted patronizing advice from everyone but Pete. Never from Pete. Whenever Danny began a question about baseball, Pete backed off. Danny knew it couldn't be out of fear of any competition. Then again, whenever Danny spoke to Pete about anything, he flinched and looked away. Except when Danny spoke to the other players. Then Pete stared with almost unblinking awe. No matter what Danny said, those round eyes would pierce him until Danny met the stare and forced the round eyes away. Danny wouldn't ask Pete why, just as he wouldn't ask Colleen why, because he still didn't want to know.

Still, after ten days he'd started undressing with the team. To make it seem as if he'd done something during the game, so Sam wouldn't continue ignoring his request to clean his uniform, Danny took to layering dirt on his uniform. Sometimes he even wore an extra pair of underwear so he would sweat more.

"Ya think I can just keep on runnin' up this team's bill for ya?" Sam had asked him.

"It's dirty," Danny insisted, shaking his uniform.

"Ya can wear it 'nother week." Sam sniffed and walked away. At least B.K. noticed the odor.

"Man, why dontcha just get it cleaned?"

"Sam won't clean it, says I don't get it dirty enough."

"You do, man, you shag some heavy flies out there, you work

129

hard. Hey, I saw that catch you made the other day in practice, real fine, really surrounded the ball."

That's because the ball surrounded me, Danny had thought. I turn every catch into an adventure. Why can't I just glide under it the way they do?

But what could he do? He didn't approach Jones anymore. He wouldn't go home, not after that last phone call with Sarah. Besides, she didn't even answer his calls anymore, which worried him. But he couldn't call his parents to ask about her because they'd lecture him and enhance his guilt. He worked as hard as he could in practice, knowing that his swing was leveling and his arm growing stronger and his catches a bit less awkward. But still not good enough. About right for a thirty-three-year-old on some sandlot, not in pro ball. He knew that, but was stuck. He couldn't go back and couldn't go forward.

Even in the house he couldn't go forward, or backwards. Some nights he would pace his room, which was really the couch, as some unconscionable music from a group called The Police assaulted him from Pee Wee's room. He'd pace, walk up the steps, pace by Pete's room, hear the muttering of words repeated interspersed with grunts, pause, shrug, start to Pee Wee's room to ask them to turn it down, stop, go back past Pete's room, hear the same vague incantations and return to his room. Except the other night when Pete had caught him.

"Danny?" he heard him call out. Danny had been midway between pacing in front of Pete's room and pacing near Pee Wee's room.

"Hey, Pete, how you doing?" Danny had finally entered, the prospect of rearranging his clothes beneath his coffee table/dresser unappealing. Though he'd invited Danny in, Pete blushed and stiffened as the door opened, then he slid a book between the bed and wall and shyly gestured for Danny to sit.

"Loud, huh?" Pete jerked his head in the direction of the music.

"No, doesn't bother me." Danny examined a row of trophies along Pete's wall. PAINTSVILLE HIGH SCHOOL MVP. ALL-KENTUCKY STATE ALL-STAR. APPALACHIAN LEAGUE ROOKIE.

"Old," Pete said softly.

"Look damn good to me."

130

"Old. Long time ago."

"Only a few years." Danny turned.

"Long time here." Pete shifted uncomfortably and Danny decided to sit, though he wasn't sure whether Pete wanted him to leave or not. He couldn't tell, because Pete didn't do anything except stare at his own feet, wait for Danny to look away, stare at Danny, then look away again.

"How long you been with the team?" Danny asked.

"Three years."

"That long for this league?"

"About two years too long," Pete said, shrugging.

"Sorry, I didn't . . ."

"It's okay, doesn't matter."

"Well, uh, doesn't mean you're not good. Hey, you're third on the team in hitting."

"Yeah." Pete played with his fingers. "Doesn't mean much."

"Could get you into a higher classification next year."

"Not what I mean."

They stared for a few seconds until Pete pulled away, allowing Danny to catch the pile of books on the desk.

"Read a lot, huh?"

"No."

"Lotta books there."

"Not so many."

"Yeah, lots." Danny peered. "Like Steinbeck, huh?"

"Yes." Pete straightened, then sagged, shrugging. "Yes."

"Me too. Read *In Dubious Battle?*

"Yes."

"Uh, well, ending was pretty good, huh?"

"Yes." Pete debated with his fingers, breathed deeply and, turning his face away from Danny, whispered, "Heavy symbolism."

"Think so? Nah." Danny's smile evaporated as Pete whirled, red-faced, and glared at his toes. "Uh, you know, symbolism's overrated, good for professors, pointy-heads?" Danny tried to lighten Pete's inexplicable color, failed, continued feebly. "To uh, examine a sentence and say the writer meant God when he used the sentence in that spot or used a semicolon."

"Sorry," Pete mumbled.

131

"For what?"

"You are a writer and I shouldn't be arguing with you about that stuff, you know better."

"Weren't arguing, Pete. You're entitled to your opinion."

"But you know better." For the first time, Pete held his stare on Danny. And he didn't know what to say.

"Uh, you'd be surprised, Pete. I just wrote for a trade magazine, not a real writer."

"You went to college and all," Pete insisted.

"So? Doesn't mean I know more than you."

"Yes, you do." Pete almost yelled.

"No, I really—I just read like you do. Go on, tell me what you think about that novel."

"Sounds stupid."

"Really, tell me." Danny didn't want Pete to think himself inferior, though Pete wanted to think himself inferior.

"Please, I don't want to, okay?"

"Okay." Or did Danny fear thinking himself superior? He didn't know as he'd moved toward the door.

"Danny?" It was a whisper and Danny paused, turning back. "Maybe sometime, uh, we could talk about, uh, Steinbeck and stuff."

"Sure, Pete, I'd like that."

"You won't laugh?"

"Don't find Steinbeck funny, do you?"

Colleen's husky voice jolted him . . . back to the present.

"I've made so many mistakes in my life. Now, I'm not saying what you're doing is a mistake." Danny tried to remember which mistake she was talking about. "Because it's what you believe in. Just—after a while—you learn to put everything in perspective."

"I can't wait until I'm old."

"You're so young yet."

"I'm not young."

"You are, Danny. You need patience."

"But I look like an asshole, the only one with a clean uniform and . . ." He wondered what she would say. "I've thought of quitting."

"Then you shouldn't."

"Tell me why."

"Because you think of it as quitting."

"What else is it? You go down, say you'll do something . . ."

"To who? Everyone else, right? They'll say you're quitting."

"And I'll say I'm quitting. Hell, should I say I'm making a tactical retreat? And I thought you don't believe in labels."

"I don't, because I'm talking about other people's labels, not yours. They can call it what they want, as long as you call it what you feel."

"I'm not that laid back."

"Oh Danny, you have this notion of me as some forty-five-year-old hippie, a reject from a commune. I'm not laid back, either."

"More than me."

"A meteor is more laid back than you. I'm talking about how you look at this. You must put everything in this neat little container of yours and then you complain because it's in a container. If you think it's wrong to stay, then leave. But at least believe your own lies."

"So I'm supposed to lie to myself."

"We all lie to ourselves. After a while, your . . . whatever, your philosophy of life—if there is such a thing, which I don't believe—allows you to accept those lies without feeling bad. That's it. You lied in the first place when you decided to try this. A lie. But then, you told me you didn't allow what anyone else thought to interfere with that. Now you do. Now you're letting impatience and fear and doubt and worry about what other people think make up your own lie. Don't do that to yourself."

"To thine own self be true?" It came out harsher than he meant. He wondered whether her expression were harsher than she meant.

"No, to thine own self, at least have livable lies. That's all."

Danny paused, studied his fingers, knew it was more than just baseball now.

"Do you want me to go?"

"No."

"Because you love me?"

"I don't know, Danny. I stopped worrying about love a long time ago. I grew content with care. I want to keep seeing you, but . . ." Colleen reddened and, for the first time, grew speechless without her vocal cords being seized by a laugh. "Do you love me?" she whispered, almost anxiously.

"I don't know if I can love two women. I'm not even sure I love my wife. You and me, we've only known each other such a short . . ."

"Then you don't. See, this is what happens. One loves, or doesn't, or neither, and they start bandying about a word when they should just do what they want and not worry so damn much."

"I'm not worrying."

"Of course you're worrying," her voice rasped. "You worry if you spend too much time with me, if we're friends or lovers, or what'll happen if you have to leave and about your wife and about everything."

"Don't you worry? Huh, a little, don't you worry about where this is all going?"

"I never used to. I was quite content to watch you."

"Don't watch me anymore, Colleen. I've spent my whole damn life watching other people, so, Christ, don't watch me anymore."

"I just want you to look at me," Sarah said, trotting over to him in a black skimpy nightie because it was Thursday and, by unspoken inertia, Thursday was their night during the week. For sex, some people called it. "Just tell me if I'm crazy and then I'll leave you alone."

"What?" Danny peered at the face drawn down by her fingers. "At what, I don't see anything." His eyes drifted past the cheek toward the neck and he thought it was about time to kiss it. So he did and she drew back.

"Not yet, I haven't put my diaphragm in yet and I still want you to look at my complexion. It's gone to shit. Over thirty and my skin is going. See those pimples?"

"I see one," Danny said, reaching for her, realized it wasn't time nor would it ever be time unless he agreed with her. "Okay, so one. I used to get more zits from one bite of pizza."

134

"So it is a zit," Sarah said sadly and Danny wondered if, for the first time in four years, Thursday night would be like Monday, Tuesday, Wednesday, Friday and Sunday. Saturday was also their night, assuming nothing good was on The Late Show. *"Shit," Sarah sighed, looking beyond him before shrugging and disappearing into the bathroom. "Be out as soon as I wash my face and use some astringent."*

Without warning, Colleen grabbed him, actually yanked him off the chair and pressed him against her chest. Her tongue forced open his mouth, not necessarily seeking out his tongue or even one spot in particular, just entered his mouth and dared him to respond—to allow his tongue to roam her mouth, her teeth, even descend into her vocal cords. Do anything he wanted.

"Could you just move over a little?" Sarah asked, shoveling Danny back across the bed. "Here." She slid her arm under his neck, he responded by laying his right arm around her shoulder. Her left arm went around his head, a bit into his curls though the fingers did little more than stay there as they kissed. Tongue to tongue. Quickly.

Danny hesitated as Colleen undressed. He saw, before closing his eyes, the large freckled breasts swooping down. Sagging just a little, but sagging because she was older and had never had any cosmetic surgery. So they sagged naturally, leaving the freckled upper chest and wide shoulders and firm arms, which now held the remains of her clothing. Panties. Panties which shook at Danny in puzzlement because he held nothing in his hands except his twisting fingers.

"Should I . . ." Colleen grinned and lunged for him. She tore at his shirt buttons, almost ripping them off as his shirt came undone, and then the pants were yanked down along with his underwear so everything fell around his ankles. He still had his shoes and socks on. Not for long, because she wrenched them off and scratched along his chest, and he still stood, eyes closed, as he reached for her breast so he wouldn't have to look at her.

Sarah dully rubbed the base of his neck. First he would kiss her neck, then peck at her shoulders so she would peck at his ear, then descend between her breasts and spend a little time on each

135

nipple. Always when he went from the right to the left, she breathed a little heavier, the breaths deepening as he moved toward her belly button and kissed around the ridges. She squirmed away because the belly contained too much flab and she didn't want him to remind her, so she tugged at his hair and he kissed her thighs.

Somehow he found himself atop Colleen. But that lasted only a minute as she flipped him over and climbed atop him.

"So soon?" Danny blushed, watching her kiss his stomach and listening to her chuckle.

"You're looking." Sarah tugged at his hair, half pulling him toward her breasts so he lay panting, wondering if he really wanted to pant. "Please keep them closed."

"Just opened them a little so I'd know where I was going."

"You should know where you're going by now." Sarah released his hair and pulled him onto her.

"Relax, Danny," Colleen said between a kiss. "I don't bite. Not yet."

"I'm just . . ." At least if she could keep her eyes closed, then I wouldn't worry if she found me attractive. Because Danny never believed Sarah found him attractive, believed they did it out of duty, that she kissed parts of his body because they belonged to her husband, and allowed his penis to penetrate because it belonged to her husband, and now this woman was heaving and squeezing him all over. Even opening her eyes now and then, and not at all repulsed by what she saw. Instead, turned on. By him. And as he half-closed, half-opened his eyes and felt a weird mist obscure his vision, he smelled her body. Not reeking of perfume but of sweat. And he stopped thinking about where his hands went. His fingers curled around her buttocks and she didn't squirm away. His fingers played with her pubic hair and she groaned and tore them up to her nipples, groaned some more, and he yanked her hair and she yanked back, until they lay side by side.

"Won't go in that way, we tried it once," Sarah said, her voice toneless as Danny tried to steady her on her side and enter at the same time.

"We could try."

136

"Danny, I'm kinda tired for experimentation tonight. Can't we just do it the regular way and try a different way Saturday night?"

Colleen squirmed around, slid under him and started guiding his penis into her. She paused for a moment and Danny peeked. Her eyes were shut. Then they fluttered and he paled, wanted to close his but didn't, and then it was too late. Her green eyes stared at him, not in curiosity or annoyance, but in what? Danny didn't know, only that he felt himself blush and smile.

"Hi." Danny hovered over her. "So I'm here."

"Huh?" Colleen's head tilted even more.

"Here, I'm coming in." Danny waited, trembling at the fingers squeezing his arms, fingers squeezing not in measurement nor searching for a comfortable place, fingers just squeezing.

Sarah smiled back, maintaining her smile until Danny could no longer tolerate the reflection of their unease and bewilderment, so he pressed his face against her neck. Mechanically, Sarah pressed her face into his neck. He pressed his penis into her vagina. She sighed. He sighed. She rubbed his back. He rubbed her back. He sighed. She sighed. He moved his penis in and out. She moved her vagina up and down. He sighed. She sighed.

Colleen laughed and Danny crimsoned. He was about to say something, but she continued chuckling and grabbed his cheeks. Pressed them together. Forced away the smile, though not the chuckle, which intensified into a lusty, delighted laugh as she kissed him and he couldn't laugh anymore. Could just stroke. But she didn't return his strokes. That confused him until he felt her hips ease beneath him and he found himself returning the rotation, not knowing what the hell he was doing because it was so damn strange. But it felt good. Very good. And he wondered if he should hug her and wondered where his hands should be, and then they just went in all different directions. As did hers. From the nape of his neck into his hair and down his spine, and he shivered. So did she as he squeezed her breasts and pulled and her mouth broke from his. A chuckle. And he chuckled back. Not from embarrassment nor from guilt, though he distantly felt those. But they couldn't enter because he was too busy laughing and groaning and, as her legs pressed him deeper, he lost him-

137

self, lost the image of Sarah and held the one of Colleen right before he went thoughtless. Totally thoughtless for a brief moment and didn't think if she had, too, because he couldn't think.

No one thought. Only groaned. Then lay still.

"Did you set the alarm?" Sarah asked, moving the ashtray between them on the bed, both of them lying on their backs.

"No. Yeah, I did."

"I'll check." Sarah ditched the cigarette, fumbled with the back of the digital and rose. They were out of matches and she spent a couple of minutes searching the tops of the dressers for one. By the time she returned, Danny was half asleep, barely hearing the match strike and the cigarette smoke and the body lean on the bed, away from him, her now open eyes staring through the dark at the digital, watching the serrated dial go round and round and tick off the seconds.

Danny tried to retrieve a random thought, found there were too many and so allowed himself to doze, very lightly, Colleen's head on his chest. He didn't feel her slipping up the blanket over his body, nor did he see the tears in her eyes. When he finally awoke several hours later and both had decided, silently, that neither was ready to spend a full night together and he'd have to leave, her tears had vanished.

Chapter 14

"I just wanted to give you some time to get your feet on the ground. Horace tells me you're doing a fine job, looking good in practice, seem to have all the makings of . . ."

What? Danny wanted to know, didn't say it, instead just stared at the photos in Antonheimer's office.

"He's a nice man," Danny mumbled. Seemed like the thing to say. What else could he say? That Jones was a brilliant manager and it was lousy players responsible for the team's last-place status? What could he say and what did he know?

". . . Day. Should be a big draw, they want to present you with something, spoke to their group, they're excited, I'm excited, you'll be excited."

"About what?"

"The Day.'"

"What day?"

"Senior Citizens Day."

Oh shit, don't let it be what I think, please don't let it . . .

"Danny, you have some problems on your mind?" Antonheimer leaned toward Danny's bloodless, slumped frame.

"Me? No, no, I'm great."

"Should be a good gate."

"Oh yeah, well, uh, what is it, they're presenting me, you said, with something?"

"Right, right, they want to make you an honorary Gray Panther. I think that's terrific, big ceremonies. We'll have an old-time vaudeville comedian as master of ceremonies, don't think you remember vaudeville, let me . . ."

"Why?" Danny squeaked.

"Why what?"

"Why do they want to make me an honorary Gray Panther? That's for senior citizens, I, I get an occasional twinge, maybe, okay, but I'm only thirty-three and . . ."

"But you're an old thirty-three." Antonheimer slammed his fist on the desk and Danny instinctively covered his chest lest it get slammed on Antonheimer's way out the door. But Antonheimer didn't move, just glared, then smiled, then giggled.

My entire athletic career is in the hands of a raving lunatic, Danny thought, slowly succumbing to nausea.

"Don't you see?" Danny did, but wished he didn't. "How many men have the courage at your age to want to break into baseball? How many?" Danny shrugged. He wished he knew someone so they could change places, right now, right here. "In our business, you're an old man. Thirty-three is goddamn old to start a baseball career, right?" Oh jeez, why does he have to rub it in? "And the Gray Panthers is an organization designed to promote the perception that you're never too old to do anything. So, then."

So then what? He still had three days before Senior Citizens Day to apply Grecian Formula 44 or devour Baby Ruths and break out in zits. But what would that do? It wouldn't change his age, wouldn't change how they looked at him, wouldn't change anything, except maybe if he looked younger the Gray Panthers wouldn't give him a cane shaped like a baseball bat. What could he do—and if he could do something, should he do it? Really, wasn't this all he was? He wasn't a ballplayer. If he were such a hot prospect he'd have been used already on a last-place team. So why not go along with it? Might as well fulfill the original intention of his contract. The gimmick. The idol to old people.

As it turned out, a lot of old people, nearly six hundred of them, made up the announced paid crowd of 931 that filled the park that night. According to the rules of Senior Citizens Day, an elderly person had to show proof of age, a birth certificate or a special seniors check-cashing card from a local supermarket. After maybe six people, the guards stopped demanding proof. So someone sixty-three snuck in. They'd surely eat and Antonheimer got a piece of the concessions. They'd make it up in beer and Cokes and franks, even if the bathroom lines were a little longer than usual.

"You going to hang up the award in the house?" Pete asked Danny, who stood in front of the dugout, bat pressed against his face, watching the old people swarm across the field and the microphones being set up and knowing it was really possible to die of embarrassment.

"Yeah." Go well with your All-State and Heddy's All-League and Pee Wee's fielding award and B.K.'s RBI trophy, Danny thought, pressing the bat closer against his face until he realized the splinters might pierce his eyeballs. It would be in character for Antonheimer to call the Braille Institute and have Danny and his seeing-eye dog shag fly balls together.

"Hey, New."

Somebody hissed at him. Someone had been hissing at Danny for several minutes now and he'd ignored it, but suddenly it seemed preferable to the walkers and canes inundating the field. Danny turned and saw a squat man with remnants of gray hair and a somewhat pleasant face, presently contorted with conspiratorial urgency, leaning over the first-base railing.

"Hey, New."

"Me?" Danny approached, pointing to his chest and glancing up and down the railing. Every Hornet seemed busy signing autographs. No one had asked Danny for his autograph since that first day he'd arrived. He'd considered tearing off his name and number from the jersey. Why should Antonheimer waste line space on the scorecard?

The man's head bobbed as he glanced nervously behind and around him.

"Yes, New." He waved his stubby arms. Even in the dreadful humidity, he wore long sleeves.

"Uh." Danny smiled, shaking his head. "It's Neuman, I wouldn't expect you to know . . ."

"I know, I know. New's better, even if Neuman is on the borderline."

"Of what?"

"You can't really tell with Neuman, what it is." He had a faint accent, maybe European.

"What is?"

"Your name. It doesn't sound quite as Jewish." His voice dipped.

Terrific, just what I needed, Danny thought, starting to walk away. The man seized Danny's arm and wrenched him back with surprising strength.

"Now be quiet, they might hear."

"Who?"

"Them." He looked at Danny. "So, you're him."

"Right, and you're who?" Danny made no attempt to conceal his irritation. Besides, it felt good.

"Rabbi Jacob Gottlieb, your brother Nathan's friend?" The Rabbi's voice stayed in a taut whisper. "He called the other night to see how you were doing, to tell me how his project was going." Gottlieb hunched forward. "Did you know he got a sign? Witnessed a four-alarm fire, broke out right in front of him. Like the burning bush, no?"

"Oh, listen." Danny sighed in pain. I need to hear about Nathan and his trek, right? "Uh, Rabbi," Gottlieb shushed him. Danny rolled his eyes and whispered, "Uh, why are we whispering?"

"You can never be sure."

"Of what?"

"Them."

"Who?"

"All around us."

Danny saw some Southern beauties, some rednecks and enough old people to fill a boardwalk.

"Them." Gottlieb waved his hand to reassure Danny, who was not at all reassured but confident of a lynching during the seventh-inning stretch. "Don't worry. Me, I'll worry for both of us."

"That's terrific, Rabbi." Danny self-consciously played with his nose. "But I . . ."

"You I was worried about, until I read in the paper about today. You were supposed to call, Nathan said, and I didn't know what had happened to you."

"Yeah, I'm sorry, Rabbi, I meant to call you but, you know."

"Who am I to question the folly of young people?"

Danny started liking him. Maybe.

"Yeah, well." Danny had no idea what to say. "So how you doing?"

"How well could I be doing?"

"I don't know."

"Only He knows."

"God?"

"Sha, please."

"Rabbi." Danny found himself watching the crowd. "I have this thing to do now but, uh, maybe we can get together sometime?"

"Wonderful. You'll come to the house."

"Yeah, okay, but right now, I have to go . . ."

"Don't worry about me, I'll sit, I'll watch. You'll hit a touchdown?"

"Yeah, a touchdown."

Rabbi Gottlieb scribbled his address and phone number on a slip of paper and shoved it into Danny's hip pocket, all the while glancing around in nervous terror.

"Now, don't lose it when you run around." Gottlieb shook his finger.

"Don't have to worry about that." Danny sighed as Gottlieb abruptly bounded up the aisle. Exactly what I needed, a paranoid rabbi. He sighed wearily as he made his way toward the dugout to spruce up. Festivities would start soon and he had to look good. He was the Man of the Hour.

"I don't understand why you wouldn't want me to see you there." Colleen had touched his minuscule chest hairs. She liked his body. Found him sexy. Him, sexy? He'd never thought of himself as sexy and now he was sexy. Maybe she was just used to older men. Older men? Now he wasn't an old man. At least with her. An older woman found his body youthful and the youthful bodies found him old. And he didn't know what to think.

"Because, okay, I'm a gimmick. I know it, okay, and I'm just embarrassed by it."

"I don't think you're a gimmick. What you've done so far takes a lot of courage."

"Yeah." Suddenly her words had their impact eviscerated.

Why? Because she cared for him and when someone cares for you, you automatically lessen their opinions in favor of a total stranger. And it bothered him to think of her as other than a stranger.

"You never want me to come out to the park."

"Because I don't do anything. You can't see me. I sit on the end of the bench and hold my bat. I never play."

"You'll get your chance."

"Oh yeah, right."

"You will, Danny. But you must believe."

And he didn't like it that she was so serious with him, either. He liked it when she laughed. Not that he didn't enjoy talking to her, but he preferred it when she laughed. If he ever told her that, though, she'd think him shallow and that he only wanted her for one thing. And she'd never believe that *that* wasn't the one thing.

"Well, I must say, uh." Danny smiled now at the Greensboro chapter of the Gray Panthers. "That I'm, well, overwhelmed by this honor and, I, uh, just hope I can continue to live up to your, uh, you know, faith in me."

The Panthers formed a circle and applauded him as he actually shuffled back toward the dugout, Danny uncertain whether he was just playing the part or whether it had seeped into his personality.

"Looks terrific, really terrific." Pete slapped him on the back and tried to read the plaque which Danny placed a foot away from himself on the bench. DANNY NEUMAN, HONORARY MEMBER OF THE GRAY PANTHERS OF GREENSBORO. "Bet Steinbeck never got an award like that."

Once the lengthy process of escorting the Panthers back into the stands had been completed, Danny settled back into his familiar grooves on the bench. Three weeks ago he could stare in bewildered awe as the Hornets took up fielding positions, could monitor the other players for their reactions so he could react, even though he already knew when to applaud or when to jeer or when to make disgusted clucking noises.

Of late, however, Danny had felt himself drifting, while at the same time developing a sense of personal interest in the game

144

totally apart from whether they won or lost. They usually lost anyway, which was one way of him justifying a lack of concentration. He knew his cheers or jeers wouldn't change anything. They were a pretty rotten team. He found he'd grown to know and like these guys, though, these kids, so he tried to concentrate because he liked them.

"No batter, no batter, he's a bum, he's a bum," Pee Wee chattered away from short. He edged back and forth on both feet, seemingly unable to hunch forward, to tense himself in anticipation of the outcome of the pitch. Pee Wee touched his cap, touched his mouth, did everything but remain motionless. At first Danny had thought it was mere nerves. He remembered back when he'd be out in the field, and his stomach would churn, and he'd pray the batter would hit the ball and end the excruciating doubt of whether the baseball would sizzle on a line straight at you or skip in drunken hops toward your left or soar on an arc over the fence.

But Danny knew it was more than nerves which bounced Pee Wee around short. He knew what it was and that made it difficult for him to watch, at the same time making it imperative he did watch.

The Spartanburg batter lunged at a low fastball and smacked it in the hole on the left side. Pee Wee had been leaning left, on his glove side, and so got a late start for the ball. He extended himself and dived headfirst, glove outstretched for a backhanded play which should've been made with his glove in front of him and his feet set up for the long, albeit simple, throw to first. He grabbed the ball, then it spurted loose, dribbled in front of him. He bounced up on one knee, picked it up and heaved a throw to first.

Heddy had already positioned himself with his rear left foot against first, his gloved right hand extended out for the throw. Heddy had obviously watched Gil Hodges play a lot for the Brooklyn Dodgers. No he hadn't, that was a lie. Heddy hadn't even known who Gil Hodges was until a coach had told him he cheated like Hodges, and Heddy had liked that, that someone acknowledged he was only cheating and not doing what he really was doing.

The runner raced down the line and Heddy's thin brown eyes darted back at the approaching footsteps, his body bending in anticipation of the throw sailing across the diamond and the steps nearing his back foot and the body a few feet from his own. Heddy crouched more, though the throw took off and, as the ball started sailing upward, Heddy sank lower and then stepped off the bag as the runner tripped over first.

"Shit," Heddy shouted and watched the ball bound up against the first-base railing. He chased after it. Pee Wee paused, still kneeling in the hole, then started toward second, though the Hornets' second baseman was already there waiting for Heddy to retrieve the ball and try and throw out the guy at second.

"Mine." Pee Wee flung himself in the air and landed a foot or two from second, bounced up and grappled with his teammate over who would get the throw from Heddy. Neither did, for Heddy, still watching the runner, kept dropping the ball and finally just gloved it in disgust. Man on second, none out.

"Make a good throw and see what happens." Pee Wee shook his head as he moved back toward his position, never once touching the dirt on his uniform.

Danny knew why they acted the way they did, which is why he allowed himself to drift after the first half-inning. He didn't want to think about it, about the real reasons for the dirt on the uniforms and the inability to catch simple balls.

He sat on the bench and recited poetry.

> Little Danny Neuman
> Sat in the corner,
> Holding his bat and glove;
> Along came a baseball
> And sat down beside him
> And said,
> "*Shmuck*, stop snoring
> I can't hear the organist."

He stopped when he found himself talking aloud and players watching him, so he started on mathematical problems. Like adding columns of figures in his head, then dividing by three, or four. Usually that lasted several innings since he had little aptitude for math and it took him a few times at bat just to add everything up.

Last of the fifth. Danny held onto the number: 53,219.

B.K. had an elaborate routine at bat. Apparently he had copied the superstitious habits of every major-league ballplayer who ever played. He'd pause exactly twenty inches from the batter's box. It was really exactly twenty inches, because on a recent road trip, Danny had seen B.K. measuring off the distance. Twenty inches where B.K. would stop and flip the bat in the air. Once, twice, each time catching it on the fat part of the bat. Then he would signal for the pine tar, rub enough to adhere a supertanker along the bat's handle, move another four inches and stop again. At this point the umpire would grow a bit irritated, as would the opposing players, which is why, Danny believed, B.K. injected religion into the procedure. He'd cross himself. Two times, which Danny thought perhaps sacrilegious, and a mite puzzling, since B.K. didn't wear any crosses around his neck, only a medallion which read OH SHIT. But he'd still cross himself, placating the umps and the other team, since they didn't want to interrupt a man asking God for a fastball waist-high.

At this point it would seem likely that B.K. would be ready to take up his stance. Not quite. He would knock the dirt out of his shoes, first the right, then the left, then the right again. Once the dirt was out of his shoes, B.K. would step out of the batter's box, look past the third-base coach's sign and off into the horizon, somewhere beyond the left-field fence. Danny often expected B.K. to point à la Babe Ruth in the '32 Series, but he never did and Danny knew why.

Finally, B.K. stepped back into the box. He wiggled his neck like Jesus Alou and stabbed his bat in the air and wiggled that, like Joe Morgan, twitching his back elbow. Then he started crouching deeply, only to bounce back up and stand erect, and Danny no longer knew who the hell B.K. was imitating at this point, only that his mother made brisket in less time than it took B.K. to get set for one pitch.

And then the pitch would come in. And B.K. would invariably try to go to right with it. Now it wouldn't matter where the

147

pitch came in, for B.K. would always try to take it to the opposite field. Danny expected someone of B.K.'s height, about six-two, and bulk, about one-ninety-five, to be a pull hitter. But he wasn't. Danny had never seen B.K. pull a ball, and that used to puzzle him until he realized that B.K. went the opposite way with every pitch for the same reason that Pee Wee was never set up right, and for the same reason Heddy rarely caught a throw unless it was within his knee-to-chest range, and for the same reason why Pete played too shallow in center.

Way too shallow, Danny half-thought, wondering if Pete believed he was a reincarnation of Tris Speaker, though he had Frank Howard's lumbering gait. More often than not, the ball would hurtle over Pete's head and he'd try to make a running, over-the-shoulder catch like Willie, and only end up flailing at the ball until it stopped around the warning track. And then Pete would fire it back in, only to see the ball die out and skip on a few bounces into the relay man's glove, rarely in time to get the runner.

Yeah, Danny knew why they were the way they were. They were detonating their own dreams. Pee Wee was five-eight, considerably taller than Herve Villechaize, only two inches shorter than Danny, yet Pee Wee had given himself that nickname. No one else. Maybe that's why Pee Wee practiced at every position and constantly managed to barely miss balls just about his leaping grab. Just like Heddy inching off the bag. He wasn't cheating. He didn't know how to cheat. Heddy was afraid of the base runner and afraid of getting hit with the ball. And that's why B.K. always went to right, because everyone expected him to be a pull hitter and he wasn't, so he became an opposite-field hitter. That's why Pete played too shallow, because he'd have an excuse when the ball went over his head and when he couldn't make the throw from deep center.

They were all afraid, kids terrified of the failure their earlier successes should devour, so they self-destructed before anyone could pin that failure upon them. The ball was too deep in the hole. The throw was too high. The pitch was low and away. The wind carried the ball. The incessant excuses told to the omnipresent Yankee minor-league instructors determined to inject

148

Pinstripe Pride into children. But the Pride couldn't conquer the Fear and that's what tore at Danny, because he couldn't stand witnessing their instinctive detonations because he liked them, and because at least they were detonating something. What the hell was he doing?

He decided to try to anticipate when the organist would thump away, perhaps his favorite game. He'd gotten good at it. Maybe that's why it was his favorite game. When he was right, he'd reward himself by uncrossing his legs. Otherwise his legs would stay bent and stiff. Not that it mattered. All he had to do with them was shuffle back into the clubhouse. And since they were bent, they'd fit easier into his tiny cubicle. At least no one bothered him.

He peered at the scoreboard. Only three zeros for each team. Coulda sworn it was longer than that. Danny shook his head, bewildered, then saw the lights had been turned on and realized the game had gone into extra innings. Huh, must have been asleep. Danny yawned, blinked again and saw there were two outs and the bases were loaded, and Jones was kicking at the water cooler and glaring at Mookie Piston, a relief pitcher and apparently the next scheduled batter.

"I can do it, Skip," Mookie pleaded.

"Jesus H., you can't even hold the goddamn bat right, Jesus H.," Danny heard Jones grumble. Danny shrugged, yawned and heard, "Neuman."

Danny yawned.

"Neuman."

Danny looked at the far end of the dugout. He rarely went there anymore, preferring this side since it was closer to the runway and he could get into the clubhouse first and take the Number 3 shower stall, which almost had paint left.

"Hi." Danny waved and looked back at the field.

"Goddamn it, Neuman, get up there, I ain't got no one left."

Danny stiffened, turning slowly and seeing the entire team watching.

"Jones, you gonna play ball today or what?" the home-plate ump shouted.

"Neuman, come on, ain't got all day, before you know it the

149

ump's angry and bored and they'll miss a call and we got a chance to win this and it's bad enough they called Kelly out at home in the eleventh so come on."

Danny laughed.

"Come on," Jones shouted.

"Danny," Pete said after sliding down the bench, nudging him in the ribs, "he wants you to hit."

"He does?"

"Danny." Pete jiggled his arm. "Come on."

Danny stumbled up, staggered. Shit, forgot to uncross them. He limped down the dugout.

"Good God, you're not hurt, are you?" Pete asked, trailing him.

"No." Danny straightened and fumbled for his bat in the rack, realized it was at the far end of the bench, ran back, grabbed it and raced back down, standing in front of Jones. The dugout half-rose. "You really want me to hit?"

"Well, what the devil else would I want you to do?"

Danny trembled.

"Uh, what, uh, kinda instructions, uh, what do you want me to do?"

Jones took Danny's chin and steered his face in the direction of third base.

"See Heddy on third?" Danny nodded. "Be nice if you got him from third to home safely, wouldn't it?"

Danny stumbled up the steps and onto the field. He stopped. I'm gonna hit, he thought, stumbling again, this time over a bat. Pee Wee, the next batter, steadied him.

"Danny, hey, you okay?"

"Sure."

"Danny, you ain't got any color in your face." Pee Wee winced. "Now listen up, this pitcher's got a shit curve, okay, no control, you see it break, lay offa it, he can't throw it for strikes. He got a fair change, but don't have much control on that, either, so he'll probably come in with smoke, intimidate you, probably on the inside corner first, then out there, setting you up, then . . . Danny, hey, you okay?"

"You never said it like that before, Pee Wee."

150

"Said what? Now listen, stay calm, okay?"

"I know what to do." Danny started toward home. At least he hoped it was home.

"Oh, Christ." Pee Wee watched Danny shuffle in a doped arc toward home, then he glanced toward the pitcher's mound, where the opposing Florence manager huddled with his players.

"Ain't that the old geezer?" Florence manager Gus Chippendale gestured at Danny, currently staring at the center of home plate.

"Don't worry." Pitcher Felipe Amos spun the ball. "I t'row it past him."

"For Greensboro, batting for Piston, number 34, Danny Neuman, number 34."

"That's me," Danny told the home-plate umpire.

"I'm glad for ya, kid," the umpire said to Danny, now digging his back right foot into the batter's box.

I've been announced. Now would they announce me if I weren't the next batter? No, course not, course they wouldn't. Would I be in this game if they hadn't run out of players? No, course not. But it was me they introduced. Me, Danny Neuman. They introduce me and lookit, outfield's moving in, thanks guys, I appreciate that, and the infield's moving in, first baseman shortening up, grinning, hah, what's so funny, huh, and the shortstop, hey aren't you even gonna hunch over a little, why, why don't you all just sit down if you think it's so funny, think the old guy's up and nothing to worry about? Well, is there? Wish I'd stop shaking. Wish I knew what to do.

Hootsie-tootsie. It popped into his head and Danny asked for time. The third-base coach wearily repeated the signs. Danny stared dumbly. Hootsie-tootsie.

> *Hootsie-tootsie, watch this stunt;*
> *Are you ready*
> *For one of my bunts?*

The fastball came in, just over the outside corner, just below Danny's waist. He scrunched, ran his right hand up the bat and caught the ball a couple of inches below the fat part, dumping it down the third-base line.

Everyone shouted. The pitcher tumbled off the mound, the third baseman raced in, the catcher dashed out, Heddy galloped down the line.

Run, Neuman, he told himself, not realizing he was running as fast as he could, straining as hard as he could with both hands flailing at his sides and his body straining forward and his sweat ripping into his eyes, as he saw the first baseman lean forward to accept the throw and, oh shit here we go, do it, you have to do it, do it, do it, you can do it, please, do it.

Danny flung himself headfirst at the bag, his left hand swiping and seizing the white bag as his body scraped the ground and he spun counterclockwise, holding onto the bag with all his strength and not looking up, not hearing anything, not even the umpire signal safe or his teammates cheering or anything. He just stood, very casually, and wiped dirt off the front of his uniform, ignoring the dirt on his face, and looked around at the happy players slapping him and knocking his cap off.

"Now can I get this cleaned?" Danny shouted, as they hoisted him atop their shoulders and carried him back into his clubhouse.

Chapter 15

Applying makeup in the morning became more than an habitual attempt to color a bored face and more of an adventure. Purchasing a one-cup Melitta coffee maker hadn't been traumatic, though Sarah had yet to use it. Scoring eighteen words a minute on a typing test hadn't been catastrophic, perhaps embarrassing, but she'd lived. Standing on line to buy tokens amazed her, though she didn't exactly know why. And she was able to stand on a crowded subway train without being raped, even as she scrutinized every male, ambulatory or not, within ten feet of her. Here she was, on a subway train stuffed with sane lunatics, on her way to work. Okay, not to a stimulating job. A receptionist's job in an ad agency. Okay, so it was mundane. But it represented progress. She had a job. Even if she didn't use her mind, which is why Sarah read all the advertisements and memorized them. To use her mind and blot out the distant fear applying makeup in an empty bathroom and buying tokens and riding the subway and working in a job filled her with.

"Stuff don't work." A voice startled Sarah. She continued reading, ignoring the voice and hoping it was aimless, like the well-tailored gentleman the other day who had harangued at the President's foreign policy to the subway window. Another directionless voice, this time not so directionless and clearly intended for her. Sarah felt a hard body stiffen against her back. Instinctively she squeezed her handbag and worried if she could save her necklace.

"Tellin' you, my Aunt Elvira tried that stuff, just doesn't do anythin'." Sarah tensed, kept her eyes on the hemorrhoid ad, so tense she didn't even sway to the ancient roll of the subway. "Ya know?"

Sarah gulped, started to turn. If she met the voice and just nodded, perhaps it would go away. But she couldn't act too abrupt because the voice probably had a hand which undoubtedly held a knife which undoubtedly would cut her heart out. Or she could just watch the hemorrhoid sign and hope the subway got to her stop before the voice started up again.

"Always go to a doctor for anythin' like that. Too many people get sick with over-the-counter stuff like that." Again the voice continued. Streetish. New Yorkish. Bordering on a cliché without the hostility—which was another cliché, except in Sarah's case. Her hostility intermingled with her fear and overtook her just enough so she half-turned toward the voice.

"Hey, how ya doin', I'm Lee Pomenzo." The voice had a face: a nice face, handsome. Olive skin, wide forehead, big round brown eyes. Dimples. Curly black hair. Wide shoulders contained within a nice, inexpensive suit, not YSL from Bloomingdale's—maybe Johnny Carson from Sears—but clean. And trim waist. And Sarah couldn't believe she was ogling this man, or kid, maybe around twenty-two, while she shook from terror. "Tell ya, think these ads do harm to people. Got no room to move on these damn subways, so it's kinda hard to read the paper. Unless you wanna read the *Post*, which, except for the sports, is a rag. So they box us in here and put us at their mercy, sort of, know what I mean? And then we gotta read ads like this and to block out alla noise and weirdasses, we think it's good stuff. But my Aunt Elvira, I tell ya, they hadda bring her into Mount Sinai. Shoulda sued, but my Uncle Carmine spoke to the druggist, then the company, and things were straightened out. Know what I mean?"

"Yes?" Sarah whispered, swiveling a little more so her body was nearly flush to his. And she reddened.

"Hey, I'm sorry. Shouldn't talk 'bout personal stuff like hemorrhoids to a stranger, but, like I said, what happened to my Aunt Elvira and all, like to help a stranger. Specially when

154

they're cute." His mouth flashed for the white teeth to show and the dimples to deepen. And she reddened more.

Cute? Her hair now crept past her ears. Her clothes no longer suffocated her hips, but marched side by side with them. Even her breasts didn't seem to sag as much. And her stomach was flattening out. She'd started using Danny's exercise bicycle.

"I, uh, don't only read that." She gestured at the sign, her fingers whitened around her handbag. "Other signs, too. Um, whatever's in front of me. I just read them, something to do."

"Yeah, ya know." Lee fished into his jacket pocket and pulled out an occult novel. "Sometimes I read this stuff. Horror stuff, know what I mean? So okay, it's garbage, but then I don't go for none of that high-level stuff. Least when I can read, I do. Or at least think. Kinda lets me escape all this crap on the subways and lets my mind ease down a couple gears 'fore I gotta go to work."

"Yes, I, uh, think, too," Sarah lied, knowing she didn't dare let her mind wander too much on the subway. "But," she struggled with words, even as she returned his level stare, returned his wide, sexy smile, uncertain where her courage came from. She knew these spasms of bravery had to be seized lest they drift away, much as she'd seized the guitar the other day, staring at the chords, knowing she knew how to play, wondering if she could.

"Maybe we can think together some night. Or kinda talk about what we think about. Could be fun."

"Excuse me?" Sarah's eyes flickered up to another sign. POWER PERSONNEL AGENCY. THERE'S A JOB FOR EVERYONE. And a picture of a middle-aged black man hauling boxes, a heavy-set Hispanic woman cheerfully answering a phone and a youngish housewife holding a meeting with four attentive men seated around a table. Beneath the housewife with the four men was a graffiti caption: SHE SWALLOWS.

"Yeah, ya know, just get together, go out to dinner. Ya know, just the two of us, me an' you."

"A date?"

"Sure, yeah." Lee grinned. "How's about it?"

A date? Someone at least ten years younger than me with a

155

heavy Brooklyn-Bronx accent and gorgeous dimples is asking me out for a date before a hemorrhoid ad on the E train? Sarah was indignant. Probably thinks I'm an easy mark. Or perverse because of my interest in the ad. Probably thinks I accept all offers from good-looking men who happen to look like Al Pacino. Who does he think he is?

"Sarah," she whispered. Lee wrote it down and waited for the phone number. Still time to get out of it. Had to be a million Sarahs in New York. Fifth Avenue stop would come any second. Race out of the car and up the steps. If he followed she'd scream and call the cops. Even if she didn't have any strength to scream or run or do anything except mumble her phone number. Not even mumble it. Okay, not exactly spit it out with authority. More out of numbed disbelief that she would give him her number, and growing shame that she hadn't remembered it only took a second for someone to ask you out for a date. That it had been so long since someone asked. That she wanted to go out with him. That she didn't know why.

"Yeah, I'll call tomorrow night, 'bout seven or so, how's that?" Lee backed away as the train stopped. Fifth Avenue. Both their stops, but Sarah wouldn't get off. Would get off at the next stop and walk, even if walking along the street still made her nervous. She didn't want to push her luck and go up the steps with him. So she managed a weak good-bye as he disappeared behind the closing doors and she returned to the sign,

FOR QUICK, PAINLESS RELIEF . . .

As always, lunchtime came too quickly for Sarah. At least during the workday, she knew what she had to do. Noon forced her into further decisions. Rarely would she eat with any of her co-workers. Twice, she'd met Sadie and Pistol for lunch. Sadie and Pistol. Sarah was still amazed they had become her friends, that a chance encounter on the steps had surmounted an embarrassed greeting and led to something resembling friendship.

Generally she'd eat alone, at one of the coffee shops, or sit on the concrete steps near the office building, eat a sandwich and watch people until they watched back and she had to lower her eyes. Today she had a luncheon date. All morning she had

156

wanted to cancel it, wanted to dial the phone, once it stopped ringing, and tell him to forget it. She had a disease, something, anything. But she hadn't, and, as he settled in across from her in one of those vinyl booths in a coffee shop, Sarah tried to cover her dread with a weary grin.

"What'll you have, *bubbelah?*" he said. Always *bubbelah*, or sweetheart. He was never cross with her, though she knew, once, she had to have done something to anger him. If she had, he'd never shown it. Sarah never knew if he really liked her or just accepted her because she was married to his son. As she started to reply, watching him slide the bulky Brentano's bag next to him in the booth, Sarah realized this was the first time they'd ever been alone. She wasn't reassured by the knowledge, however, even as he folded his hands and smiled tenderly, showing Danny in the eyes, back when Danny was tender, when his face had spread in gentleness unencumbered by bitterness.

"Salad, maybe?" Sarah smiled back, wished her mother-in-law were there to shovel stuffed cabbage down her throat, or Danny were there to quip sarcastically. Danny. She couldn't bear to think of Danny, but knew she had no choice since she was sitting with his father and since this luncheon was designed to reprimand her for not calling Danny. God, what if Mr. Neuman knew what she was doing tomorrow night when the phone would ring? He wouldn't know because she wouldn't answer the phone. Or if she did answer the phone, she'd refuse the date.

"So, how have you been?" Mr. Neuman asked as the waitress deposited two salads.

"Fine, okay, I think. You?"

"Good, fine, okay."

They twisted their fingers and waited for a third person to say something.

"Job good?" he asked.

"Okay. Not exactly my life's ambition," Sarah replied, not knowing what her ambitions were, beyond letting her hair grow and taking the subway and answering phones and refusing dates from gorgeous men she wanted to go out with. Shit.

"Uh, I thought we could get together. I—we never talk, I

157

thought we could talk, that is why I called last night. I didn't wake you, did I?" he asked, apologizing as if to assuage the coming disapprobation.

"No." Sarah picked at her salad. "Mom okay?"

"You know your mother-in-law." So much for that. "And you, you are okay, you, uh, look okay, have a job, ever hear from Daniel?"

"No." Sarah looked down, steadying herself. "I don't."

"He doesn't call you?"

"No."

"Uh, you call him?"

"No."

"Maybe you should?"

"Maybe he should call me."

"So, maybe he's afraid because you don't call him."

"Did he tell you that?"

"No." Now Mr. Neuman looked down. "He doesn't say."

"So does he say he misses me?"

"Your mother-in-law doesn't say. Neither does Nathan."

"What does he say to you?"

"Nothing."

"About me, nothing?"

"I haven't spoken to him."

"You don't speak to him?"

"No. He never asks for me." His eyes still didn't bob up. "I thought maybe you could call him, see how he's doing."

"Doesn't he tell Mom and Nathan he's doing fine?"

"Would he tell them the truth? You he would tell the truth."

"I can't." Sarah stabbed a tomato. "I—it's better we don't speak, lets him do what he has to do, lets me do what I have to do."

"Maybe it's pride, okay? Maybe if you made the first effort, he would respond, this, this split would be patched up. So call."

"I can't call him, Dad. I just can't. I have enough on my mind here, figuring things out, trying to see if I can do anything by myself. I, I can't call him. It wouldn't help. I . . ."

"I worry about him."

"Please, I worry about him, too."

158

"If he eats right. He wouldn't tell your mother-in-law if he isn't eating right. Sleeping, drinking, who knows what. Maybe he's an alcoholic by now. They all are, those athletes."

"Shit, I can't, okay? I think about him, you think I don't, that . . ." Sarah glared at a cucumber, rolled it about her bowl. "I have my reasons for not calling and, and I can't. It'd ruin—" She stared at him. "Why don't you call him?"

"You should call."

"Why can't you?"

"He talks to my wife, to Nathan, that's good enough."

"Obviously it's not or you wouldn't ask me to call him."

"Am I thinking about me or your marriage?"

"I don't know. Which? Why won't you call?"

"He would talk to me?"

"Why not?"

Mr. Neuman chuckled weakly and shook his head.

"Please call him."

"I can't. He has to do what he must do and I have to do what I must do."

"And why must you both be alone? Why must Daniel be alone?"

"His choice, Dad, damnit, he decided to do this. I respect it enough to let him do what he wants, so should you."

"And I don't respect him? He's my son, I respect what he does. I just want to hear that he is fine."

"Then you call him."

"We never . . . it was silly. I'm sorry I interfered. I should mind my own business."

"It's your business, too, right?" She squeezed his hand.

"What? Your marriage."

"You, too, right?" She studied him so intently he turned his face. "You're not only concerned about our marriage, but about Danny, how he's doing. If you are, then you should speak to him."

"I just thought . . ."

"Don't make me call him, Dad. I didn't stop him, don't stop me from doing what I have to do. Okay?"

"So, this job of yours," he sipped coffee, "they pay you well?"

"Terrible." Again she squeezed his hand. "Call him. It would make him happy, I know."

"What is it that you do in this job?"

"I'm not sure," she sighed, releasing her grip, comforting both of them.

Chapter 16

"You look fine," Pistol squealed.

"No." Sarah shook her head, her eyes, swollen from applying and removing and applying makeup for the last hour, peered into the mirror. "Need more. I just don't look good."

"How'd you look on the subway?"

"Like this."

"Thought you weren't wearing as much makeup?" Sadie asked.

"Yes, but I want to look good."

"If you hadn't looked good originally, do you think he would have asked you out?" Pistol searched her eyes. "You want us to stay down here with you and meet him?"

"Oh yeah, that's a great idea, would you do that?"

"No." Pistol grinned. "Got to do this on your own."

"No, really, I, I'd like you to tell me what you think of him."

"Don't you think we might scare him off?" Sadie smiled. "Not everyone is as liberal as you."

"And if he's scared off because my friends happen to be transvestites, well then, so, who needs him anyway?"

"You do, sweetie."

Only a date, Sarah kept telling herself. Just a harmless little date. Then why was she driving herself crazy preparing for it when it was only a date? Because she hadn't had a date since her hair was frizzy and she played the guitar and only worried about how to pass one of her psych courses? Was that it? Only a date. Nothing major. So she had told herself two nights ago as she paced crazily near the telephone, waiting for him to call, dressed in a shabby nightgown and black fishnet stockings, waiting for the call which should have come at seven but came instead at eight.

"Yeah, so hi, how ya doin'?" Lee's swift voice had driven her hands to cover the nightgown.

"Oh, okay, uh, you?"

"Good, good, listen. I hate the phone, so okay? Anyway, what do we say I pick you up, dunno, say, 'bout eight or so Friday, go out to eat, do something afterwards?"

"Like what?" she snapped.

"Dunno, anything you want." He chuckled faintly. "Maybe go dancin', somethin' like that, maybe a movie?"

"Dancing?" Sarah rubbed her thighs. Dancing? With these legs, dancing? Last time she'd gone dancing was with Danny. Another simple date. Their wedding. "Yes, uh, we could do that."

"Yeah, ya know, we'll play it by ear, know what I mean? So okay, Friday around eight?"

"Yes. Uh, Lee?"

"Huh?"

"Uh, for dinner, where are we going, how should I dress? Uh, skirt, pants, what?"

"Hey, just wear what you did on the subway, that'd be fine, you looked real good that way."

I did? Sarah laid down the phone and managed to light a cigarette. Was I too sexy? Too alluring? Stop it, Sarah, you haven't been alluring in ten years. Then what? What was he after? My money? Did he think I was a grieving widow still wearing the ring and forced into riding a crowded subway to a menial job to support several children? So he thought she was desperate. She wasn't desperate. She didn't even want to go out on this stupid date and ruin an hour of her life putting on, taking off and putting on makeup so she looked like some washed-out werewolf. And what did she need this for, anyway—going out with some sex maniac who'd probably drive her into the closet and violate

162

her. Good God, Sarah, you're not Mother Theresa. Violate your womanhood, she considered the thought, appalled by the sensation it evoked, and quickly thought of Danny. As she'd done for the past twenty-four hours. Think of Danny and maybe start yet another letter.

Dear Danny,

How are you? I am fine. Tonight I am going out with someone who looks like Al Pacino. Hope all is well with you.

Just like all the other letters she'd started, then destroyed, knowing why she began them and why she destroyed them. Silly, pointless letters she felt obliged to write, like the ones she'd been forced to write when her family had gone to the bungalow colony in the Catskills. Teenage counselors seeking ways to keep their charges busy so they could make out near the swings, telling the little children in the bungalow-colony day camp to write letters to their parents, who were a mere fifteen feet away, grouped around bridge tables, playing canasta and mah-jongg and gin. Sexually segregated gambling. Unlike the other children, Sarah had taken great care in those silly letters. Unlike the other children, Sarah had never shouted for her parents' attention, instead had written those stupid little letters day after day. And unlike the other children, Sarah hadn't had the good fortune of her parents beaming dutifully and shoving the letters in a purse or jacket pocket only to throw them away an hour later.

"Love is with an *o*, not a *u*, honey," the tall gentle man with the kindly face would say in that half-whisper of his. "Always have to learn the right way, Sarah."

And she'd nod, fighting the tears as she averted her eyes from the gentle gaze of her father the giant. The giant, even if he was only five-seven with a shock of gray hair and thin blue eyes. Her father. Always the right way to her father. Irv Golden ran his law practice that way, offering gentle admonitions to his clients, few of whom could ever afford his services. Assuming he charged them, of course, which he rarely did—or such a small amount that it didn't matter to anyone but his wife. His payment was their relief, from a ruthless landlord or obstinate bureaucrat or conniving employer. His passion for the poor never extended to

163

overt antiwar marches or civil rights activism, because Irv Golden didn't believe in publicizing his passion. So Irv Golden donated money. To the NAACP, to B'nai Brith, to John Kennedy's campaign. Anonymously. So anonymously he never even told his wife.

And her mother never asked why the clients rarely paid or where the small savings account went every time a liberal ran for office. Her mother was a quiet sufferer, seemingly more at home in a shtetl, peddling herring in a Kiev marketplace, than surviving in America. Even if both were second-generation Americans, her mother could never match the assimilation of her husband. As much as Irv Golden could assimilate from his conscience. So her mother tirelessly accepted the poverty of a lawyer-husband, when she'd been taught a lawyer-husband should bring a home in Scarsdale. To contain her disappointment over not having that home in Scarsdale, her mother had reverted to Old World values she'd never experienced. This quiet suffering she had tried to pass on to Sarah, never once discussing it, merely refraining from the subject so that her lesson of suffocating emotions through silence had impacted upon Sarah and created contempt. Not for her mother, but for her father, that he had somehow forced this upon her mother. Sarah lived in a house of concealed concern until the day Irv Golden died. Then her mother became the grieving widow, sobbing, rolling her eyes, startling and frightening eighteen-year-old Sarah because she found she couldn't join in the pain, and so felt guilt and confusion. Even then, she had no one to share it with because her mother, perhaps out of her own guilt, or perhaps out of homage to Irv Golden, took the decent-sized insurance policy and moved out of their Forest Hills home to Minnesota during Sarah's freshman year. Not Miami, because all Jewish widows moved there. Not to the Sunbelt. No, Minnesota, as if by suffering through the final years in the cold she could make up for all those years of quiet disappointment. But Sarah's father couldn't hear, didn't know. His grave was in Jersey.

The doorbell rang, startling Sarah. She stared at the door, wondering what to do. Why not ignore it, she thought. Then you can stay home and wonder what would've happened, and add it

164

to all the other wonderings about what you should or should not have done.

Just answer the goddamn door, Sarah, try not to shake too much and for God's sake, smile.

"Hey, Sarah, how ya doin'?" Lee held out a single red rose. She took it, held her wavering smile and stepped back, examining him. She expected his shirt to be pulled open to reveal a Saint Christopher medal or some Italian good-luck charm resting amid the mat of black chest hair she'd already imagined him to have. He wasn't dressed that way. Instead, Lee stepped into the apartment attired in a blue cotton suit and beige dress shirt—neither able to contain his wide shoulders—dark blue tie accentuating his dark brown eyes, and neatly polished shoes. It was his shoes Sarah stared at for a moment, until her gaze traveled up the lean, muscular legs and rested for a second on his crotch. For more than a second. It had to take more than a second for Lee to catch her stare, cough and drag her blushing face up to his. She looked away, shaking the rose.

"Um, so hi." Sarah swallowed, avoiding his curious stare, focusing instead on a point off his eyes. His cheeks. Freshly shaven, dimpling as he grinned and she blushed again, or maybe just darkened more because the first blush had never left.

"You look real nice, Sarah."

"Yeah?" Hope not too nice. Don't want him excited before we even get out the door. Why not, you are. No, I'm not, just curious. Just don't want to stare right at him, so I'm trying to find some innocuous place to look, like his arms which are sort of bulging out of his suit. Shit, why does he have to have such a good body? Sarah thought, stumbling back as he pressed closer into the apartment. Lee glanced around, shoving his hands in his pocket, smiling at her. She smiled back, stared at the strong hands filling the pockets, and again her eyes drifted to his crotch and she didn't know if he caught it or not because she swore she wouldn't look anymore.

"Nice place. I kinda gotta couch like that." Lee pointed into the living room.

"Yes?" Sarah dropped the rose into a vase on a rickety table. The vase didn't have any water. Didn't matter. She had to get

165

him out of the apartment before he tried something she'd succumb to.

"Uh, ya know, hey, Sarah?" Lee stood behind her as she fumbled in the closet. Not really fumbling, more staring at her coats, and Danny's jackets. Staring unblinkingly at Danny's jackets as she smelled Lee's cologne. Jovan. God, Jovan, smells so good, Danny used to use Aqua Velva. So what difference does that make? It must, because why haven't I budged from the closet if his cologne doesn't matter and I know I won't look at his crotch anymore? "Maybe we should kinda go, 'cause I did make reservations and well, ya know?"

"I'm ready." One arm was in her coat, the other loose by her side. He was half a foot away. Too close. Close enough to smell him. Close enough for him to kiss her. Still too close for her eyes to wander so they stayed upon his mass of curly black hair and fell upon his broad forehead and rested upon those deep, very deep, dark eyes which twinkled in flattered bewilderment.

"Uh, ya know." Lee stepped back as she struggled to get into her coat. He started to help her but she yanked away. "You look kinda nervous, know what I mean?"

"Me? No, silly, no," Sarah chuckled and bounded past him toward the door. "I'm not nervous, this is always the way I am."

"Yeah?" Lee frowned. Sarah caught the frown, a mere glance because she was determined to keep her eyes on the floor. So she heard and then saw his puzzled feet go past her. They paused. Why? Out of fear he'd asked out a lunatic? And why would he think she was a lunatic, just because she half-whispered into her purse, shook her keys and announced three times that she had to lock the door and make sure to turn on the burglar alarm, which was, of course, piped directly into the local police precinct, where her uncle the chief of detectives kept a special team of men on twenty-four-hour guard watching for her security. Why should that make him nervous?

"My Uncle Carmine's." Lee started the engine of the white Lincoln.

"Uncle Carmine?" Sarah said faintly.

"Yeah, ya know, told you 'bout him. Married to my Aunt Elvira, ya know, she had the problem?"

166

Sarah examined the sleek automobile with its rich leather and electronic signals and the olive-skinned hand which shifted the car into drive.

"What?" Sarah asked, the radio on.

"Just borrowin' it, gotta old Torino. Tranny just went so to save three hundred bucks—can't afford it—my cousin Vinnie, he works atta garage, he's gonna go in this weekend and fix it onna sly, save me labor costs. Just parts. Me and Vinnie are real close, grew up together, kinda like brothers and he wanted to lend me his car tonight—gotta Nova—but, ya know, thought this might look nicer." He waited for her reaction.

"Nice." Sarah remembered her father's Studebaker without a muffler and dented sides, and how it had embarrassed her mother who had never complained. "You like big cars?" Sarah stared through the windshield, saw the light turn yellow, turned to see his reaction, which was to speed up. She stared at the foot pressed down upon the gas pedal and the way the thigh muscles bunched up from the tension of speeding through the intersection.

"Yeah, don't you?"

"No." Sarah watched his right arm command his right hand to gently turn the wheel. "Hate big cars. Eat up gas."

"Yeah, I guess. Stop-and-go traffic burns the fuel pretty bad in town."

"Terrible the way they make the engines, still eating up fuel." Sarah kept her eyes riveted to the radio. "These, these big cars, what with energy so precious and they make these big cars so men can feed their macho image."

"Yeah, well, just kinda like the way they handle, know what I mean?" Lee played with the wheel and Sarah glared at his long, strong fingers.

"Should get rid of big cars." Again her eyes were back on the road. Where were they going? "Abolish them, should abolish all cars."

"Well, ya know, guess wouldn't hurt to abolish some of 'em, but it's still not a bad way to get around." He chuckled, not faintly but huskily, seductively.

"Mass transit. Instead of building the West Side Highway

167

they should pour money into mass transit." Sarah chopped the air with her fist, hoping she wouldn't inadvertently bang against his solid shoulder. "Improve the subways, bus systems, improve the rail lines instead of feeding the auto and oil companies." Calm down, Sarah, she told herself, pressed into the cushiony seat which evoked shivers and a wailing splintering to her voice. "It's criminal, that's all, criminal." She squirmed on the seat. "The way everyone gives in, criminal, that's it." She squeezed the door handle, pressed the fingers of her left hand into her thigh and dared not look at him.

"I dunno," Lee said softly, and she shuddered, praying her gasps weren't audible. "I don't think my Uncle Carmine would do anythin' criminal."

"Why, you never know." Her voice kept fading as the radio grew louder. "You, you don't know." She didn't know—what she was talking about or why she was acting this way when she wanted to turn to him. "I mean, not that, uh, your Uncle Carmine, would but, you don't, he's not a criminal, I'm sure"—what is he?—"but what does he do?" Probably manufactures calzone and numbers on Mulberry Street.

". . . detective at Manhattan South." They stopped at a light, the distant jolt of the car failing to penetrate Sarah's acute sense of numbed stupidity. She just sat there, afraid to move as he leaned over and took her hand. "Hey, ya know, Sarah?" She swallowed and felt his hand take her chin, felt the fear intensify to such a pitch that it evaporated once she looked at him. "Uh, I kinda got the feelin' that you're not so hot 'bout goin' out with me and hey, that's okay, ya know, if ya want I can take ya home and that'd be okay. Kinda got the feelin' you think you're out with a criminal or somethin'. I'll take ya home if ya want. We could call your uncle the chief of detectives and make sure they don't turn no floods on us and no dogs bite my leg off. Or ya can run a check on me, don't have a record, worst I ever done was pocketing some comics when I was eleven. Even then, I gave 'em back after my Mom beat my ass black and blue."

Sarah saw him fight back the smile, a bemused grin which flooded into those large eyes and evoked dribbles of tears down her cheeks, large brown eyes which followed the tears and

168

wiped them away, eyes not reacting to the honking of horns behind them.

"Huh? Whaddaya say?" He allowed the grin to pop out, dimpling his cheeks, and she found herself grinning back.

"After all the gas you wasted picking me up?" she whispered,
still afraid, still confused.

Chapter 17

"I'm not scratching." Danny moved his hands away from the tailored Le Dixie coveralls and placed them on his bow tie. Also designer, of course.

"You been scratching all day," shouted the little director with the one brown and one blue eye. "You wanna see it on film? You want this entire crew to sign affidavits that you scratch?"

"I told you not to shove straw in my pockets."

"Straw gives it the look."

"What look, hives?" Danny looked around for an ally, and found none among the skimpily clad cowgirls, the wooden cow or the steel Caddy arrayed upon the set. "I told you to put, I dunno, put in something else. You have to put straw in my pants so I scratch?" He'd scratched through two hours until his body was a mass of red hills. Danny was afraid to take off his clothes and see what had happened to his body.

"I don't want you to scratch anymore. You think we can go through one take without you scratching?"

"Okay, okay, I won't scratch, then. Maybe you could give me some lotion?"

"We're not budgeted for lotion."

"Solarcaine, baby cream, anything. I'll give you a couple of bucks, go to the drugstore for me. I'm sorry, I'm just not used to straw."

"Oh sure, couple of bucks. Go and fling your money around. You ballplayers don't understand economics. Think because you're making a mint we all have money to toss around, huh?"

Jeez. Danny shook his head, reached into his pocket for a bill and instead forced straw beneath his fingernails. Jeez, it wasn't supposed to be like this . . .

"So how's it feel to be thirty-three and get your first professional hit in your first professional at-bat in your first professional game?" some kid reporter had asked him three weeks ago, a kid who probably hadn't even been around for the 1960 World Series when Bill Mazeroski had broken every heart in the Bronx. A kid who probably didn't even know that Danny had gotten three punchball home runs, hammering them out of angry frustration, right after Mazeroski's bottom-of-the-ninth homer.

"Real good," Danny had mumbled, his body drenched with sweat and the Boone's Farm Apple Wine every player had taken turns pouring over him. Around him, players had showered, screeched, laughed, celebrated victory. Before his cubicle, Danny had furtively slid the towel onto his lap, exposing his stomach. Wasn't such a bad stomach, Danny had thought. Except for a few stretch marks.

"Why'd you bunt?" another kid had asked him. He'd considered the question, leaning back, smoking a thin cigar and trying to look like a jock.

"Well," Danny had formulated an answer, half-hearing Jones take credit for the bunt, not realizing at that time that his response would never make the papers because no one really cared why he had bunted or whether he'd noticed the third baseman playing back, or if he'd been guessing fastball or curve ball. Only that he was thirty-three years old and a hero. But that night, delirious with triumph, Danny had ignored the obvious and so framed an intelligent reply, even as reporters interrupted each other, asking him if the other players came to him for advice, if he felt out of place amid all the kids.

What kids? Danny had wanted to know. He was one of the kids. Every bit one of the kids, now dousing Pee Wee with wine and slapping butts with wet towels and thinking up dirty jokes. And when they had marched into the bar to celebrate, no one had sat according to age. No special seats, even if he was the guest of honor. All they had done was order pitcher after pitcher with cheap Scotch chasers and relive the dramatic bunt until it had taken on legendary proportions. As well it should have. As well Danny should have gotten looped out of his mind and danced on the table and clapped his hands together and screamed to the country music, music he hated, except that night, because that night he loved everyone, including himself. Because he was a member of the Greensboro Hornets, a productive member, even if it would be short-lived and wouldn't survive the next morning's hangover.

"Gotta go," Danny slurred sometime in the middle of that night as the players stumbled off toward B.K.'s van.

"Gosh dang, Danny, get on back here, where the heck ya goin'?" Pete shouted to him. Danny giggled, staggered away, barely felt Pete and Pee Wee grab him by the arms and try to haul him back to the van, vaguely heard his own words of protest.

"Gotta see her." Danny yanked himself free, put up his fists to fight, half fell down, then stumbled up and took off on a drunken run. They let him go, having no idea whom he was going to see, since all those nights Danny had gone over to her apartment, he'd told them he was just going out for walks. And that night wasn't the time to explain why he'd never told anyone about her, assuming he knew. Drunk or sober.

"Hey, lemme in, hey, guess who? Doo-dah, doo-dah, lemme in, hey, it's me." Danny banged.

"Shit, Danny, you're drunk." Sarah grimaced and stepped away from the doorway.

He wasn't drunk. Three drinks with Norman. He wasn't drunk. If he had an extra glass of apple juice, Sarah thought he was drunk.

"Not so." Danny giggled, spilling through the door and wavering in the foyer. "Not drunk, just had a couple of drinks, that's all."

"Uh-huh." Sarah nodded, going up the steps. He forced himself to follow. He had no choice. The bathroom was upstairs.

"Two drinks." He wiggled his fingers at her turned back. She whirled, saw the fingers, stared them back to his side and folded her arms, glaring.

"Danny, you're drunk. Just admit you're drunk. Shit, can't you ever just admit anything when you're wrong?"

172

"What, wrong, why am I wrong? Make me sound like an alkie, jeez, had a few lousy drinks." He started sobering himself up, more out of instinct than reason.

"Missed a good movie tonight." Sarah now sat on the edge of the bed, her voice small.

"You tell me about it?" Danny grabbed the doorway.

"And would you remember tomorrow morning if I did?"

"If I saw it already, did I ever see it before?" God, why was she confusing him?

"No, course you didn't. First time on TV."

"So tell me." He braced himself near the bureau.

"You're not even coherent, how the hell can I talk to you if you're not even coherent?" she shouted.

"Am too, just—can't I just go out and relax once in a while, that so bad? You go out, you do, you know."

"I don't go to some damn bar and get drunk and talk about the good old days as if today, this, is so damn bad, okay?"

"This isn't so bad."

"Uh-huh." Sarah lowered her face for a moment and, unable to bear the lie, bounced her narrowed eyes back at him. "Just why can't you go out and do something normal instead of getting drunk?"

"What, once a year I do it."

"You did it in July." It was then November.

"That's what, long time ago."

"Can you count the months?"

"Am I getting a drunk driving test?"

"Shit, just, just go puke your guts up, okay?"

He wanted to, but didn't. Instead Danny started toward her, stopping at the foot of the bed as she whirled away and faced the wall.

"Why are you mad at me?" he whispered.

"Not mad, Danny, just . . ."

"What?"

"Nothing."

Colleen exploded in that boisterous, soothing laugh of hers—leaned back against the wall, bathrobe open, skin exposed, and kept laughing. And all he could do was grin, shuffle foolishly,

173

half-stumbling through the door, and giggle. She made no attempt to steady him or lead him anywhere. Danny could just stand in the hallway, fall and get up all night if he wanted. That was fine with her, as it was fine with her that he managed to half-crawl to the couch, fling himself over the arm and lie there, barely breathing, nose into the fabric. Colleen stood above him, chuckling. He looked up, expecting a question when he should've known there would be none. Nothing like why was he so drunk and banging on her door and now humming a song neither could recognize, but both could laugh at. Colleen kept her laugh until his had turned into a weak chuckle, occasional giggle and snore before doing anything.

Then, she placed a bucket by the couch, a blanket over his deadened body, and took a seat on the chair near him. This time she only watched him for a few minutes before turning off the lights and going to sleep. She worried he would wake and see her watching him.

Unfortunately, Danny couldn't stay forever. After a quiet breakfast during which Colleen forced food into his stomach which only came back up, Danny went to the stadium. As soon as he entered the clubhouse, Horace, with a combination grin-leer, said Antonheimer wanted to meet with him.

"I'll take care of everything, just trust me." Antonheimer folded his hands across the desk, leaning forward as Danny leaned, or slumped back. He still felt green and wondered if he would ever feel unhungover again.

"About what?"

"You."

"What do you mean?"

"Just don't worry about anything."

There wasn't anything he could worry about, except whether his stomach would ever hold anything stronger than farina again. Danny grinned weakly, mind still numb and unable to comprehend the knowing smile across the desk.

"I'm not worried." Danny swallowed quickly, hoping it would help his stomach. "Just not with it today, kinda did a little too much celebrating last night and . . ."

"As well you should've. Now, I'll give you a couple days to get yourself in order. Let you adjust to this new fame. As I said, don't worry about anything, I'll make the arrangements."

"Fame?"

"Naturally, fame."

"Only got one hit," Danny said, irritated he would have to belittle it. "Don't really see what . . ."

"Don't worry, just go out there and play baseball."

"Why?" Danny peered at Jones a few minutes later, back at the lineup card, then again at the manager, who shrugged and looked away.

"You ask me, I tell you one thing, you think, it's simple, the human body is complex, ballplayers ain't simple, if their bodies were as simple as their minds I'd have no problems and probably be managing in the bigs right now instead of this league, so you tell me."

"Just because I got one hit?" Danny asked the lineup card, which kept answering with his name, NEUMAN, his position, CF, inside the number-five slot in the batting order.

"We're just lucky to have you, to step right in. People think the starting eight win the games, don't agree, need depth, we got depth with you."

"Yeah, but . . ." Again he asked the lineup card, which changed its answer to KELLY, LF, in the sixth slot in the order. Danny turned and looked down the bench at Pete, hunched over a pad, scribbling wildly. Probably more poetry, Danny thought.

"Told me he has a bad arm, can't make the throws from center, need his mind and bat out there, so I hadda put him in left."

"Didn't know he had a bad arm," Danny muttered, staring at Kelly.

"Things happen. Don't you worry none about him. Take care of yourself. Now," Horace whispered into Danny's ear, "I know you did a little bit of drinkin' last night, hadda good reason though most players I've known never had good reasons to hit the bottle though they told themselves and anyone who'd listen they did and before you know they got the bellies, can't run and are back pumping gas somewhere. So, between you and me, just watch the sauce, okay? Don't want to see you ruin yourself."

"Yeah, sure, no more Mr. Booze for me," Danny mumbled back and slid next to Pete.

"Hey, hello." Pete smiled. "Do you have one minute?" Pete

cradled the pad so no one would see. "I will read it very quickly. I think you'll be proud of me the way I have structured this poem. I have tried to infer something . . ."

Imply, Danny wanted to say, but he wouldn't correct Pete's word usage. Nor would he correct his grammar, nor would he ever hurry Pete's speech up as he struggled to say every word clearly and perfectly, even though he failed half the time. For Pete looked up to Danny, admired, respected and was maybe a little awed by him. They never discussed baseball, because Pete always changed the subject and Danny had never felt comfortable enough to talk about something he wasn't—at least until yesterday—capable enough to discuss. So they discussed literature. Pete, digesting books with simian precision, asking Danny questions. And Danny, politely, perhaps condescendingly, responding. Never would Danny let the conversation go beyond Pete's capabilities. He listened, offered monosyllabic responses which Pete took for profound wisdom, read Pete's wildly naive, incoherently florid cartons of poetry and proclaimed them to be promising, insightful. Danny hated himself for the way he acted with Pete because deep down he liked him, genuinely liked him, and half didn't care if they really did discuss baseball, or even literature or theology. As long as Pete wouldn't look up to him like that and feed his ego and nourish the guilt at wanting someone to admire him so much.

"How's the arm?"

"Fine. Little tender. Found I can write with both hands. Does that mean my mind is ambivalently dextrous?"

"Yeah, probably."

"Gosh." Pete caught himself, flushed. Danny leaned closer, took the pad and placed it on his left side, away from them.

"Doctor look at it?"

"What doctor?" Pete took back the pad and studied it, smiling to himself, then frowning. "Don't think this is too good. Would you read it?"

"Since when did you have a sore arm?"

"Just a little tender. Made that long throw the other day, must have twitched it a little. I don't know." He stared onto the field, oblivious to the practice session, even to Danny, just drifted away and seized himself back.

176

"When will you be back in center?"

"When my arm is better. I read Dylan Thomas the other day, like you suggested."

Danny could've pushed it with Pete, but he was afraid, and not just that. Fear he could take, in small amounts, at least, but along with it was guilt, uncertainty, confusion. The Four Horsemen of the Neurotic.

So he wouldn't push Pete into admitting there was nothing wrong with his arm, not force him to confess that Antonheimer must've told Jones, who must've ordered Pete, to fake a sore arm so Danny could play in center, the glamour position. Nor make Pete admit that he was doing this out of friendship for Danny, sacrificing his position so he would continue to have someone to talk to and someone to read his poetry. So he didn't. Not with Pete, not with Antonheimer, not with Jones.

He hung back as Jones clapped his hands and urged the Hornets to take the field. The players poured out, diffusing toward their positions. Danny wanted to hide behind them, to go to center by way of third, maybe round toward home, dash down first, race toward second, hoping that someone's body would shield him from the sparse, inattentive crowd. He knew people would be watching, though, and that's why he panicked and tried to remember how he used to saunter. Loll the shoulders, swing the glove, skip the feet. Careful not to touch the first-base line because that was superstition, even if Danny wasn't superstitious. But then again, he wasn't certain and didn't want to wake up tomorrow morning and find his glasses electrified. So he stepped gingerly over first as Pete hustled off toward left and B.K. ran away to right and forced Danny to dash up the middle, slanting into center. Where he now stood. In center field.

He wasn't as nervous as he thought he'd be. He was terrified, of course, but nervous? Why should he be? He hadn't been nervous when he was eleven and the punchball king of the Bronx. *Robert Kohner.* That name popped into Danny's head as Pete tossed a warmup throw toward him. Robert Kohner, a man of wit and grace and, ultimately, cleverness, because when he chewed his cold hamburger sandwiches in the sixth-grade lunchroom, mouth open and agape with ketchup and half-cooked meat, the rest of the table willingly surrendered their food to

177

him. Clever and physically blessed because he had the largest thumbs in the world, two potato pancakes affixed to the end of his fingers which could indent a spauldeen and make it flutter and flip and so frustrate the opposing batters that it allowed fielders like Danny time to contemplate important matters like hitting. Which is what Danny tried to do right now, contemplate hitting a punchball with his balled fist, until he realized he should be concentrating on the lead-off batter. This wasn't punchball, it was his first professional start. That thought leaped into his head and made him ill, so he pushed it aside.

Danny hunched forward, glove on his left knee, right hand loose, albeit trembling, by his side. He was ready. If he was so ready, why wasn't he shouting?

"No batter, no batter," chattered Pee Wee.

Heddy babbled in Spanish. Pete and B.K. hollered. Everyone hollered except Danny, suddenly fixated on an eleven-year-old mouth chomping on cold hamburger, until he decided it was time to shout.

"Hit a homer."

What a silly thing to say. Aside from the obvious fact that it wasn't a good way to develop friendships with your pitching staff, it was a silly thing. Not that Danny wanted the other team to score, just that the first thing that came to his mind was a home run, so he wouldn't have to make an effort to catch the ball. He was afraid. Why should he be afraid? Because he didn't belong? He could catch it like anyone else. He could do it. He hunched forward.

The diamond wavered, almost became a New York City playground with chubby, prepubescent legs squirming in imitation of the idols of the day. Shortstop looking like Kubek. Third baseman like Boyer. Heddy emulating Skowron. Richardson over at second. Yogi was in left today because Ellie was behind the plate. Maris over in right. The Mick in center. Danny looked down at his feet, recognized his size-nine-and-a-halfs and knew they didn't belong to the Mick. Nonsense, he thought, self-conscious about his feet. And more nonsense, because those names meant nothing to these kids, only to Danny. He didn't want to get caught showing his age by emulating a player long since retired, and he couldn't very well emulate Mantle, anyway, because this wasn't a punchball game, this was a real professional game, and he thought about maybe emulating Mumphrey when the lead-off batter cracked one in his direction.

Oh my God, oh my God, Danny thought, frozen until he suggested his legs move, or at least make the appearance of moving. They, and Danny, inched back until desperation took over and all of them raced back, the ball soaring over his head, and he kept running and running toward the warning track in right center. He half-heard B.K. call him off, less than half because Danny never let up, maybe half-hoping he'd smash through the fence and be on his way back North again.

Up went his glove, his eyes widening as the ball popped against the tip and, instead of bounding away, came right back at him. Off his chin and onto his forearms. Then the ball and his forearms and the rest of Danny Neuman crashed into the fence. He splattered to the ground, much like a fallen tree.

Unfortunately, fallen trees don't have large black right fielders groping for a baseball under their broken body. Nor do fallen trees feel immense pain.

"Shit," Danny groaned, trying to get to his feet and catching a glimpse of B.K.'s relay throw back to the infield, much too late to do anything except confine the runner to third. "Shit."

"You okay?" B.K. helped him up. Presently Pete came over. And the entire team, though he was standing, if not fully cognizant.

"Man, you can really cover ground," Pee Wee said in admiration.

"Huh?" Danny peered.

"You okay, kid?" Horace asked. Danny nodded. "Sure you're okay, don't want you playin' with a brain fracture or anythin' like that which wouldn't show up right away until maybe three games later and then you're at bat in a crucial situation and you drop dead."

"No, no," Danny squeaked, suddenly alert. "I'm okay."

"Good try, Dan." B.K. slapped his rear as he, and the others, resumed their positions.

Hah, Danny grunted to himself. Got a late start on the ball.

Could've killed B.K. by not allowing him to make the catch when he called. But why shouldn't they say all that? Humor me, huh? I know you know why, and you know I know why, I'm starting.

He didn't want that knowledge to become overt, however, and in the days that followed, the only way he could be sure of it was by participating in their rituals. Being one of the boys. He went about being what he wasn't, so others would think he was what they wanted him to be, even if then others wouldn't let him be what the others wanted him to be. One horseman pulled ahead of the pack.

"Neuman, hey, you comin' or what?" Pee Wee poked his head through the Shelby motel doorway. He didn't look at Pete nor did Pete look up from his book—*Nausea* by Jean-Paul Sartre—but Pete did flinch and half-glance at Danny, who was sitting in a chair, staring out the window. When he stared out the window he didn't have to decide between Pee Wee's offer and Pete's hurt.

"Um." Danny looked between them. Pee Wee grinned, Pete frowned and slid down a bit on the bed. "Uh, yeah, I guess, we'll be ready in a sec."

Pete shook his head.

"You comin', Pete?" Pee Wee asked, a bit surprised.

"Nah, kinda bushed. Might like to just sit a while here and read." Pete peeked at Danny, now standing in confusion.

"Uh, we'll meet you down in a few minutes, Pee Wee." Danny waited until the door closed. He also waited before saying something because he knew Pete didn't like socializing. It was Pete who couldn't understand why Danny wanted to go drinking.

"You're staying?" Pete asked hopefully.

"Come on, have a few beers, we'll get back early enough."

"No." Pete tightened his grip around the book. He'd been on the same page for fifteen minutes. "I have a headache."

"C'mon, few beers won't hurt us."

"I would rather read. Or go if I knew we could talk."

"We don't always have to talk. I'll drink, you bring the book."

"I can't read in a bar."

"Why not?"

"Too dark. Besides," pause, "you know how they are. First round of beers it'll be okay, next round the book'll be in a pitcher of warm beer."

"Afraid they'll make fun of you?"

"Yes."

Danny felt awkward at the honest admission. He didn't know what to say because he knew Pete was right. They would make fun of him and he knew how sensitive Pete was. Maybe another reason why he was so careful with him, which made him edgy. But then he couldn't desert him, not after what Pete had done for him. Or maybe he should desert him, so Pete'd get angry and tell Jones his arm was fine and force Danny back to the bench. And then make Danny win the position on his own merit. But maybe Pete was deep-down afraid Danny would beat him out on pure athletic ability, so it was safer for him this way. For both of them.

Or maybe it was none of those and Danny had to figure out some cautious way to get Pete to a sleaze-ball bar in Shelby. He, Pete and Jean-Paul.

"Lookit, we'll reserve some time to talk," Danny said.

"Said that the other day. After one sip you were telling dirty stories and picking up girls."

"I said I was sorry, okay? Didn't I apologize? Didn't we come back and talk for three hours?"

"You'll do it again."

"Why don't you believe me when I say we'll talk?"

"Because you're afraid of them," said Pete.

"Bullshit." Danny put his hands on his hips. "Not afraid of them."

"You care what they think of you."

"Do not."

"Then why do you go drinking with them all the time? I know you don't enjoy it. Why?"

"Maybe I do enjoy it."

"I thought you were better than that, wasting your mind drinking and making idle talk. I thought more of you than that."

Great, the son I never had. Danny bit back something harsh, tried for something kind.

"I swear we'll talk. I swear I'll stick up for you if anyone says

181

anything about the book, or reading, or whatever. Just come."

"Why do I have to come?"

"Because I'll feel guilty if you're here all alone, reading and not having any fun."

"I thought we would talk. Now you're talking about having fun."

"Don't we have fun when we talk?"

"Yes. I do. Do you?"

"Sure," Danny lied. "So come, okay? Make me happy if you come. It'll be fine."

"I hate being a jock, don't you see, gosh, damn," Pete exploded. "Don't like that whole ammabience of it. Been doin' that my whole life and don't wanna do it no more. You go on, still new for you, all this." Pete gestured around the room with its bolted-down furniture. "I'd rather read."

"So then read. Okay, so then read. Turn into a brain, just go on. Read all you want, but you still need to talk about it and you'll only talk to yourself and you'll go fucking crazy doing that, so, just go and read, okay?"

Danny stormed out of the room, met the players and walked to the bar, two blocks away. Pete joined them ten minutes later, without the book. Once Danny saw him, he vowed to talk to him. Pete was right. It didn't last past the first pitcher.

"You're the ballplayer, aren't you? I saw you in the papers," she said. B.K. had hauled her and some friends over. Pete inched away shyly, forced a smile to his girl and shot Danny a dirty look. He was tempted to ignore the girl, but feared the reaction of the players. Feared them disapproving him. Feared them thinking him different. Feared them saying the word aloud he said silently every day.

"Yeah, it's me." Danny blushed. Same thing would happen that had happened on the other stops on this first famous road trip. He knew why they wanted him. To them, he was Number 34. Face in the paper. Figure on the field. A hunk of meat. Once he would've been flattered to be the object of such feminine attention, but not now. Still, he knew, as he bought her a drink and ignored Pete's wounded stare, that he wouldn't have to do anything with this groupie, just as he hadn't done anything to the brunette in Spartanburg or the blonde in Florence.

182

He acted as if he would do something, allowed her to squeeze his thighs and play with his zipper and lure him back to her apartment. But then there he stood, red-faced and naked, behind a chair, telling this lovely girl with big breasts and puzzled expression the same story he had told all over the South Atlantic League, hoping it would work one more time.

"I don't understand." Her name was Laura, he thought.

"See, I had this operation when I was a child and well, you know."

"You mean . . ." She gestured at his groin, hidden behind the back of the chair, so her waning lust focused on aged cotton.

"Yeah."

"What happened?"

"I, I was just born and, well . . ." Danny faked tears. Was he faking tears? "The doctor, uh, had to cut off . . ." She shuddered, seemed to recoil even as her neck craned forward in case he let her look at the deformity. "Part of it."

"It?"

"Yeah, it." Danny patted the chair.

"A big part?"

"Enough."

"But why?"

"Doctor said I needed a *brith.*"

So he used that long-ago memory of a rabbi and a doctor and his parents crying as they snipped off his foreskin as an excuse not to impregnate some groupie in Shelby. So as not to further confuse him, because he had enough trouble dealing with cheating on Sarah with Colleen without cheating on both Sarah and Colleen with an eighteen-year-old.

It was bad enough that, as soon as he took the field, he heard the chorus of shrieks from the stands. Already he'd become a celebrity in the Jewish community, even if he'd assiduously avoided accepting Gottlieb's dinner invitations. No matter. Once he bounded up the dugout steps, he heard the Hebrew and Yiddish cries and felt the *tefillin* flail his back. He personally brought the sports section of the *Greensboro Jewish Press* from the back page to the front. He shattered the hopes of thousands of canasta players who gained their satisfaction from winning a

183

tournament and making their way into the newspapers, all because the sportswriter, a fourteen-year-old kid continuing with his Hebrew School education, had gone berserk in lavish praise of Danny.

ALTE MEIN HITS HOMER. SANDY KOUFAX NEUMAN GETS A SINGLE. HANK GREENBERG NEUMAN STEALS SECOND. DANNY ART SHAMSKY DOUBLES AND TRIPLES.

After a while the kid ran out of famous Jewish ballplayers to compare Danny to, and so: DANNY DAYAN CATCHES FIVE BALLS.

In the eyes of the Greensboro Jewish community, Danny was one step behind Menachem Begin, inches ahead of Henny Youngman. Not only was Danny a hero in the Jewish community, but a source of inspiration to middle-aged men, a beacon of sensual maturity to young girls. To everyone, it seemed, Danny Neuman was a star, except to himself, maybe because they had robbed him of that splendid moment when he settled under a fly ball or dived headfirst for a twisting line drive or felt the fat part of the bat meet the ball. Maybe because the organist's tune of "Hava Nagila," sounding suspiciously like "Home on the Range," still rang in his ears, drowning out the crack of the bat and forcing him, not his legs, down the first-base line.

But what could he do? If he hustled 150 percent, he feared the players would think he had to go to such extremes just to keep up with them. If he tried nonchalance, he feared their resentment and worried they'd think this wasn't important enough to him. So he just tried to play naturally, even if he wasn't certain what natural was anymore. He stood in center and ignored Pete's feigned winces every time he had to make a throw from left. Danny knew Pete only winced when he watched him, so he would think he really did have a sore arm. Naturally Pete wouldn't wince when Danny wasn't watching. Whom would he have to wince for? The other players? They knew. Horace. He was in on it, too. The plot to exploit the gimmick. The old man. Soon Danny would graduate from Le Dixie coveralls commercials to speeches at local nursing homes and then, who knows, perhaps a national Geritol campaign. Perhaps even make the cover of the *National Enquirer.*

184

DANNY NEUMAN IS REALLY SEVENTY-FOUR, the headline would read.

If only he could accept his position. If only he could really believe he was out there on his own merits, then maybe he could handle the flailing *tefillin* and waving Confederate flags. But he knew he wasn't. He knew why the home games and even some of the road games were sold out. All to watch the ageless wonder maybe break a hip diving for a line drive, the ageless wonder hitting a mere .280. Which is why he didn't want her coming to the games. Which is why she didn't understand.

"Why not?" Colleen had leaned forward, near the half-empty bottle of wine on the half-sloppy coffee table.

"What?" He hadn't been listening, had been thinking about Sarah, allowing himself to wonder what she was doing and if she were all right.

"I want you to tell me why you don't want me to come to the park to watch you."

"Just don't." He still feared confessing how he viewed himself to her, for she would surely reassure him, and that would surely tighten a relationship he was afraid of.

"Don't you think I'd like to go see you, to cheer you in person instead of cheering at the television or radio?"

"I don't do anything so hot. You're reading the papers, thinking I'm doing something so terrific when I'm not."

"Or"—she paused, then went on breathlessly—"is it that you're ashamed of me, hmm, is that it?" Colleen crossed her legs, maintaining calm. "Danny? Is that it? That you're ashamed of me?"

"Why, that's ridiculous." Is it?

"I'm not sure. Maybe it isn't. You know, we never leave the apartment. You're content to stay here and talk. That's fine by me, Danny, really. I don't want you to feel you have to take me out. Or that I have to take you out. Or that we have to do anything special. But I do think the age difference bothers you. Am I right?"

"Why should it?"

"Because"—she laughed in exasperation—"because I'm older than you."

"I never think about it."

"You're lying to me."

"So, okay. I'm lying to you."

"Then it does bother you."

"No."

"A little? Maybe just a little that you can't get someone your own age?"

"I can get anyone I want. Didn't you hear? I'm a star."

"But it must nag at you. Admit it, Danny. Admit my body isn't quite as firm as a younger woman's or that maybe I don't have quite enough energy for you. That I'm really not your contemporary and it gnaws at you to hear me talk about the good old days that you only experience in yellowed newspaper clippings. At least admit that."

He shook his head, honestly. If anything, she had too much sexual energy for him and he, lately, fought against impotence. Not from exhaustion but from guilt—the guilt of sleeping with someone other than his wife, the guilt of not enjoying it as much with Colleen as he used to, the guilt of fighting back their growing relationship. And from faking orgasm. From breathing deeply, from faking groans, and from the pained confusion of realizing that his feigned groans and heavy breaths sounded exactly like Sarah's. And wondering whether she had faked it all these years. And whether Colleen faked it. And if she wasn't, then why was he, and why couldn't they just talk the way they had in the beginning and not engage in these conversations where he had to say things he didn't want to say?

"It isn't as if I want you to say you love me, Danny. Do you understand that much?"

"No. Because I think I do."

"Which doesn't make you too happy, right?"

"It does."

"It can't, Danny. I can tell. For example." Again she crossed her legs and Danny grew irritated at her vague, pedantic manner. "Like when we're in bed, how uncomfortable you feel."

"I'm uncomfortable with everyone in bed. Christ, I've been uncomfortable when I've masturbated."

186

He grinned and she ignored it, sighing instead, sipping her wine, measuring her words. He tensed.

"Look, Danny, maybe we should just let this out, okay? You tell me what you expect from this relationship, I'll tell you what I expect. Once and for all, it'll be out in the open."

"Can you go first?"

"Would you like to pick straws?"

"Please, Colleen . . ."

"No, you listen, okay? I don't know, see, I'm talking like you now."

"Thought I had a cute accent."

"Damn, Danny. I just want to be your friend, okay? I don't want a lasting relationship with you because that isn't possible, because of what I want out of life, because of what you have in life, okay? But I care for you and all you worry about is where this relationship is going, so we waste time instead of just enjoying it. Isn't that so? You talk to me and I can see how you begin sifting how much you can say, suddenly you're on guard with me. It's all backwards. We should just be able to talk. We should just be able to have sex, to enjoy each other's body. Share things. Not everything. As much as I want to share with you and you want to share with me."

"That's just hippie shit."

"Lousy thing to say."

"You, you think you can just sit back and, I dunno, things aren't that simple."

"They are if you let them be. But you can't just let them be. I can feel it, the tension. And it wasn't there when we first started . . . whatever."

"Whatever what?"

"I don't know." Colleen sighed.

"See, you don't know either."

"Must there be a name for this?"

"There is a name. Called cheating on your wife."

"Finally it comes out."

"No, no, not that."

"No." She bolted forward, almost off the chair. "No, come on now. You don't think about Sarah when we're together?"

187

"Of course I do. Can I help it?"

"No, certainly not. All I ask is that you be honest about it."

"Colleen, look, I don't know. I might be in love with you, okay, I really might. I—but—I have this, concept of . . ."

"Concept, prearranged idea of what should be and what shouldn't be. Like not watching television with me?"

"We, we could watch TV if . . ."

"What about the other day when I went to turn on the TV and you started sulking, wouldn't talk for an hour?"

"I don't like *Three's Company.*"

"Go on, hide your emotions."

"What do you want from me? You want to pull my guts on the table, is that it? Is the only way we can have a relationship is for you to wrench my guts onto the coffee table so you can sift through everything and say you know me, is that it?"

"No, I just want to feel like I can share what you're going through. That you aren't ashamed of me when we go out. That you won't mind my coming to the park. If all you want is a shrink and a lay, find someone else, because I'm past that point."

"Look, please, just—let me work up to you coming to the park, okay? I, I'll do something special when you finally come, okay? Something crazy, just for you, to show you I know you're there. Is that good? Just don't press it, okay?"

Since he had no intention of inviting her to the park, he knew he had to do something, which annoyed him because he felt obligated to enough people and things as is and wanted one thing for himself. Even if he couldn't have it. So he opted for a cease-fire, which is why he accepted Rabbi Gottlieb's invitation and decided to bring Colleen with him. So she wouldn't think he was ashamed of her. So Gottlieb wouldn't think him a traitor to his people . . .

"And don't touch the bow tie, it's arranged perfectly, just stand there, keep smiling and read right off the cue cards," the director said.

"Anything you say," Danny replied wearily.

Chapter 18

Lee touched her cheek and Sarah shuddered, wanted to recoil, yet instead returned the touch. Her still trembling fingers ran up and down his strong hand, playing briefly with his thumb. She met his gaze and he grinned, his dimples deepening and his teeth flashing, and Sarah reeled on her seat at the rear of Angelo's of Mulberry Street.

"Ya know," Lee began and her eyes half-closed, as they always did when he started to speak and she tuned him out. Unless, of course, he said something about her. He did. "I'm really glad you don't wear all that stuff on your face like you did the first time we went out." Sarah opened her eyes, smiled, then closed them again as he started talking about his car.

It had to be purely physical, Sarah had concluded about their three-week-old relationship. They had nothing to talk about, nothing in common. She didn't know how to respond to his discourses about engines and football, and she wouldn't discomfort him by talking about things that mattered to her—not that she knew what mattered to her. So whenever that sensual voice oozed toward her, Sarah half-closed her eyes and waited. If he discussed something about her, Sarah gave him her full attention. If not, Sarah drifted off, remembering to nod and offer propitious monosyllabic responses.

Lee didn't like her with all that makeup, so she ceased wearing all that makeup. Sarah liked to think it was because she herself wanted to change the way her face looked, but she wasn't certain and it was easier for Lee to tell her he liked her better without the makeup. Or that he liked the way her hair lay. She thought she looked like Bozo the Clown. He didn't, so she stopped worrying as much about her hair, or worrying when one of the jerks in the office praised her for the coffee, or a client told her what a sexy voice she had on the phone. Sarah didn't think there was anything particularly difficult about making coffee or answering the phone or occasionally typing a near-perfect letter. Others did. Were they right? Sarah wondered, at once relieved others had decided for her, then struggling back to the conclusion that, while she was allowing others to define her, at least she had placed herself in a position to accept complimentary definitions.

Maybe that was why she liked a job she hated, or went out with Lee. Because at work no one knew her to be Danny's wife. When she spoke with her mother-in-law, she received lavish praise for her courage in coping with an emergency situation. With her father-in-law, well, they'd only had that one talk and he was never home when her mother-in-law called, and Sarah felt uneasy calling just to speak to him. When their friends called and asked how she was doing, she was the abandoned wife supposed to fall apart. If Danny had still been home no one would've thought to ask how she was doing. Obviously they, like everyone else, still perceived her in terms of Danny. Except Lee. He viewed her in terms of Sarah, or so she thought. Pretty, cute, funny Sarah, though she rarely said anything funny and rarely did more than caress his fingers and stare into his eyes and wonder why she was going out with him. She knew why. Primal lust. She wanted to tear off his clothes and leap into his pants. Pure and simple, she wanted to fuck him. This is what she told herself as she did all she could to maintain the semblance of a date and hold back from too passionate a good-night kiss. She held back because she knew that, if Danny were still home, she wouldn't be going out with Lee Pomenzo and so, even Lee, even this gorgeous hunk with the bulging crotch, even with him it was in terms of Danny. Which is why she told herself she felt bad dating him. Told herself it was wrong, this simplistic lust. That she

190

should be home knitting and watching television because she had never been told she should feel this way about someone ten years younger.

Told herself and told them.

"You're being ridiculous," Sadie had insisted the other night when she'd escaped to their apartment after midnight. Did they ever sleep? Sarah wondered, also wondering if they wondered about whether things were right or wrong or if they had so formulated this cohesive moral structure that everything fell neatly into place.

"Sadie, it isn't right."

"What isn't? What are you doing so wrong?"

"Look, I know I'm putting you guys, uh, people in a bad position because you are also Danny's friends."

"And yours," said Pistol, skating back from the kitchen with espresso.

"And mine. So I don't want you to take sides."

"We want both of you to be happy and I think, if you like this guy, you should go out with him." Pistol sighed, adjusting his turquoise bathrobe. "Do you have fun with him?"

"When I let myself."

"Then do it."

"And how do you think Danny would feel if he knew?"

They lowered their eyes, Sadie busying himself with the espresso, Pistol fumbling with the Famous Amos cookies. Sarah watched them ignore her and she shivered. They knew something. She always knew they knew something about Danny, because they had spoken to him on the phone. Twice. And each time they spoke to him they'd mention it and she'd just nod and never ask beyond if he was okay. But they did know something more than whether he was just okay and she felt they wanted her to know, or else these consummate actors/actresses wouldn't have gone to the trouble of even subtly acting uneasy. They would have skated over it. They wanted her to know, or ask, and Sarah didn't know if she wanted to know, or ask, or maybe if she should just go downstairs and lie in bed and think about Lee's naked body, and masturbate, and fret about that though it felt good. This, she knew, wouldn't feel good. That, she wasn't certain would feel good until she tried it. But this, no, this couldn't feel good.

"But, it's more than just enjoying myself, right?" She somehow managed that, waiting for their response. There was none. Again she breathed deeply, knew it would be painful the way everything had been painful, but somehow she'd found a job and rode the subways and made her bed and kissed a strange man and had espresso with transvestites after midnight. Somehow she'd survived all that when she wondered if she'd survive breakfast alone. So she moved forward, not knowing whether to be wary or persistent, angry or hurt. Only scared. "Affair," she squeaked it out and they kept their faces down. Still down and she resented them, felt unbearable hostility because she felt they were testing her, and she was growing damned tired of being tested—tested by the E train and tested by the goddamn coffee maker and the three phones which only rang in unison at the office, and now tested by her friends. "Right?" Sadie glanced up, not at Sarah but at Pistol, who exchanged a glance and then stared directly into her. It didn't make her recoil, only made her angry and it felt damn good to feel angry. "Danny's having an affair down there and that's why you want me to go out with Lee, because if Danny's having one so should I?"

Now she waited. For them to lie to her and for her to lose respect yet feel reassured. Or for them to tell her the truth and for her to cry or laugh or whatever and then go ahead full blast with her so-called relationship with Lee, knowing damn well that the motivation for the sudden lurch into the bedroom would be vengeance.

"Do you want us to tell you?" Pistol whispered. Four narrowed mascaraed eyes drilled into her.

"Yes." No.

"Sure?"

"No." Yes.

"Would you rather not know?"

She picked at her fingers and wanted to curl her hair or kick over the coffee table and so, comforted by anger, she leaned forward and snapped, "By your saying that, you're telling me Danny's having an affair."

"No, we're not," Pistol said it. "If we say we have no knowledge, then you won't believe us and then our relationship will change. If we emphatically say no, you'll always wonder what else Danny could be doing down there to satisfy his urges. And if we say yes, you'll hate Danny. So what do you want us to say to you?"

"Okay." Okay what? "So tell me." No, please don't. I don't want to know. I really don't want to know what he's doing down there, because somehow I have to escape this linkage our marriage created and I've been doing it incrementally, so please don't re-form the link and make me think in terms of Danny again. Once, in terms of Sarah. Just once. "But, uh, if you tell me, are you betraying a confidence?"

"Yes."

"So you make it that I'm asking you to break a confidence?"

"Yes."

"So then I wonder if I ever told you something, then maybe you would tell someone like Danny or the mailman and then I would trust you less, so maybe I shouldn't push it?"

"No."

But she had taken temporary refuge behind that. She had given up, had disappointed them and, more so, disappointed herself. Maybe it was a good thing she had disappointed herself. Maybe that night as she had lain in bed having erotic fantasies of Lee, she had begun to wonder what it was she had left that she could think of solely in terms of Sarah.

"You know, Sarah, uh." Lee fiddled with his wineglass. Sarah picked up her own glass, played with the stem, then laid it down. At least she could fidget with something different. "So okay, we been going out for a few weeks now and uh, I dunno, like . . ."

"Sex?" Sarah thought she said it, knew it didn't come from any of the other tables in Angelo's. It certainly hadn't popped out of Lee's mouth, because he merely reddened and let his lips part until he could recover something of his composure.

"Uh, I wasn't talkin' about sex, I mean."

"Then?"

"No, just, I know you got a husband and all and, ya know, I

mean, I really like you and just wanted to be kinda honest how I felt about you."

"I like you, too," she said. How much of a lie was that? How bored was she with him? Very bored. How long could they continue going out without the real reason she went out with him coming out? Not long. Maybe not after tonight.

"I'm not sure you do." Sarah started to protest but Lee held up his hands. "Hey, sometimes, so okay, I know I bore you. Lookit, I know we don't have a lot in common but, I, ya know. Probably not even your type."

"You're my type."

"Nah, you know better."

"You are my type," Sarah insisted with more emphasis than she'd ever displayed with him. I don't have a type, Sarah realized as she watched him, holding her gaze on that handsome face. Danny was my type, but that was a long time ago and the only other types I'd ever thought about had been movie stars, which weren't types but fantasies. It had been too long since she'd had to define a type in reality. She didn't like, or at least wasn't accustomed to, forming her own definitions, and it had been a lot simpler to think that Lee was her type as she stole glances at his crotch. And that was it, she thought. Why she didn't push it with Sadie and Pistol. Because she didn't want to know about Danny and didn't want motivation for the only thing over which she had total control to be warped by vengeance. And that was—she smiled at this sexy street kid from Sheepshead Bay—that she wanted to have sex with Lee. Free, frivolous sex, as she used to have.

"Here, in here," Sarah said, opening her dorm door, her body filled with excessive quantities of quaaludes and alcohol, and let the kinda cute, also very wasted junior into her room. "Here," Sarah giggled, allowing him to take her to the bed and then ravish her as the blouse fell off and her panties disappeared and thank God she used the Pill. And thank God that cute junior couldn't look into her mind, could only hear her groan as she moved beneath him and thought of someone nice making love to her. So when did you ever have frivolous sex, Sarah? When were you ever freed from those silly romantic notions? Never, really. With

Danny there was romance until the candles burned down and the overhead lights came on. For seven years. Now you start deluding yourself you can have romance with this character out of *Godfather II* and you know that's a lie, too. That maybe you wanted romance because you feared frivolous sex. That maybe right now, the only thing you really own is sex, unencumbered with the need for romance or for someone to light a candle or uncork the wine or remark about how the fireplace shines across your face, when you never once lived in a house with a fireplace. Never once a fireplace or frivolity or any of that. So now control. Total control.

"Sunday night," Sarah said softly, staring into her zuppa inglese.

"Huh?" Lee's head bobbed up.

"Sunday night." Sarah smiled and took his hands. "Okay?"

Chapter 19

Danny had to blink rapidly to adjust to the lights. In the past few days he'd taken to wearing sunglasses to preserve his anonymity—not that he was incessantly besieged, but just in case, just for those moments when yet another middle-aged man, never an eleven-year-old, would stop him on the street.

"I just wanted to shake your hand and thank you, Mr. Neuman." A man of nearly fifty with ruddy features and stooped shoulders and bulging stomach had pressed him against a parking meter.

"Danny, please."

"Thought you were a regular guy, one of us. I could tell and I just wanted to thank you, Danny. Sure Danny's okay?"

"Yeah, absolutely. Dan, if you want. Daniel. Whatever, doesn't matter."

Danny had clutched the grocery bag as he stood outside Piggly-Wiggly and prayed the ice cream wouldn't start dripping down his leg and spoil this man's illusions.

"Dan, well, I just wanted to thank you, that's all."

"For what?"

"For getting me out of the hammock. I used to lie there, every weekend, lie there and allow myself to turn into a physical you-know-what."

"I can imagine." Out of the corner of his eye, Danny had seen several other people move toward him. Trapped.

"But you got me out of that hammock. Hell, now I bowl every week, here, feel this." The man had extended his bicep.

"Rather not." Danny had clutched the bag closer.

"Just feel it, see what you've done for me." The man had seized Danny's bag so he could feel the bicep. Danny had felt it, three times, taken back the bag and nodded. "See, this is what you've done for me," the man had continued. "Your example that you're never too old."

Hallelujah. Reverend Rabbi Daniel Neuman of the First Fundamentalist Yiddish Church-Synagogue of Greensboro, by way of the Pale of Settlement. Heal the old, the infirm. If you can do it, anyone can.

So he wore shades: shades when he walked out during the day, shades when he walked out at night. Shades in the frozen food section of the supermarket while he stared at Sara Lee cakes, unable to see, believing it was better to suffer frostbite from frozen cheesecakes than to heal some middle-aged man battling menopause.

Naturally, he hadn't thought to bring sunglasses to Rabbi Gottlieb's house. It had been difficult enough bringing Colleen.

"He said I could bring a friend, so I'm bringing you."

"Danny." Colleen had shaken that red hair. "Is it that you're afraid to go alone?"

"What, no, that's silly. A friend, I'm bringing a friend. You always say we never go out, so here we are, a night at the Gottliebs', should be fun. Maybe he'll show slides of his trip to the Golan Heights."

"I just want you to be honest about why you want me to go with you. Suddenly."

"I am being honest."

"You could bring Pete."

"Pete, Pete, he'd be too embarrassed to eat. Set back Judeo-Christian relations five hundred years, probably evoke a rebuke from the Chief Rabbi of North Carolina, be in all the newspapers, gentile refuses to eat at Jewish house, smears ketchup on gefilte fish. Colleen, please, it's important to me that you go."

"When you tell me why."

"I am."

"No. You know if you bring me, they'll wonder about our relationship."

"Let them wonder, since when did I care?"

197

She had almost sneered.

"The Rabbi is a friend of your brother's. He'll mention that you brought me to your brother, your family will wonder, it'll get back to Sarah."

"And if my wife knows?" Danny never used her name with Colleen. "So no, I, I want you there, I don't want you to think I'm embarrassed by you, please, okay? They don't have to know our relationship if it'll make you uncomfortable. You can just be my friend, my shrink, the team mascot. We'll hold hands, we can fondle each other and play perverse games with the matzoh—whatever you want, just come."

"It isn't what I want, because you're the one trying to prove something. You're the one upset over your publicity, uneasy about our relationship. Inviting me to this dinner is your way of showing you're not upset or uncomfortable, maybe that you have nothing to hide. Isn't that so?"

"No," he had lied, desperately seeking something to hide from her. "Just come, okay? They can think what they want. Who are they anyway?"

"Then why are we going if they don't matter?" Colleen had sighed.

Good question, Danny had thought back then. Even better one now, he wondered, staring beyond the table at the harvest of candles strewn across the dining room and pouring into the living room. Rabbi Gottlieb and his wife, Myra, who insisted they call her Myra but seemed more pleased by Mrs. Rabbi, were candle freaks. At least it seemed that way to Danny, though the Rabbi had a ready explanation.

"With each visitor, I like to light a candle. A tradition in my family," he'd explained.

"I thought there weren't going to be any visitors or anyone but us." Danny had glared at the opened carton of waiting candles.

"*Ach,* a few people, they would like to meet you, for a handshake and hello. Some important people, the *machers* in the community. No one big."

So they had come. At first they were only the *machers* in the community. The Cantor. The Temple Board Members. This large contributor and that large contributor, even though neither attended services anymore. Still, they were *machers*. And with each visitor another candle had been lit until Danny was certain they'd exhausted both *machers* and candles. He'd been wrong. Every *macher* had a relative or a friend and suddenly Danny was talking to the great-aunt of Mrs. Rabbi's canasta partner. Gladys. Getillah, she had insisted on the Yiddish monicker, explaining it was her way of paying homage to her great-grandfather, slain in the 1903 Russian pogroms.

Whereas Danny had been dazed by the guests, Colleen had been invigorated. Through it all she had been incredibly charming, disarming those wary of her obvious Christianity. Never once had she stooped to exchanging Yiddish slang grown so common in American speech patterns that few really knew what *shmuck* actually meant. Nor had she condescended and expressed admiration for "you people's great attributes and dedication to family and education and success." Nothing like that. Colleen had spoken to them as people and they had almost responded to her as a person, albeit a person who might be the *shiksa* girl friend of the famous Jewish ballplayer. And Danny knew how charming she was because he had watched her through the blazing candles. That's why he'd wanted her there in the first place. To test her, for her to give him a reason not to like her because she had displayed condescension or subtle anti-Semitism or spoken with Mrs. Rabbi, over sixty, as a peer. He hadn't expected to fall more deeply in love with her.

At last, the guests had left, though the candles remained. So there they were, Danny seated between the brisket and stuffed cabbage, to the right of Mrs. Rabbi, who had gefilte fish between her and Colleen, who had the latkes and gefilte fish separating her from the Rabbi.

". . . Rarely fry, Jacob and me, the frying, what with the grease, it goes straight to our stomachs and comes right back up . . ." Colleen heard Mrs. Rabbi say. She half-heard herself offering something out of *Hints from Heloise,* and studied Danny.

She'd found it intensely difficult, being charming to all those people. Some were nice, some weren't and Colleen wouldn't have minded so much the politeness she extended to those—

what was the word—yentas, if she hadn't resented so much being forced to be nice to them.

That was what hurt, that she had to be unnatural, all because Danny had forced her into this situation. She really wanted to tell everyone exactly what their relationship was, that she wasn't loosely affiliated with the team or doing a magazine piece on him or the aunt or mother of one of the players. That she and Danny were lovers, that's what she should have said. But didn't. All because she cared about Danny, and that confused her more because she never would've put him in any position like this in which he had to be other than himself. And what if she had? Perhaps he, too, would've refrained from saying what was on his mind. Would've been phony, would've lied. And did she resent him putting her in this position, or did she resent the fact that they might, after all, have formed something of a conventional relationship? She had tried to deceive herself that they didn't have a conventional relationship, that it wasn't like all the other idiotic relationships she'd had with other men who had demanded she satisfy some role and of whom, she had to admit, she had demanded that they satisfy a role in return. With Danny, they could just be themselves. Maybe that's why he feared going places. Maybe he was wiser than she. Maybe she'd never counted on what had happened to them actually happening, and couldn't decide whether it was just that she couldn't remember how to deal with it or whether she simply didn't want to deal with it.

Colleen paused, two plates in hand. Mrs. Rabbi had insisted she didn't need help, to which Colleen had countered she would be hurt if she couldn't help, to which Mrs. Rabbi had relented with a heavy sigh. But Colleen didn't bound toward the kitchen as quickly as Mrs. Rabbi. She just held the two plates, then, abruptly, startling even herself, kissed Danny on the top of the head and then rushed after Mrs. Rabbi, not glancing back to see his reaction. He merely blushed and smiled weakly at Rabbi Gottlieb, who rolled his eyes and smiled the smile of near-sin, which deepened Danny's cheeks.

"So." Gottlieb stared past Danny at a needlepoint of an ancient, gray-bearded rabbi hanging on the wall of the study.

Danny followed the object of the stare, turned to Gottlieb, expecting him to break the look and turn his way. Gottlieb didn't. Just kept staring. "I enjoy staring," Gottlieb said, staring. "I find it relaxing, after a big dinner, to sit in my study and stare. Allows my food to digest."

"Yeah, well, you think, uh, maybe we could talk first, stare later?"

"Stare with me for a while." Gottlieb's eyes never left the wall. "It helps order your thoughts."

"Rabbi Gottlieb, my thoughts are beyond order."

"A few more moments, Danny."

"I haven't time," Danny pleaded.

"We all have time, Daniel."

"Not cosmic time, earth time, you know, Eastern Standard Time?" Danny listened to the sounds of dishes being washed.

"To talk about what you wanted to talk about when you phoned?"

"Right, I, I'd hoped we could've spoken earlier but . . ."

"Responsibility, duty, obligation. Your people wanted to meet you. That is more important than anything you or I could ever discuss." Gottlieb kept staring, so Danny stared at Gottlieb until the Rabbi's eyes finally wandered back across the room and fell in faint bemusement upon Danny, squirming in his chair. "You want to talk about her?"

"Yeah, her, Colleen."

"She is your girl friend?"

"Yeah, well, sort of."

"Sort of? How can there be a sort of girl friend?"

"There can, believe me, okay? I—could you maybe . . . I don't know, see, I'm married and . . ."

"I know."

"My brother?"

"Your wedding ring."

"Right." Danny wanted to take it off, had never wanted to take it off but wanted to now, in the presence of the Rabbi. Not to throw it away, but just to take it off so he could decide, on his own volition, whether to put it back on again. "Married, right, and well, see, I've never cheated on Sarah before, that's my wife's name, Sarah, she's really, well, I never did before and now this has happened and I well, see, I'm falling in love or am in love or at least care about Colleen and I can't shake the guilt when I'm with her but don't want to give her up and . . ."

"Guilt? This is about guilt?"

"Yeah, guilt. You know, guilt."

"Guilt. This guilt bothers you?"

"Shouldn't it?"

"No, guilt is healthy."

"What's healthy about guilt?"

"Guilt is God's way of giving us ambition. We would do nothing without guilt. Either we are guilty for not doing something, or guilty about doing something. In either way, guilt motivates us."

"Or gives me heart palpitations."

"At your age?"

"Rabbi, listen, I don't feel too good about guilt, okay? I feel miserable."

"Why? Guilt, I tell you, young people do not understand the wonder of guilt. It is a divine gift, guilt. Do you think hungry people would be fed without the guilt of those who have? Do you? No, guilt is God's great equalizer. His method of taking from those who have and giving to those who need."

"I'm not talking about taking or giving away anything, I'm talking about being miserable. There's a difference."

"No difference." Gottlieb shook his head. "Obviously this guilt of yours makes you examine your feelings for this woman. If you didn't feel guilty about what you call cheating on your wife, perhaps you would not be giving this thought such attention. Or if you were not cheating on your wife, perhaps you would feel guilt about how well you are treating this woman. The by-products of guilt are infinite, as He wants."

"Just wait, okay? I don't want theology. I'm coming to you for help."

"And I am giving you help. I am telling you that guilt is healthy. You should feel guilt. Over everything."

"I do and it drives me crazy, so what you're saying doesn't help. I just want an answer, okay? Some answer. Am I doing wrong?"

"Do you feel you're doing wrong?"

"I don't know."

"And you want me to tell you?"

"If not you, then Him. Make Him tell me."

"Ah, so you think He would talk to you directly? That is how *goyim* think, with their revelations and saints, that God speaks to them as if He had a WATS line. It doesn't work that way. So"— Gottlieb leaned forward—"do you love her?"

"Yes, I think so."

"Would you be certain if you weren't married?"

"No."

"Do you love her because you're lonely? Afraid, confused?"

"Keep going, I don't think you're done yet. Try bewildered. Uncertain. Terrified. Maybe we should use a thesaurus."

"Daniel, Daniel," Gottlieb chuckled. "If this woman gives you pleasure, then accept the pleasure. If she gives you joy, then accept the joy. There is so very little of that. But to expect that there can ever be pleasure without guilt is nonsense. You want a perfect world. Such a world doesn't exist."

"I want one black-and-white, okay? Just one. I'll take the other grays, just give me one black-and-white and I'm happy."

"I cannot give you that which does not exist. If you wish to go into the desert to find such a black-and-white, then go. But here, in this world, there is no such thing. It is all gray, all cluttered, all confusing. To accept the confusion, to exist in this confusion, that is the key."

"Great." Danny sank into the lining of the chair as the women entered. Mrs. Rabbi took the seat next to her husband and Colleen slid another chair near Danny. He glanced quickly, questioningly at her. She just smiled and studied him. He nodded and turned away. Now he had nowhere to look.

He sat stiffly as Gottlieb filled his pipe, leaned back and smiled.

"Now, Daniel, I have a favor to ask of you."

Uh-oh.

"Myra told me . . ." Colleen began.

"Mrs. Rabbi," she corrected without looking up.

"Mrs. Rabbi told me in the kitchen." Colleen's eyes twinkled. "I think you'll find this one interesting."

"How interesting?" Danny ignored the elderly couple.

"Very interesting." She grinned.

"Thanks," he muttered, allowing her to take his hand, allowing her to squeeze it, yet not allowing her to withdraw it even though it only made him feel worse.

"As you can see, to those in our little community, you are something of a hero down here," Gottlieb said softly. "*Ach*, a Jewish athlete, in North Carolina, you can't imagine what it means to us. It isn't like in New York, where everyone, gentiles included, forgive me, Colleen, I say this without reproach, is Jewish."

"I understand." She smiled.

"You do?" Danny asked her.

"I'm Irish, remember?"

"So?" What did that have to do with anything and why was everyone smiling at him, even Mrs. Rabbi, who had laid down her needlepoint to smile at him.

"Just listen, Danny," Colleen replied, still smiling, sighing a little as she kept the grin.

"Do I have to?" he asked, returning the grin. Her expression went harsh and he didn't know why, or why her fingers pulled away from his, only that it frightened him and it was bad enough some impending request was about to come from a Holocaust survivor who preferred staring at needlepoints to talking.

". . . Masked Hebrew couldn't make it, he has a big match in Roanoke, for the Mid-Atlantic Heavyweight title. He was very upset, I was upset, Raymond Mendelssohn, the entire Mendelssohn family, everyone was upset Masked Hebrew couldn't make it, may God give him strength to win back the title from that *shmendrick* Cowboy Watson."

"Masked Hebrew," Danny repeated dully. Masked Hebrew, a professional wrestler who trotted out attired in the blue-and-white colors of Israel, the Star of David flag draped across his huge carcass as he jettisoned his muscular arms outward to the shrieks of his adoring fans. Masked Hebrew, who Danny knew, from his wrestling writing background, to be Jerry Walker, an Episcopalian. A fraud. A gimmick. Remember glass houses, Neuman.

"So," Gottlieb continued, "we hoped that maybe you could make young Raymond's bar mitzvah this Sunday evening. We know your game is early, you should be finished in time, we already, forgive me for the insolence, consulted with your boss. A nice man, Antonheimer, Jewish maybe?" Danny shrugged. "And he agreed it would be a marvelous thing if you would speak at Raymond's bar mitzvah, say a few words."

"A *mitzvah*," muttered Mrs. Rabbi.

"I do think it'd be wonderful, Danny," Colleen said breathlessly. "To participate in something like this, something so hallowed with tradition. There is so little tradition left. Mrs. Rabbi said, if you agreed, I could come. I've always wanted to see a bar mitzvah."

"It is a glorious moment," Gottlieb said to Colleen, who smiled and turned back to Danny, who fought an impulse to stare at the rabbi on the wall.

"See, uh, I'm not too good speaking in public," Danny actually whispered.

"What, you do those commercials, you speak to reporters. This is for your people," Gottlieb persisted.

"Danny." Colleen took his shoulder and spun him toward her. He had started listing to one side. "It's important, you know?" Colleen frowned and shook her head tightly.

"I just don't," now he sputtered. "I, I don't know what to say," he said to all of them.

"Wait, I think I know why Danny is a little reluctant," Gottlieb said quietly, refilling his pipe. Danny trembled, knowing on a rational level Gottlieb couldn't possibly know. "You are a little hurt that we didn't ask you first, that you are second choice to Masked Hebrew, is that it?" Gottlieb smiled.

"Uh, well." Danny felt limp. Not a bad lie, he thought, nodding and smiling stupidly. "See, I, not really that, a little, just, I'm so uncomfortable with those sorts of things that, I . . ." he made the mistake of turning to Colleen for help.

"Danny, you complain about all the commercialism you go through. Finally you have something without commercialism. Something holy, I think you could submerge your ego and realize how very important this is to your people here."

I don't want to do it, Danny thought. He held that thought through coffee and pound cake, through the ride home with Colleen, through a sweaty sex scene during which he kept losing his erection, through a nightcap of anisette and through the walk to the 7-11 three blocks from her apartment.

At that phone booth, Danny slipped dime after dime into the slot, time after time hitting the coin release because it was, after all, just another thing he couldn't do. Even if he did desperately want to call her. He knew why he kept dialing the suddenly unfamiliar number. He wanted to talk to her because—what? Did he really want to talk to her or was he just frightened and needed to hear her voice? Did it matter, his motives? Wasn't it sufficient he was the one to make the first move?

On the ninth try, he let the dime stay. The phone rang seven times before Danny finally gave up. Not home. Brilliant deduction. So where is she? And who am I to question where she is, when I'm calling my wife from a phone booth three blocks from my girl friend's apartment?

Chapter 20

Colleen was neither a reckless nor a cautious driver. Simply, she had no idea how to drive a car. When her tubercular Ford started drifting into opposing traffic, Danny thought it a good time to shout in protest.

"Will you watch how you drive?"

"Danny." Colleen peered at the oncoming, honking cars, shrugged and eased across her left lane into the right, cutting off another car. "Relax. I know what I'm doing, try not to be so nervous."

"I can't help it, I am nervous," Danny said.

"And I don't want you to be nervous," his father smiled, adjusting Danny's tie. "You'll do fine." He undid Danny's tie and remade it, making Danny even more nervous because he didn't want to start worrying about ties, and his father's preoccupation unnerved him.

"Pop, do I really have to talk in front of all those people?"

"Daniel, you'll be fine. I did it. Your grandfather did it. Jews for time immemorial have done it."

"But why?" Danny shuddered. "I mean, can't I just—I don't know, maybe, not do it?"

"It's too late," Colleen said as they approached the synagogue. "You made a commitment. You have to honor your commitments."

"I do honor my commitments," Danny insisted, squeezing the door handle. "Do you see me jumping out of the car, huh?" He had thought of jumping out of the car, but had always feared being crippled and having people wheeling him around or incurring irritation from bus passengers as the bus eased its front end to the ground so his wheelchair could make it up and he delayed traffic. "I'm going."

"You could be a little more excited," she insisted. "This is a great day for you. Participating in a holy event. God, I envy you."

"If you envy me so much, why don't you go up there and do it?"

"I will be there," his father assured him, pleased with the tie on the fourth effort. "I will read from the Torah with you, don't worry, I'll be nearby."

"Yeah, well, could you stay real close to me? That rabbi, he doesn't like me."

"Nonsense, he's a rabbi, why shouldn't he like you?"

"Daddy, he doesn't like me."

"So again, why shouldn't the rabbi like you?"

Mr. Neuman didn't know of Danny's disobedience in Hebrew School. Never knew how Danny would crack walnuts or read comics or wisecrack from the back of the room until the exasperated female sabra instructor would order him to the rabbi's office. And Danny would go, not content to sit and wait, instead determined to exact revenge for being forced to attend Hebrew School when he had enough homework from junior high school, when it was still nice out and bright enough to play baseball. No, Mr. Neuman didn't know how Danny tore the wires out of the wall of the rabbi's office, how he dumped tobacco into the rabbi's jacket pockets, how he rearranged the books and fiddled with the Hebrew notes in the margins of the books so they would be illegible and maybe drive the rabbi insane. No, Mr. Neuman never heard the time Danny crawled onto the ledge and closed the window behind him, so when the rabbi came back in, expecting to deliver another weary lecture, he found an empty office. No one had seen Danny go past the rabbi's upstairs classroom. No one downstairs had seen Danny leave the building. Nor was Danny in the attic. He was nowhere, which frightened the entire school and sent them on a forty-minute search for Danny. Fi-

nally, he crawled back from the ledge, slid into the office and calmly waited for the frantic rabbi to reappear. No lectures that day because the rabbi was too worried maybe the Cossacks from the Grand Concourse had gotten him. No, Mr. Neuman knew none of that.

"What if I get laryngitis?" *Danny persisted.*

"All children get laryngitis." *His father took him by the hand as they walked to the synagogue.* "Then God takes over. He gives you strength. He gives you courage."

"Yeah, so how do I know for sure? What if God's busy that day, what if there's another bar mitzvah he's gotta take care of?"

"God is omnipotent. All-powerful. And so on."

"So if he's so powerful and so understanding and everything, why can't he say the Haftorah instead of me? Wouldn't that be a better bar mitzvah, God up there instead of me? It'd be a miracle. Be in all the papers. I'd do that for God."

"Tradition," Colleen said, patting his arm as they ascended the wooden steps of the ancient synagogue. Danny half-hid behind her. He hadn't brought his sunglasses. "Tradition. You Jewish people are lucky to have this sort of unbroken, unchanged tradition. To have a bar mitzvah in the same manner, with the same words, the same holiness as has been done for three thousand years is exhilarating."

"Yeah, well, let's not get silly, okay? They didn't exactly have prime ribs when Judah the Maccabee was bar-mitzvahed."

Colleen sighed as she started to open the door. Danny remained two steps down and she beckoned him up.

"Don't look at it like you're someone so special. Look at it like you're just another guest, like me, except that you have been honored to say a few words."

He didn't want to follow her into the *shul*, but had no choice, since he couldn't stand on the bottom step and cringe all day. So he accepted her outstretched hand as she led him in. He should've stayed on the bottom step.

"Danny, Danny, so good of you to come." Rabbi Gottlieb seized him by the hand. Danny kept his hand in Colleen's, even as Gottlieb shlepped him through the crowd and brought him toward a well-dressed couple flanking a small little boy. "I want you should meet the Mendelssohns. Here, Mr. Mendelssohn, Mrs. Mendelssohn, little Raymond Mendelssohn, this is Daniel Neuman, the famous ballplayer."

"Pleased to meet you," Danny mumbled as they told him how much they enjoyed his hitting and he murmured it was nothing, all you had to do was be old, and they chuckled in confusion. So did Colleen as she studied him, enhancing his dread. Dread and fear. Dread and fear combining to bring about an irresistible physical impulse.

"Daddy, I have to pee," Danny whispered at they approached the podium.

"Not now."

"If not now, when? I have to."

"You're just nervous, don't pee now, pee afterwards."

"I gotta go now."

"Daniel, you can't think of peeing on your day of manhood. It isn't right."

"Don't men pee? You pee, why can't I? I should be allowed to do whatever a man does."

"When you finish your Haftorah, then you can pee, then you are a man."

Danny stared at Raymond Mendelssohn as he began his prayers. Raymond Mendelssohn looked like all other bar-mitzvah boys. Short, chubby. Bar-mitzvah boys were always chubby unless both their mothers and grandmothers were dead. Also an aunt, just to make sure. Then they would be short and skinny. Danny had looked like Raymond Mendelssohn. Danny wondered if Raymond Mendelssohn had yet learned how to play with his pecker, as all bar-mitzvah boys are supposed to know. Except Danny. He hadn't yet learned what to do with his pecker, though his friends told him all about pulling your *putz* and jacking off and whacking off, though Danny didn't know what any of that meant. So he had opted for just playing with it, until his grandfather had taken him aside and told him not to touch it so much because when it finally grew out it would like like rigatoni. Danny didn't know what rigatoni was, either, but it had frightened him, so he had refrained from playing with his pecker.

210

In fact, the first time he had ever masturbated wasn't by playing with his pecker. He had been six months past his bar mitzvah and had been lying in bed, watching *Gilligan's Island,* when he'd begun to study, really study for the first time, both Mary Ann and Ginger. And while he'd studied them he'd rubbed on his mattress because he'd been lying on his stomach. And the more he'd studied the stranger his body had felt, and soon a weird sensation, frightening, puzzling and wonderful, had shot through his pecker and he'd come. Though he hadn't known that was coming because he hadn't played with his pecker, and didn't know anything could happen if you didn't. So for the next few weeks Danny had lain on his stomach and thought of Mary Ann and Ginger and *I Dream of Jeannie* and Barbara Feldon and come. Except that his bed had been on wheels and it had kept hurtling across the room, banging into opposing walls as he had come without playing with his pecker. What must his parents have thought as they heard the bang, roll and crash from one wall to the other? That he was playing with his pecker, probably. Then Danny had grown frightened someone would find him, so he'd gone into the bathroom and tried to figure out the right way to play with his pecker. He never had because anyone he had ever discussed playing with his pecker with had been surprised. Danny rubbed it against his thigh. To this day, hair didn't grow on one spot on his upper right thigh.

But that had been six months after his own bar mitzvah. He had finally been expelled from Hebrew School. Not actually expelled. Danny had complained the workload from his classes had been too much combined with Hebrew School, and his parents had sent him to a private tutor. There, Danny couldn't pull wires out of the walls, or dump tobacco in the sallow-faced instructor's pockets, because the sallow-faced instructor had always been in the room. And, Danny realized, neither could he learn Hebrew. So he had learned his Haftorah phonetically. BA-RUCH. AW-TAW, AH-DOE-NOY. And that had pleased his instructor and his parents, all except the rabbi of the Hebrew School who had resented Danny's loss of tuition.

Raymond Mendelssohn finished and the Rabbi began to speak. *"And so to you Jeff Froberg,"* Danny's rabbi had said to his partner in the Haftorah. Jeff Froberg had been born on the same day so they split the ordeal. Danny didn't know what had happened to Jeff Froberg. He'd heard from someone that, after high school, Froberg had gone into the headband-making business. And, from that same source whose name Danny couldn't remember, that Froberg had dropped out of that business once Joplin, Hendrix and Morrison died and headbands were no longer in vogue. Last Danny heard Froberg was a chiropractor in Pompano Beach. *". . . who is now a man in the eyes of God." And Danny's rabbi presented Froberg with expensive books and other stuff he'd never read but would look nice on his parents' bookshelves. Then the rabbi turned to Danny. Gone was any sacred warmth. Instead, a sinister stare which told Danny he knew who had pulled out the wires and dumped the tobacco and hid on the window ledge and hadn't paid the Hebrew School tuition. Danny knew he knew and couldn't speak, could only wait and hope he was wrong.*

"And to you, Daniel Neuman, who is not yet a man in the eyes of God, I . . ."

So Danny did little else than freeze and look for help. He looked straight at his father, standing beyond his grandfather to Danny's left. His father looked back at Danny, then at the rabbi as the congregation sort of gasped in bewilderment, but what did they know anyway, because the rabbi knew more than them, so maybe Danny wasn't really a man yet and would have to wait a few more years to pee. Mr. Neuman kept staring, his face losing more and more color until he almost leaped off the ground.

"Momzer," he screamed the Yiddish word for bastard. "You dirty momzer," again he shouted and started for the rabbi, inching away in fear. No one knew what to do, so they let pandemonium take over. Danny's grandfather holding back his screaming son-in-law, aided by Danny's mother's brother whom Danny never liked, also assisted by several cousins Danny never liked and by big fat Aunt Gussie, who was really Danny's great-aunt but he called her Aunt Gussie and liked her. All of them pressed against Mr. Neuman and led him, still screaming, off the podium or whatever it's called in shul. Danny didn't know. Only that he was proud of his father.

"I take great pleasure," Rabbi Gottlieb spoke into the microphone. From their seats in the fourth row, Colleen squeezed Danny's hand and he shook, looking off toward the closed oak doors beyond the Rabbi and little Raymond and Raymond's father and grandfather, where Danny knew the chopped liver and pound cake awaited them. "Great, great pleasure"—everyone strained to look at Danny as he slid down in his seat—"in introducing a great man, a wonderful athlete, a member of our faith who can be considered one of the all-time great Jewish ballplayers of all time, a man who must rank with Hank Greenberg and Sandy Koufax and all the other great Jewish athletes too numerous to mention." You're almost done, Danny thought. "And who has been kind enough to come here today, to celebrate in Raymond Mendelssohn's day of manhood. Would you please welcome, with a big, big hand, Danny Neuman, star center fielder of the Greensboro Hornets."

"Well, uh," Danny said shakily, grasping the microphone, praying for a sign from God. He stared down at Raymond, eyes wide with admiration. What are you looking at, you little *putz*. What? You think I'm so hot? I'm just a bush-league ballplayer and you can't even flip my baseball card because I'm not on one. I'm not a real major-leaguer, you little *shmeckle*, you. "Raymond, this is a big day for you." What crap, Danny thought. He'd rather be watching television than doing this, rather be watching reruns of *Gilligan's Island* and getting hot over Mary Ann and Ginger than doing this. "Today you are a man, right, Raymond, Ray now, I guess, because today you are a man, right?" Raymond nodded, and so did everyone else. "And uh, today you are a man because it was written that you are a man, thousands of years ago and, uh, because it was written, then they tell you that you are a man. Doesn't uh, everyone think Ray, no, Raymond is a man now?" Heads bobbed gravely. "Well uh, Raymond, do you think you are a man, feel like you are a man?" Heads held their bobbing and Raymond tilted his head, examining Danny.

"So uh, I'd like to talk about being a man. Uh, you know, there's this artificial dividing line in our faith and, uh, our society says that you are a man at a certain age and uh, well, Raymond, today you are a man and do you know what being a man is all about?" Heads tilted forward, expecting profundity. Only Colleen squirmed. "Do you? Maybe you think you do because you said your Haftorah nicely and got checks and leaky pen sets. Well, I said my Haftorah nicely and got checks and leaky pen sets and you know, Raymond, you know something? I didn't know what the hell being a man was all about when I was bar-mitzvahed, because I wasn't a man and the whole thing didn't mean a damn thing to me, and maybe I would've appreciated it more if I were older, or maybe I wouldn't have because the whole thing is silly, yeah, silly." Danny was shouting now as several people rose toward him. "Look at this kid," Danny screamed, pointing his finger at Raymond, who half-smiled in glee. "He's just a kid, you know? What the hell does he know about anything? Has he ever had real disappointment like a man's supposed to have?" Three men came toward Danny. "Or has he ever had a woman, jeez, Raymond, you ever play with yourself?"

Hands grabbed him, but Danny resisted, kept his twisted mouth in front of the microphone. "You half-believe you're a man, Raymond," he had to shout, because all around him people were screaming and he had already been dragged away from the microphone. "Don't feel bad because I was brainwashed, like we're all brainwashed about artificial truths and artificial lies and this is this and that is that." They were dragging him down an aisle, but he kept his face twisted directly at Raymond, the only person in the whole synagogue, except maybe Colleen—who was sitting with her face buried in her hands—still listening to him. "And we're all covered by thousands of years of bullshit and it isn't true, Raymond, damnit. You're not a man like I'm not a man and I'm thirty-three years old, and you can't listen to all this bullshit, and don't let them make you do stuff you don't want to do because you're supposed to be a grownup, because believe me—" he shrieked above the din, resisted against the arms dragging him toward the door, though his eyes and Ray-mond's were still locked—"they don't know what the hell they're talking about, and they don't want you to have fun be-cause they don't but you have to, you have to have fun and hit a

214

baseball and get dirty or cop a feel or play with your pecker and that's all you should want to do." He was a few feet from the opened door and could no longer see Raymond, though he still shouted. "And you should do it because all you should care about is scraping your stupid knee, which they say you can't do anymore because they can't, so just do it, Raymond, damnit, Raymond, listen to me, for Chrissakes, just go ahead and get zits, just get zits."

And now all he faced was the closed door. Inside, screams gradually subsiding into muttered hate. He would be excommunicated. That much was certain, as it was certain the mob anger would subside into food for months of disbelieving gossip and Raymond would go along thinking he was a man. That was about all Danny could think about as he sagged onto the bottom step, found a stale cigarette in his dark blue suit and lit it, not knowing nor caring where he was supposed to go, only that what he had done felt good, even if it had accomplished nothing. Or maybe it had.

"God, Danny." She breathed it, didn't say it, just breathed it as she stood on the top step, closing the door behind her and heaving her huge breasts up and down. "God."

"I wouldn't try to talk to him in my presence," Danny said, waiting for her to sit beside him. She didn't, though she did move down the two steps so she at least stood next to him, glaring down not in anger but overwhelmed disbelief. "So go ahead"—Danny shook his head—"I'm ready, tell me the bad thing I did."

"You really felt that, didn't you?" she whispered.

"I guess."

"You guess?" she hissed. "You did that and you guess it was what you felt?"

"Okay, okay, I did." He strained to look up to her, then stood. "Yeah, it's what I felt, okay? I know I embarrassed you, caused a war in there, certain excommunication, my picture'll probably be in every deli in the Diaspora because . . ."

"Enough."

"Enough what?"

"Jokes. You did it, didn't you? You did it because you had to do it, because you felt it and were honest and so, just did it. God."

"Didn't do it to you," he snapped.

"Yes, you did," she said vacantly, eyes fluttering.

"What, I did it to my people. Don't care if you're Irish, you're still not one of us."

"I couldn't believe you did it."

"So, I'm sorry to you. Sorry I upset you, I'm . . ."

"Don't apologize." Again that distant voice.

"Well, then what?" He reached for her and she allowed him to squeeze her shoulder, just allowed him out of such distant acquiescence that he had no choice but to pull away. "What, tell me what?"

"You know I love you," she whispered, without any emotion or with so much emotion it had flattened itself out. He trembled, still not knowing what do do. "I do love you."

"And I love you, so, hey then, come with me to New York when this is over, or, or, I'll—we'll move in together, okay?"

"I love you." Now her eyes were closed tight. "Live together?" Colleen chuckled as if she'd read his words, instead of hearing them. "I love you. I can't."

"Can't what, live together?"

"We'd be doing it out of fear."

"What fear, not fear, damnit, love, commitment. Isn't that what you want?"

"Yes, it is what I want and no, that's why I can't do it."

"Jeez, what's that mean, you do and that's why you won't?"

"Danny." Colleen touched his arm and he shuddered from the distant warmth. "I can't live with a mirror. You're my mirror."

"I'm your mirror," he said, sullen, irritated because he was losing her and she wouldn't tell him why. "I know why, because I did that, because I embarrassed you, right?"

She laughed softly.

"Because you showed me that I'm not what I thought I was, Danny. I thought I was some tough middle-aged broad able to bounce from man to man and instead you showed me I wanted a normal relationship. Which I don't, really, or if I do it should stay submerged, Danny, stay buried beneath me, do you understand?" Colleen stroked his cheek and he could do nothing but cry onto her fingers. "Little Danny," she whispered. "Sad little Danny." Colleen shook her head. "A crazy little boy who doesn't understand that people don't like to be told they've been lying to themselves." Colleen kissed his forehead, turned away, so she wouldn't have to watch his tears, so he wouldn't see that she had no tears, so she wouldn't have to cry in his reflection.

Colleen bounded away, reassuming that stiff, determined manner he hadn't seen since that first night in the bar. And Danny took a step after her until he realized he couldn't follow her, nor could he go within the synagogue. Could only hear the rejoicing from within the *shul* and watch Colleen calmly drive out of the parking lot and down the street. Probably to a bar, Danny thought, feeling envy, then hurt, then a puzzled relief which spilled into forlorn emptiness as he sagged onto the bottom step and lit another stale cigarette retrieved from within his suit.

Danny would sit there for another hour until he realized he had nowhere to go, so he had to leave.

Chapter 21

Sarah tore open the hotel drawers. First the desk, then the small
bureau. Nothing. Terrific. *Even the Gideons aren't here to save
me.* She stood, still in her coat, her small valise containing the
Bloomingdale's artifacts lying at the foot of the bed she still
hadn't the courage to go near. *Has to be here,* she made one
more search of the room. *How can the Gideons have missed this
room?* Sarah glared about the small corner room at the Statler
Hilton.

*Should've expected it. And why are you looking for the New
Testament to save you? You wanted this. Your decision. Everything done by you. Picking the night. Picking the hotel. Making
the reservation in your name. And getting here first so you could
try out the room, lie on the bed, so it would be your bed and
your sheets because it was your decision. A decision which terri-
fies you, which is why you're now opening the closet and pressing your fingers into the back wall searching for the secret com-
partment where the Gideons have hidden the Bible—so why
don't you just stop and calm down and get undressed?*

So she did get undressed. She had half an hour before Lee was
to arrive, so Sarah struggled out of her coat, entered the bathroom, closed the door, for no reason except growing paranoia,
and slipped into her black lace nightie. Somehow the sheer material exposing her nipples and cutting away from her vagina
didn't look quite as sexy as it had when she'd tried it on this afternoon at Bloomingdale's. Maybe because all she'd had to im-

218

press was her own reflection, and not the suddenly real prospect of Lee's attention. But he wasn't supposed to matter. Whether he thought it was sexy or not was incidental because it was what Sarah thought that mattered. And now she wasn't so certain how good it looked and it was certainly too late to rush out and buy another nightie, though it wasn't too late to flee the room and leave some touching note.

Sarah started out the bathroom, again back to the desk and toward the hotel stationery, to write Lee why this really wasn't such a great idea, because she was a married woman and had never had an affair, and this seam on the nightie was irritating her right breast and besides, she heard him knock.

Perspiration dripped down her arms. She cursed her new improved deodorant and thought it a particularly ridiculous thing to ponder when someone was standing outside her door, knocking three times now, and she wasn't certain if she was going to let him in. Maybe he'd go away and she could get out in time.

"Yes?" Sarah leaned against the wall adjoining the door, her hand on the knob.

"Hey, it's me."

"Lee?"

"Yeah, sure, Lee."

"Uh, are you alone?" No, he brought all of Brooklyn with him.

"Sure, what do ya think, I'm alone."

"Okay."

Sarah started to open the door. She knew what was supposed to happen. He would enter by himself, even if that was impossible because only she had the key. She would be sprawled upon the bed, legs spread, which was silly since the bedspread was still on and there had to be an annoying seam near her crotch as well. He would smile gently, though by now he must be wondering why he was still standing in the hallway. She would smile alluringly, even if she was presently forcing her lips to stay in one place for more than a second. He would come to her. But he was out in the corridor. She would see his quickening excitement, at present impossible because all she could see was a notice to guests to take their key with them whenever they left the room. She would feel her own quickening excitement, right now

219

more nausea than anything else. He would lie beside her and stroke her flesh, though now he was playing with the outside door knob. She would rip his clothes off, instead of peeling at the wallpaper on the wall. That had been the plan.

"Hey, Sarah, c'mon, open up. I feel kinda silly out here, know what I mean?"

Sarah rushed back to the desk chair and draped her light cotton jacket over her nightie before rushing back to the door, fumbling with the lock and letting it open. She stepped back as Lee entered, holding a bottle of champagne and two glasses. Sarah took the bottle and half-hid it within her jacket. French champagne, of course. She looked at it. Upstate New York. Lee frowned slightly as they jostled for position in the tiny corridor.

"Champagne, huh?" Sarah inched back a bit so now she was closer to the door than he was.

"Yeah, champagne, figured it'd be nice, uh . . ." Lee watched Sarah press against the door. "Hey, Sarah, you comin' or goin' or what?"

"Coming. I, I got here first. Uh, you know, to get here first."

"Yeah, I guess." He smiled. She smiled. He would now drape his strong arms around her waist and kiss her hello. Actually he clasped his hands in front of his groin and squirmed from side to side as Sarah, who should have wrapped her arms around his neck, trembled from the cold champagne pressing against her chest.

"Uh, you look nice." Sarah touched his light blue suit, shivered, withdrew her hand, almost pressed through the wall. "New, right?"

"No, uh, wore it at dinner some night, I think." Lee grinned. Neither had moved yet. "You look nice, too."

"I do?" Nice? Grandmothers look nice. I'm supposed to be appealing, sensual. He is supposed to be bulging with animal lust. Neither of us is supposed to be standing in the hallway as if we were waiting for the subway. "Uh"—Sarah tossed her hand out toward the room—"nice, the room."

"Yeah, I guess." He craned forward to look at it, spent some time examining it from his limited view in the corridor.

"It's not there, you know," Sarah said sadly.

220

"What?"

"I looked for it, not there."

"What isn't?"

You're a fool, Sarah.

"Bucket of ice."

"We need it?"

Of course.

"No. Seems cold." Sarah could no longer feel her breastbone. "Uh, so, maybe we should, uh, drink the champagne, okay?"

"Yeah, sure, that's why I brought it." He chuckled. Still neither moved. Who was supposed to go first? Sarah waited for him, he waited for her, they exchanged smiles and stared at the opposing walls until Sarah coughed and inched forward a step. Lee inched forward a step. Sarah took another step and Lee took another step and now they had left the corridor and were in the small room.

"Nice, good room," Lee said, hands still clasped.

"Yes." Sarah watched him as his eyes fell on the bed. "Why don't I put this on ice?"

"Thought we didn't have any."

"No, we don't. Then we should open it before it gets warm."

"Yeah, so okay." Lee smiled, took the bottle, laid it on the desk and popped it open. Where was the music, Sarah thought, and dim lights? She wouldn't dare dim the lights. In fact, every lamp in the room was on. He should turn off the desk lamp illuminating the foamy champagne. The very desk lamp suddenly covered with foamy champagne. The very desk lamp Sarah started cleaning as Lee poured out the champagne and extended it to her and she took it, a damp Kleenex in her left hand, her right hand, trembling, clinking her glass to his. Again they smiled.

"So." Lee moved near her. Sarah gazed into his eyes, shook, wanted to caress his cheeks and instead bumped her behind into the desk. "Uh, a toast?"

"Yeah," she said too quickly. To love, to pleasure, to sin, to us.

"To me and you." Lee grinned, Sarah grinned, they sipped, and she wondered when she should slip off the jacket. She didn't have to wonder too long because he laid down his glass and took off her coat. Her eyes fell on the floor, in the same direction of the jacket, until his hands cupped her chin and brought her face to his.

He kissed her without opening her mouth, just a gentle kiss. No tongues thrashing about and arms locked around each other. Merely a gentle, inviting kiss. It should be tongues thrashing about and arms pulling at clothes, because that was the way it should be and the way Sarah imagined it, and she was allowing him to take the lead when it was her night.

"Hey, Sarah, you nervous or somethin'?" Lee whispered.

"Of course not." Liar. "Not at all." Touch him, you can't go any further back on the desk. "I've been thinking, uh, about this for a while." Undo his clothes. She did. Quickly unknot his tie. She couldn't, instead caught her fingers in a loop and he had to extricate her quivering fingers so they could manage to daintily release his buttons. She wasn't dainty nor could she undo his buttons, because her fingers got curled about in his chest hair. Should've stayed in the chest hair but hurried down the shirt, nearly popping off a button as his hands grazed up and down her hips. She was supposed to giggle and feel goose bumps and press her body against his. She did giggle but it was out of fear, and the goose bumps emanated from her lowered body temperature, and she did press against him but that was because she couldn't believe how many buttons he had on his shirt.

Then his pants fell down around his ankles. His shirt was open, somehow his jacket was on the desk, barely missing the spilled champagne. Pants around his socks and shoes, shirt ajar, leg hair rising up and twisting about his skimpy black bikini shorts. So far that was the only thing that was the way it was supposed to be. Not the only thing. Through her feeble fumblings Sarah hadn't even realized that her nightie was off and she was completely naked. He wasn't. She was. He got first look. His smile widened in joy. Not lust. It was supposed to be lust. No, it was supposed to be her lust, but she had to fight back a laugh because he looked so silly with his pants around his shoes.

"What's so funny?" He chuckled.

"Nothing." She chuckled nervously, reached for him, more stumbled than reached, and since his pants had trapped his feet

222

she fell atop him and onto the bed. Finally something was the way it was supposed to be. She atop him. He didn't let that last too long, because he had to ease her off him so he could pull off his shoes and socks and pants. Sarah watched his broad back as he removed the remnants of his clothes and she started to slide up the bed, stopped, wondered if she should just lie on her back, didn't, just lay on her side and stared at the door and waited for him to slide his own strong fingers down her back. He jabbed her in the small of her back.

"Uh, ya think maybe we could switch sides, I kinda like to stay on the right side of the bed." Lee sat up, motioning to Sarah.

"Right side?" She stared at him. Naked. Broad, hairy, olive-skinned upper body bristling with well-defined muscles sloping down to a flat, hard stomach which descended into a forest of black pubic hair containing a semierection, which now turned more semi than erect because she stared at him.

"I—okay." She crawled on her knees and hands over to the left side and he crawled onto the right side. Now she turned back to him as he turned to her. She should've taken him in her arms, but he took her in his arms, once more pressing her against him and kissing her neck. She was supposed to kiss his neck. She did. Concentrating on kissing his neck. Cautiously, methodically kissing one side of his neck as his tongue slithered down her neck and moved just above her breasts. She spent careful moments on his neck before she realized she was supposed to nibble on his ear because the ear was in the general direction her tongue was taking her mouth, and she thought it was the same way she spread cream cheese on a bagel. Or vacuumed each and every corner of the carpet, cutting the carpet into little squares and ensuring each and every square had been annihilated of dirt before moving on to the next one.

Lee giggled as she bit on his earlobe.

"Makes me laugh," he said in explanation.

"Should I stop?"

"No." He grinned and kissed her mouth as he clambered atop her. Her hands grazed up and down his back with methodical precision, as she had always finished every bit of food in her refrigerator before going on to the next bit of food, even if the food

223

she was eating was on the verge of going bad. That is how she grazed his strong back as he wildly kissed her shoulders.

"You uncomfortable?" Sarah asked.

"No." Lee tried to balance himself flush upon her. "You?"

"No. A little."

"Want me to lean on the side?"

"Can you?"

He didn't say anything. Just leaned on his side and grabbed her right breast. Her 34B right breast. No freckles or moles or birthmarks. He didn't seem to search for them, just allowed his tongue to dart around her breast as he cupped the other one and she squeezed his thick hair, starting on one side, then moving to the other. Always in order. Always called friends in order. Alphabetical order. No one had ever caught on. Lisa never realized that Sarah called Annie and Donna and Harriet before Lisa. No one ever knew. Maybe Sarah didn't even know, maybe Sarah suddenly realized that as her hands dug into his hair and she felt something like a moan escape her lips. A moan not forced as it had always been with Danny, just a moan that came from somewhere within her and wasn't ordered and was prompted by this young man with broad shoulders she was having an affair with. Broad shoulders that weren't quite as broad as she'd imagined once he took his shirt off. So she closed her eyes and his shoulders broadened. As did the tongue that caressed her and the mouth that kissed her, and she knew she would have to, eventually, grab his penis, and wondered if it would be as long as it really was or as it should be. Or shriveled like her father's when she'd stumbled into the bathroom while he was getting dressed. So she started opening her eyes, quickly saw the penis, then closed them again and just grabbed this person's penis. It didn't matter whose penis it was, could've been her father's or Danny's or Lee's, or just someone's, for all that mattered was that it was a penis the size she wanted and a body built the way she wanted. And the penis entered, straight in, straight out, and the body leaned and rotated up against her and she heard a deeper moan. Whose moan? A woman's moan. Not a moan from down the hallway, muted by rock music. Not a moan from down near her parents' room, muted by guilt. This was her moan she heard. Her

224

body she felt. And then it started happening and what was it? A fantasy? A reality? No, her orgasm. Her orgasm. It kept building and spraying over her and from somewhere she heard a man grunt and cry out as she cried out and then it was over.

"So." Lee rolled over, handed her a cigarette, which she wanted to refuse, started to accept, finally refused.

"Yes?" Sarah held his hand, squeezed it tenderly, feeling sorry for him that she had used him so, just to satisfy herself. Not guilt over having an orgasm but over not knowing who had produced it.

"I knew you were thinkin' of your husband, huh?" Lee asked softly, so soft it was almost a whimper.

"No," Sarah whispered back. "I didn't think about Danny. Not really about Danny."

"Then me?"

Sarah stared at him and he winced. Or maybe she just thought he winced. Maybe she wanted him to wince because he should wince.

"Someone else?" Lee blew smoke in the air.

"No, no one, I . . . no one else. I thought of my father a little. Weird, huh?"

"Dunno." Lee paused. "Sure just your father?"

"I don't know who I thought of. I'm sorry, I hurt you."

"No, s'okay." He smiled.

"No, it's not, tell me, I hurt you, I didn't think of you, please, you can tell me."

"Ya know, Sarah . . ." He measured his words. "I dunno, maybe you think of me as some kinda macho type, I dunno, really. But, ya know, I kinda felt you weren't here, that's all . . . that, sounds strange, but you were making love to yourself."

"I think I was." She didn't whisper, nor did she shout, just said it casually because there was no need to whisper or shout. No need to do anything except hold his hand. For the last time because there would be no more hand-holding with Lee. Danny was supposed to come home. And there might be no more hand-holding with him, either. And then what? If I can make love to myself, can I live with myself? By myself? What if this entire

225

summer had only been bearable because you knew he was coming home. And if that wasn't true, then where do you go from here? To more hotel rendezvous? No, because you haven't come this far just to have an orgasm. That wasn't why you've done all this.

But then why have you?

Chapter 22

In a few hours, it would be time to clean out his locker. Unlike the others, Danny had no place to bring his locker contents to. He wasn't going to the Puerto Rican Winter League or some instructional league in Florida or Arizona. No other organizations had scouted him with the thought of drafting him at the winter meetings. All he had to take out of his locker was his glove and white socks. He'd already disposed of all the fan mail, disposed of it by throwing it away and never answering any of the letters. Not that the others had much more to clean out, but at least they had hope.

"Don't look," B.K. snapped at Danny as they stood near the batting cage before the last game of the year.

"At what?" Danny had just been examining the stands, suddenly incapable of focusing upon practice.

"At him." B.K.'s round eyes hardened. "Scumbag from the Atlanta organization's up there, scum who cut me, said I couldn't make it, didn't have it. Scumbag is up there."

"Where?" Danny started to look, but B.K. clumped his elbow with the bat.

"I said don't look. In the fifth row, flowered shirt, wart on his neck, right side, mean eyes, ugly mother, hate his guts. Want you to watch him for me when I take my cuts, want you to tell me if he reacts, if he takes notes."

Danny started to look, again B.K. rapped him with the bat.

"Don't make like you're looking, okay?" he ordered, stepping into the cage.

Hope. At least they had the false hope. The hope of another year in which a few points were added to a batting average, the hope of a few more homers or runs batted in or someone from either the Yankees or another organization taking notice of them. They still had hope because they were still young.

Danny heard the crack of B.K.'s practice swings and watched the ugly man with the wart put aside his scouting pad and stare at a voluptuous blonde with breasts dangling out of her halter top. Danny stared at the man and hated him, despised him for hurting B.K., maybe more than that, despised him for making him lie to B.K.

"So?" B.K. rapped his bat against Danny's side.

"What?"

"What'd he do? You see them shots of mine, shit. So, his wart bulge out?"

"Oh yeah, mother's wart nearly came off, shoulda seen him, B.K., you really impressed him, really did a number on him."

B.K. considered this while staring at the end of his bat.

"Know something, I'd like to have them draft me just so I could refuse, shit, so I could tell 'em to shove it up their asses and have it come outta their noses, shit." B.K. stomped in a tight circle. "Really made notes on me?" Danny nodded. "Good. Shit. Heard they could use a right-handed hittin' outfielder. Mothers. Once I get into their camp, show 'em what I can do."

"Bet he'll regret reporting to cut you in the first place."

What was one more lie to them? Or him? He'd spent the entire summer lying, so why not end it on a coherent note? Another lie to B.K. and when the Atlanta organization didn't draft him, he'd ascribe it to racial prejudice or personal animosity from the scout instead of the simple fact that B.K. was nothing more than a Class A ballplayer. But at least he wouldn't have to know that, unlike Danny, who had to know that for all his ravings last night at synagogue nothing had been accomplished except losing Colleen, that this entire summer, in fact, had produced—what? He didn't know. He did know he loved Colleen. Didn't love Colleen. Missed Sarah. Didn't miss Sarah. Still couldn't hit a curve ball. Could hit a curve ball.

And, as the last game of the year entered the fourth inning, with Greensboro already having clinched last place and opponent Shelby destined to finish fourth, Danny had accepted everything. Even though he hadn't. But no matter what, there was nothing he could do. Or so he thought.

He hadn't expected some acne-ridden kid in a Shelby uniform to provide the catalyst for what Danny mistakenly thought would be an avenue to truth. Surely the kid with acne didn't know that. Nor did Danny, nor did Pete. No one did. No one thought anything of the racing line drive hurtling up the alley in left-center field because it looked like any other line drive which would come between Danny and Pete, and Danny would call Pete off and make the catch and throw it back in, so Pete would gratefully wink from over in left field.

And that was how Danny viewed it as he waved his arms to signal for the ball. Pete started slowing down. And Danny looked at Pete, at the poet, at the friend who had sacrificed a season of his short life for him. Danny also slowed as he watched Pete, watched Pete's sudden puzzlement, watched Pete's growing alarm because Danny had stopped still. Stood in place because Pete could just as easily catch the ball, could just as easily fire it back in and try and keep the Shelby base runners affixed to second and third. Pete could do it. And Pete was going to do it, was going to face up to it, even if Danny couldn't. Pete was going to make the catch.

But Pete didn't make the catch. He, too, slowed, then stopped as the ball raced between them and bounded up against the wall, and the startled Shelby runners raced home and Jones screamed from the dugout. Screamed and raved as Danny and Pete just looked at each other.

"Get it," Danny yelled.

Pete didn't move.

"Get it." Danny half-started to the ball. Pete half-followed. Danny seized Pete's arm and almost flung him against the wall. Pete bounded back, the ball resting at their feet.

"Danny, please throw it," Pete pleaded.

Danny stared at the ball, then up at Pete. Harshly, mercilessly.

"Throw it, damnit, you can, you know. Just throw it this one time, let me see, throw the damn ball!"

"I can't."

"Throw the fucking ball!"

The runner sped around third, too late for a throw from either of them to do any good. Pete glared at Danny, reached for the ball, then kicked it viciously so the ball bounced against Danny's knee and skittered along the wall away from them. Danny didn't watch the ball, just watched Pete storm back to his position.

They all shook their heads as Danny and Pete walked past the cubicles and into Jones's office after the game. Pete received sympathy, Danny hostility. He could understand neither, but then again, didn't care. He knew why he'd done it, knew it was wrong, but then, it was wrong of Pete to care about him so much to sacrifice so much for him. That had been embarrassing to him. Now it would end, along with everything else, the friendly condescension and the friendly lies. Everything would end because he'd gone against his instincts and forced Pete to throw the ball.

"Lousy, I have seen them all. I have watched the greats, the near-greats, those who thought they were great and weren't and those who were great but didn't know it and I ain't never seen such nonsense as that, so why don't you tell me what the hell you were doing out there?" Jones ranted. Danny started to speak, realized that Jones had been looking directly at Pete all this time, that the question didn't include him. Maybe he didn't even belong in the office. When Horace had shouted into the locker, he'd only mentioned Pete's name, not Danny's.

Fuck that, Danny thought.

"Horace, it was . . ." he started.

"Talkin' to Pete." Horace didn't look at Danny, who didn't look back, who didn't know where to look except at his shoes.

"Don't know what I was thinkin' 'bout, Horace," Pete said, shaking his head. "Coulda sworn that dang ball was mine, but I kinda got inna way of Danny and he was gonna t'row it in, but I kinda accidentally like kicked it with my dang feet."

Why was he talking like Gomer Pyle? Danny wondered, knowing Pete had always talked slightly different with the others, but never quite as pronounced a difference.

"It was your ball, Kelly," Horace said coldly. "You know this field better'n him"—he jerked his thumb at Danny—"and you know how the ball skips around but that ain't even the worst

230

part, kickin' the ball was the worst part and maybe you forgotten you ain't playin' no foreign soccer game but good old American baseball."

"Got confused, Skip," Pete said softly. Danny stared at him.

"Or maybe you just can't throw the ball, huh, that it? Been watchin' you all year long now, keepin' my eyes on you and everytime you hadda make a throw, you let Neuman make it for you, played on his sympathies because he's a nice guy."

Oh right, nice guy, Danny thought. Really nice guy. If you're such a sweetheart, then you should stick up for him.

"Not true," Danny said quietly. "I never . . ."

"Danny." Now Horace's voice was almost tender, almost deferential. "Maybe you can just wait outside for a while, okay? I got somethin' to talk to you about, tell you later, why don't you just wait outside for a while, okay?"

Stay, Danny thought as he rose. Show some guts. You had enough guts with some bar mitzvah, have some guts here. You have nothing to lose, damnit, stay and defend your friend the way he's defended you all year, damnit, stay.

Danny walked out the door, ashamed of himself. Ashamed of Pete for making him do something to shame himself. Ashamed of Horace for picking on someone as vulnerable as Pete. Ashamed of the team because they all glared at him and instead they should've placed him in a torture chamber. Ashamed of the whole world.

"Danny, if you don't put those ugly white socks in the wash today, I can't wash them in the machine anymore if you don't put them in right now, right this instant," his mother shouted as Danny sat on his bed, holding his graying white socks behind his back.

"They're not dirty."

"Daniel, don't aggravate your mother like this. Let her clean your socks."

"I don't know if I can anymore, they'll stink up everything. So I'll have to wash them by hand, so I'll have a little extra housework, who cares anyway?"

"No." Danny shook his head. "You'll wash the luck off."

"You can't wash luck off," his father chuckled. "Maybe a little

bit will come off on our clothes. You think maybe you'd like to give your father some luck, maybe turn one of my boxer shorts into lucky shorts, I should have some mazel." His father held out his hand.

Danny clenched the white socks, held them above his valise, didn't drop them in or do anything, because all he could do was stare into his locker.

"Hello." Pete sat beside him. Danny couldn't look up. He was too angry at both of them to look up. "Could leave a few things, there, okay? You'll be back."

"Yeah," Danny chuckled. "Real soon." He forced himself to look at Pete. "Sorry I got you in trouble."

"Okay. Couldn't hide it much longer. Wanted to ask you, though, uh, if you were sticking around for a while."

"I don't know." Danny shook his head. "I don't know anything anymore."

"See, on Wednesday, I have to go to the doctors and I need a way out and, I, I wondered if you could cover for me. You're a writer, you can come up with some excuse to get me out of it. Something credible. Maybe we can consult Steinbeck, see if he can help with a good story."

"Why?" Danny peered. "Why not just go?"

"You know."

"No. Just go. What's to worry about?"

"Don't want the team to know."

"Know what?"

"About my arm."

"Nothing wrong with your arm," Danny snapped. Jeez, enough already.

"Who said so?" Pete frowned. "Course there's something wrong with my arm. You knew that. That is why I couldn't throw well, because of my arm."

"Pete," Danny hissed. "Damn, Pete, okay stop? Huh, stop, I know you faked it, that's why I did that today, because I'm a shmuck."

"Isaac Singer uses shmuck, doesn't he?"

"Yes." Danny sighed. "So, please."

"Please what? You think I do not have a sore arm? You crazy or somethin'?"

232

"Yeah, well, probably. I do know the story. How Antonheimer told you to fake an injury so I could play center and . . ."

"Gosh darn, you are one stupid Yankee and here I thought all you Jews were supposed to be so dang smart," Pete shouted. "You think I would fake an injury? How come?"

"Because they told you to. Because I was the gimmick. Because you cared about me and this didn't mean as much to you as to me."

"Bullshit. You t'ink I'd go through all this horseshit all these years and give it up for you? T'ink I wouldn't wanna play center 'cause I feel sorry for you? You crazy or somethin'? You must be, man."

"You were really hurt?"

"Damn straight I was hurt and I was countin' on you to cover for me so them team doctors wouldn't go 'round pokin' at my arm, so's I can go back to Kentucky and get it treated and so's I don't come to camp next year as the guy with the bad arm. Sheet, you really thought I was fakin' it?"

"Then I was playing center on my own?"

"Shit, no, Danny, shit no." Pete purpled. "You can bet your butt if my arm was okay I woulda kept you onna bench. Don't care none how good friends we were, ain't no way I'd ever give up the only thing that's ever got me up inna mornin's for you. Gosh dang, Danny, you're a goddamn fool."

"What if you were healthy, what if I was healthy, what if I did beat you out on my own skills, what then?"

"Hah and hah shit to that, man. Even if you did beat me out, I know's I woulda beat you out 'cause the day I stop thinkin' I ain't the next Winfield is the day I stop doin' all this." Pete panted, recovered, tried to retrieve the remnants of their friendship, suddenly dead. He asked, unable to plead, actually harsh, "So cover for me."

"No." Danny shook his head. "No."

Pete whirled away and stomped to his cubicle, angrily flinging articles into his bag as the clubhouse remained still, until Horace's booming voice shattered everything.

"So, Neuman, whatdaya think?" Horace clasped Danny on the shoulder.

"About what?" Danny stared into his locker.

" 'Bout yourself, huh? I know, you did a helluva job for me, that's all, a helluva job. Could put you in any situation and you'd come out there with your head on your shoulders."

"Yeah, well, you helped me a lot, Horace."

"Think so?" Danny didn't see how Horace beamed.

"Oh yeah, been real good."

"Taught you stuff, right?" Danny nodded. "Hittin' and throwin', finer points of the game, right?"

"Absolutely." Danny turned to watch Pete finish cleaning out his cubicle.

"Think I was a good manager?" Danny nodded. "Ain't easy bein' a good manager. Everyone's got gripes, can't please everyone." Danny saw Kafka drop into Pete's bag. "So you'll tell 'em that, how good a manager I was to you?"

"Yeah, sure, Horace, I'll tell all my friends." Danny winced as he saw *The Grapes of Wrath* clunk into Pete's bag.

"Friends? Hell, who cares 'bout your friends? Tell 'em up there." Horace pointed upward.

Danny followed the raised finger. Great, six months to live.

"When I go up there, I'll mention you to Saint Peter, Horace, I promise, soon as I check in."

"What's with Saint Peter?" Horace laughed. "Them, up there, not up, up there. Just up there."

Whatever noise there had been, died. Whatever had occupied the clubhouse evaporated as all turned to stare at Danny's stiffened back, though he was aware of only one pair of eyes.

"What are you talking about?" Danny whispered, knowing it couldn't be what he thought.

"The big club."

"Big club?"

Pete just froze and stared at Danny, who was already frozen and staring into his almost empty locker.

"Which big club?"

"Yankees."

"Who?"

"Sure, the Yankees, gotta join 'em in New York, gotta blow town, get onna big bird and catch some currents and hit your Apple Town. Heard they got big plans for you."

234

"The Yankees?" It wasn't Danny but Pete who said the words, said them for Danny.

"Why?" Danny asked his locker. Horace answered for the locker, explaining in rambling fashion how the Yankees had suffered another wave of injuries and were scouring the system for replacements and besides the Boss was displeased with the team's poor showing and wanted to clean house and . . .

Danny listened, vaguely, even as he brushed past Horace to stand, even as Horace continued babbling and players approached to congratulate him, even if he didn't want their congratulations, because he didn't believe what was happening, so how could you accept congratulations? Holding his valise, now completely filled with the contents of his cubicle, Danny walked over to Pete, hunched over, just staring, maybe jealous, maybe hurt, maybe confused, maybe none of the above. Danny would never know what was coursing through Pete Kelly at that exact moment. Nor did Danny know what was coursing through him, why he unzipped his valise and removed the white socks, removed his copy of Steinbeck, and dropped the socks upon *In Dubious Battle* at the bottom of Pete's cubicle as he walked past the shocked handshakes and out the door.

Chapter 23

Steam. Everywhere the steam. Fogging the windows. Trickling beneath the door. Obliterating the sign, NEUMAN'S CLEANERS—SAME DAY SERVICE. GROUP RATES AVAILABLE.

He stared at the familiar steam, the familiar fogged windows, the familiar sign as dumbly as he had stared at the phone booth last night, wondering whom to call, whom to tell of his wonderful news. He had dialed Colleen's number, but it had been busy. Dialed again, again it had been busy. Once more . . .

"Hello?"

He had hung up, searched for another dime. This time he had dialed Sarah, collect. No answer. He had waited five minutes, tried again. No answer. Then who? His parents, no, not his parents, because his brother would be there, and he didn't want any disparaging words from his brother about the bar-mitzvah riot. About then, Danny's own steam had misted and he had realized he really couldn't call anyone. To call anyone and share this moment would have only lessened it somehow. It would no longer belong solely to him. Someone's congratulations and joy or even puzzlement would intrude upon what he had done. What should he do then? Get drunk? No amount of alcohol could match his own sober intoxication. Shout? Someone would notice and partake in his joy, or berate him and minimize his joy, or scare him. And he was joyfully terrified enough. He was a New York Yankee. What exactly did that mean?

"Now Young's already mentioned you in his *Post* column this morning," said Yankees PR Director Paul Peterson upon meeting Danny at LaGuardia. "He'll probably stop by the clubhouse early, Dave Anderson might want to do a column on you, both WCBS and WNBC want a minute or so, still working on WABC. So you've gotta get to the park reasonably early, I'll go over everything with you, suggest things for you to say."

"I know what to say." Danny had scooped his luggage off the rotating luggage bin. "Don't worry, I know what to say."

Of course he didn't know what to say. What could he say? Probably depended on what they asked, but he knew what they would ask. How it felt. Jeez, how the hell was he supposed to know how it felt? He couldn't describe it, but they'd demand he put it into words. With fear and some sort of resentment he couldn't quite place, Danny had darted away from Peterson, promising to arrive early, even extra-special early because supposedly the Boss himself wanted to talk to him. The Boss had big plans for him.

"People say we're out of the Division race, but I don't believe we're out of it yet and this team better not believe they're out of it yet," the Boss had screamed beneath the screaming *Post* headline, MIDDLE-AGED PHENOM TO START TONITE? Couldn't the headline at least not have had a question mark, Danny thought, scurrying past the Boss's comments about complacency and long-term contracts and infusing the team with fresh blood. He had stared at the print, fighting back the urge to stare at his own photo on the back page of the *Post*. Danny Neuman, a slightly foolish grin, still wearing a Greensboro Hornets cap and uniform. Soon to be wearing the uniform of the New York Yankees. A New York Yankee. A mistake? No. He was a New York Yankee. Really and truly a New York Yankee. And because he was really and truly a New York Yankee, Danny found himself opening the door of his father's store.

The bell tinkled but the bent frame of his father didn't leap around from behind the pressing machines. Maybe he'd gone deaf from too many years of too many bells tinkling and permitting too many people to hand him their dirt. Maybe he didn't want to hear the bell anymore. Danny stood off to the side, looking around at all the clever little signs like IN GOD WE TRUST, BUT NOT YOUR CHECKS or IF CLEANLINESS IS NEXT TO GODLINESS, IMAGINE HOW HOLY MARTINIZING IS. Danny read the signs he'd never really seen before, though he had seen them a thousand times, and avoided the irritated stare of a fat, ugly woman clutching and crinkling two huge, ugly dresses.

"Could you bust?" she snapped at Danny. Yes, he could, he wanted to tell her, but didn't and looked at his shoes. Shoes, not sneakers, and he felt even more uncomfortable, the woman's mutterings not helping. "Ten minutes already I've been here, a loyal customer for all these years," he heard her say as he intently stared at his shoes.

"Just an hour, Danny," his father said as Danny shrank, squishing the baseball into his glove.

"Daddy, I gotta game."

"So? They can't wait for you. They can't wait maybe an hour?"

"I really gotta go. But, you know, if you really need my help. . ."

"No, no, not too busy, go, play your baseball. I just thought you might want to stay here, maybe . . ." Mr. Neuman had shrugged, his face seized with the sadness of a man whose sole legacy to his son is a last name. "Just be home on time for dinner. Your mother's making brisket and you know how you aggravate her when you're late and the food isn't hot."

"Jack, *nu*, you still there or what?"

Danny watched his father move toward the counter, saw the kindly expression grow disarmingly placable, then stiffen as he saw Danny, no longer looking at his shoes, no longer looking at his father but at some point beyond him.

"Danny." He bounded around the counter, brushed past the woman and stopped in front of his son. They stared, too old for a hug, too intimate for a handshake.

"Jack, I have a beauty parlor appointment, what do you think?" The woman rescued them as Jack Neuman backed toward her, still looking at Danny, half-smiling, as Danny half-smiled.

"Esther." Jack motioned to Danny and he moved forward half

238

a foot, still securely away from both of them. "Esther, this is Danny, my son, Danny."

"The rabbi?"

"No, not him," Jack said, harshly, fiercely. Danny flinched, startled by the tone, embarrassed for his father because he couldn't possibly top the introduction of my son the rabbi with my son the what. "No, my youngest son."

"I didn't know you had one."

"I told you all about him," Jack said, reddening and seizing Danny by the elbow. "The uh, he's a . . . what?" his father asked him. "He's a . . ." Now Danny coughed to interrupt.

"Writer." Danny shook his head at his father, who peered in possible comprehension, in certain disappointment.

"Oh?" Her voice rose. "And so what do you write?"

"Stories. Good stories for good magazines. A good writer, Danny is." His father said this with strained conviction and tossed guarded annoyance toward Danny, who fielded it and turned upon Esther. By now, her interest had waned. Obviously Danny wasn't an important enough writer. Obviously any comparison between her son David, who was probably a podiatrist whom she called doctor, and Danny was so mismatched as to embarrass Jack. To whom she had been a loyal customer and from whom she needed these two dresses by tomorrow. He quickly wrote up the cleaning order, kept scribbling on the pad until she left, then moved back behind the counter, looking at Danny.

"I could've told her," Jack whispered.

"What, that I'm a ballplayer?"

"Is that a disgrace?"

"No."

"So then?"

"Just didn't want her to know."

"Why?" Another question. His father had actually asked him two questions.

"Because if she asks a question I have to give an answer, and I don't want to give an answer and be rude and louse up a loyal customer of ten years for you, okay?" He said it too sharply, both regretting and enjoying his tone.

"Or that you think I don't talk about you, that it?" Jack fiddled with his pen, the same black pen Danny remembered. "I do, you know, all the time. Talk about you."

"Yeah, okay."

"I do, she doesn't know, she's just senile from sitting under a hair dryer every Friday for God knows how long. I do talk about you," Jack said softly.

"I believe you, Dad."

"No, you don't." Jack fiddled with his pad now, leaning against the counter, Danny on the other side.

"Yeah, sure, I do. It's okay. Besides," Danny forced a smile, "what's better than the son a rabbi, huh?"

"And what's wrong with the son a ballplayer?"

"And what's wrong with just a son?" Danny returned the hostility.

So again they both looked away.

"Nothing," his father said quietly. Still examining his pad, he asked, "So you're here for long?"

"Until I fuck up, I guess."

"Are you planning on fucking up?"

"Never heard you swear before," Danny said, slipping both hands in his back pockets.

"You did once."

"When?"

"*Momzer. Feshtay momzer?*"

"*Feshtay,* so what?" Danny peered, removed his hands from his back pockets and sought something to play with, like the glove and ball he had always brought into the store. He no longer had them, but his father still had the pad, and that angered Danny and drew him closer to the counter. "What's that mean, I heard you say bastard?"

"Because I heard," his father muttered.

"Heard what?" Right, he heard. The bar mitzvah. Colleen. What else? What is he hearing and what is he talking about?

"That Gottlieb told Nathan what happened."

"Nathan? I thought Nathan was in the Middle East."

"The Arabs canceled his visa."

Great, another reason not to like Camp David.

240

"And of course Nathan told you."

"Did you think otherwise?"

"I don't know."

"Did you care?"

"If it upset you and Mommy, yeah, I care."

"So then why?" Now Jack's tone lost its sharpness, evolved into pained curiosity.

"Because. Because I had to, okay?" Danny played with his thumbs. "So, what's new with you, how's Mommy?"

"She's fine, she bakes, she gets pains. I press. I steam. Other things."

"What other things?"

"Why won't you tell me why?"

"I dunno." Danny sighed. "Maybe I don't want a lecture, okay?"

"Have I ever lectured you?"

"No."

"So then, what else? Never a lecture. A talk. Did we ever have a talk?"

"Sure."

"When?"

"I dunno."

"Remember once."

"I can't." He couldn't remember and couldn't bother pretending he had merely forgotten.

"Then, so why? Tell me why you did it?" Abruptly his father reddened and Danny feared he would have a stroke, drop dead over his pad, his damn pad and his damn leaky pen.

"I just did, okay? I couldn't go through with it, damnit, okay? I'm sorry I brought disgrace."

"What did you do so wrong?"

"I . . ." Danny blinked, studied his father. "The bar mitzvah down there, right, isn't that what we're talking about?"

"The bar mitzvah." Jack's voice was hoarse.

"So, that's what I'm saying."

"Which bar mitzvah?" His father's lips pulled and tugged, bit nervously and Danny recalled the nervous nibbling of the lower lip, not from his father but from one of his own schoolyard

241

teammates who had told him he always nibbled on his lower lip whenever he was behind on the count.

"What are you saying?" Danny shouted, wanted to reach behind the counter but couldn't.

"Your bar mitzvah."

"Mine?"

"Yours. Your bar mitzvah. Remember? You did that at that Southern bar mitzvah because of what happened at your bar mitzvah, right?"

"Partly. Maybe. Other stuff, okay? A lot happened to me down there. I just got fed up, probably took it out on the wrong occasion, should've—I dunno. You feeling okay?"

"Why won't you talk to me?"

"Because I don't want to go into it, okay, that good enough? How's Mommy?"

"You call her yet to ask in person?"

"No."

"You call Sarah yet?"

"No one."

"Me first. You come to me first, why? To watch me press and steam? You never wanted to before."

"I'm sorry for that."

"Why? Because you didn't want to watch your foolish father press and clean other people's filth? What is there to apologize for? I don't ask you to stand and watch, I want you to talk to me."

"I don't want to talk about that, okay, okay, okay? Good enough, *feshtay* okay, huh?"

"So then when? On my deathbed will you talk to me? Or maybe I'll squeeze your hand good-bye and you'll talk about the weather?"

"Will you stop being so fucking morbid, jeez, deathbed. Will you just . . ."

"No, you just." His father bounded back around the counter and now stood inches from Danny. "Maybe I want to talk to you. You ever think that, maybe I want to talk to you, maybe I have things to talk to you about?"

"Since when?" Danny glared. "Jeez, you just came back from

242

behind the fuckin' counter to talk to me, you never did before, you always stayed behind the goddamned counter whenever I came into the store. You, you would hold the pad, like you wanted me to take off my jeans so you could clean them, so I wouldn't be any different from Esther with her beauty parlor appointments. So now you want to talk to me, huh, well maybe I don't want to, okay?"

"Hebrew School," Jack flushed and muttered.

"What?"

"I knew. About Hebrew School. I knew."

"Hebrew School? What I did in Hebrew School this is about? You want to talk about that, why, you want to punish me?"

"I never punished you."

"But why are you so damned angry?"

"I'm not angry," his father shouted.

"God damn you, you're not making any sense," Danny screamed back, squeezed his father's arm, felt the bone beneath the hanging flesh, felt frightened and tried to pull away, but his father grabbed Danny by the hand. "Talk sense, please."

"I am. I knew."

"What?"

"I knew about you, but you never knew about me. Never. I knew how you faked your Haftorah, I knew it. You loused up. You gave yourself away. I knew it. Maybe everyone knew it. I knew how you accented it, you did it phonetically, right, tell me, right?" Danny nodded dumbly. "Me, too."

"You?"

"I did. Cheated on my Haftorah. Why, you want to know? Because I had to, because my father forced me, because he said I had to and I never asked him about it and he never explained it, so I went to the *shul* and studied there, phonetically. All right then, but I went to the rabbi but, no, not you, you wouldn't obey me, never obeyed me."

"I'm sorry, I . . ."

"You don't listen to me?" Jack screamed. "Why should you obey me when the only time I ordered you to do something made you so miserable you had to cheat. Do you think I care you cheated, no, not that, not that . . ." His face started turning away and Danny seized it as severely as he'd ever seized anything, thought his father's face would crack in his hands.

"Then what?"

"*Feshtay momzer?*" Jack whispered. "*Momzer.* I wanted you to know why, that scene I made. For twenty years I wanted you to know why I made that scene."

"Because you cheated?"

"No, no, does it matter what I ever did, or didn't do?"

"Don't say that about yourself." Danny tightened his grip on the arm.

"I'll say what I want, okay, what I want. I made that scene for show, okay? I listened to you read the Haftorah and heard myself at my bar mitzvah. I heard the same wrong accenting of the *baruchs* and *awtaws* and knew I had done it, but no one ever caught me. You were caught."

"Come on, you know the only reason the rabbi was pissed was because I didn't go to his lousy school and give him the tuition."

"And I shouldn't have made you go. But when he said that, I had to do something. Something for you. Something so you would know about how I . . . what else? To come up to you afterwards and say it was all right? I never did that, so how could you know? Only when you slept. With your croup. I sat with you when your mother had already gone to sleep. Then I would talk to you, when you couldn't hear me."

"I thought that was Mommy," Danny whispered.

"Never your mother, she was too busy fainting. Me. In the chair. Remember the chair? Talking to you when you couldn't hear and maybe when I couldn't hear, either. So I had to do something for you. I made myself angry. But I wasn't angry. That was a fakery. I couldn't just sit there, as always, like some lump on the log, so I bounced up and I did it for show, because I thought that was what a father should do, should protect his son, even against a man of God in the Lord's house. I thought I should do it but I never felt the angry feelings, never. Only now, when I realized why I did it, that I could've knocked aside your grandfather and your Uncle Seymour and Aunt Gussie, if I was really mad. But I wasn't, so I let them hold me back. Even when I faked it I didn't do it right, but I did it anyway, because I thought a father should do that. Maybe you would know. You never did, so what good was it?"

"I was proud of you, Daddy." Danny clasped his father's shoulder. "That day, boy, was I proud of the way you helped me."

"I didn't do anything," Jack whispered, half-leaning against his son's chest until Danny gently pushed him back and squeezed both his shoulders.

"Doesn't matter why. Just that you did it."

They exchanged awkward grins, kept their hands upon each other.

"So, Dad."

"So, Daniel."

"What other things?" Danny grinned.

"Things. A thing or two."

"Like?"

"Like I'm reading more. Accounting books."

"You are?"

"Don't get so excited." Jack returned behind the counter, picked up his pad and pencil, maybe waiting for Danny to join him back there. Danny didn't and Jack shrugged lightly. "I read up on the books. It got so my mind was so soft I couldn't handle the *TV Guide* anymore. I thought, maybe, Jack, you're not that old yet, you should read something. Not garbage, something that interests you."

"You going to school?" Danny walked behind the counter, took away the pad and pencil and forced his father to stare straight at him, pad, pencil, glove and ball gone.

"What, school?" Jack chuckled. "No. I read myself. So this way, that accountant of mine, he can't fool around. I can read the books better now. Nothing big."

"You never know." Danny smiled. "You still could end up with Price, Waterhouse, you know? Still count the Academy Awards."

"Ah." Jack shook his head, grinning. "Me with movie stars, what would I say to Robert Redford?"

"Something. I think you'd find something to say."

"Something, yeah? For thirty-three years all I could ever say to my son was not to bother me when I'm watching wrestling, when some bastard was beating up Bruno Sammartino, breaking his neck that time."

"Sammartino never got his neck broken, Dad."

"No?" Jack's smile widened. "Sprained maybe? Had to be at least a bad sprain."

"Right, Dad. A sprain. A bad sprain."

Chapter 24

There'd been no shock when she'd heard. Only hurt. Or so Sarah thought, because she started crying, and she'd always been taught that you only cry when you're hurt. And don't cry out of joy because that's a waste of time, nor out of frustration because that's self-defeating. Only hurt. Hurt at seeing his face flashed on the eleven o'clock sports report, accompanied by some mindless drivel. Hurt at him not telling her. Hurt at him coming home.

She sat crying, motionless, long after Danny's face beneath a Hornets cap had disappeared from the screen and the final American League scores replaced it. Then she rose, at first forcing it, then lurching away from the chair and the television, and stormed into the kitchen. She reached beneath the sink, pushing aside the protective barrier of paper towels and sponges and soap pads she'd erected before the poisonous cleansing fluids so the ammonia wouldn't be susceptible to a child's reach, as her mother had done. She knocked aside this fortress and removed every cleansing fluid, laying them upon the counter. Then she marched into the living room. By now Mr. G. was telling the television audience tomorrow would be sunny with a high in the upper seventies. Sarah dragged the vacuum past Mr. G., plugged it in, left it there for the high-pressure center rolling across Pennsylvania and dashed up the steps into the upstairs bathroom. Once again the fortress of sponges and Brillo toppled to the ground as Sarah removed them and laid them out on the bathroom sink. Almost done, she thought, for there were no other thoughts, only almost done and the mindless search for clean sheets, which she found and flung onto the unmade bed.

My hair, Sarah thought dimly, touching her hair, touching her face, knowing what she was doing was extremely foolish. Not just her hair or her face or the plugged-in vacuum cleaner or the Ajax liquid. Just everything. She stared at the wall, hands at her sides, and tried to remember why she was bothering to clean the house when she hadn't made more than a superficial effort all summer. But now she was cleaning. Now she was playing with the frizz of her hair. Now she was imagining what had happened to her face. As if her hair didn't belong to her, or her face. They did belong to her. But the vacuum cleaner didn't. It belonged to this house. His house. Her house? Their house?

Which was it and why was she so surprised he was coming home tomorrow? She'd known he was coming home, eventually. She had it on her calendar, had circled the last day of the South Atlantic League season when he'd left—and then had forgotten about it. She had only glanced at it on her way around the kitchen, purely coincidentally, something to look at as she half-washed the breakfast dishes or folded back the *Times.* Just something to glance at and now the calendar leaped off the wall and told her he was coming back to New York.

No, she wouldn't meet him at the airport. She wouldn't wait there, because he hadn't called her and asked her to. Simple enough. And since he hadn't called and asked her to meet him, Sarah didn't think about whether she really wanted to, because that would only confuse her. So she allowed him to decide when they would meet.

But she didn't know what time his plane would land because she wouldn't be there to greet him. And she wouldn't call the airport because then she might wonder if she wanted to meet him and it had already been decided. So she would have to wonder what time he would arrive home. Would he march into the apartment in the middle of the afternoon, try and surprise her? That would be like Danny. And it would be like her to be waiting, angry because he hadn't called her, even if she hadn't called him. So he would stumble in and she wouldn't be angry, because she wouldn't be home but at work, and he'd wonder where she was. And maybe she would come home and he would already be gone, perhaps he would leave her some melodramatic note saying he wanted to talk to her. And what if she didn't want to talk to him? What if by the time he came home after the game she was asleep? Then she would have to wake up and then she would be bitchy. Maybe she was being bitchy by demanding he somehow compromise with her. Or defer to her. No, it wasn't that she wanted him to defer to her, but that she would defer to herself. Go about her business as she'd done all summer. If they happened to bump into each other in the next day or week or so, then they would talk. If she wanted to. But she wouldn't make the first move and didn't expect him to make the first move. Assuming he did come to this home, Sarah thought, inching beneath the covers, forgetting to turn off the television or put back the Ajax, only thinking ahead to the next day when her subway would let her off and she'd walk those blocks and up the few steps and into the apartment.

Danny stiffened as the key entered the lock. He'd locked the door behind him. Maybe he just wanted to examine the house before she came back, and thought by locking the door he would have more privacy. But he didn't examine the house, just sniffed at the bottles of Ajax and Fantastik upstairs, at the upright Hoover in the living room, at the paper towels and Brillos scattered about the kitchen. More than that he didn't have to see, because he couldn't quite figure out what all that meant, much less anything else he might find as he opened every closet. For what? Another man's jeans? Shaving lotion in the medicine cabinet or a different brand of toilet paper or some such foolishness, when he knew if another man had been living there, then Sarah would have had the good sense to hide it from him?

If she knew he was coming back, that is. But he hadn't wanted to tell her, had wanted to surprise her, as if they were playing some silly little playground game—which they had been playing all these years: Ring-O-Leavio with emotions. Maybe there wouldn't be any more games. Maybe they would just look at each other and the games would end. He knew that wouldn't happen. You didn't just up and forget a summer of silence and an affair and all those years of marriage. Even if it were over, it required one final scene, maybe with some screaming and yelling and swearing, even if he didn't feel like screaming and yelling and swearing but only like having her there waiting for him, making dinner and knowing the meal would be quiet and they could conceal things again. Even if he didn't want that, either. Even if he didn't know what he wanted as the door opened and he stiffened, looking at his wife.

"So hi," Danny said, standing in the foyer as Sarah stood by the door. She made a great effort of removing the key from the lock and turning her back on him as she closed the door. Then Sarah turned and shook her head, not with real vigor, but just enough so the frizz of her hair shook and he would see what had happened to her hair and maybe ask a question about only that.

"Hi." Sarah managed a weak smile which turned into an irritated blush before his examining stare. "What's the matter?"

"Nothing, uh, you just look different." How?

"In what way?"

"I dunno." He didn't, feared saying the wrong thing until he could figure out a safe answer, so he just shrugged. "Different different, nice different."

"It's my hair, right?"

"Well uh, yeah, I think, your hair, right, it's . . ."

"Longer? I'm letting it grow out."

"That's it," Danny said too quickly.

"I was thinking of getting it cut." Shit, he hates it.

"You cut it short so it grows long?" Lost weight. Lotta weight.

"Yes." Shouldn't have mentioned it. "So," Sarah said, staring at the key. "Been here long?"

"Just got home."

"How long?" Sarah worried about the condition of the apartment. "Place is a mess."

"No, looks okay." Looks like Woolworth's basement. "Fine, seems clean."

"If you'd called I could've cleaned some more."

"Yeah, I'm sorry, I'll call next time."

"Well, I wouldn't have been here if you had."

"Where would you have been?" Jeez, where does she go?

"Out."

"Out where?"

"At work."

"You work now? Work?" Sarah works and Sarah works without much makeup. That's it. I can see her face for the first time in how long and why does it frighten me so?

"Receptionist at an ad agency."

"You like it?"

"You don't have to interrogate me."

"What was I saying? I asked about your job."

"Pays the bills."

"Does it pay enough? You look kinda thin."

"How thin?"

"Thin, I dunno, thin, different, nice different." He held out his hands to forestall another outburst. With hands still out, Danny stepped forward and touched her cheek with his fingers. Sarah closed her eyes, started to return the touch and moved aside swiftly, ripping open the closet door and flinging her jacket onto the floor. She slammed it shut. Now they'd reversed positions, she by the closet, he closer to the door.

"I'm sorry," Danny blurted suddenly.

"For what?"

"For not calling all summer."

"You don't have to apologize."

"Then you didn't care?"

"Of course I cared."

"But you didn't miss me."

"Damnit, Danny, of course I missed you."

"So why won't you let me kiss you?"

"I didn't stop you."

"Did too."

"Maybe you didn't try hard enough."

"Oh, oh, I see, maybe you'd like it if I threw you on the ground, huh?" Danny stepped toward her. She flinched, didn't retreat. "That what you're into now, spent the summer getting into S&M and leaving Ajax around the house?"

"If you don't like it then you should've cleaned all goddamn summer." Sarah's hands reached for his biceps as his hands wavered near her face.

"I was in goddamn North Carolina, how the hell am I supposed to clean long-distance?"

"If you would've called once, I could've told you it needed a

251

cleaning." Her hands pressed his arms away while her fingers squeezed his elbows.

"Then maybe you should've written me a letter and told me how filthy it was." He grabbed her mouth and pressed it against his. Both trembled, shook, too much to embrace, too much to allow their mouths to part or to hold each other's quivering bodies. Sarah almost pulled away as Danny almost pulled away and they were left just staring at each other. Neither seemed able to handle that and they stepped back.

"Great," Danny mumbled.

"What, not good enough?"

"No, my father was more passionate. I shlep all the way from North Carolina and my own wife doesn't even kiss me right."

"Oh, right, you came back just to kiss me."

"Maybe, partly. Doesn't seem to excite you too much."

"Not when you just grab me like a lump of meat."

"I always took you like that." No, you didn't.

"And I never liked it." He never did.

"So it's my fault?"

"It's no one's fault."

"Has to be someone's fault, always someone's fault."

"Not this time and don't scream at me."

"I'm not screaming."

"The veins on your neck are standing out."

"What's wrong with my neck, it's too skinny, that it, that why you won't kiss me?"

"God, you're insane, I didn't say anything about your neck."

"You never liked my neck or, or my body, that it?"

"You never liked mine."

"Yes I do. Who's the one trying to kiss who?"

"You're kissing me only because you haven't seen me all summer, that's why."

"Isn't so, I always went to kiss you when I came home from work."

"Where, what fantasy is this? You never did."

"I always reached down to kiss you, but you were always too busy."

"Ever think you didn't make enough of an effort?"

252

"So again it's my fault."

"It's no one's fault what's happened to us."

"What's happened to us?" Danny blanched. "I'm trying to kiss you, that so terrible?"

"Kissing me won't solve anything, don't you see?"

"It's a start."

"It isn't anymore." Sarah waved her arms about. "Okay, it isn't anymore, I don't know what you're used to but . . ."

"What?" Danny stepped back. "What's that supposed to mean?"

"Nothing."

"Okay then."

"See, see."

"What?"

"You give in too easy."

"You won't tell me."

"Because you don't want to hear."

"You haven't said anything." How could she know?

"Just that you might not have come back if the Yankees hadn't called you up, that's what." Say it, damnit.

"I didn't take a long-term lease there, you know that?"

"Not what I mean. You, you know what I mean."

"No I don't."

"Then you don't."

"Oh, now you're giving up."

"You won't talk to me."

"Who am I talking to?"

"You're yelling."

"Again with my veins, with my neck, with my shrimpy, pot-bellied, unattractive body. Shit, you know, it's not so bad a body, you know, maybe you're wrong about it, yours isn't the only damn opinion in the world."

Danny stopped, waiting for her to urge him on, to force him to confess. She didn't force him, didn't even look at him, instead stared at the floor. Yet he couldn't retreat because he'd gone too far and knew no safe route out of it. He simply couldn't say it.

"What was her name?" Sarah whispered.

"Who?" Danny trembled.

253

"Your girl friend. Just tell me her name and I'll be happy."

"She has no name."

"No name?" Sarah looked up, tearfully.

"I didn't have a girl friend," Danny whispered.

"Didn't fuck anyone?"

"No."

"You sure?"

"You don't believe me?"

"No."

"Good."

"What?"

"I said good because, because . . ." What?

"Because you're lying to me," she whispered. Danny nodded. "Why?"

"Because I don't want to make you angry."

"Angry?" Sarah shook her head. "Angry." Her voice faded, rose haltingly. "That's it, huh, angry, don't want to make me angry?"

"You got upset when I said that about the house. I . . ." Danny shrugged as she took a tentative menacing step toward him. "What would I . . ."

"The house is the same as an affair?"

"To you, yeah."

"And the same as my cream cheese, right?"

"Huh?" Danny was frightened by the expression on a face he hadn't seen in so long. "What's . . ."

"Cream cheese. Or the Ajax bottle lying about or the rug not vacuumed or not enough milk in the refrigerator or buying the wrong kind of bagels or having an affair, all that makes me angry," she whispered harshly. "All the same to you, right, like it's all the same to me?"

"No, I don't . . ."

"Yes you do," she said with encrazed gentleness. "You do, you think that of me. That brave little Sarah doesn't even get the privilege of real tears for important things, because Sarah doesn't have real emotions, and when her husband tells her he had an affair she'll get angry and maybe give him a list of how to end the affair, right? Number four behind picking up the cleaning, is that what you think of me?"

254

"I love you." It arose out of such horrified sincerity, such rightful misplacement that Sarah swung a fist and slammed him in the shoulder.

"Me too," she screamed, afraid she'd lost it, and him, afraid the suffocation would grab her again and devour yet one more truth, and she'd regret not having said it, and regret saying it, because this would mean the end. But she had no choice. "Me too, I did."

"Love me?" Danny whispered hopefully.

"Have an affair, fucked him."

"What?" Danny stumbled back. "Don't have to be so damn graphic . . ."

"Fucked him." Sarah pushed Danny toward the door. "Do you like that, how does it feel?" She punched him in the arm. "Does it hurt, huh, does it hurt you like it hurts me? But I'm not supposed to hurt, only you and your goddamned"—again she punched him—"problems, but not me, shit, I fucked him." Now she clubbed Danny about both arms, bouncing him against the door. "And I don't want to tell you about it, because I don't want to go back in the past anymore, so you see, huh?" Sarah started one last punch. Danny just stood there, defenseless. She could have hit him anywhere, but her hands fell to her side. She started up to grab him as she wanted to, to hit him as she wanted to, but she did neither, just whirled away and bounded up the steps. As she'd raced down the steps the day of his tryout. This time he didn't go after her. He couldn't go after her. He couldn't make her do anything she didn't want to do.

Danny walked out, toward Yankee Stadium.

255

Chapter 25

No one looked like a Yankee. The Left-Handed Pinch-Hitting Outfielder who, at eighteen, was to be the next Mickey Mantle chewed tobacco and looked like a rancher. The Hard-Throwing Relief Pitcher sniffed at his roll-on deodorant and wailed "Nine to Five" and looked like someone who used to chase Danny home from Hebrew School. The Muscular Catcher slapped a dry towel in the air and looked like a waiter at Patsy's. The Handsome Shortstop autographed pictures of himself as a Handsome Shortstop and murmured encouragement to those pictures of himself as a Handsome Shortstop, looking a great deal like one of the would-be male models who traipsed down Fifth Avenue with sweaters wrapped around their necks, even in February when their lips were blue. The Gold Glove Third Baseman kept pressing down his curly auburn hair while shoveling a huge sandwich into his mouth, as if he thought it bad manners to eat when he went on his next insurance sale at some wealthy person's house. Certainly not at Danny's house, because he wouldn't have let him in. He wouldn't have let any of them in, because no one looked like a Yankee. Only the Coach with those pockmarked, endearingly ugly features who had been one of Danny's favorites, and whose soft drink Danny had become addicted to at the age of nine, until his dentist had warned him he would have false teeth for his high school graduation unless he laid off the Yoo-Hoo—only the Coach looked the way he was supposed to. Somehow that relieved Danny as he sat at the far end of the carpeted clubhouse. That they didn't look the way they were supposed to. That they looked normal. Not as they did on television or on baseball cards or on television interviews or in the newspapers. Normal people. None of whom had said one word to him as he sat before his locker. 57-NEUMAN-57.

Maybe no one knew who he was. Maybe they thought he was the new batboy or a writer or delivery boy. Maybe that's why no one had spoken to him. Actually, he was relieved no one had said anything to him, thus far, because he was still soaking in the utter disbelief of dressing in the Yankees clubhouse because he was a New York Yankee. Even if no one ever spoke to him, he was a Yankee. Officially. A Yankee. So he shouldn't be nervous, his fingers shouldn't be trembling as he reached for the pinstripes he had dreamed about, for the undershirt and cap and warmup jacket and socks and everything. He shouldn't be terrified because he belonged. He hadn't forced anyone to call him up.

Then why do I want to throw up? Danny murmured to himself, half-watching the Lean Second Baseman dress because Danny wanted to do it right, half-watching several reporters pause in the doorway, men Danny recognized. One a famous columnist from the *Times*. Another a reporter from the *News*. And then the birdlike, gray-haired columnist of the *Post*. They surveyed the room full of Yankees with casualness until they sighted Danny and started toward him, and he prayed that in the time it took them to reach his locker someone would send him home.

"Danny?" asked the columnist of the *Post*. "How you doing?"

"Great." It came out falsetto and Danny heard a player chuckle and wondered if it were for him. It wasn't, it was for a joke told by the First Baseman to the Reserve Catcher, who relayed it to the Fireballing Left-Handed Starting Pitcher, who cackled near his locker. Danny would've liked to have known the joke. He would've liked to have known any joke other than the one which seemed to capture these three esteemed gentlemen of the Press.

"So what does it feel like to finally make it up here?" asked the columnist of the *Times*.

257

"Um, amazing, if I could steady my hands to tie my shoes."
Danny grinned weakly and they laughed. Funny, Danny
thought.

"When you went out for the tryout, did you ever, in your
wildest dreams, imagine you'd be up with the Yankees in September?" asked the reporter from the *News.*

"Well, I, uh, did well down there, uh, you know." Yeah? .274,
two home runs, thirty-one RBIs. Even a couple of stolen bases
when the sight of Danny speeding toward second paralyzed both
catcher and pitcher. "So, I, I wasn't too surprised when I was
recalled."

"You weren't?" persisted the reporter.

"No, I, well . . ."

"Do you think of yourself more as a man approaching middle
age living out a dream than as an actual athlete?" asked the reporter.

"No, no, I am an athlete." Danny held up a poorly tied shoe.
"See? An athlete. See?" Danny brandished toward his locker—
his locker in the Yankees clubhouse, as the anger and resentment
grew at these frustrated bastards jealous of what he had done,
who dared to mock him when he mocked himself enough. "I'm
here, so, I'm here. Right?"

All three exchanged skeptical grins and continued their bar-
rage. What was it like living in the minors? Have you spoken to
the Boss yet? Have you heard any plans the Boss might have for
you? Do you expect to get into a game? Have you made plans to
write an account of this summer? And, silently, each asked, do
you need a ghostwriter?

To these Danny offered monosyllabic answers. He wanted to
be somewhat rude, maybe because most baseball players, in fact
most athletes, are rude to journalists. But that wasn't the only
reason. Fear played a great part, along with anger that they
would ask him these questions and minimize what he had done,
or had tried to do. Also creeping upon him was something on the
order of disappointment, as he looked around the clubhouse
once the reporters had left with promises of returning. He
looked at all the Yankees and realized that, if they looked really
no different from normal people, and he was normal, more or

258

less, then he was really no different than they were. Which meant, somehow, that he was no different from anyone else who might be watching the game—that everyone was the same and any differences were always imagined. He kept assuring himself with this profundity, though he didn't believe any of it, as the Lean Second Baseman approached and extended a wiry black hand.

"Hey, how are you?"

"Yeah, hi," Danny said, staring into the face he'd seen closeup shots of on Channel 11. "I, I just got here." Danny apologized for his half-dressed appearance.

"I can tell by the way you're standing there." The Lean Second Baseman grinned. "You can walk around, you know, might as well make yourself feel at home."

"They won't mind?"

"Who?" The grin widened.

"I mean, uh, the players. Me walking around, don't want them to think I'm spying or looking where I shouldn't."

The Lean Second Baseman laughed.

"Need anything, give a holler, okay?"

He left, as several of the other players started drifting out the clubhouse door. Batting practice. Danny didn't want to take batting practice, because he wasn't certain he could hold his bat. Or stand. So he kept staring into his locker and tried to finish dressing, wondering why he didn't have that magical feeling he'd imagined for so long when the Millionaire Left Fielder approached.

"Dan Neuman, right?" Danny looked up, realized a quick glance up would only make it to the man's groin, and since he didn't need a suspicion of homosexuality, he kept craning his neck until he met the mirthful gaze some six feet, six inches from the ground. Danny should've stood but felt too embarrassed by the height difference and knew he shouldn't stand on his stool. So he rose anyway, blushing. The Millionaire Left Fielder didn't seem to mind either way.

"Yeah, hi." What else could he say? "How, uh, are you?"

"Good, good." The mirth intermingled with seriousness. "Heard you jumped all the way from Greensboro."

259

"Yeah, by plane, I think."

"So how's it going with you?" The Millionaire Left Fielder contained a chuckle.

It? Danny wondered. What's it?

"Fine." He swallowed. "It's going fine."

"Good, good. This is a good, tight team. Good people, no matter what you read or hear, bunch of good people."

"I haven't read or heard anything, at all." Good, feed my paranoia.

"Well, just wanted to say hello, let you know this is a good team. People keep their own area, everything's fine, don't worry about the Boss, isn't that bad once you get to know him." I don't want to know him. "So, just wanted to introduce myself. Any advice, any problems, come by."

Yeah sure, Danny nodded to himself. The Boss? Danny started considering the Boss, praying the Boss wouldn't talk to him because that would be the end of him. All he needed was the Boss.

Soon Danny was all alone in the clubhouse. He could no longer delay. He started out the door, down the sloping incline and into the dugout, where he froze.

He had been there before, but that had been different. And a long time ago, that day of the tryout. This time the Yankees were all around him. Several TV camera crews were readying themselves on the field and Danny had a sinking feeling they were intended for him. So he sat down on the bench. In the dugout. The Yankee Dugout. Where Babe Ruth had sat. Where Lou Gehrig had sat. Where Joe DiMaggio and Mickey Mantle had sat. Danny sat there, too, transfixed by the tradition of it all, by the sweeping sight of the ancient, beautiful Stadium they had no need to remodel. The depth of the outfield walls, the grandeur of the sweeping stands and the flagpole blowing back late summer winds somehow lost a bit of its impact, though, because Danny stared at the players and realized they weren't much bigger than he, not that much broader. A few were even shorter. Then he realized that he didn't want to think of them in those terms, so he pushed it aside and leaned back against the dugout and glanced off to his left. No one was there, so Danny imagined Casey pacing back and forth and Bill Dickey laughing with Tommy Heinrich and Whitey Ford cracking jokes and Tony

Kubek overhearing them. He imagined that and tried to think of a good joke that even the Babe would find amusing, when he felt someone squish beside him.

"Heard about you," said the Handsome Shortstop while twirling his bat.

"You did?" Danny weakened.

"Yup. Getting a lot of attention, right?" Danny nodded, shrugged, didn't know what to say. "Should capitalize on it while you're hot."

"Hot about what?" Now Danny forgot the joke he was going to tell the Babe.

"Goes quick." The Handsome Shortstop nudged him. "I'd check into all possibilities, investigate every avenue you can think of. Even give you the name of someone who can help."

"I, I don't need a name." Have enough. Babe, Lou, Casey . . .

"Well, suit yourself, just suggesting you act on endorsements while you can. They forget you awfully quick."

"Yeah, well . . ." Danny watched the Handsome Shortstop shrug and wander onto the field. Then he glared at the Handsome Shortstop. And glared at all of them. He didn't want endorsements. He was a Yankee now, what did he need with endorsements? Shouldn't he do something before he endorsed something? Something more than telling a good joke to Babe Ruth? Even if Danny forgot what the joke was and started wondering what would've happened if he told the good joke to Babe Ruth and the Bambino farted. Didn't the Bambino fart? Or did Joe D. ever pick his nose, maybe as the current center fielder was picking his nose near the batting cage which no one would ever take a picture of? No, Joe D. would never pick his nose. Or have bowel trouble. Or phlegm. Maybe the Babe would fart, but if the Babe could fart and Mickey be surly, as Danny had read and ignored, then maybe Joe D. could pick his nose. Someone must've picked their nose on this bench. Fred Whitfield or Frank Tepedino or Horace Clarke? Those who didn't belong on the same bench as the Babe and Lou, and if they didn't belong how could Danny? So he bounced off the bench, looked back in wounded love, because he could never again look at it the way he once had, and that was wrong. Someone was to blame, and who was it he should blame?

He should blame the Yankees for speaking like normal people, for speaking English instead of some alien language only someone who had been in the majors five years could decipher. He should blame the Yankees organization for planting press stories about his middle-aged phenomenalness, if there were such a word, instead of placing him amid the other routine September recalls so his name could be sandwiched between Freddie Divine, shortstop, and Allan Bugglaccio, pitcher. It should've read Danny Neuman, outfielder.

He should blame the press for bothering him with silly questions about how he felt, talking to him like a peer instead of like some dopey hick from some dopey hick town somewhere in a state Danny would never visit. Montana, maybe. He should be spoken to as if he came from Montana or Alabama or even the South Bronx. He could blame them, or he could blame the television people for grabbing him for interviews and asking him such questions as, "Do you have anything to say to those guys on the easy chair who wish they were like you?" and for forcing Danny to think such nonsensical thoughts as, "It is better to have climbed into the pit of battle and emerge defeated and soiled," or, "I dream things that never were," or "Don't take any wooden nickels," so his mind was so feverish with confusion and fear and disappointment that he just giggled and said something which sounded like, "Never give up the ship." Which brilliance the WCBS-TV announcer applauded, as did the WNBC-TV reporter who asked the same thing, as did the WABC-TV reporter who asked the same thing.

Or he could blame the batting cage, poor inanimate batting cage, for not sparkling like gold and having Mel Allen announcing his swings. Or he could blame the Coach for just smiling at him and not asking if he still drank Yoo-Hoo. He could blame all of them individually or singly. There was a lot of blame to go around. Oh, and he almost forgot how he could blame the Manager. He could blame the Manager a lot because the Manager hadn't inspired disappointment or confusion or irritation. No, the Manager had inspired terror without saying one word. The pencil is mightier than the sword and all that drivel, because it was the Manager's pencil which had made the notation on the second rectangle on the lineup card affixed to the dugout near the bat rack. In that rectangle on the lineup card affixed to the dugout near the bat rack was a name.

NEUMAN. CF.

In a very short while, NEUMAN CF would be starting his first major league game in a New York Yankee uniform.

And while NEUMAN CF had sat in the Yankees clubhouse awaiting both the start of the game and the dread exhilaration to kill him, the Coach had stopped by his locker, pausing, perhaps thinking Danny's lowered head between his spread legs indicated prayer instead of incipient gastroenteritis.

"Hey kid, don't be so nervous," the Coach had said to him. Danny had looked up, smiled weakly, started to formulate some flip response to one of his idols but his lips failed and only saliva dribbled down his quivering chin. "Ya look nervous, kid, relax, ain't nothin' to it. Everyone's nervous their first time. Take it easy, kid."

"I wanna throw up," Danny had whispered, amazed by his intimacy, fearful the Coach would tell the Manager who would tell the Boss who would put him on the disabled list, which maybe wouldn't be such a bad idea. But the Coach had just cackled.

"So? Lotsa guys throw up."

"You? You ever throw up?" Danny had wanted a yes and a no.

"Nah, never did. But plenty of guys I know used to throw up before the game. Sometimes they couldn't throw up, so they jammed their fingers down their throat, you should try that."

I haven't jammed my fingers down my throat since I was a kid and wanted to simulate sickness to throw up. Either that, or smelling gefilte fish provoked sickness. But Danny hadn't said that, only muttered hopefully, "Like who?"

"Dunno, lotsa guys."

"Could you name one? Maybe I know him, maybe I had his baseball card, just one name?"

The Coach had considered it.

"Lots. Hard to remember who 'cause they tried to sneak into the bathroom and when they came back they'd already cleaned themselves off and were just white, so you couldn't tell if they was white from nerves or white from throwin' up. But try it, it'll

263

help. Maybe make you a bit weak, but then when you get out there, you'll think you're weak from throwin' up instead of bein' scared shitless."

Danny wouldn't throw up, wouldn't succumb, though he wished he had by the time he found himself in the dugout, dully watching the managers exchange lineup cards, one of which had the second rectangle filled with NEUMAN CF. The umpires laughed with the managers and Danny wondered if they were laughing at him, and if she were there.

He had left tickets at the gate. He figured his father would be there, his mother, undoubtedly Nathan and his wife and probably Sadie and Pistol. So would she dare not come, and expose herself to charges of treason? And if she did come, would that be the only reason, and would that have to be one more thing he'd have to worry about? But how could he find out? Could he just step out of the dugout and glance up in the stands and search for her, knowing if he didn't see her in the box seats he'd be crushed and relieved, and if he did he'd be happy and wondering?

"Sure you can, make sure you're back in the dugout before the manager comes back because it won't look good and, besides, he leads us out today." The Lean Second Baseman jerked his head toward the Gold Glove Third Baseman. Danny didn't want to offend anyone, was afraid to move out of the dugout because it seemed so safe, but he knew he'd be dashing onto the field any minute now and wouldn't know if she were there, which might not be such a bad thing.

Danny peeked above the Yankees dugout, not looking where he thought she'd be but allowing his strained, casual stare to drift further back toward the reserved seats beyond the third-base line. He froze, blinked, stared, shook his head because he saw her there, didn't think it was possible he could locate her among the nearly twenty thousand who'd gathered, presumably to see him, but he did see her. And maybe he saw her because deep down he was looking for her, deep down knew she would be there. So he stared and hoped she didn't see him, even as he hoped she did. And slowly, ever so slowly, her eyes fell on him. She didn't smile or wave, just stared because that was sufficient. From her end, at least, because he had a bargain to live up to

264

and he knew he had to do it. Even if the Manager saw what he was about to do and yanked him from the lineup, and the players thought he was insane, and the fans hissed and laughed at him, he had to do it.

So Danny started spinning around and around, seizing his cap as he spun and flipping it in the air and catching it, placing it back on his head sideways. And Colleen made no acknowledgment of his signal that he knew she was there, just rose and walked up the aisle and disappeared through the exit ramp. Danny waited until she had exited before returning to the dugout, unconcerned about the puzzled looks the team gave him, because he knew he owed her that one small thing.

"Why did Danny do that?" Mickey Neuman nudged her husband. Jack shrugged.

"Must be some kind of honor they gave him. I didn't see any other player get to do that."

Danny was the last Yankee to take the field as the team raced out for the top of the first inning. He was the last because he had paused to savor the sensation of dashing up those dugout steps, and the last because he was terrified of dashing up those dugout steps. Once he crossed the first-base line, he ran full speed out to center field, then stopped and looked around. Now what? he thought, expecting the Right Fielder to play catch with him or the Left Fielder to play catch with him, or at least for himself to feel larger than he felt. For he felt minute. And huge. Minute because the immensity of the Stadium swallowed him, because he knew on television and from the stands he was an insect, and from the perspective of over eighty years of tradition he was an insect. Knew he didn't belong out there, and so he bent to pick up a pebble as a souvenir, then stopped, knowing he was wearing the Yankees uniform and didn't need any souvenirs, that he should just act nonchalant even if he could barely stand.

But huge. He did feel huge because he was at the apex of it all. He was in the midst of center field. Everyone was watching him out there. Would watch what he did, if he could catch, if he could run, if he could throw. And he remembered how it looked when he had sat in the bleachers, how huge that Number 7 on the back of the Mick's uniform had looked, and he wondered if his Number 57 looked as big. And then he stopped wondering if he felt huge or minute, because the National Anthem had been played and the umpire had screamed "Play ball" and he had to concentrate.

Concentrate? Danny allowed the Coach to position him toward right center for the Boston lead-off batter. Concentrate? How can I concentrate when I'm not sure if I'm hunching over right? I never used to think about how to hunch over or where to place my glove, because all I ever had to do was emulate the Mick. But now I can't emulate the Mick because I'm in center field, and will look damn foolish if I act as if this were some punchball game because I'm supposed to be a major-leaguer. A major-leaguer. A Yankee. Yup, a Yankee, so come on boy, hit it to me, no don't hit it to me please don't, yeah hit it to me give me a hard one, no not a hard one maybe a little looper which I'll have to run for and trip and fall down, so give me a long one I can run back for, but I won't run fast enough and it'll drop over my head, so how's about just an old-fashioned fly ball where I don't have to move, unless I misjudge it and it bounces away and I have to chase it near the wall and have the monuments laugh at me, so don't hit it, for Christ's sake pitcher, strike them all out, please strike them all out.

Not quite. But the Veteran Left-Handed Pitcher with the Rebuilt Arm got the first batter to ground out to short, the second batter to foul out to first and had a one-ball, two-strike count on the next hitter when Danny heard the bat crack and saw a fly ball travel to the outfield.

Oh my God, he thought, starting for the ball, running at full speed, glove outstretched and feet and heart racing as he propelled his body in the direction of left-center field, only stopping when the Left Fielder made an easy catch, turned and winked quizzically at Danny, who felt like a damn fool. To lessen his feeling of being a damn fool for running full tilt for a ball which wasn't even near his ability to catch and which he never could've caught since The Left Fielder had only to move a few feet to his left to make the catch, Danny tried trotting casually off the field and toward the dugout. It didn't work, because by the time he got into the dugout, the players were waiting.

266

"Way to hustle," cackled the Millionaire Left Fielder. "Thought you were gonna swipe my ring the way you chased after me."

Danny blushed and played with his bat.

"You got somethin' in your contract says you have to retrieve foul balls, too, some kinda bonus clause?" grinned the Muscular Catcher.

Danny gulped.

"Man oh man, we do need his hustle," giggled the Lean Second Baseman as he moved ahead of Danny. He turned back, grinning at Danny standing almost motionless in the on-deck circle. "Hey, man, you awake enough to hit?" Danny nodded. "Good, don't want you goin' into any kinda coma on us up there, right?" He smiled, and Danny felt grateful for this sudden friend, who maybe wasn't really his friend but just afraid Danny would miss the hit-and-run sign if he led off with a single and he'd get cut down at second base, or who maybe was Danny's friend because the Lean Second Baseman was just another human being, as Danny had been before he had been left alone on the on-deck circle. By now, Danny wasn't a human being, because blood circulated through human beings' hearts, which also worked, and blinking was instinctive and Danny displayed only automated responses. Like staring at the Boston pitcher. Like staring at the Lean Second Baseman fouling off three straight pitches. Like staring at the left-center field wall. Like nodding stupidly when the Lean Second Baseman went out of his way to stop by Danny after he'd popped to short. To wake him up. To make sure he made it to the plate. To Home Plate in Yankee Stadium. That is where Danny suddenly stood.

"For New York, number fifty-seven, Danny Neuman, center field."

It wasn't his own voice which said that as he stood poised to meet the spauldeen during a stickball game. Or stood at bat during a high school game. Or college. He wasn't announcing himself. The Yankees Public Address Announcer was announcing him. Him, Danny Neuman. Him, a New York Yankee who was really standing up at the plate. The Plate. The Plate where he still stood semiconscious, nodded stupidly at the signs from the Third-Base Coach and watched a fastball split the plate for strike one.

Him, Danny Neuman. He was there. No one had made a mistake. He hadn't appealed to the President for this honor. He hadn't paid money to do this. So maybe he wasn't the next Mickey Mantle, but he was still standing at bat in a major league game, and so what if he was a gimmick, did that matter as long as he was there? Did it? And what if it did matter?

Another fastball split the plate. Strike two.

What mattered was he was up at bat and it was really no different from any punchball or stickball or high school baseball game he had ever played, because the Public Address Announcer sounded just as Danny ever had, and he wore the same official uniform he'd worn when he was eleven and held the same sort of bat and they threw the same sort of ball and he still had to hit the damn thing. Maelstroms of anger engulfed him for ever thinking differently, or thinking that Colleen or Sarah or his father or Horace or Pete or Antonheimer or Norman or Sadie or Pistol or any of them had or could or would change this unalterable fact of sameness. Which is the thought that went through Danny's mind and would last only a few seconds, until he came back to his senses.

The third pitch came hurtling toward him. It was big, fat, white and ugly. Very ugly and Danny wanted to smash it into a million little pieces, and as he swung he didn't think about whether his front foot stepped forward properly or his swing was level or his hips went into his swing. Or even about the swing because it was majestically fleeting, as was the very sweet sound of the fat part of his bat hitting the ugly white ball and propelling it on a high, high arc down the left-field line.

Danny didn't move. Not because he was so sure it was going to make it, but because he couldn't move. And shouldn't have moved, because he had done all he possibly could do. So he had to stand there and just watch the Boston left fielder run back for his ball. Just watch the outfielder race back and back as the ball soared and straddled the imaginary lines of the fair pole. Just watch that left fielder instead of watching the fans for their reaction, because it was the left fielder who had all the power now, the left fielder who could leap up into the stands and make a sensational catch and deprive Danny, and then he knew, he knew he wouldn't be deprived of this, that left fielder would never make the catch in a million years and that goddamn ball would stay fair and, just to make sure, Danny thought, please God, I'll owe you one if you give me this.

But God didn't give it to him. Nor did the left fielder who perhaps didn't jump as high as he could, nor did the Boston pitcher who had thrown that fastball down the center of the plate, nor the Boston catcher who had signaled for that fastball.

This one was Danny's. His home run.

He leaped high in the air near home plate and landed several feet up the first-base line as people applauded and the Boston pitcher kicked the mound in disgust. He tried to remember the perfect, nonchalant home-run trot he had practiced all these years, the casual way one is supposed to round the bases. But he didn't. Not because he forgot, but because he knew this was really and truly different and not imaginary and, damnit, he was going to run and maybe stumble and giggle and shake his fist and do whatever the hell he wanted to do. Which he did. Laughing as the first-base coach slapped his rump as he rounded first. Giggling hysterically as he nearly tripped over second, winking at the shortstop, then rolling his eyes at the third baseman as he rounded third, accepted another slap from his third-base coach and then started slowing down as he neared home. Knew why he was slowing down and that filled him with momentary grief, but it couldn't be helped, and should be ignored, so he made one final dash and the Millionaire Left Fielder rubbed the top of his cap and the cleanup batter shook his hand and the players grouped about the bat rack to congratulate him.

DANNY, DANNY, DANNY, flashed the scoreboard. He looked at it and just knew, didn't know how anyone was going to react to what he would do, only that he was going to do it because he had to. Not stumble onto the field. That wasn't planned. Someone just shoved him out and he turned, took off his cap and saw her. Saw her because he looked for her. And Sarah looked back, her prideful apprehension creasing into puzzlement, then moistening into vague understanding as she watched Danny doff his cap to the applauding crowd, then shove the Yankees cap into his back pocket and vanish down the dugout steps.

"Wasn't it nice the way he took off his hat so everyone could see his nice hair?" Mrs. Neuman asked Sarah, who ignored her. In broad, careful strokes, she wrote "HR" next to Danny's name, folded the scorecard and looked at Sadie and Pistol. Fortunately they did nothing, didn't grin or nod or any sort of encouragement. She was thankful for that.

Danny played with his glove as the players continued walking in front of him, tossing knowing grins which only enhanced his discomfort. He desperately wanted the inning to continue, wanted the Millionaire Left Fielder to get a hit, so the cleanup batter would get a hit, so the next batter would get a hit, and the next and the next, and mercifully the inning would end without him having to come up again. But it didn't last as long as he hoped, or as he had any reason to hope. The Millionaire Left Fielder grounded to third and the cleanup batter lofted a high fly to center and the inning, and everything, was over.

The players scrambled onto the field. Danny didn't move, couldn't move, wouldn't move until he sensed someone was about to hurl a quizzical look his way or, God forbid, say something to him. So he had to act before anyone did anything. Slowly, Danny rose and started back down their dugout, paused, cast one final look out over the Stadium, and started up the sloping incline leading back into the clubhouse.

"Hey, where you goin'?" the Manager shouted after him. "Take a leak next half inning." Danny didn't stop, not now. "Hey, Neuman, where the hell are you going, you gotta play the field."

No, he didn't.

Danny paused at the Yankees players' exit and stepped outside, the police barricades already in place. A few kids hung around, the way Danny used to. They'd come, as Danny used to, hoping a player would give them a free ticket and, once disappointed, stayed for the remainder of the game, listening to it from outside the Stadium, hoping to catch a glimpse of the players afterwards. So it didn't surprise him to see about five kids clustered down by the bottom of the barricades, swapping baseball cards and autographs and dirty jokes. Nor did it surprise him to see her there, though it did.

A huge cheer bellowed out of Yankee Stadium as Danny paused before Sarah.

"Missing the game," he said softly.

"Yeah," she paused. "Well, you guys already had one run. Figured you'd win."

"They would, huh?" Danny searched her, she searched back. "How'd you know I'd leave?"

"I didn't."

"Just guessed?"

"No." Again Sarah paused, this time smiling. "You know how I hate baseball."

He laughed, unaware of the ten-year-old by his elbow. "So, you hungry?"

"I don't know." Sarah shrugged. "You?"

"Guess. Maybe we could get some pizza?"

"To eat there or bring home?" Sarah waited and he shrugged, which she understood, as they understood why they walked side by side, grazing each other, hands not touching.

"Hey, Yankee." The ten-year-old materialized again by Danny's left side. "Gimme your autograph."

"Not a Yankee." Danny laughed, slowing down. The kid kept pace.

"I seen you inna papers, c'mon, how's 'bout an autograph?"

Danny looked at Sarah and she turned away. He smiled at that.

"Listen, kid, you can't get around the block with my autograph."

"Come on, man, just one, take a sec."

Now Danny halted, listened to the cheers from within, sighed, took the pad and scribbled. The kid grinned after Danny as he and Sarah continued walking away, his hand on her arm, her fingers by his hip.

The kid looked down at his pad, scowled, then glared at Danny and Sarah, nearing the subway platform.

"Mister, hey you, what kinda shit is this, you ruined my fuckin' autograph pad." The kid started running after them.

271

Sarah started to turn but Danny held her firm and quickened their pace.

"Hey," the kid screamed, now stopping. "You bastard." He shook the pad. "You bastard you, you ain't Mickey Mantle."

Danny slowed, ignoring Sarah's spreading grin as he turned and looked at the kid. And smiled.

Though Gary Morgenstein grew up six blocks from Yankee Stadium and could always hit a high fastball, he never tried out for the Yankees. His family suggested more concrete careers, which is probably why he left law school after his first year to pursue journalism and fiction. He spent three years at *Newsday* covering high school kids who couldn't go to their glove sides as well as he could, and six months at the *Cincinnati Post* writing news and searching for bagels. In 1980, while working as a boxing and baseball magazine writer, his first novel, *Take Me Out to the Ballgame*, was published. Since then, he has been freelancing for such magazines as *Inside Sports* and *Palm Springs Life* And ho can still hit a high fastball. More or less. He lives in New York.